APRIL WEDDING

by

Sara Hylton

Magna Large Print Books
Long Preston, North Yorkshire,
BD23 4ND, England.

British Library Cataloguing in Publication Data.

Hylton, Sara
    April wedding.

    A catalogue record of this book is
    available from the British Library

    ISBN 0-7505-1689-5

First published in Great Britain in 2000 by
Judy Piatkus (Publishers) Ltd.

Copyright © 2000 by Lilian Unsworth

Cover illustration by arrangement with P.W.A. International Ltd.

The moral right of the author has been asserted

Published in Large Print 2001 by arrangement with
Judy Piatkus (Publishers) Ltd.

Magna Large Print is an imprint of Library Magna Books Ltd.

Printed and bound in Great Britain by
T.J. (International) Ltd., Cornwall, PL28 8RW

00363059

APRIL WEDDING

Three months before the wedding of Ginevra Midhurst to Dominic, the Marquis of Chayter, the bride is having serious misgivings about her husband-to-be. Three of Ginevra's closest schoolfriends are invited – Kathy fears the gossips will be out, for it is common knowledge that her aunt's lover paid for her education; Alanna knows that after two failed marriages the press will be looking for her latest conquest; Jane is not convinced Dominic is as perfect as he seems.

The 'wedding of the year' will be a turning point in the lives of all four girls ... for better or for worse?

To my good friend Ron

Ginevra

Chapter One

The large portly man hurrying down the main street was red faced with exertion as he raced to beat the Royal Mail van on its way to the village post office. In his hands was a large parcel which he hugged to his bosom in a singularly protective fashion and with minutes to spare he hurried through the door which a departing customer held open for him. Even as he recovered something of his breath the van pulled up outside the door.

From behind the counter Mrs Pearson eyed his arrival with open-mouthed astonishment, tinged a few seconds later with annoyance when she saw him handing his parcel to the van driver himself.

'Have you nothin' in there that wants registerin'?' she asked him sharply.

'Nothing at all Mrs Pearson. All stamped and correctly addressed I think.'

'Aye, well, I likes to handle things for meself, folks don't like 'avin' to pay extra for letters that arrive without a stamp.'

He smiled at her benevolently. 'I'm sure you do your job very well Mrs Pearson. I'll take some stamps whilst I'm here, two pounds' worth, half of them first class, half second class.'

He watched while the van driver collected his parcels and emptied the letter box, then he went to the counter to pick up his stamps. Mrs Pearson favoured him with a smile and a few words of caution. 'You shouldn't be runnin' down the street at your time of life Mr Charlton, it must 'ave bin something highly important.'

He smiled.

'I didn't want to miss the van and I saw him further up the road.'

'I suppose those were Lady Ginevra's wedding invitations?'

He smiled again.

There was no point in trying to deceive Mrs Pearson, she knew everything that went on in the village and she knew everybody. He had defeated her anticipation of viewing the recipients of the wedding invitations, but he had no doubt she would avidly investigate the envelopes when they began to arrive with their replies.

By the time he reached the gates the mist was clearing from the hills and the morning snow had begun to melt along the drive and on the short grass. In the distance he could now see the herd of fallow deer grazing beyond the mere; Saunderscourt looked enchanting in the morning sunlight.

He felt intoxicated by the keen wind that swept down from the hills and he viewed the panorama with as much pride as he might have done if he had been the owner of the stately pile. He had come to Saunderscourt a young man whose father was the coachman to the present earl's father and whose mother had been a senior housemaid. He knew every stick and stone, every article of furniture, every picture on the wall and for the past twelve years he had been the butler with every ambition he had ever nurtured finally realised.

He had married late in life, a spinster lady, headmistress of the village school, and his Lordship had been most generous in handing over a charming stone cottage on the edge of the estate.

As he walked unhurriedly along the drive his thoughts were on the conversation he had had with his wife only that morning.

He listened to her views carefully because he knew she was a wise and astute woman, as any woman might be who had had the nurturing and training of a great many young souls for a good number of years, and Margaret's face had been thoughtful as she sat across the breakfast table looking earnestly into his eyes.

'Do you think Lady Ginevra's happy with this marriage?' she had asked him, and seeing the surprise on his face she had smiled gently.

'I haven't been listening to gossip, Steven, you know I never do that.'

'Then why ask?'

'I've seen her around the village, walking the dogs, and she looks anything but happy. Three months to her wedding, she should be as happy as a lark.'

'She's always been a reserved sort of girl.'

'She seemed happy enough with that Harbrook boy. I used to see them laughing together, walking with their arms round each other, riding their horses, now I never see him and out of the blue she's engaged to somebody else.'

'Young Harbrook was a nice enough lad but he

9

wasn't exactly Midhurst material.'

'His father's a baronet.'

'With very little money and most of that he's gambled away. He's got that large house that's been in the family for centuries and it's falling to pieces round his ears. His son needs to marry money to restore it, but the Earl doesn't want it to be his daughter.'

'But if the two young people care for each other...'

'You'd like it to be that simple, wouldn't you Margaret? Unfortunately in their world it isn't.'

'Then they're asking for trouble. The divorce rate in the aristocracy is exceedingly high.'

'And not only in the aristocracy.'

'No, perhaps not. But we really shouldn't interfere, they shouldn't interfere.'

'Oh I don't know. I was forty-five when I got married and I knew what I wanted and what was right and proper, you can't tell me somebody younger who is in love with love has the right know-how.'

Margaret had smiled and changed the subject. Now when he thought about it he knew she was right. Ginevra did not seem as happy as she should be. The atmosphere over the dinner table was far from amicable; Lord Midhurst was tetchy, his wife was silent and Lady Ginevra wrapped within her own thoughts.

He liked the girl, he had seen her grow up from a pretty, jolly young girl who was kind and thoughtful into this patently troubled young woman.

He had almost reached the house when he saw

his employer strolling across the grass from the stables. The Earl was wearing an old tweed jacket and battered felt hat, and in spite of the lingering snow there were bedroom slippers on his feet.

He greeted Charlton with a bright smile however, saying, 'Well I expect by this time it's all over the village who we might expect to join us for the wedding.'

'I don't think so, sir, I intercepted the van driver so Mrs Pearson didn't get a chance to handle the invitations.'

Lord Midhurst chortled appreciatively. 'Good for you Charlton. She'll keep a sharp look-out for the replies I've no doubt, but we've thwarted her for the moment and that's very good. Mrs Charlton in good health this wretched weather?'

'Yes, my Lord, she's very well.'

'You did very well for yourself there Charlton, nice woman, pretty too. Why wasn't she snapped up years ago?'

'Invalid parents, but lucky for me though.'

'Rather. I'll get out of these old clothes and go into the library. My wife can't stand to see me dressed like this. Bring me a hot toddy Charlton, well laced with malt.'

Charlton smiled as the two men entered the house together. As he made his way to the back of the hall and the servants' quarters, his Lordship glanced around him quickly before going into the gun room to change his apparel. He need not have worried, his wife was in her private sitting room writing letters and the apparel of her spouse was the last thing on her mind. She was worried about Ginevra. She was so apathetic

11

about the wedding, she hadn't even discussed with them who she had invited personally. Oh, all the people who should be there would be there, but there were Ginevra's old school friends and she wanted to be sure about those; there were two of them at least who were suspect. As soon as possible she had to speak to Ginevra about them. Now what were their names, Kathy was one, now who was the other?

The atmosphere over the dinner table that evening was far from congenial. Now and again Lady Midhurst glanced at her daughter with something like apprehension. Ginevra, immersed in her own thoughts, pushed the food around her plate with little appetite for it. His Lordship, oblivious of the tension, requested more wine.

Smiling at his daughter he said, 'Charlton managed to get your invitations off without the intervention of that pesky woman at the post office. Nearly broke his neck to get there before the mail van.'

Ginevra looked at Charlton and smiled her thanks.

'I do wish you'd decided to get married in June instead of April, dear,' her mother said wistfully. 'June is so beautiful here and April can be unpredictable; besides, it's too close to Easter.'

'We talked about it, Mother, April suited Dominic's family better.'

'I can't see why.'

'Well, his brother is hoping to go on safari early May and his sister and her husband have to go to America in June. His grandmother preferred April, she hates travelling in hot weather.'

'I should think the old girl's too long in the tooth to contemplate attending,' Lord Midhurst muttered. 'The last time I saw her it was like launching a battleship, it took three of them to walk her into the Abbey.'

Ginevra looked up as the servant removed her plate. 'I don't think I want anything else at the moment, I'll have coffee in the study, Mother.'

'But you've hardly eaten anything,' her mother protested. 'I do hope you're not sickening for this influenza that's going about. What will you be doing in the study?'

'I have a few letters to write, Mother, really I've had quite enough but I'd like coffee.'

With a brief smile she rose and left the table.

'I'm worried about her,' her mother said, 'she's hardly eating enough to keep a sparrow alive.'

'Wedding nerves,' his Lordship muttered.

'Hardly. It's four months off, the wedding.' Rising to her feet she said, 'I'll take coffee in the study with Lady Ginevra. You don't mind do you dear?'

'Yes, I jolly well do mind. Sit down and tell me what's been worrying you ever since you sat down to dinner,' and turning to the servants he said, 'we'll ring when we want coffee.'

Charlton ushered them out of the room in front of him and closed the door discreetly behind him.

'Now,' said the Earl, 'what is all this?'

'I'd like her to talk about this wedding. We don't know who she's invited, we don't know if her guests will be suitable.'

'Suitable! Well of course they'll be suitable, who

does she know that we don't know? If she wants to invite Harbrook's son then we can't stop her; after all we know the lad even if we didn't think she should marry him.'

'I'm thinking about the girls.'

'Girls! Which girls?'

'I have a feeling she's invited the girls she was at school with.'

'Well, what's wrong with that? She invited them at one time or another and I saw nothing wrong with them. We know Fortesque's girl Jane and the other two were right enough. There was that blonde pretty one and that sassy American girl.'

'I'm not objecting to Jane Fortesque, it's the other two I'm worried about.'

'Why, for heaven's sake?'

'Well there was that awful scandal about the one you call the blonde one, surely you remember that?'

'No. What scandal?'

'Oh, James, you're hopeless. You know Lord Fortesque as well as I do, surely you remember that quite awful scandal? It's still going on I'm quite sure.'

'I don't remember any scandal concerning Johnny Fortesque, purer than the driven snow he's always been, had to be with that wife of his, she's enough to turn the milk sour!'

'That's an awful thing to say. Elspeth has never been the subject of any scandal.'

'I'm sure she hasn't, for a woman who resembles the horses she's so fond of she did remarkably well to capture Johnny Fortesque. Now what's all this scandal you're talking about?'

'Johnny Fortesque's had an affair for years with a woman from the village near the hall. I don't quite know how it started or why, but I do know that he educated Kathy, Ginevra's school friend, the little blonde one you mentioned, and that he set this woman up in a house just outside the next town.'

'You mean this girl's his daughter by this woman?'

'No. She's her niece, and she asked him to get her educated. Apparently the girl was her brother's daughter and she was very very fond of her.'

'Isn't all that Fortesque's business, nothing the girl can help?'

'James, we've invited the Fortesques to the wedding, Johnny and Elspeth and, hopefully, Jane. It will be diabolical to include this girl Johnny's spent a fortune on, it would be too hurting for Elspeth.'

'If Elspeth has tolerated the arrangement all these years I don't see why the situation can't be tolerated for just one day. You don't know if Ginevra's invited this Kathy?'

'No. That was what I was going to find out when you prevented me asking her in the study.'

'Oh well, go on in and ask her if it's worrying you so much. And ask Charlton to bring me a hot toddy into the library.'

'Don't you want coffee?'

'No. I want to forget about this wretched wedding for one evening.'

She found Ginevra standing at the window staring out at the parkland glistening with frost

15

under a dark jewelled sky. A log fire burned in the grate and the room felt cosy and deliciously warm. Ginevra turned to smile at her mother, then she pulled the cord that drew the long velvet curtains across the window.

'I was thinking how beautiful the park looked tonight, Mother,' she said.

'Yes dear, it looks very nice from inside the house. I wouldn't like to be out in it.'

'Have you written your letter?'

'No, I haven't started yet. Are you having coffee with me?'

'Yes, dear, that will be nice. And we do need to talk about the wedding.'

'Mother, it's months away and everything is ordered.'

'I've been having thoughts about the invitations; you haven't told us who you have included.'

'If you're thinking of Larry Harbrook, Mother, I have invited him but I don't think he'll come.'

'Oh surely he will, he can't be that insensitive.'

'I thought I was being insensitive in inviting him.'

Changing the subject rapidly her mother said, 'Actually, darling, I wasn't thinking about Larry, I was thinking about your school friends. I know you've invited Jane, she was included on her parents' invitation, but what about the other two?'

'Kathy and Alanna? Yes, I've invited them.'

'Do you think that was entirely wise, dear?'

'We spent seven years together, Mother, eating, sleeping, studying, playing games. Sisters couldn't have been closer.'

'Did you always get along?'

'Most of the time. If we hadn't it would have been hell.'

'Were you all in Switzerland together?'

'No. Kathy was clever, she went to university to get a law degree. She was the one who needed a job, we needed to speak a little French, ski a little, ride a horse and exchange polite conversation.'

The satire in her daughter's voice troubled her.

'Really, Ginevra, I thought you loved Switzerland. It was meant to put the polish on all that had gone before.'

'The only polish it put on me was the feeling that it was all a waste of time, particularly when Kathy got a BA Honours degree the first time round and Alanna went off to America to marry the first man who asked her.'

'That's another thing, Ginevra, what about Alanna? She's been an absolute gift to every gossip columnist for years. Two disastrous marriages and God knows how many affairs. Darling, we want your wedding day to be for you, not a meeting place for reporters and photographers to dish the dirt on your guests.'

'Don't they do that at weddings generally?'

'Not if there's nothing to attract them.'

'Well, you'll just have to hope that neither of them will come, won't you. I've invited them to bring an escort. With Kathy I've no idea if there is someone, with Alanna it could be anybody.'

'You see darling, you've lost touch with them, you don't know anything about them these days, unless it's Alanna who is seldom out of the gossip columns.'

'Mother, it's my wedding. I've been more or less told who I should marry by you and father, I've been instructed by Dominic's family that April is an appropriate month for it. Nobody on earth is going to interfere with my choice of guests.'

'No,' her mother said resignedly. 'I can see that.'

At that moment a manservant came in with the coffee and the two women took their seats in front of the fire to drink it. Lady Midhurst was troubled. She wanted this wedding to be a peaceful, dignified affair, but the prospects were anything but rosy.

The silence was an uncomfortable one, and, putting her coffee cup down, Lady Midhurst said, 'I think I'll join your father now Ginevra. He's as worried about this as I am.'

'Surely not, Mother, he doesn't usually worry about anything outside his money and his horses.'

Her mother made good her escape.

His Lordship was in a benign mood. On his third whisky and soda, immersed in the *Financial Times*, thoughts on his daughter's choice of wedding guests was hardly uppermost in his mind. His wife however was prepared to shatter his complacency.

'It's as I thought, Ginevra has invited those two girls; there could be all kinds of repercussions,' his wife began.

'What repercussions? We're surely not responsible for Ginevra's friends, or who she wants to come to her wedding.'

'What about the Fortesques?'

'Well what about them?'

'What is Elspeth going to think, what is Jane going to think?'

'I'm sure Jane will know all about it. Ginevra's not invited any of them to be a bridesmaid, they'll simply mingle with the other guests and there'll be enough of those to hide any problems.'

'I wish I could think like that.'

'You're worrying about nothing. I'd like to know a bit more about Johnny Fortesque's affair, didn't think he had it in him. Have you met the woman?'

'Of course not.'

'Kept her under wraps did he?'

'They travelled abroad together, they spent time together. I do know people who met her.'

'What was she like then? It wouldn't take much to make her prettier than Elspeth Fortesque.'

'Prettiness has nothing to do with it. Elspeth is a good woman, there's never been any scandal attached to her. She's been a good wife and mother and I don't want her feeling uncomfortable because Ginevra's been thoughtless.'

'I'll have a talk to her.'

'It's too late, James, the invitations have gone out.'

'Well, it's no use worrying is it? Perhaps the girls won't come.'

'The newspapers will get hold of it. Not so much the Fortesque affair, they'll have to dig a bit deep to sort that one out, but Alanna. There's been nothing but scandal attached to her.'

His Lordship permitted himself a smile. He remembered Alanna. Beautiful, over-confident and decidedly sassy, even as a young girl.

His wife was saying, 'Ginevra's told them they may bring escorts. Heaven knows who Alanna will bring.'

His Lordship sat back in his chair to contemplate matters. His daughter's wedding promised to be more of a challenge than he had expected.

Chapter Two

Similar thoughts were being expressed by the Earl's butler in response to his wife's opinion that she had met Lady Ginevra riding her horse along the lanes leading from the village and the young lady had seemed intensely preoccupied.

'She was like that over dinner, in fact she left to write letters, but you're right, she doesn't look as happy as she ought to.'

'Are her parents aware of it, do you think?'

'I'm sure her mother is. I'm not so sure about the Earl.'

'I wonder who she's chosen to be her bridesmaids?'

'Children I think. Nieces, nephews, daughters of friends.'

'Really! Children can be such a nuisance at weddings, I would have thought she'd have chosen friends, girls she was at school with.'

'Well, she could hardly have chosen Miss Van Royston, the scandal surrounding that girl would have detracted from the occasion, nobody would want that.'

'What did you think about the girl, Steven, you met her of course?'

'Well yes. She came to the hall for holidays instead of going home to America. She was lively, a bit of a tomboy, but likeable enough.'

'Then there was Jane Fortesque.'

'Yes. Lord Fortesque's daughter. She was a nice sort of girl, rather reserved, not as jolly as the other two.'

'Two?'

'Why yes, there was another girl, Kathy, pretty girl, bit of a mystery surrounding her.'

'Mystery?'

'Yes. Something about her family, a bit obscure I think.'

There was a small frown on his face as he tried to remember the talk at that time, but for the moment it defeated him, and his wife said, 'I'll make coffee, Steven, aren't you having a whisky and soda?'

He smiled. Margaret was a comfortable person to be with, her mind was as uncluttered as his home.

Margaret Charlton had always been an independent sort of woman, her father had fostered that in her. He had been the headmaster of a boys' school in the next town and he had largely reared his only daughter in the same way he treated his boy pupils.

She'd been a bright girl. Winning a scholarship

21

to university and going on to teaching in the village school where she'd risen to be head-mistress. Her mother had been a semi-invalid for years before she died and Margaret had always been a dutiful daughter.

There had been several men who had thought her attractive, and with expectations of being more to her than friends, but one by one they had gone out of her life and only after her mother died had she felt free to make decisions about her future. Her father had died at the age of fifty-six so she was now alone in a large stone house at the bottom of the hill leading out of the village.

She had met Steven Charlton at a village fête where his Lordship had been generous enough to allow one of his fields to be used for the event and where her Ladyship was showing her prize cocker spaniel and his Lordship was presenting the awards for village crafts and prize cattle. She knew little about the noble family whose ancestral home dominated the village and the surrounding landscape, but that afternoon she learned considerably more as she sat next to Steven Charlton in the marquee over a cup of tea and home-made scones.

She learned that he was the butler, and as the time progressed he pointed out several members of the family as well as a great many of the servants. She was introduced to the cook and the housekeeper, and between them they kept her entertained about the comings and goings at the hall, all of them most circumspect and avoiding tittle-tattle.

Over the weeks and months that followed she

saw more of Steven Charlton. At the church where he sang in the choir, around the village and at meetings of the musical society, and for the first time in both their lives they fell in love.

The Earl and his Countess had been most generous. They were given a handsome wedding present in the shape of a very large Wedgwood urn which rather overpowered the living room.

Whenever she met Lord Midhurst in the village he favoured her with a bright smile. Indeed Steven had informed her that the Earl had said that she was a mighty attractive woman and very fanciable. That his Lordship had an eye for the ladies was very evident. His wife on the other hand favoured Margaret with an absent-minded smile, but Lady Ginevra had always seemed to her to be a nice friendly girl with a merry laughing face and a sense of fun about her. The fact that this was now so evidently lacking was causing Steven some apprehension.

When Margaret took the coffee into the living room Steven sat slumped in his chair entirely wrapped in his own thoughts, and it was a part of him she had never been fully able to understand.

That a grown-up intelligent man should tie himself so closely to a family that was not his own, and a house that would never be his, seemed ludicrous in Margaret's estimation, and yet she knew that it was something in him she would never be able to change.

She placed his coffee on a small table besides his chair and he looked up with a wry smile. Margaret sat opposite and when he sank back into lethargy she said, 'You're worried about

Lady Ginevra, Steven, and it's really nothing to do with you.'

'I suppose not, but we're all a bit concerned. The sparkle seems to have gone out of her and it's less than four months to her wedding. She should be on top of the world.'

'I wonder if her parents are concerned?'

'They must be. If the servants have noticed the atmosphere surely they have.'

'Well, worrying about it isn't going to alter things. I thought she was supposed to have pulled off the catch of the century, a marquis to boot, and wealth beyond anybody's wildest dreams. The fact that he's getting on for forty and she's twenty-two doesn't seem to be important.'

'That's just it. Is it going to work out?'

'Well, isn't it something royal and noble families have always done? Marriage and love seem to be things apart. They marry for expediency and look for love outside it.'

'That's a very cynical way of looking at it, Margaret.'

'It's also a very truthful way of looking at it. Before the media had a hand in it we were largely living in ignorance, now we're being more and more aware of it. If we persist in telling people when they have to marry and who they have to marry what can we expect.'

Steven leapt quickly to their defence as she knew he would. 'His Lordship and the Countess have been a most happy couple, there's never been a hint of scandal about either of them.'

She smiled. 'But scandal there has been, Steven. What about these two girls that you don't seem to think are suitable wedding guests?'

'Well, one of them is American so she's not a member of the nobility.'

'And the other one?'

He frowned before answering. 'I'm not sure exactly what happened there. Is there more coffee?'

She knew better than to continue the conversation. There had to be no criticism, no post-mortems on past scandals, so instead she said, 'The Abbey will be full I suppose, I can't think why they didn't decide to marry from the London house. Saint Margaret's would have been far more appropriate.'

'Oh no, I rather think they wanted it here where the family is so well known, and the groom's parents mustn't have objected. I suppose Lady Ginevra's brothers will be back long before the day.'

'Are either of them married?'

'Yes. One of them's in the Guards, the other in the Navy. Nice boys they were, very handsome. Their wives are very nice, and the children.'

'Lucky they didn't fall in love with the two girls who are suspect then.'

His look of incredulity amused her.

'That wouldn't do at all,' he said firmly. 'Lady Ginevra invited the girls here for long weekends and holidays in the summer, but the boys were never around.'

'Then we must hope that they view their marriages with rather more enthusiasm than their sister appears to be viewing hers.'

'Oh, I'm sure we're all imagining things.

Wedding nerves, nothing more is what she's suffering from.'

In her bedroom Lady Ginevra was assessing the clothes in her wardrobe. What did one take for a long weekend in Northumberland in late January? She'd never been there, but Dominic had told her that his grandmother lived in a bleak stone castle on the coast and she was a stickler for protocol. Ginevra had already been inspected by his father's side of the family, now it was his mother's side she was being expected to meet.

What did people do in remote castles miles from civilisation, particularly an elderly woman more or less crippled with arthritis? What would she expect from Dominic and his fiancée?

She supposed country tweeds would be appropriate, skirts and sweaters, and the odd afternoon dress, but what about the evenings? Dominic had said his grandmother dressed for dinner and had retained some sort of style within the crumbling sixteenth-century pile.

Her father had been predictably scathing.

'It'll be church on Sunday, inquisitions on the forthcoming nuptials and your guest list,' he'd said, 'so get yourself prepared. I remember the old girl, Victorian, proper and something of a martinet.'

'You've met her then,' Ginevra had asked.

'Yes. She figured prominently at school prize-giving and later at Cambridge. She knew more than the dons put together.'

In some annoyance her mother had said, 'Don't take any notice darling, you can hold your own against anything Dominic's grand-mother can throw at you. You're his choice, never forget it.'

She wasn't at all sure that she had been Dominic's choice. Rather they had been thrown together like two peas in a pod. He needed to find a suitable wife, she needed to get Larry Harbrook out of her life. As the son of a womanising baronet who had largely gambled his inheritance away Larry was hardly a suitable proposition for an earl's daughter.

Love had nothing to do with it. That Larry was charming and incredibly handsome carried no weight with her father, and Dominic had appeared on the scene at exactly the right moment.

Nobody seemed to quite know why Dominic had never married, why there had never been anybody serious in his life, and Larry had been sceptical.

'He's sexless,' Larry had asserted, either that or worse. There had been so much pain in his anger, anger her parents had anticipated.

'I know what he's been saying to you,' her father had said. 'Just because a man doesn't elect to get married out of the schoolroom doesn't mean he's queer. There were a great many things that stopped Dominic getting married, his grandfather's death, a mountainous pile of death duties, his father's illness. Besides, he probably never met the right woman.'

Larry on the other hand said, 'He's probably run the gamut of a multitude of women looking for the one with the most money.'

'There are girls with more money than me,' she'd answered.

'Probably in his age group, but he wants a young woman capable of providing him with an heir, not some woman who's past her sell-by-date.'

It didn't matter what she might say Larry had an answer, and always behind it she saw his eyes filled with hurt and he was finding other girls in an effort to make her jealous.

She had been introduced to Dominic at Goodwood; at Christmas the family were invited to stay in Shropshire, where they became engaged and where she met the rest of the family. All except the grandmother, hence the forthcoming weekend in Northumberland.

She eyed her wardrobe with a dissatisfied air and quietly closed the doors. Her mother would have a better idea on what she needed to take.

As she crossed the hall she could hear the telephone ringing in the library so she went to answer it. It was Dominic.

His voice was clipped. 'I'm glad I've found you in, Ginevra, it's to do with the few days we're spending at grandmother's. If I pick you up on Thursday morning will that be satisfactory?'

'Well, I don't know; isn't it rather a roundabout journey from Shropshire?'

'I'm in London. I'll drive north from there.'

'Oh, in that case Thursday will do very well Dominic.'

'How are you Ginevra, and your parents?'

'We're all very well, Dominic.'

'That's good. I'm looking forward to seeing

you. I've heard from Grandmother, she too is looking forward to seeing us.'

'That's nice.'

'Goodbye dear, until Thursday, around eleven.'

Ginevra sat down weakly on the arm of a large chair. This was how it always was, passionless, precise. Whenever Larry had telephoned her there had been teasing laughter and warmth. Words of endearment had sprung easily to his lips, not the conventional stilted conversations she had over the telephone with Dominic.

She couldn't begin to think about the weekend ahead of them. A grandmother she didn't know and a fiancé she had yet to discover.

In the drawing room her mother was working at her tapestry. Her father was not in the room. Lady Midhurst smiled saying, 'I saw you going to answer the telephone dear, was it anybody special?'

'It was Dominic.'

'That was nice. What had he to say for himself?'

'Nothing Mother, it was about the weekend. He's picking me up on Thursday morning.'

Her mother smiled. Distances didn't mean anything to her mother. The mere fact that his home was on the other side of the country didn't register, and she saw no reason to tell her he was driving up from London.

'I've been looking at what I might need to take,' Ginevra said. 'I've never been to Northumberland and his grandmother is very old. What do you think I shall need, or will we even be setting foot outside the place?'

'Of course you will. It's quite beautiful up

there, I went once with your father to north Yorkshire, it's in the same area I think.'

Ginevra didn't enlighten her. 'Then what do
you think I'll need Mother?'

'Oh, some nice country tweeds and woollies.
I'm not sure if the old lady will approve of
trousers, different generation and all that, but
you'll need to take one or two dressy things for
the afternoons and evenings.'

'I wonder if she has horses?'

'I'm sure she had at one time, she may not have
now.'

'I should have asked Dominic.'

'Why didn't you dear? Can't you ring him
back?'

'Where's father?'

'At some hunt meeting. He'll be late back.'

'The tapestry's coming along, Mother.'

'Well yes. I hate finishing them and starting
another. I thought I'd give this one to Aunt Dora
for her birthday. Dominic's mother was admiring
it, I suppose I might just think about giving one
to her. Did Dominic mention the wedding at all?'

'No, I only spoke with him for a few minutes.'

'The replies will be coming in now. I can't help
wondering how your two friends are going to
respond.'

'Stop worrying about them, Mother. I'd like
them to come, both of them. After all we were
friends once and I'd like to know what life is
doing to them. I sent Jane Fortesque a separate
invitation from the one going to her parents.'

'Why did you do that, dear?'

'Because she may want to bring somebody. I

30

don't know what Jane is doing with herself these days.'

'Did she really get along with that girl her father was educating, Ginevra? It wasn't very loyal to her mother was it, after all, would you have been as amenable if you'd found yourself at school with a girl your father was supporting?'

'I don't know any of the circumstances, Mother. Kathy came and at first none of us really tried. She came from a different background and we were a lot of silly snobs. She was clever, brighter than any of us, and we came around.'

'On your own?'

'Well, I rather think Miss Prothero had a hand in it, and then when we got to know her we liked her. She was intelligent and beautiful and as I said, brighter than any of us.'

'And what about Alanna?'

Ginevra laughed. 'We only know what the newspapers said about her. Husbands, lovers. A mother who was too rich, a father who was involved in one scandal after another. How can we even begin to blame Alanna for the way it's turned out.'

'I don't want her goings-on interfering with your wedding.'

'How could they do that?'

'Well, you've invited a great many people, she could have been involved with any one of them, or caused disruption to their lives.'

Ginevra laughed. 'At least she'll bring some excitement into the proceedings. Everything seems so flat. I don't feel engaged, I can't even think that in less than four months I'll be a married woman, and when I do I can't visualise Dominic beside me.'

Her mother frowned anxiously. 'Ginevra, do get that Harbrook boy out of your thoughts. He's the reason you think like this, try telling yourself that Dominic is a far better proposition. Your father would never have agreed to you marrying Larry, it was inconceivable. You'd never have had any money and you couldn't expect your father to bolster Larry at the expense of your two brothers.'

'We hadn't got around to thinking it was serious, Mother. We simply enjoyed being together, I'm worrying myself sick that I shall be spending a long weekend with a man I hardly know. What shall we talk about, what shall we do?'

'You're worrying unnecessarily. Give Dominic a chance, darling. I'm sure after this weekend you'll come to realise everything is going to be wonderful.'

Nothing would convince her mother otherwise. Back in her bedroom Ginevra started throwing things on to the bed. Tweed skirts and hacking jackets. Cashmere sweaters and sturdy country brogues. She selected only two dresses that might just do duty for afternoon or evening. They were both plain heavy georgette that might respond to jewellery to give them some sort of glamour.

Impulsively she decided to telephone Larry. She didn't enjoy being bad friends with him, and he'd had a few days to cool down.

A man's voice answered the telephone and she recognised Harvey, baronet Harbrook's manservant. He had a broad north-country accent and he was a man totally different from Charlton. Charlton was tall and dignified, a kind gentle man with a nice smile, but Harvey was a small cocky man who Larry said had never been averse to boxing his ears as a boy whenever the occasion had demanded it.

She asked to speak to Larry, and after a few moments his voice came to her mildly cautious.

'Are we going to be friends Larry?' she asked him.

'I'm not coming to your bloody wedding.'

'All right, that's your prerogative, you've been invited.'

'When did you last see him?'

'We're going to spend a long weekend with his grandmother in Northumberland. Thursday until next Tuesday or Wednesday I think.'

'That'll be the Dowager Duchess won't it?'

'She's the one member of his family I haven't yet met.'

'Well that's a thrill to look forward to. Northumberland in January, and an old girl getting on for ninety and probably gaga most of the time.'

'I believe the old lady is rather deaf, but otherwise has all her faculties. Larry if you're going to be peevish I might as well hang up.'

'Please yourself Ginny, good luck for the weekend, don't spare me a thought.'

'I won't.'

Chapter Three

Ginevra watched Dominic parking his car on the lower terrace, a long dark-green Aston Martin that must have cost the earth, and she compared it with Larry's rakish and decidedly more flamboyant sports car that was a good few years old.

As he climbed the steps he raised his hand to wave to her and her mother said encouragingly, 'Do go out to meet him Ginevra, show a little welcome.'

It was difficult. All morning she had been apprehensive about meeting a fiancé she hardly knew. A week at Goodwood, three long country weekends in the homes of friends and relatives and now this one she was hardly looking forward to.

He was very good-looking and his smile was charming, and yet she was remembering the laughter in Larry's eyes, the way he lifted her off her feet, swinging her round in rapturous delight. Dominic took her hand and bent forward to kiss both her cheeks, and with something like impudence she wondered how he might behave on their wedding night.

He was greeting her mother with the right degree of courtesy and correctness, taking her father's outstretched hand, responding to his jovial smile with a more restrained one of his own.

'Nice to see you my boy,' her father said. 'Time for a sherry or are you wanting to get away?'

'I think we should get away sir, we have quite a long drive ahead of us.'

'I'm sure you're right. Ginevra's been ready and waiting since early on, standing at the window waiting for your arrival.'

Ginevra seethed, Dominic grinned and Lady Midhurst eyed the rest of them with a cautious smile.

Ginevra loved the car – who wouldn't have – and she sat back to enjoy the drive and the scenery. Dominic was a good driver, without Larry's aplomb, but then Larry was a bit of a show-off when he got behind the wheel. He was like that with everything, horses, boats, even people. Larry would never acknowledge that other people were more experienced, better able to cope.

He bought a horse one day, considered entering him in the National the next, then weeks later was forced to sell it through lack of funds. It was the same with boats. He came back from Cowes, more proficient than men who had spent their lives sailing the seven seas; if Ginevra grew impatient with him he would merely laugh and continue to believe in himself.

She shouldn't be thinking about Larry. She should be concentrating on Dominic.

'This is a lovely car, is it new?' she asked.

'New since I saw you last. I've always fancied an Aston Martin and I had a bit of a windfall. Great-Aunt Sophia died and left me a fair bit otherwise I doubt if I'd have bought it.'

In Dominic's circumstances Larry would have

been the big spender, there would have been no limits to what he would buy for himself, but here was this reserved aristocrat admitting to being careful about his money.

He turned to smile at her. 'I do hope you're going to enjoy this weekend, Ginevra, Grandmother is hardly exciting company. Don't be at all put out if she asks you a lot of silly questions.'

'Silly?'

'Well yes. When we were young she interrogated my brothers and me about our school, our university, everything under the sun that she thought she had a right to know about. When we knew she was coming to stay with us we made every excuse under the sun to get out of her way.'

'And will she still be like that?'

'I can't think she'll have changed much. She's still got a keen mind even if she is arthritic and becoming more forgetful.'

'What sort of questions is she likely to ask me?'

'I can't begin to imagine, but she will.'

The forthcoming weekend was becoming more and more daunting and by the time they were driving through the gates with the long narrow drive before them Ginevra was wishing she were miles away.

The dark-grey stone castle loomed ahead of them menacingly through the low-lying mist and to the girl sitting staring through the windscreen it seemed like the epitome of every horror story she had ever read.

Several lights shone from the windows into the dusk and as they drew nearer she began to appreciate the fairytale structure of the castle with its turrets and towers. Heather and bracken ran riot over the boulders and now they were driving through an arched bridge into a cobbled courtyard.

Dominic looked down at her with an apprehensive smile. 'Well, is it what you expected?' he asked her.

'It's like something out of Sleeping Beauty, a castle the Brothers Grimm could have written about.'

'Isn't it. Or somewhere Dracula could have lived.'

'Is it always so gloomy?'

'Actually no. Don't forget you are seeing it for the first time in January. In the spring it can be enchanting, and at the other side it overlooks the North Sea. You might not believe it now, but there are formal gardens and in the springtime they can be quite beautiful. Come along, we should get into the castle and hopefully some warmth.'

'It must cost a bomb to heat that place.'

'It probably does. But the old lady likes her creature comforts, I think you might be pleasantly surprised.'

He took her arm as they walked across the cobbles towards the front of the house and the great dark oak door with its ancient bellrope.

The sound of it echoed eerily behind the closed door; then they were aware of footsteps on flagged floors and bolts being withdrawn before the door opened to reveal a tall bearded man wearing impeccable Scottish tartan. Leathers and kilt, and he was smiling, holding the door wider and ushering them in before him.

'You're looking well, McPherson,' Dominic said genially. 'May I introduce you to Lady Ginevra Midhurst, my fiancée?'

Ginevra smiled up at him and McPherson bowed over her hand, saying courteously, 'I am happy to meet you, Milady. Her Grace has been looking forward to your arrival.'

'How is my grandmother, McPherson?' Dominic asked.

'Well enough, my Lord. Her arthritis is not good, but then in January what can she expect. Nothing affects her mind, she's as bright as she always was.'

'That's good.'

'Perhaps you'd like to see your rooms and get unpacked before you see her Grace. She was asleep in her chair the last time I looked in on her.'

'That's a good idea McPherson. Have you put me in the room I usually occupy?'

'Aye, that I 'ave sir, Mrs McPherson's put Lady Ginevra in the turret room that overlooks the sea. If you don't care for the sea view Milady we can find you another room.'

'I do like the sea, I'm sure I shall be quite happy there.'

'Aye well, there's sea and sea, I doubt you've bin accustomed to our sort Milady, it's wild and grey today, not your Mediterranean sea.'

Ginevra smiled. 'I wasn't expecting the Med, McPherson.'

At that moment a small slim woman came hurrying from the back of the vast hall and Mc-

Pherson introduced her to Ginevra as his wife. She bobbed a quaint country curtsy and asked Ginevra shyly to follow her while Dominic and McPherson, carrying their luggage, walked behind.

In the turret room Ginevra looked around her with interest. A large four-poster bed hung with rich damask to match the curtains at the windows. There was a preponderance of heavy dark oak furniture, but a fire blazed in the hearth and a warm rose-red carpet covered the floor.

Mrs McPherson fussed around, ushering Ginevra into the bathroom which was half the size of the huge bedroom and where the bath was a huge white one on four claw feet.

Back in the bedroom Mrs McPherson said, 'I con send ye up a maid Milady, but she's only a housemaid, nairy a lady's maid so to speak.'

'That's all right Mrs McPherson, I really don't need anyone.'

'Aye well, the old lady has her own maid who's bin with her for monny a year, and when the family visit the ladies bring their own maids with 'em.'

'Have you been with her long, Mrs McPherson?'

'Aye indeed. Me husband's father worked on the family home in north Scotland, up beyond Inverness, and Dougal was born on the estate. I lived in the village and went as a young housemaid and we got married fro' there, then when we got the chance to come to work for the Duchess here we took it. Neither of us wanted to work i' London, this place is as near to Scotland as we're likely to get.'

Ginevra smiled. 'You've been happy here then?'

'Oh aye. The old lady's exactin' and she doesn't get any better with the years, but we understand each other and Dougal's a good honest man.'

'I'm sure he is. It will take some time for me to find my way round this place.'

'Ye dinna need ta worry Milady, Master Dominic'll come for ye to escort ye down to dinner.'

'Master Dominic!'

'Aye. We always addressed the boys as Master Dominic and Master Andrew when they were small and addressin' them as anythin' else is hard.'

'I'm sure it is.'

With another little curtsy Mrs McPherson opened the door. 'Ring for anythin' ye might want, Milady, the bellrope's over there near the bed.'

The wardrobe was a huge walk-in affair and after Ginevra had unpacked and hung up her clothes they only occupied a small space in it. She went to kneel on the rug in front of the fire, luxuriating in its warmth, eyeing the rest of the room with some degree of apprehension. She was suddenly aware of a long low-sounding noise coming at intervals, a sound that fell upon her ears like the eerie hooting of an owl, and jumping to her feet she went to open the curtains.

Mist swirled across the window obscuring any view there might have been, and in the sound she recognised the moaning of a foghorn. Beyond that mist surged the North Sea, and she was glad to pull the curtains together and return to the warmth of the fire.

There was a timid tap on her door and then it opened to admit a young rosy-faced housemaid carrying a tray. Ginevra got to her feet to watch her placing it on a table and pulling up a chair.

'Mrs McPherson's said ye'd be wantin' tea ma'am. There's hot buttered scones too and shortbread.'

Ginevra's face lit up with pleasure. 'Do thank her, it looks lovely.'

The girl smiled and curtsied.

The tray was filled with a large teapot, milk and sugar and matching china. There was a large silver cake stand piled with buttered scones and shortbreads, and for the first time that day Ginevra felt a sense of welcoming warmth.

She decided she would wear the French navy dress which was a favourite of her mother's. Lady Midhurst thought she looked well in navy and she had the pearls her father had given her for her twenty-first birthday.

What sort of girl would the old lady be looking for in her grandson's fiancée? She thought about her own grandmother who constantly moaned about changing values. Dresses that were too short and too scanty, respect for other people which seemed to have flown out of the window, and too much American slang that she found totally deplorable.

At one point she opened the door and looked out along the corridor beyond. It was silent, almost eerie, and when she closed the door she

41

could still hear the low insidious sound of the foghorn.

The maid came to collect the tray and she decided it was perhaps time she bathed and changed for dinner. The water was hot, which cheered her considerably, and the towels in the bathroom were huge and pleasantly fragrant, and when at last she stood in front of the cheval mirror she felt reassured by what she saw.

The heavy georgette dress was exquisitely cut even though it was plain, and the colour did show up her dark blue eyes and bring out the lustre in her light brown hair. She was not strictly beautiful, not like Kathy had been beautiful or Alanna, but in her tall slender figure and air of gentility she had a certain allure.

She sat in front of the fire to wait for Dominic, and as she had surmised he was wearing a dinner jacket and his smile of approval told her she looked the part.

'I hope you like this room Ginevra,' he said. 'My mother always wanted to stay in this room, it was her favourite.'

'Yes, it's lovely. Did you hear the foghorn?'

'Yes. The mist comes down very suddenly along this stretch of coast and we'll probably be hearing it all the time we're here. The weather forecast isn't good I'm afraid.'

'What shall we do with ourselves?'

'Oh, there's always something. I know this part of England very well. Perhaps the fog will lift and tomorrow we can drive out somewhere. We're to join Grandmother in the drawing room, dinner is at eight.'

She nodded, and with a smile he said, 'You look very beautiful Ginevra, Grandmother will think so I'm sure.'

Ginevra was anything but sure, but as they walked down the long wide staircase he took her hand in his and held it fast. At that moment she felt for the first time a sense of belonging.

Ginevra looked around her with interest. The large hall was panelled in dark rich oak and there was a flagged floor and several oriental rugs. Suits of armour stood cheek by jowl with solid oak chests on which reposed huge bronze ornaments, mostly of ancient Roman gladiators and centurions.

When Dominic saw Ginevra's interest in them he said with a smile, 'Apparently my grandfather and his father before him had a great interest in anything to do with ancient Rome.'

A huge log fire burned in the massive stone fireplace and the flames from it dispelled much of the gloom created by dark wood and bronze, however well it had been cared for. The lighting was dim, but Dominic said, 'We'll go into the drawing room, Ginevra. I doubt if the old lady will be down yet.'

The drawing room was considerably more cheerful. Here were velvet curtains and faded chintz, here too were vases filled with red autumn leaves and bright red berries. A log fire burned in the grate and above it on the wall hung a huge picture of a Scottish loch with its heather-clad braes and Highland cattle.

Dominic stood on the rug looking up at it.

'When I was a small boy I loved this picture. I'd

43

spent a lot of time in Scotland and this picture seemed to embody everything I loved there, I always hoped that one day it would be mine; now I have to ask you if you would want it.'

Ginevra went to stand beside him so that she could look at it.

'We have one or two pictures of Scottish lochs, but I always thought they were too dark and dreary. This one is different, it comes to life.'

'Does that mean that you would like it?'

'Yes, very much.'

'In that case I'll go on staking a claim for it. Andrew liked it too, but I am the eldest.' His smile dispelled any hint of superiority.

From outside the room came the sound of footsteps across the flagged floor.

The old lady entered on the arm of her butler, who took her to a chair near the fireplace and immediately placed a rug over her knees before leaving. Dominic went to embrace her, then he held out his hand to Ginevra.

Her first impression of the Duchess was that she was tall and thin with a lined aristocratic face and fine blue-grey eyes. There had once been great beauty in that face, but now all that was left was fine bone structure and dignity.

'Come into the light so that I can look at you,' she demanded, and dutifully Ginevra obeyed.

'You're very young,' she said. 'How old are you?'

'I'm twenty-two, your Grace.'

'There's no need for you to address me with my title, you are going to marry my grandson. I suggest you call me Grandmother as he does.'

'Thank you, Grandmother.'

Looking up at Dominic she said, 'How long are you staying? The weather is bad, I'm told.'

'It's misty and rather grey, but that is no problem.'

'You would have done better to have visited me in the autumn instead of leaving it until January, don't you think so my dear?'

'Yes, but I think this was the first time Dominic could manage it.'

'I suppose so. Always too much going on, too many calls on his time. When did you arrive?'

'Around half-past four,' Dominic answered.

'Did Mrs McPherson give you something to eat?'

'We had afternoon tea, Grandmother, she looked after us very well.'

At that moment the sound of the dinner gong echoed round the room and the old lady said, 'Ah dinner. Give me your arm Dominic. These chairs are so low and at this time of the year my arthritis is bad.'

Dominic collected her rug, gave her his arm, and Ginevra walked behind them across the hall and down a wide passage into the dining room.

Like everything else in the castle it was large and dark, but on the long dining table candelabras holding ten candles each burned brightly and the table glistened with crystal and silver.

'You still dine in some style, Grandmother,' Dominic said with a smile.

'I usually dine in a smaller room, tonight I am entertaining guests.'

'You needn't have gone to all this trouble for us.'

'Indeed I should. I am meeting a new member of the family, I wanted her to see that I may be old and largely forgotten, but I can still muster up some style.'

'You're never forgotten Grandmother, why do you say you are?'

'Because I rarely see any of you. How is your mother, it's months since she's been to see me.'

'She's very well, but Father hasn't been well and he gets querulous if he's left on his own.'

'Does he indeed, and when is he ever on his own with a house full of servants and a lot nearer to civilisation than I am.'

She took her place at the dining table, indicating where Dominic and Ginevra should sit.

McPherson appeared with two younger men who proceeded to serve the meal and the dinner wine. When the old lady refused it Dominic said, 'You don't want wine, Grandmother?'

'No, I never touch it now. I'll have brandy with my coffee.'

The meal was excellent and Ginevra reflected that probably the old lady would settle for nothing less. She was one of the old school, not unlike her own grandmother, and as she watched the Duchess delicately crumbling the roll on her plate she felt that there was a timelessness about her. Indeed the entire castle and its inhabitants could have descended from another age, an age of inflexibility and impeccable good manners.

The meal was eaten mostly in silence and it was

only when McPherson asked if the Duchess would like coffee served in the drawing room that she said sharply, 'No, we'll have it in here, McPherson.'

When Dominic looked at her in some surprise she said with a smile, 'After dinner I want to talk to Ginevra while you go into the billiard room. You can knock a few balls about surely for half an hour or so.'

Ginevra's heart sank. She wondered what sort of questions this indomitable old woman would ask and what her replies might be.

Chapter Four

Dutifully McPherson came to take the old lady's arm, but shrugging him on one side she said, 'That's all right McPherson, Lady Ginevra will look after me, I'll ring for you later.'

Instead of her large comfortable chair the Duchess selected the couch, patting the cushions for Ginevra to sit beside her.

'My eyes are not what they were,' she explained. 'I can't see you at the other side of the fireplace. I couldn't see you properly in the dining room, the lighting is very dim. I keep promising myself that I must have something done about it.'

'Wouldn't that detract from the charm of the place?' Ginevra asked.

'Perhaps. I don't suppose I'll bother, not with the little time I've got left.'

There was no self-pity in her voice, she was simply stating a fact and Ginevra deemed it wiser to remain silent.

'You're very like your grandmother you know,' the Duchess said with a little smile.

'Yes, I've often been told so. Did you know her well?'

'No. She was one of the bright young things who came out later. I was a long-standing married woman by that time. They were a merry throng that year, we had to look to our husbands. I was nineteen when I married the Duke, he was Lord Tarleton in those days. I was head over heels in love with him and he was nearly thirty and he'd lived a little.'

Ginevra waited.

'I didn't know him very well. We were encouraged to marry young men with titles and fortunes. I was told that I'd pulled off the catch of the season. I was living in a state of euphoria.'

'Were you happy?' Ginevra ventured.

'For those very few months exceedingly so. I gave him a son and a daughter, Dominic's mother, I had a beautiful house in Berkshire as well as this place and a house in Mayfair. I had riches and servants, indeed I had everything my parents had wanted for me, but there were cracks in the structure. It did not take me long to learn that my beautiful, perfect world was flawed and people were at pains to tell me so.'

'Wasn't that a bit unkind?'

The old lady smiled, and as she viewed the girl sitting beside her something like pity appeared in her eyes.

Ignoring Ginevra's comments she said, 'Tell me about you, my dear, when did you first meet Dominic, and how well do you know him?'

'Our parents have known one another for years, but I first met him in the summer at Goodwood. We were house guests at the home of mutual friends.'

'The Garvestons?'

'Yes. Do you know them?'

'Oh yes. Not the younger element though. So you met Dominic at the Garvestons when you were all at the races together?'

'Yes, that's right.'

'And you were thrown together and left alone to get on with it. It would seem that even after all these years times don't change much.'

Ginevra remained silent. She felt strangely uncomfortable with her companion's astute summing up of those first few days of her meeting with Dominic. He'd been nice, kind. They'd enjoyed the races, talked and laughed together. Her parents and his had beamed at them benevolently, and after that week Dominic had telephoned constantly, accepted invitations to long country weekends, and asked her father for his daughter's hand in marriage.

It had been sweet and charming. He had embraced her with respect and Ginevra believed that out of it love would grow for both of them. She wanted it to grow, she was more in love with him than he was with her.

She suddenly realised that her thoughts had occupied a time of silence and, looking at her companion quickly, she said, 'Please forgive me,

I was miles away.'

'You have a lot to think about my dear.'

'It all seems to have happened so quickly, I hadn't thought to be getting married so soon.'

'What did you expect?'

'Dances and house parties where I would meet a host of young men. When I was at finishing school in the Bernese Oberland we talked about the fun we would have when we arrived back in England. Not that there would be somebody like Dominic after a week at Goodwood.'

'A man much older than the young blades you'd visualised?'

'Well, yes.'

'Dominic was always a nice boy, reserved, thoughtful. Totally unlike his brother Andrew. Have you met Andrew?'

'Oh yes. I've met all Dominic's family now.'

'Andrew was always the mischievous one, I expect he's had a multitude of young women in a very short space of time.'

Ginevra smiled.

'There are some family photographs on the piano Ginevra; if you'll bring some of them over I'll tell you who they are and where they were taken.'

Obediently Ginevra went to collect the photographs, placing them on the cushions between them, and the Duchess picked them up one by one.

There were studio photographs of Dominic's mother in silks and satins, with tiaras and feathers in her hair, and groups of family photographs. His sister Prunella and her husband and children, Andrew in the company of a group of young people on a climbing venture, and several others with Dominic and his family, a much younger Dominic, handsome and smiling, and a girl, dark and very beautiful, hanging on to his arm, gazing into his eyes.

Puzzled, she laid them back on the cushion and, meeting the Duchess's eyes she said, 'These were taken a long time ago, I've met them all except the girl.'

'Melinda Fallon.'

Ginevra waited expectantly.

'She was the most beautiful girl I ever saw,' the old lady went on. 'She had everything going for her, beauty, brains, wit and breeding.' Suddenly her voice trailed off and she looked at Ginevra out of sad old eyes. 'Talk to Dominic my dear, if you don't others will talk to you like they talked to me. Don't go blindly into this marriage, if you are lucky we are talking about a very long time.'

Ginevra nodded gently, then picking up the photographs she stacked them together and went to replace them on the piano.

Her mind was filled with confusion. She had not come to Northumberland to have Dominic's grandmother fill her heart and mind with un-certainties, and yet there had been kindness in the old lady's face, and as she returned to her seat the Duchess said, 'Please pull the bellrope Ginevra, I am feeling very tired, McPherson will help me up to my room.'

'Can't I do that?'

'McPherson is stronger. You would be sur-prised how much strength is needed.'

McPherson had been anticipating the call and Ginevra watched as he manoeuvred the old lady out of her seat and across the floor. At the door she turned to say, 'I will see you tomorrow for dinner Ginevra. I hope the day is fine and Dominic can show you something of Northumbria.'

She went to stare at the photographs on top of the grand piano. Melinda Fallon was beautiful with a gay laughing face framed by dark hair. Slender and tall, she was gazing up at Dominic with rapt admiration and he was gazing down at her with the same sort of absorption. When he looked at Ginevra it was with an expression that was gentle, kind and without the deeper emotion of love.

The old lady had warned her to be careful. She too had taken this journey into the unknown a long time ago and found it fraught with uncertainty.

As she looked down at the photographs the door opened to admit Dominic and quickly she turned away. She did not want him to see her looking at the photographs. Tomorrow there would be time to talk.

Ginevra slept badly that cold winter's night. Outside in the darkness the sound of the foghorn's persistent moaning penetrated the stout walls and windows covered by their long curtains, and occasionally there was another sound which she recognised as the crashing of the sea against the rocks.

She had to know about Melinda Fallon. After all Dominic was thirty-nine years old so obviously there had been women in his life, so why hadn't he married a girl like Melinda Fallon, and was he still nursing a love for her? Where was she? Why hadn't he married her?

The Duchess was right, there had to be honesty between herself and Dominic. She would refuse to marry a man who was nursing a longing for some other woman. If that was the case the engagement had been a mistake.

Tossing and turning she thought about what he might say. Admit it, refute it, or would there be more, some strange reason why it had all gone wrong. Dominic would be honest with her, she would stand for nothing less, and yet she was half afraid of hearing the truth.

Did his grandmother know the truth, and had it been so distasteful that she thought Ginevra should hear it from Dominic himself?

She slept at last. It was a fitful tormented sleep, but on awakening she could not remember her dreams. The foghorn had stopped and when she opened the curtains a thin watery sun was trying to dispel the remaining mist.

She gasped with delight as she looked down through the gardens at a sea rolling gently in towards the rocks, at a long green lawn leading down to the boulders where thrift and heather would bloom rampantly in the springtime. Suddenly she felt an urgent need to get out of the castle and into the countryside.

The castle with its medieval turrets and suits of armour was as dark as her thoughts. Away from it they could talk about normality and even if the sun shone out of a wintry sky, at least it was better than this old dark castle which would

53

forever remind her of a restless night and the darkest deeds her imagination might conjure up.

Dominic was already sitting at the breakfast table and although his smile was warm he was aware that her answering smile was unduly cautious.

Relaxed conversation came easily to his lips. 'Did you sleep well?' he asked her.

'Fitfully I'm afraid. I was very conscious of this dark castle and the sea crashing on the rocks.'

'I know. But it is a nice morning so we should be able to see something of the countryside. Did my grandmother subject you to an alarming inquisition?'

'Not really. She talked about her youth and her marriage.'

'I never think of grandmother's youth, it seems to me that she's always been the age she is now, probably because she was always censorious and critical.'

'Perhaps marriage did that to her. She was very young, only nineteen.'

'And my grandfather was extremely pompous and overbearing. Is that all you're having for breakfast?'

She had helped herself to orange juice and toast, and Dominic was eyeing her plate with some alarm.

'I never eat much breakfast, my father is always telling me off about it.'

'Yes well, we were always advised to make a good breakfast, it was the best way to start the day.'

He smiled across the table at her. 'You look

very nice this morning Ginevra, I'm glad you brought tweeds and sweaters.'

'The views from my bedroom are beautiful, I can imagine they will be even more so in the springtime.'

'Yes they are, then the castle doesn't look quite so forbidding. Did Grandmother subject you to all sorts of questions about the wedding?'

'Some.'

'And did she say if she was going to make the effort?'

'I didn't ask her. I assumed she would come.'

'We should get off soon Ginevra, these winter days are short, I'll bring the car round.'

'There's no need, I'll come with you.'

'You'll need a warm coat.'

'It's in the cloakroom, I can get it on our way out.'

She was glad of the warmth of her sheepskin coat because there was a strong wind blowing across the parkland, and glancing up at the sky Dominic said, 'There's snow in the wind, we'll keep an eye on the weather. It can change so quickly in this part of England.'

They drove along the winding roads towards the sea and Ginevra was charmed by castles crumbling on sweeping hills and ancient abbeys. It seemed that the ancient Romans had left a legacy of their presence everywhere and before lunch they were standing on the wall that separated England from Scotland and Dominic was saying, 'Can you even begin to imagine those men from sunny Italy facing an implacable enemy on these windswept hills? When I was a boy I loved this place, so much of our history is contained along that majestic wall.'

Lunch was a companionable affair taken in an old inn with low ceilings, dark oak rafters and glowing log fires.

She had enjoyed their morning together, the sort of morning she would never have experienced with Larry. Larry liked driving, but at the end of it there had to be horse-racing or motor-racing. Crowds of people and noise. Her morning with Dominic had been filled with solitude, apart from the sound of the wind, and Dominic had said, 'Can you feel it, Ginevra, those Roman soldiers standing here on the wall listening to the wind and the cries of the vengeful Scots?'

On the way back he smiled down at her saying, 'You're very pensive Ginevra, have you been terribly bored?'

'Oh no, I've loved it.'

'But you're very quiet.'

'Yes. I've been thinking about something your grandmother said last night, but I don't quite know how to begin.'

'Well, I do remember when my sister married that Grandmother posed questions nobody else had even thought about. I can't think that we have escaped. What exactly did she say?'

'She said she had thought her marriage perfect, it wasn't and other people were only too anxious to talk to her. She said I mustn't let that happen, that I should talk to you, Dominic.'

'You know you can talk to me about anything, but what particularly?'

'She told me to look at the family photographs on the piano.'

'It's years since I looked at them, what did she mean?'

'One picture Dominic. A group of young people, one of them was you, and there was a girl, lovely and dark; in spite of there being a group you and she were together.'

She was suddenly aware that he was very quiet, his gaze concentrated on the road in front of them, and a feeling of anguish and remembered pain. She was wishing she'd ignored Dominic's grandmother, some things were better left alone, sometimes living in a fool's paradise was preferable to knowing the truth.

They had driven for some miles in silence, then to her surprise Dominic pulled into a layby with the sea below them and the old castle standing gaunt and strangely beautiful on the hillside in the rays of the setting sun.

'What exactly do you want to ask me Ginevra? Plainly there are things in my life you feel you should know about.'

'Dominic, I'm sorry, they have nothing to do with me, I shouldn't be asking about them.'

'Obviously my grandmother thinks you should know and perhaps she's right. If we're to journey on together we should have no secrets, particularly secrets that some other person might reveal. The photograph, you want to know about one of the people in it?'

'Yes. Melinda Fallon.'

He didn't look at her. The expression on his face was distant, but after a few seconds he an-

57

swered, his voice strangely flat and unemotional.

'I met Melinda soon after I came down from Cambridge and she'd erupted on the social scene in a whirl of balls and house parties. She was very beautiful, the most shining light in that year of beautiful debs, and she was both witty and charming.

'Most of the young men were in love with Melinda, vying for her attention, and she could have taken her pick from any of them. She fell in love with me and I with her, it seemed inevitable.

'We were inseparable. My family and hers were delighted, her father was an Irish peer, her mother was French. They had a beautiful house in County Clare where her father bred race horses. We spent long ecstatic weekends there, sailing and riding, and I discovered that Melinda was fearless. She liked unpredictable horses and sailing in rough turbulent seas. In the winter we spent holidays on the ski slopes. It seemed that wherever Melinda was there was excitement and adventure.

'We were the beautiful golden couple on whom the sun shone with an increasing brilliance, and we announced our engagement at a ball our respective parents laid on for us at the London house.

'Perhaps we're not meant to find perfection in this world, it was never meant to last.'

His expression was bitter. He had forgotten she was there, all his thoughts were in the past and it would seem the past belonged to Melinda. Ginevra waited, her hands clenched tight against her knees, while Dominic sought for words to tell her of the thing that had destroyed his world.

After a long silence he began to speak again. 'We were spending a long weekend in the Lake District. There'd been dancing and it was a beautiful night in early August, warm, and the lake was calm and beautiful. Some of them suggested taking boats out, they were all pretty merry, but it was late and I had to leave early in the morning so I said I wouldn't join them and I tried to persuade Melinda to stay behind too.

'She suddenly decided she wouldn't go out in the boats, she'd swim in the lake. Again I tried to dissuade her, but she simply said, "Dominic darling don't fuss, it's a beautiful night and I feel like swimming. I'll see you at breakfast."

'It didn't really bother me. She was an excellent swimmer and she'd swum in the lake many times before. So I went to bed and the next morning I was the first one down to breakfast. The rest of them arrived laughing and talking about their time on the lake. Melinda didn't appear and one of them said how unusual it was for her to sleep in, she was usually wide awake and ready for whatever the day would bring.

'One of the men said, "I think we hit Percy in the water last night, the local fishermen will be relieved about that."

'Percy was a gigantic pike that had been the bane of local fishermen for years.

'I finished my breakfast and decided to collect my things. Melinda still hadn't arrived so I said I'd go up to her room to say goodbye. I knew we'd be meeting in a few days' time when she was up in London.

'When there was no answer when I knocked on her bedroom door I opened it. The bed hadn't been slept in, the dress she had worn the evening before was thrown over a chair, her shoes and the rest of her clothes lay in a heap on the floor. I was suddenly aware of a feeling of terror. I ran down the stairs to tell the rest of them, and they all left the breakfast table and we raced through the gardens and down to the lake. Melinda's body lay in the shallows; she was dead, her neck was broken.'

Ginevra remained silent, she couldn't intrude in a moment that had brought the past back in all its disastrous trauma. Dominic was reliving that fateful morning.

After what seemed like an eternity he turned to look at her. His eyes were still filled with pain and she waited patiently for him to leave the past and re-enter the present.

At last he said 'Is that what my grandmother wanted me to tell you, Ginevra?'

'I think she believed it was something I should know about, Dominic.'

'It happened fifteen years ago.'

'I know, but the pain is still there, isn't it? The story had to come from you, not from somebody else in a moment of malice or trivial conversation.'

'And now that you know, does it make a difference?'

'I think so. Now I shall know why you can't love me like you loved her. Now neither of us will have to pretend.'

'Pretend!'

'Of course. That is what we were doing isn't it, Dominic? We don't really know one another and no amount of socialising is going to make it any different. There was a girl I was at school with, her father was an Indian rajah and she'd known since she was six that one day she would marry a boy seven years older than herself and whom she could not ever remember meeting. She didn't seem to think there was anything wrong with the idea, I thought it was terrible, but then I was romantically inclined, very much in love with love, and expecting life to play fair.

'I hear from Shanta from time to time. She's married with two sons so she's more than fulfilled her side of the contract. Doesn't that just about sum up our contract Dominic?'

His expression said it all. Doubt, uncertainty, even shock, and with a little smile she said, 'Have I been too explicit?'

'I was hoping we could establish a great deal more to our marriage. That between us there would be respect, affection, a hope that out of it love would grow. Love doesn't always have to be that headlong flight into ecstasy which often falls at the first hurdle.'

He covered her hand with his and his expression was warm and thoughtful. 'I'd like to believe that we do have a loving future together Ginevra, I'm older than you, and I probably have considerably more patience. You are young enough to want everything and want it now.'

She nodded. At that moment she couldn't trust her voice, and after a few moments he started up the engine and drove out into the road.

Chapter Five

It was raining by the time they reached the castle and Dominic let her out of the car in front of the door so that she could hurry in out of the rain. She was glad to escape up to her room unobserved and hopeful that she would not meet Dominic again before dinner.

She bathed and changed into the other evening dress she had brought with her, but all the time her actions were automatic, she had too many things to think about.

The housemaid appeared with tea and scones and before she sat down she opened the dressing table drawer and took out a leather-bound wallet. She couldn't have said why she'd brought it with her from home, but it had been a constant companion for a good number of years. She opened it and brought out a page from a magazine, one of her mother's society magazines she had loved as a child. She spread the page out across the dressing table top. It was a photograph of several groups of people at a London ball. Young men in uniform or formal evening dress, girls in satins and silks wearing their glittering jewellery and one picture larger than the rest of Dominic Hartington, the Marquis of Chayter.

Young and incredibly handsome, there had been no mention of Melinda Fallon, he had simply been a man she had dreamed of. Avidly she had continued to scan her mother's magazines for news of him, but there had been nothing, and now it appeared she knew the reason why. After Melinda, Dominic had withdrawn from the social scene and the next time Ginevra had seen his face was across a crowded room at the Garvestons during that week at Goodwood.

He was still handsome, but there had been an aura of remoteness about him that had appealed to the romantic in her. They had been introduced and she had made herself agreeable, flattering him with her fresh youth and ingenuous chatter. All that week she had sought him out, and her parents and his had watched their friendship grow and decided that there was a chance something concrete might emerge from it.

She hated Dominic's grandmother for spelling it out to her. He had asked her to marry him because it was time he married, time he produced an heir, and everybody in their world thought she'd done very well for herself.

Dominic too was troubled. He had changed, and was ready to go down to dinner, but he wasn't sure of the evening's normality. There was a soft tap on the door and he thought immediately that it was Ginevra with her anxieties as acute as his own. He was surprised to see his grandmother standing outside the door, leaning heavily on her stick, and then she was in his room limping slowly toward a chair. They faced each other without speaking for several moments before she said. 'I know what you're thinking, Dominic, that I'm the same sort of meddling old woman that I've always been. You're probably right, but I've only ever meddled when I've thought it was called for.'

Dominic remained silent.

'Well, say something,' she demanded.

'I don't see that your meddling has served any good purpose, Grandmother. Everything would have resolved itself in time.'

'But time is in very short supply isn't it. How well do you know this girl, a few long weekends in other people's houses, usually with a fair-sized house party? That's how it was with me, and in Ginevra I see myself.'

'But you don't see my grandfather in me.'

'No. On the other hand what do you know about him?'

'Rumours have always been flying around. That he had other women, that he was charming and ruthless and completely immoral for most of your married life.'

'It's true, Dominic. I was nineteen, starry-eyed and head over heels in love with him, then after a few months he began to grow bored with his child bride, and waiting were a string of available women only too convinced that his marriage would collapse.'

'There are no other women waiting to surface in my life, Grandmother.'

'Perhaps not, but there is Melinda Fallon.'

'Melinda is dead, the dead don't come back to harass the living.'

'But you haven't forgotten her. All these years when you've wilfully erased women from your life because you couldn't get her out of it, you

64

never tried, you never wanted to get close to another woman because it would destroy Melinda's memory; now because your family have become impatient with you, because they are demanding more than you have to give, you suddenly decide that this young artless girl will fit the bill.'

'It isn't like that, I like Ginevra, I will like her more, we will grow together, make our marriage work.'

'And suppose you don't? The lack of love in my marriage destroyed me. It made me old and bitter before my time, turned me into the sort of meddling old martinet you despise.'

'Then you think this engagement is a mistake, that we should put an end to it now before it's too late?'

'You think that's better than trying? Dominic, Melinda Fallon is dead and she is not coming back. You have a young, beautiful girl who needs to get to know you, you need to get to know each other, surely at least you can try.'

'There isn't much time.'

'Give yourself time. Not on the telephone, not in other people's houses, not where there's too much of a crowd and not enough of you.'

When he continued to stare at her searchingly she said, 'There are romantic places you can take her to even in the depths of winter, places where you can be together, where you can talk to each other, learn a little more about each other.' Then with something approaching humour in her voice she said, 'I should stay away from the Lakes; they would do no good at all.'

'Perhaps Ginevra will find she's no longer interested.'

'Where is all that charm that landed Melinda Fallon? It can't all be dead.'

'And suppose your therapy doesn't work, suppose we're no nearer needing each other than we are now?'

'Well, at least you'll have tried. Your grandfather never tried with me. He knew I was unhappy, he didn't think I was worth the effort, not when there were other women with whom he didn't have to make an effort. Now you can take me down to dinner.'

'What about Ginevra?'

'I asked McPherson to escort Ginevra.'

'You've thought of everything, haven't you, Grandmother.'

'I'm not sure. My memory is not what it was, I have to be spurred on to doing things, but I do have an instinctive feeling about being right.'

Dominic laughed. For the first time in all the long years he had known his grandmother he felt close to her. He had never seen the wisdom behind her carping, the astuteness underneath her meddling.

The family had always said his grandfather had turned to other women because of his wife's peculiarities; now he was coming to realise that her peculiarities had been a result of his philanderings.

He helped her gently out of her chair and walked slowly with her to the door. Her slight frame felt heavy on his arm and a wave of pity swept over him. She looked so frail, and yet underneath that fragility was a hint of steel. His grandmother was a survivor. She had outlived her husband by twenty years and for the last few years of his life she had been the one person in it he had esteemed.

Dominic could hear him saying, 'We'll have to ask your grandmother,' or 'Your grandmother wouldn't like that,' and they'd laughed about it, saying he couldn't do anything without consulting her. Now he understood that by sheer willpower and courage she had earned his esteem, and probably his love, although that had come too late.

Ginevra was already in the dining room and they went forward to meet her.

She kissed his grandmother's cheek and offered him a sweet but hesitant smile. Seated at the dining table the Duchess said, 'Now tell me what sort of a day you've had. What do you think of Northumberland, Ginevra?'

'It's beautiful. It must be even more so in the summer.'

'Yes it is, and strangely enough not too many people have absorbed its beauty. They go to the lakes, across the border into Scotland. They only seem to pass through here.'

'Then they don't know what they're missing.'

'You must come in the summer. I don't have any horses now, my riding days are over, but McPherson will get me two decent ones from Lord Cresswell's stables, then you can really get to know the countryside.'

'I'd like that.'

Across the table her eyes met Dominic's and he smiled.

The Duchess heaved a sigh of relief. At least there was hope. If they could think about the summer all was not lost.

'And how do you propose to spend the rest of your stay?' she enquired.

'Weather permitting I thought tomorrow we might drive over to Lindisfarne. It's years since I wandered round that old abbey. Do the monks still make the mead Grandfather was so fond of?'

'I expect they do. It was far too sweet for me, and you have to watch for the tides, they can be treacherous at all times, but more so in the winter.'

'How do you spend your time in the winter?' Dominic asked her.

'I read a little. Those books with large print are a boon, but Mrs McPherson doesn't always choose them too wisely. She selects those she likes herself, silly frothy love stories, and I've told her time and again I like historical novels. I keep promising to get a television but I never do.'

'You should, Grandmother.'

'The servants have one and McPherson prefers to spend his evenings at the inn because there's nothing he wants to watch.'

Conversation was not easy in that vast dining room where servants moved around softly or stood in respectful silence.

'We'll take coffee in the drawing room,' the Duchess announced, and as before Dominic offered his arm to escort her while Ginevra followed behind. They were half-way across the hall when the telephone erupted in the silence and McPherson was hurrying into the library to answer it. He returned quickly saying, 'It's for ye Mr Dominic, I'll look after her Grace.'

As he settled her into her chair she asked, 'Who was it, McPherson? Not my daughter I hope.'

'I canna be sure, whoever she was she sounded agitated.'

'Have them serve the coffee in here, McPherson.'

After he had left she said, 'It sounds like Dominic's mother. She's guaranteed to sound agitated at the least thing. When his father suffered that mild heart attack it might have been the end of the world.'

Ginevra smiled politely.

They looked up expectantly when Dominic came into the room, and instinctively knew he had received no good news.

'It's Father,' he explained quickly. 'He's been out on the estate and fallen on some thin ice. He hasn't broken anything but he's badly bruised. Mother's afraid it might set off another heart attack.'

'So she wants you home?' the Duchess snapped.

'You know Mother. I tried telling her there was nothing to worry about but she doesn't agree with me.'

'So, when will you leave?'

He looked at Ginevra with a reluctant smile. 'I'm afraid it will have to be tomorrow, dear. I am sorry.'

'It doesn't matter. I understand, Dominic.'

'Isn't Andrew there to give support?' His grandmother asked.

'We didn't mention him.'

'Oh, well, you can only do what you have to do. Let me know how things go.'

It was evident that the Duchess was not pleased at their early departure and after Dominic had drunk his coffee he rose to his feet saying, 'I was going back to London on Wednesday so I do have several telephone calls to make. Will you please excuse me?'

Ginevra felt bemused. Dominic was going back to his family and she had no means of knowing when they would meet again. Their wedding was in April and it all seemed a confused leap in the dark. Something of her confusion transmitted itself to her companion, and the old lady said, 'I spoke with Dominic earlier on, Ginevra. I expected him to accuse me of being a meddlesome old woman. He didn't, but the implication was there. What had he to say about Melinda Fallon?'

'He told me how she had died, he told me that he had been desperately in love with her and unable to get her out of his mind.'

'This happened fifteen years ago, plenty of time to forget her.'

'If Melinda was alive, Grandmother, I would feel that the competition was fair. How can I fight a ghost?'

'My dear, in the long run the cards are stacked on your side. You're alive, with warmth and beauty. But don't do it as I tried to do it. I rebelled, I fought the opposition with tears and tantrums that my husband abhorred and didn't know how to deal with, but then I was a naïve girl who nobody had even thought to caution and I was up against worldly-wise women who dismissed me as unimportant.

'It isn't going to be easy my dear, but in the early stages be satisfied to be a good friend, a warm and loyal companion, from that I am certain that love will grow and Melinda Fallon's shadow will become dim.'

'I wish I could think that.'

'But you will try?'

'Yes, I'll try. I'm so glad we came here this weekend, I feel you've been a very good friend. There's nobody else I can talk to.'

'Not to your parents?'

'No. They're quite happy with the situation. If they know anything about Melinda I'd be the last person they would talk to about it.'

When Dominic came back to the room he found them sitting in comfortable ease enjoying a glass of sherry, and he went to pour himself a whisky and soda.

'I suppose you'll want to be off early in the morning,' his grandmother said.

'I'm afraid so. It's a long drive to Berkshire and then across country to Shropshire.'

'Your mother never had any idea about geography.'

Dominic laughed and Ginevra said, 'My mother isn't much better, she thought Yorkshire and Northumberland were one and the same.'

'Your mother panics, always has done,' the Duchess went on mercilessly. 'Where is your brother in all this, and how about Prunella, they're within driving distance.'

'They are also in Chamonix, Grandmother.'

'I'm tired, I shall go to bed,' the old lady announced. 'I didn't sleep well last night.'

'I'll take you up to your room,' Dominic said.

'No, ring for McPherson. Talk to Ginevra, you came up here to give yourself time together, there isn't much time left so make the most of it.'

They both embraced her and she said, 'I shan't be up to see you off so I wish you a pleasant journey.'

'We will see you in April, Grandmother?' Dominic asked.

'It will depend on my state of health. Why people elect to get married in April I can't imagine. It's one of those indeterminate months, too close to Easter and the weather can be any way.'

'We've ordered lashings of sunshine and warm breezes, Grandmother.'

The old lady merely sniffed, and, taking McPherson's arm, she limped painfully out of the room.

'Another inquisition, Ginevra?' Dominic asked.

'No. I hope your father is not seriously injured?'

'I don't think so. If he cuts his finger there are panic stations.

It took all Dominic's skill as a driver to cope with the weather conditions as they drove south the next day. Icy winds bringing sleet and snow swept across the countryside and a grey rumbling sea and low hanging clouds promised nothing better as the day progressed.

They pulled into a deserted hotel car park midday, and the empty dining room did nothing to dispel their misgivings. When Dominic felt disposed to apologise for the weekend, the weather, and their hasty summons home Ginevra said evenly, 'It's not your fault, there's no need for you to apologise.'

'Even so, it was a mistake to come. Every year Mother invites Grandmother to stay with us for the winter months, but she refuses.' He reached across the table and covered her hand with his.

'There's so much we have to talk about and so little time. As soon as I know what the position is at home I'll telephone you. We have to meet again very soon.'

'Another house party, when we hardly ever find time to talk?'

'That's another thing Grandmother said, "Too much of a crowd and not enough of me".'

'Yes well, it was easier in a crowd wasn't it. No need to rehash the past, and the future would take care of itself.'

'Something like that. It was hopeless to think it would work.'

'Oh I don't know. We could have got married in April, got along perhaps, and then slowly and painfully over the years I would have been asking myself what was wrong with our marriage.'

'You think there would have been something wrong with it?'

'Of course. I'm a young romantic woman with all sorts of dreams about the prince who would kiss my dreaming heart awake, and I'm not sure that you would have known how to pretend.'

'And now?'

'At least now I shall know that I have to earn your love Dominic. It might not be instant, it might never be at all, but I know about Melinda, nobody else is going to enlighten me. It would have been worse if she'd been alive.'

They had gone back to the car and Ginevra sat huddled under the rug listening to the wind beating around them, and the hypnotic windscreen wipers attempting to cope with the icy rain. Normal conversation was impossible, so Ginevra permitted herself to think about her future. Such a short time she had before the wedding. She would stand beside Dominic in front of the altar in the huge Abbey surrounded by guests and onlookers, and they would make promises that only one of them could believe in.

Would Dominic look down at her and picture Melinda? Would there be others in the congregation who would remember her, think what a mistake they were making?

It could have been worse. Melinda was dead. It could have been some woman in the congregation waiting to get back into his life when the first enthusiasm for their marriage had passed into oblivion.

When they drove at last through the gates of her home the rain was still dancing on the terrace and Charlton, armed with a huge umbrella, was running down the steps to help with her luggage.

'Are my parents in?' she asked him.

'No, my lady. They went over to stay with Lady Oakwell for the weekend; they didn't expect you home until Wednesday.'

'No, circumstances altered our arrangements.'

Charlton hurried up the steps carrying her case and Dominic walked with her, sheltering them both under his umbrella. At the door she asked, 'Would you like tea or something, you still have a long way to drive.'

'No I'll get off now, it will be dark before I get home. I'll ring you this evening to let you know the score. We'll meet again very soon.'

She watched him hurrying back to his car, responding to his final wave before he drove swiftly towards the gates, then she went into the house and Charlton was waiting to take her coat.

His first impression was that she looked pensive and preoccupied.

'There's a warm fire in the study, Milady. What time will you want dinner?'

'I'm not hungry, we had something on the journey but I would like tea. Did my parents say when they were returning?'

'No. But I'm sure it will be before you were expected back.'

She stood at the morning room window with the curtains open looking out into the wet misery of the night. She could see in the light from the window the pelting rain and she was thinking about Dominic driving the long route into Shropshire.

She drank her tea sitting in front of the fire and gradually she thawed out. For no explicable reason she decided to telephone Larry Harbrook. They hadn't parted on very good terms and their last telephone conversation had hardly been harmonious. At that moment however she simply wanted to hear the cheerfulness in his voice, even

75

the sarcasm that crept into it.

She could never talk to Larry about Dominic and the phantoms that pursued him, but Larry could make her feel worthy, Larry had loved her.

Chapter Six

Larry was his usual brash self. 'I didn't expect to be hearing from you,' he said airily. 'Wasn't the weekend going to extend until Wednesday at least? It's only Sunday.'

'Dominic's father had an accident on the estate and he had to get back.'

'Don't you really mean you were bored to death with each other?'

'No I don't, and if you're going to be unpleasant perhaps it was a mistake to ring you.'

'Actually I don't want to be unpleasant. I've had a very lucrative weekend; put some money on a couple of horses that came in first and met a very delightful girl.'

'I'm glad Larry. How much did you win?'

'That's not important, ask me about the girl.'

'All right, who is she and what's she like?'

'Beautiful, with legs that go on for ever and she's got great style. You don't know her.'

'How do you know I don't?'

'Because she doesn't exactly move in your exalted circles. She's a dancer in some American show.'

'She's American?'

'No. She's Scottish. She comes from Ayrshire.'

'You're invited to bring her to my wedding Larry.'

'I'm not sure about that, I told you I wasn't intending to come.'

'I'm sure you'll change your mind. What is your new girlfriend called?'

'Annie, but she prefers to be called Anita.'

'Why, for heaven's sake?'

'It does more for her professional image.'

'Well, I'm inviting her to my wedding. If she's all you say she is she'll liven the affair up no end.'

'How's Dominic? Don't tell me, I can imagine. Haughty, remote, very much the aristocrat, outmoded and Out of It.'

'And your jealousy shows in your sarcasm.'

'I'm not jealous. Don't flatter yourself. I admit I was jealous when I thought you were my girl, but I'm well over that now. How bad is Dominic's father? If it's bad enough you could end up marrying a duke.'

Suddenly she found Larry tiresome and infantile. It had been a mistake to ring him. In a resigned voice she said, 'I'm hanging up now Larry, I'll speak to you again one day.'

'You mean it when you say I can bring Anita to your wedding?'

'Of course.'

'She's beautiful, she won't let the side down.'

'Bring who you want, the invitation was for you and some other. I was so sure you'd find somebody.'

'Yes, well, life goes on doesn't it.'

In her bedroom she found that Polly, her maid,

77

had put away her clothes and turned on the electric fire. The room felt pleasantly warm and Polly had turned down the bedspread and her robe lay draped over the bed. She decided she'd had enough for one day, she would go to bed and try to get interested in her book.

A while later there was a knock on her door and Polly's smiling face appeared round it. 'I wasn't sure you were in bed, Milady,' she said, 'would you like something to drink?'

'Yes please Polly. Hot chocolate or something like that.'

She was back within a few minutes carrying a small tray which she placed on the bedside cabinet and Ginevra said, 'I suppose it's still raining.'

'It was when Mr Charlton went home, Milady, simply pouring down. He'd get very wet walking across the park.'

Polly smiled and wished her goodnight, and Ginevra sat up in bed to drink her chocolate. Dimly she could hear the wind whistling round the chimney and she wished Dominic would telephone.

Dominic faced his mother across the breakfast table and in a slightly aggrieved voice she said, 'You were very late arriving Dominic, I expected you earlier.'

'You do know Mother that it is some distance from Northumberland. Ginevra was with me so I had to take her home first.'

'I thought you'd have left the night before.'

'And drive through the night, a particularly

dreadful night? As it was the day journey was horrific enough.'

'I suppose your grandmother was against you coming home at all.'

'She had nothing to say on the subject.'

'Did she say if she intended to come to the wedding? It's in April, and she's coming a long way, I suppose Andrew will have to go up there to escort her down here?'

'I rather think she'll ask McPherson to bring her.'

'As well as his wife and probably some other servant. We're all staying with the Bannisters, we can't impose on them for all and sundry.'

'Grandmother is hardly sundry, Mother.'

'I know, but I really do think she should realise her limitations and stay at home.'

'And I would like her to come to the wedding, so would Ginevra.'

His mother raised her eyebrows. 'Really. I wouldn't have thought they'd have much in common. What on earth did they talk about?'

'They got along very well. The weather was bad, a lot of mist about, but I did manage to show Ginevra something of the countryside.'

'I've always thought it rather gloomy, all those old ruined abbeys and Roman remains.'

'We went up on the Wall. Ginevra was pretty impressed in spite of the wind that was blowing.'

'It's always blowing up there, we've never had a good day there yet.'

Dominic smiled. It was useless to argue about anything his mother had made up her mind about.

'I'm glad your father's so much better. I suppose you think I shouldn't have sent for you, but after last summer and that heart attack I had to be sure.'

'Did he ask you to send for me?'

'No. He said he had a few bruises, nothing more, but I had to be convinced. He makes light of everything if he thinks he's going to be confined to bed.'

He watched while she started to open her mail, which gave him the opportunity to attend to his own.

After a few minutes his mother exclaimed, 'This is lovely, Dominic, Margaret Ambrose is inviting us to spend a long weekend in Bath at the end of February and there's another one here from John and Mary Fletcher inviting us to another long weekend in Cheltenham. They're all dying to meet Ginevra before the wedding.'

'Have Ginevra and I been included in the invitation?'

'Yes, of course.'

'Mother, I don't think it's possible. Our wedding is in April and Ginevra and I have to spend some time together.'

'Well, you'll be together in Bath and in Cheltenham. What more do you want?'

'When I say together Mother, I mean exactly that. We need to get to know each other.'

'You have the rest of your lives to get to know each other.'

'You think that's all right, do you?'

'Of course. It's what your father and I did, it's what your grandparents did.'

'I'm amazed that it worked out so well.'

She stared at him uneasily. 'Has somebody been talking to Ginevra about Melinda?'

'She saw her photograph on the piano at Grandmother's house.'

'She should have had the good sense to see that it was removed before Ginevra got there.'

'You mean you would have preferred us to get married and have some other well-meaning souls tell her about Melinda later?'

'They wouldn't.'

'Oh, yes they would. Isn't that how Grandmother found out about Grandfather's nefarious pursuits?'

'Well, you've never had any nefarious pursuits as you call them. There's only been Melinda and she's been dead a great many years.'

'Perhaps that doesn't make it any easier. Grandfather's women were available predators waiting for the main chance. He got them out of his system, Melinda left too many memories.'

'So in less than four months you are hoping to convince Ginevra that nothing of the past remains, that you are ready to love again, and love her?'

'I'm hoping to try.'

'So what do I tell the Ambroses and the Fletchers?'

'You'll think of something, Mother. It doesn't stop you and Father going. Why not take Andrew? Penelope Fletcher's been mooning after him for some time.'

'Andrew's hopeless. He's got abominable taste in girlfriends and he'll make some excuse not to get involved.'

81

Dominic went to the side table to help himself to coffee, after his mother declined more of it. Her eyes followed him uncertainly. This was Ginevra's doing. Girls laid so many rules down these days. When she was a girl parents made the rules and they obeyed them, now girls were wanting the moon and accepting nothing less.

'Where do you intend to take Ginevra so that you can get to know her better?' she demanded.

'We'll think of something. Somewhere where we can be together, less of a crowd and a little more of me.'

His mother frowned. 'I see your grandmother in this Dominic,' she snapped.

Ignoring her last remark Dominic said, 'Ginevra was intrigued with the castle and you have to admit it has a certain gothic charm.'

His mother shivered delicately. 'I expect there was a gale blowing, Ginevra would hardly be impressed.'

'Actually, she was, Mother.'

'Are you saying she's a bit of a bluestocking?'

'No, but neither is she one of these dollies who are interested in nothing outside their appearance and living it up.'

'She's cleverer than I thought.'

'How do you mean?'

'She's evidently realised you wouldn't be attracted to a dolly and she's trying hard.'

'No. I think Ginevra is too sincere for that.'

'You've changed, Dominic,' she said drily.

'What exactly do you mean by that, Mother?'

'Well, harking back to Melinda and without any disparagement whatsoever, Melinda was both

82

beautiful and volatile. She enjoyed life to the full and she was well aware that she was beautiful. You were fifteen years younger than you are now and it didn't matter then that Melinda could often be superficial.'

Dominic frowned. 'Melinda was twenty, she acted her age.'

'And Ginevra is twenty-two. Did you ever take Melinda on to the Wall?'

'I don't remember.'

'I never heard you mentioning it, but you did talk about other things, the race meetings and the parties, weekends in Deauville, and Cowes Week.'

'Can we change the subject?'

She smiled. 'I'm merely pointing out, darling, that you've grown up a lot, growing up was forced on you, don't make Ginevra pretend, let her be herself.'

'I wouldn't expect her to be anything else. Now that Father is much better it wouldn't upset you if I went away for a few days?'

'You've only just come back!'

'That was a duty visit, this will be just Ginevra and me.'

'Where will you go at this time of the year?'

'We'll think of somewhere.'

'Well, I wouldn't advise you to go skiing, broken limbs and winter chills could put a real blight on the marriage ceremony.'

Dominic smiled. 'I wasn't thinking about winter sport, Mother, but Ginevra was at school in the Bernese Oberland; she probably skis very well.'

She was aware that he was teasing her but that

she would get nothing out of him. Of her three children Dominic had always been the most reticent. For the first time she was aware of a feeling of anxiety. Suppose they spent time together and didn't get on? The great advantage of being with people meant that they could mingle, not become too involved, be part of a jolly crowd.

That's how it had been with her and Dominic's father. They'd been entertained here, there and everywhere. They'd both known they were destined to spend the rest of their lives together so why burden it all with something more weighty.

If they didn't get on would they cancel the wedding arrangements at this late stage? The mere thought of it was horrific.

'When will you leave?' she demanded.

'I'll telephone Ginevra this evening, if she's agreeable, probably in the morning.'

'Have you mentioned it to your father?'

'No, but I will. I'm sure he'll understand.'

Malcolm would not understand. He'd see a thousand and one reasons why they needn't go to the Ambroses or the Fletchers, and she wanted to go. It was weekends like that that livened up the winter, she really would have to have words with her mother about interfering.

The atmosphere over the dinner table at Saunderscourt was considerably more congenial than it had been of late and Charlton eyed the family with something like relief.

Ginevra was smiling and her mother asked, 'Who was that on the telephone dear?'

84

'Dominic, Mother.'

'Oh dear, I do hope his father is feeling better.'

'Yes, actually he is, much better.'

'What a pity you had to cut short your stay with his grandmother, if we'd known you were coming back early we wouldn't have been away.'

'It doesn't matter, Mother.'

'We did half promise Jean Oakwell that we'd all spend a long weekend with her at the beginning of March, she does so want you and Dominic to be there too.'

'I don't know Mother. Dominic has suggested that we go off somewhere, just the two of us.'

'Where?' her father demanded.

'We haven't decided. He's coming over on Friday morning, we'll decide then.'

'Not back to Northumberland I hope,' the Earl said sharply.

'No. I don't think so.'

'I wouldn't have thought you'd want to be anywhere for too long, there's an awful lot to see to with your wedding coming up, it really is too much to leave to me, Ginevra,' her mother said plaintively.

'We shan't be away long, Mother, but we do have to get to know one another a little better than we do now.'

'Get to know one another!' her father exclaimed. 'You're marrying the fella aren't you? Isn't that enough?'

'No, Daddy, it isn't.'

'Well, can't you get to know him in the homes of friends when they've been kind enough to invite you?'

'It isn't the same.'

'You've just spent a weekend with him in Northumberland, didn't you get to know him there?'

'Perhaps a little, but not enough.'

'Is this the old girl's doing, has she put her two-pennorth in?'

'It has nothing to do with Grandmother.'

'So she's asked you to call her "grandmother" has she?'

'I liked her, we got along fine.'

Her mother was throwing warning signals across the table at her husband, but, oblivious of them, he went on, 'Most people know she had problems with her husband and it's no doubt left her a bit bitter and ready to interfere with other people's nuptials. What did she have to tell you?'

Ginevra smiled sweetly at him, 'Nothing at all Father. We actually didn't spend much time with her, she rested most of the day and we went out on to the Wall the day after we arrived. We only really saw her at dinner.'

'I should have thought being on the Wall would have allowed you to get to know Dominic very well. There isn't anything else to do up there,' he snapped.

They had told Ginevra that they were afraid his grandmother might have told her about Melinda, it was pretty evident that they knew about her. Her mother looked decidedly worried, her father not in the best of humour, but Charlton standing near the door where he could keep an eye on the servants attending to the family felt nothing but relief that her parents' discomfort caused her no problems.

When he related the incidents to his wife later that evening she said, 'Well at least Ginevra and her fiancé appear to be taking matters in hand. You say she looked much happier?'

'Oh yes, more like the girl we remember.'

'And they're going away somewhere?'

'It would seem so.'

'I wonder where at this time of the year. Probably somewhere warmer than here.'

Dominic too was thinking on where they should go. He was remembering the long weeks and weekends he had spent with Melinda so it had to be somewhere different. He wanted no memories of the past to interfere with their time together.

With Melinda there had been so many places. She had loved the boulevards of Paris and the castles along the Rhine, the winter snows of Zermatt and Gstaad and in the summer the exotic delights of St Tropez and Antibes. He hoped Ginevra had leanings to none of these places. One thing was sure, she would not be so insensitive as to suggest the English Lake District.

Larry Harbrook telephoned Ginevra to inform her that he was spending a long weekend in London so that he could visit the theatre where Anita was a dancer.

'What sort of a show is it?' Ginevra asked.

'You know, one of those girlie shows. They must like her, she's in the front row and has a bit part.'

'That's good then.'

'Of course. How's Dominic?'

'Very well. He's coming here in the morning.'

'You mean he's staying there for a few days?'

'You needn't sound so surprised.'

'Actually I am. You've never spent time with him like you spent with me.'

Ginevra didn't answer.

'Why is he coming? Do you want him to come?'

'Of course I do, we're going away for a few days, or perhaps a little longer, I don't know until he gets here.'

'What, just the two of you?'

'Of course.'

'Things are getting serious.'

'They are serious Larry, we're getting married in April.'

The telephone went dead, Larry had heard enough.

Chapter Seven

Lady Midhurst stood in the window of the drawing room watching Dominic and Ginevra strolling across the parkland in the direction of the stables. He had arrived in time for lunch, which had been a stress-free, amiable meal when Dominic had been charming, her daughter pleasant and her husband jocular.

They had talked about horses and dogs, politics and the health of Dominic's father and grandmother. At no time was the forthcoming wedding discussed.

Immediately after lunch Dominic had expressed a desire to see his host's latest hunter and Ginevra had been quick to say she would go with him to the stables. When Lord Midhurst had suggested going with them his wife had given him a decidedly telling stare which had occasioned him to change his mind.

He'd been grumpy, stomping off to his study immediately they'd left and after informing his wife that he didn't see the need for all the secrecy. If they didn't know each other well enough now they never would.

'They don't know each other all that well,' his wife had said and that had sent him off in high dudgeon.

In an effort to placate him she joined him in the study where he sat in front of the fire, a whisky and soda beside him, and a newspaper folded on his knee.

'I'm sure everything is going to be fine, dear,' his wife said gently. 'Young people are different these days, they're more go-ahead than they were in our days and probably more capable of organising their lives.'

'That's rubbish and you know it,' he retorted. 'They're more silly, and Dominic is hardly a boy.'

'I know, but Ginevra has to be sure. Do you suppose she learned anything about Melinda Fallon from the grandmother?'

'Surely the old girl wouldn't introduce the subject.'

'Perhaps she would. Ginevra liked her, perhaps

she had their future welfare at heart.'

'Well, something's upset the apple-cart and that's for sure.'

'It was years ago, surely he can't still be carrying a torch for Melinda? If he is he shouldn't have asked Ginevra to marry him.'

'Did you ever meet the girl?' the Earl demanded.

'Of course. She was a shining light on the London scene that year, beautiful, intelligent, entertaining. Irish father, French mother.'

'I've never heard either of our boys talking about her.'

'They were rather younger than Dominic and Melinda. I doubt if they knew her.'

'Didn't she die in an accident? Was it on the hunting field?'

'No dear, she drowned in Windermere.'

'What was she doing in the lake, was she on her own?'

'She'd gone swimming after a house party, apparently some of the other young people were out in a boat and she was hit by it.'

'And you tell me young people are more organised these days. If you ask me they're incredibly more foolish. You'd never have gone swimming in Windermere in the dead of night, you'd have had more sense.'

'Yes I would. But I still maintain that girls are different these days. Ginevra wouldn't do it I'm sure.'

'And I'm not. Young Harbrook's getting a name for himself over one misdemeanour after another, and he was very close to Ginevra at one time.'

'I expect Larry was very unhappy about Ginevra; this could well be his way of coming to terms with it.'

'Damn funny way if you ask me.'

Dominic was impressed with her father's latest acquisition to his stable, and Ginevra watched him stroking the long velvety neck of the hunter.

'He's a beauty,' Dominic commented.

'Yes, his name is Jupiter.'

'Very appropriate,' Dominic said with a smile. 'The king of the gods.'

'This is where my father's happiest. With his horses or tramping round the parkland with his dogs.'

It was cold in the stable yard and Ginevra shivered, pulling her coat collar closer round her throat, and Dominic said, 'You're cold, Ginevra, would you like to drive somewhere or can we talk in the house?'

'I'd rather drive if you don't mind. My parents will monitor all the time we're together in the house and worry themselves about what we're talking about.'

He laughed. 'I know, my mother would have done the same. Come along then we'll go for a drive, you'll have to direct me, I don't know this area too well.'

'We could drive up to the Downs, they're very beautiful and there'll be hardly anybody there on a day like this.'

They drove, largely in silence, along the country lanes and up the gentle hills until they had the Downs before them and the ruins of an old stone castle, and it was there that Dominic stopped the car and, reaching behind to the back seat, brought out a thick woollen rug which he spread attentively across her knees.

She wanted him to love her, she wanted him to put his arms around her and assure her that he had forgotten Melinda, that there was no other woman past or present except her, but he was looking out at a landscape sparkling with frost and at a pair of kestrels sailing on the wind.

After a few minutes he said, 'My mother thinks we are being foolish, we have the rest of our lives to get to know one another. I have convinced her that it isn't enough.'

'I suppose she thinks I'm being very foolish.'

'Perhaps, me too I suppose, but we have to make our own decisions about this. I agree with you that these last few months haven't been long enough. I like you more than any girl I have met in a very long time, I want to like you a lot more, I want to love you Ginevra, do you feel the same?'

'Yes I do.'

'Then we have to get away from people and find ourselves. Have you any ideas where you would like to go?'

'No. Not in January when it's cold, wet and miserable.'

He smiled. 'Then how about Madeira. It will be warm there and the island is lovely; have you ever been there?'

'No, never.'

'Well I know a very charming hotel there on the outskirts of Funchal. We'll hire a car and explore

92

the island. One part of it is lush and hospitable, some of it is wild and barren, but we'll avoid the crowds and the fleshpots, we'll search for ourselves. Is that what you want, Ginevra?'

'Yes, that's exactly what I want.'

She loved his smile. It was warm and charming. The smile on a face that smiled too much was unremarkable, on a face that was often remote and serious it was enchanting.

Impulsively she leaned forward and put her arms around him, holding her cheek against his, and after a moment he responded by holding her close, and it seemed to Ginevra that the moment went on and on so that when he released her it was like the sudden closing of a door. His expression though was tender and he said gently, 'Do you want to go back now? I don't want you catching cold before our holiday in Madeira.'

'When shall we go?' she asked him.

'I'll go home tomorrow, pack a suitcase and make our travel arrangements, then I'll telephone you. What about your parents?'

'I'll tell them when you've gone, I'll make them understand.'

'I'll tell them tonight.'

'What will your parents think?'

He laughed. 'My father will think about it and say nothing, my mother will bemoan the fact that we're not weekending with several friends who have invited us. Any excuse for a party where Mother is concerned.'

'Oh dear, if I do become her daughter-in-law I could disappoint her sorely.'

'I wouldn't worry too much about that. When

93

you become her daughter-in-law she'll be glad to have got me off her hands.'

Ginevra sat back to contemplate that he had said 'when' and not 'if'.

Dominic spoke to her father after dinner that evening and Ginevra spoke to her mother, who said, 'Won't everybody be surprised that you've gone off with Dominic so soon before your wedding, dear?'

'It's nothing to do with anybody but ourselves, Mother.'

'Of course not dear. Your father'll have something to say.'

'I suppose so. It won't make any difference Mother, we've decided.'

'How long will you be away for?'

'As long as it takes.'

'And if it doesn't work out?'

'Then all those people we invited are going to be disappointed.'

'Oh dear, I do hope it doesn't come to that.'

'I hope so too, Mother.'

Her mother stared at her uncertainly. 'You're certain aren't you Ginevra, it's Dominic you're not sure about?'

'Yes.'

'What has he said?'

'I know that you and Daddy know about Melinda Fallon. You would never have said anything to me about her, you'd have kept quiet hoping it would never be necessary for me to find out, but other people might not have been so charitable. I want Dominic to love me like he loved her, but if he can't I'd rather we ended it. It would be terrible to go into the marriage and wonder for the rest of my life if he cared enough, and then have somebody tell me why he didn't.'

'Surely nobody would be so unkind?'

'Oh, yes they would. They were unkind to his grandmother. They told her about the other women in her husband's life, women she hadn't known about. What do you think that did to her?'

'Your father was convinced the old lady had had a hand in it.'

'She showed me Melinda's photograph. She needn't have bothered, I already knew that there was something or somebody preventing Dominic loving me as Larry Harbrook loved me.'

'Larry Harbrook!'

'Yes, Mother. Larry did love me in his own fashion. He wanted to make love to me, he put it into words, he adored me.'

'Did you love him?'

'No. I enjoyed being with him, he was fun, we had good times together. I'm very much afraid that I've hurt him tremendously.'

'He's the sort of boy who'll get over it.'

'I know, that's what I hope for anyway, but don't you see I want Dominic's eyes to light up when he sees me, I want him to sweep me into his arms and really want me. I'm not going to be satisfied with anything less than that.'

'Oh, my dear, I do really hope you get what you want. Fighting Melinda Fallon's ghost is going to be awfully hard. Dominic built a wall around himself for so many years, shutting everybody out. That he liked you so much we really hoped meant he was coming alive again.'

95

'And not just responding to his father's urges to find himself a wife capable of producing heirs to the dukedom?'

Her mother had the grace to look embarrassed, and Ginevra laughed, 'Don't worry Mummy, I know how it is in our exalted circles, it simply isn't for me.'

'That's the study door,' her mother said, 'Perhaps we should join them in the drawing room. I hope your father's taken it well and that he's in a good mood.'

Whatever Dominic had said to her father, the Earl was reasonably benign, giving Steven Charlton every opportunity to report that all was well to his wife later that evening.

'I'm so glad,' she murmured. 'I hoped you were worrying needlessly.'

The next few days passed quickly. Every morning in the company of her father or one of the grooms Ginevra exercised her horse and walked the dogs, but immediately lunch was over she spent time in her bedroom sorting out the clothes she would need for Madeira.

'Shall I need evening dresses?' she asked her mother.

'Well, of course dear. I'm sure Dominic will have chosen a very superior hotel, probably Reid's, and when I and your father went there the women were fashion plates.'

'I'm not so sure that Dominic will want that sort of place.'

'Of course he will. His mother will have advised him to book in there.'

96

'I don't think I'll drive down to London, I'll take the train and meet Dominic there.'

'Why can't he come here for you?'

'Mother, it isn't convenient from Shropshire, I suggested meeting him in London.'

'Oh well, you'll have your own way I'm sure, but your father and I will drive you to London and see you off.'

'Mother, there's no need.'

'It's our duty, besides it's a gesture that Dominic should be aware of.'

'I expect some of the responses to our wedding invitations might be arriving while we're away, will you open them Mother?'

'Of course, they were sent out in our name, dear.'

'You're still worried about Alanna and Kathy Marston?'

'Yes, I can't help it.'

'I wish you wouldn't. However Alanna chooses to live her life is none of our business or anybody else's for that matter. I'm sure she's had her own reasons for behaving the way she has. Alanna wasn't a fool.'

'Have you mentioned either of them to Dominic?'

'No, why should I? He gave me a list of the people he wanted to invite and he didn't seem at all interested in my guests.'

'I'm sure he would be if you'd mentioned them.'

'Mother, I doubt if Dominic has even heard of Kathy and if he's heard of Alanna he would understand my wanting to invite her. I'm sure there's the odd skeleton or two in his cupboard.'

'I've never heard of any.'

'Well, his grandfather was not exactly circum-spect.'

'His misdemeanours were hardly splashed all over the newspapers though, not like Alanna's. What happened to her last husband? We were treated to several pages about her wedding to some Polish count. the divorce, then more pages concerned with her wedding to an obscure Austrian prince, then an equally lurid account of their separation. Did she divorce him?'

'I have no idea. When she comes to the wedding you'll be able to ask her.'

'So there will be a wedding?'

She smiled. 'Poor Mummy. I promise I won't keep you in suspense any longer than is neces-sary. Is that all about Alanna?'

'I suppose so. I'm still not too happy about Jane Fortesque in the company of a girl her father educated.'

'Jane has spent a number of years in Kathy's company, I'm sure she'll be able to cope with just one day.'

'Surely you're taking that turquoise dress you had for Jane's twenty-first ball?'

'It does take up rather a lot of room, the skirt's voluminous.'

'Well, take another suitcase dear.'

'We are going by air, Mother.'

'Oh well, these things are not weighty. I shall be worried sick all the time you're away, simply wondering if there's going to be a wedding and what we shall say to people if there isn't.'

'I know. I'm sorry to be doing this to you but I have to be sure. I'm not like Alanna. She was always the harum-scarum one who leapt before she thought. She was always in trouble with the teachers because she was impulsive and easily led. I don't want to marry Dominic then find out that he could never love me. It's not for me, Mother.'

With a rather doubtful smile her mother turned away and left her. As she walked down the stairs she thought about her own marriage. She'd been thrilled to have captured the Earl of Midhurst. He was handsome, popular and a leading light among the young blades of his generation. She'd been pretty, well connected, and reasonably rich.

Marrying well had been important, love was something that was never really discussed, it was only assumed. If there had been other women in his life she realised they were hardly likely to cause any problems. She was his wife, she was the mother of his children, he knew come hell or high water he could depend upon her loyalty and she'd never let him down.

In their middle age they were totally devoted to each other. She'd learned to overlook his little foibles and when she'd chastised him in private he'd been apologetic and quick to tell her she was the only one that mattered, then he'd shown her most generously by some quite ostentatious gift of jewellery that he meant it. Why couldn't Ginevra have settled for something like that?

As she crossed the hall Charlton was taking a pile of envelopes off the table where the post was always kept and with a smile he said, 'The replies are coming in, Milady, shall I take them into the drawing room?'

'I'll take them, Charlton, I'll look at them over tea.'

He handed them to her and she was surprised to see that they were quite substantial. They would be coming in steadily now, and as she sat down in front of the fire she leafed through them quickly in search of a foreign stamp. When she didn't find one she heaved a quick sigh of relief. Obviously, Alanna was in no hurry to reply.

As a student of human nature Charlton had correctly assessed her Ladyship's anxiety. There were two invitations that might cause problems; he really didn't see why she had to worry, with so many people milling around on the day the two young ladies concerned were hardly likely to cause any predicaments.

When Ginevra joined her mother for afternoon tea she too looked quickly at the replies. Some of them she didn't even know. Dominic's relatives, women who had been nannies to the children in both families, friends of long-standing relatives, but Ginevra, seeing her mother's expression, smiled.

'You look relieved, Mummy. None from Alanna or Kathy?'

'No, not as yet.'

'Ah, well it's early days. I really don't know where Alanna is, I sent the invitation to her house on Long Island, she may not even be there.'

'Was it her home or her parents'?'

'Her father's I think. The last I heard her mother was living in the south of France. When

Alanna was in New York she stayed with her father.'

'Didn't she have a home of her own?'

'She lived with Ivan in Switzerland and with Claus in Austria and Italy. Where her permanent home is now I have no idea.'

Her mother raised her eyes heavenwards and Ginevra laughed.

'By this time she could be in love with an Argentinian playboy or a fully paid up member of the Mafia. You have to admit she's good entertainment value.'

'Her face is as well-known as the Queen's. Everybody at your wedding will know about Alanna.'

'But not everybody will know about Kathy.'

'No, but Jane will, and her mother too I suspect. I'm surprised at Johnny Fortesque, he was always so nice, charming and genuine, it goes to show that you really never know anybody.'

That was the moment afternoon tea arrived and while the servants attended to it Lady Midhurst shuffled the letters of acceptance into a pile and Lady Ginevra helped herself to hot buttered toast.

'It doesn't look as though your father will be in for tea,' her mother commented.

'He's happier with a hot toddy. Tea was never Daddy's style,' said her daughter.

Kathy

Chapter Eight

Market days in the small Midland town where Kathy Marston lived with her widowed father didn't change. The stall holders came early to set out their wares, their fruit and their vegetables, and as usual Friday morning was the busiest day in the week.

Kathy sat eating her last piece of toast when her father came in with the morning post. A tall, slim man with a nice smile, iron-grey hair and dressed immaculately in a clerical grey suit, white shirt and dark red tie. Kathy reflected that he'd looked exactly the same for as long as she could remember, except that perhaps his hair was a little sparser and greyer.

'There's one here that looks interesting,' he said putting a large cream-coloured envelope down in front of her. 'It's addressed to you, love.'

She picked it up to look at the postmark then turned it over to examine the coat of arms on the flap.

Her father was looking at her curiously and with a little smile she reached for a knife and slit the envelope open. She took out the thick gold-embossed wedding invitation before looking up at her father in some surprise.

'Well?' he said encouragingly.

'An invitation to Ginevra Midhurst's wedding, Dad.'

'Really. When is that then?'

'After Easter. Mid-April.'

'That's going to be one wedding present that'll set you back a bit. Who is she marrying?'

Kathy referred to the invitation. 'Dominic, the Marquis of Chayter.' She passed the card over so that he could read it himself.

'It's nice of them to ask you, love. You'll go of course?'

'I'm not sure, I'll have to think about it.'

'What do you have to think about? Obviously if she's invited you she wants you to be there.'

'I haven't seen Ginevra for years. They all went off to Switzerland and I went to university. There have been Christmas cards but nothing more.'

'But you were good friends at school.'

'Eventually, but the first few months were awful.'

'Kathy, none of it was your fault and in the end they realised it. She invited you to spend holidays at her parents' home, and you did get along with Jane. Who was the other girl?'

'Alanna.'

'Ah yes, the American girl, the one who's never out of the newspapers.'

'I wonder if she's invited Alanna?'

'Well, if she can show her face, Kathy, I'm sure you can. After all none of it concerned you, you were never responsible for what Josie did.'

'Jane will be there with her parents.'

'Well, what does it matter, it's all water under the bridge, love.'

Kathy was staring down at the invitation with a frown of perplexity on her pretty face. Albert

Marston was proud of his daughter. She was pretty and intelligent. She had a first-class law degree and worked for the best firm of solicitors in the town. Her friends had been pampered rich girls, she'd been the one with the brains.

'I'll get off now Kathy, we'll talk about this some other time,' he said, shrugging his arms into his raincoat.

'I'll drop you off Dad,' she said quickly.

'No need love. I like to walk it and the street will be very busy this morning.'

She stood in the front window watching him stepping smartly down the road just as she had watched him as a child. He worked at the oldest gents' outfitters in the town, where, since the owner had retired, he was in charge. He'd never worked anywhere else having gone there straight from the schoolroom, a boy who brushed the floors and cleaned the shelves, rising steadily through hard work and application to his duties. Other men had come and gone but Albert had remained steadfast in his loyalty to the shop. He was an institution in the town.

For years she'd been trying to encourage him to move house, somewhere on the outskirts of the town, a house where there were not so many memories, but he always said, 'I like it here Kathy, it's handy for the shop and if you want to get a place of your own I really don't mind. You'll know where I am and I'll know where you are.'

Over the years he'd made alterations to the house. New furniture and bathroom. Kathy herself had installed new kitchen fittings, and gone were the long lace curtains from every window which had been her mother's pride and joy. She had grown up in this house, with a father she had adored, a mother who had not been the easiest person to get along with, and an aunt, her father's sister Josie, who had considerably brightened the life of the little girl who had idolised her.

Josie was her father's younger sister. It had been their parents' house and when they died it seemed necessary that Josie continue to live there even when her brother had recently married. She didn't get along with Edith, Albert's wife, which meant that there were constant battles between the two of them, and Kathy had often felt herself to be caught in the middle.

Edith was a woman of rigid principles. An ardent chapel-goer and enthusiastic server on a good many committees in the town. Albert and Josie were Church of England, but even when Albert capitulated and went Chapel, Josie never did.

Edith had a sharp tongue in her head and she had firm likes and dislikes on anything from brass band concerts to the way women dressed. She dressed plainly, her style never varying, and when Josie appeared in anything less than circumspect her disapproval was made evident.

Josie Marston was beautiful, with dark red wavy hair and a pale porcelain complexion. She had green eyes, the colour of chipped jade, and a slender willowy figure that did justice to anything she wore.

Edith regarded her as a bad influence on her one young daughter.

As usual on Friday morning the roads were busy and the large impressive offices of Greavson and Johnson, Solicitors, was in the centre of the main street. Fortunately there was a parking place behind the offices and Kathy was lucky enough to find the only spot left.

As she parked her car she was hailed by a young man waiting on the steps by the side door and she waved back with a smile.

Anthony Greavson had joined his uncle's firm in the summer with a law degree taken at Oxford and several years' experience with a law firm in London. He was good-looking, affable, charming and very taken with Kathy Marston.

At eleven o'clock every Friday morning the principal called a meeting of everybody who worked there, and it was quite a ceremony over morning coffee. Kathy was the only qualified female solicitor on the staff and she was popular with everybody, from the juniors who made the tea to the partners themselves.

Everybody aired their views, nobody was left out, and as one after the other addressed the meeting Anthony treated Kathy to warm smiles which did not go unnoticed by James Greavson, his uncle.

Immediately the meeting was over and they all moved back into their respective offices Anthony caught up with her.

'Any wiser?' he asked with a grin.

'I think so. Same old grouses from one or two of them, the coffee was good.'

'Mother has invited you to tea tomorrow Kathy, can I pick you up at half three?'

'I thought you wanted to drive into Cheltenham tomorrow afternoon.'

'Well, we did talk about it. However, when
Mother suggested this instead I was sure you
wouldn't mind. Can I tell her you'll come
Kathy?'

'Yes. It is nice of her to invite me.'

'Three-thirty then, you know where we live, it'll
take us about half an hour to get there.'

Kathy was well aware where they lived. An area
of big imposing houses with large green lawns,
huge conservatories and sweeping driveways. She
knew that Anthony's father was a well respected
doctor in the town; she had no idea what his
mother was like.

She knew that Anthony fancied her from the
first moment he had joined the firm. She liked
him, she liked being with him, beyond that she
didn't really know where their mutual liking for
each other was going.

It was later in the day when James Greavson
entered her office carrying a file of papers which
he placed on the corner of her desk while he took
the chair opposite her. Kathy believed that the
file was unimportant, Mr Greavson quite evidently had something else in mind.

'No problems at the meeting Kathy,' he began.

'No, none.'

'It's good for the staff to have these little get-
togethers, keeps us all on our toes, don't you
think?'

She smiled.

'You appear to be getting along very well with
young Anthony?'

'Well yes. He's really very nice.'

'Oh Anthony's all right. His father's a nice chap, one of the best. Do you know him at all?'

'No. He isn't my doctor, but I know that he's very well thought of.'

'Not met the family then?'

'No. His mother's invited me to tea tomorrow.'

'Has she indeed.'

She looked at him doubtfully. His face was reflective and she hoped he would embroider his remark.

'John is my younger brother you know, we've always got along very well, I'm not so sure how you'll get along with Clara, she prefers to be called Clare, God knows why.'

'You don't like her?'

'I tolerate her for the sake of all concerned.'

'Oh dear. You're making me wish I hadn't accepted her invitation.'

'I just thought I should warn you, Kathy. My sister-in-law is a terrible snob. I won't bore you with details, I'd prefer that you found out for yourself, but don't let her get to you. You're a clever intelligent girl with a good head on your shoulders. If she starts talking down to you just remember that.'

'Is she likely to talk down to me, do you think?'

'Anthony is her one lone lamb. I doubt if she would consider a member of the royal family good enough for him. She has her own ideas of the sort of girl he should marry. Aristocratic family, loads of money, and that is no reflection on you my dear.'

'But evidently not some girl who lives in an old

terrace house near the market and opposite the bakery.'

He laughed.

'I'm going to be very interested in this, Kathy. I'm not sure how grown-up Anthony is, whether he's been too long conditioned to take considerable notice of his mother and her foibles, or if he's prepared to please himself.'

Her expression was doubtful and with a smile he said, 'I didn't want you to get too involved, Kathy, without knowing what you were up against.'

'I'm not looking forward to tomorrow.'

'You'll like his father and you like Anthony, just take her at face value and be yourself, pretty and intelligent and nobody's fool.'

With a warm smile he picked up his file of papers and left.

As she drove home Kathy wondered how long it would be before Anthony's mother became aware of the scandal surrounding her family. In the small provincial town people were still ready to talk about Josie Marston and her long-standing affair with Earl Fortesque. Her mother had maintained that she had contaminated the rest of them for posterity. She hadn't. Her father was still a respected figure in the town and Kathy had been accepted.

She had few friends in the town of her own age. She was the girl who had left her home town to be educated at some superior school none of them had heard of, the girl they had seen little of until she came back to live with her father after leaving university.

112

The girls of her own age gave her a wide berth. They thought her superior and when she joined the firm of solicitors in the High Street, too hifalutin. Her profession was something they didn't try to understand. In the small town, girls served in the shops or went in for hairdressing. They became clerks in small offices or worked as home helps. The few high flyers in evidence were products of high schools in nearby towns, not girls who went to boarding school and seldom came home.

The evening traffic was heavy and by the time Kathy arrived home her father had left for his Lodge meeting and she ate her solitary meal from a tray sitting in front of the television.

The streets outside the house became quiet as the stallholders went home and she could hear rain pattering on the window. Idly she looked again at Ginevra's invitation addressed to Miss Kathryn Marston and escort. What escort? She couldn't ask Anthony, it would look as though she thought of them as a pair and it was really too soon. James Greavson had thought to warn her about his mother and already she was wishing she was not going. Something of those early years at Martlesham still lingered when she'd been something of a curio and when a classroom of aristocratic and moneyed girls had looked askance at the young woman who was being educated by Jane Fortesque's father.

It had taken a long time, and in the end it was Jane Fortesque who had made the first move, sensing her loneliness and insecurity. After that, one by one the others had begun to accept her.

She'd left them all standing in the classroom. She had never had anything to do with horses but she'd tried and in the end even horses had posed no problems. Ginevra's family had accepted her, she'd never known Alanna's parents and Jane's had only been discussed by Aunt Josie.

She found herself remembering those old Friday evenings and the sound of girls' voices and their laughter echoing down the street as they made their way to the church hall where Friday dances were held.

Aunt Josie would be in her bedroom getting into her best frock and her mother would be scathing, calling them getting-off places, and her face would be bitter and disapproving as she sat with her knitting needles clicking ominously.

As always her father would attempt to pour oil on troubled waters saying, 'They're only young once, love, we can't begrudge them a bit of fun.'

'They go there to pick up boys and they don't know what they're getting into,' her mother complained.

'I'm sure Josie's got a good head on her shoulders. Isn't Alec Dawson her current boyfriend?'

'He won't be there, the Dawsons are away for the weekend. Some family party. If he'd been serious about Josie he'd have invited her.'

'Well it isn't serious is it. Josie's only eighteen and he has his way to make.'

At that moment Josie appeared in her glad rags, short silk dress and high heels. Beads round her neck and newly styled shingled hair, and her sister-in-law would look at her with jaundiced disapproval saying, 'The dress is too short, I'd be afraid to stir outside the house in that.'

Kathy would look at her aunt in rapt admiration. Josie looked beautiful in a dress that had not been expensive, but whatever Josie Marston wore looked somehow right. She wished her mother was only half as glamorous.

She smiled at Kathy saying, 'Wait until you're a few years older love and you'll be coming with me.'

'Indeed she will not!' her mother snapped. 'She'll be helping me in the house and learning to cook and sew. Frittering her life away at Friday night hops won't help make a good wife out of her.'

Her father had smiled. 'The child's only eight, Edith, there's plenty of time to think about what makes a good wife, and she should have a bit of fun before she thinks of marriage anyway.'

Her mother sniffed. 'Alex Dawson's gone off with his parents this weekend so who will you be with tonight?' she asked, fixing Josie with an intent stare.

'I'm with my girlfriends, Edith. I don't belong to Alec and he doesn't belong to me, we're nothing more than friends.'

'Well, he'll hardly expect you to be going to that dance in his absence.'

'He doesn't own me. I can go where I please.'

'And that's a sure way to lose him.'

'That wouldn't worry me, and it will hardly worry him,' Josie retorted.

They'd watched Josie shrugging her arms into her new tweed coat with its brown fur collar. Her mother and Josie had already had words about that when Edith had proclaimed it a wicked extravagance when she should be paying more for her board.

'Tell me how much more you want,' Josie had demanded. 'I can probably afford it.'

Indeed Josie had a decent job at Silverstone's, the only department store in the town where she worked in the ladies' fashion department, and where old Mr Silverstone believed she was a commendable asset.

Women bought clothes because Josie wore them beautifully and in the hope that they could look like her. They never did, but she was a kind girl with great charm and a keen desire to advise them on anything they purchased.

A discreet tap on the front door sent her hurrying out after giving them a cheery smile.

'I've got my key,' she called out, 'but I don't expect I'll be late, the dance finishes at twelve.'

With her departure Kathy had always felt that something warm and glamorous had gone from her life, and her mother had cautioned her to get on with her homework and then get off to bed.

She would open the window in her bedroom wider than usual so that she could hear the music from the dance drifting on the night wind, and she would think about Aunt Josie waltzing with some quite wonderful man. She could never put a face on him. None of the local boys fitted the picture, not even Alec Dawson who was plump, a little bit spotty and who was at least two inches shorter than Josie.

One day she would go to those Friday night

dances in spite of her mother's strictures. Her mother didn't know that when she was out at her Mothers' Union meeting Aunt Josie was teaching Kathy to dance. She would roll up the kitchen carpet and wind up the gramophone which years before her mother had relegated to the attics. She loved dancing. She could waltz and do the fox-trot, and now Aunt Josie was teaching her the tango where they laughed uncontrollably at the postures they adopted. Thanks to Josie she knew all the latest dance tunes and Edith knew nothing of the latest records hidden at the back of Josie's wardrobe.

Once her father had caught them in the act, but he had merely laughed and Josie had invited him to dance while Kathy looked on in admiration. She hadn't known that her father was an accomplished dancer, but then he and her mother never went to dances since her mother deemed them to be sinful.

Fortunately Edith Marston had been the last to know when things started to change. Almost from that night Kathy had known that something had changed in her aunt's life. One minute she was full of joy and happiness, the next filled with despair, but none of them could believe that from that innocent village hop Josie's life would change irrevocably, and Kathy's also. To a lesser extent her parents' life changed too, but it was the way it changed that caused the greatest scandal.

It had been a church hall dance like every other with a gaggle of girls arriving chattering about how they had spent their day, who they were

117

hoping to meet, what each of them was wearing.

There was a small four-piece band made up of local boys with a smattering of talent.

The girls would sit decorously at the side of the hall, the men would stand in groups or sit in chairs in a row opposite, and then when the music started they would either stride out boldly across the room or remain shyly waiting for some encouragement from the opposite side.

It would never have occurred to any of them present on that evening that from such commonplace beginnings notoriety would be born.

Chapter Nine

It had started out as a Friday night like all the others. Most of the boys were diffident about asking Josie Marston to dance, she was too pristine, too beautiful, and they selected the plainer girls instead. Some of the brasher, bolder ones approached her, then when she danced with them they bragged about it and invented myths that she fancied them.

Half-way through the evening she was wishing Alec Dawson was there. At least they met on equal terms, she was pretty, he was the son of a town councillor and owner of the local *Gazette*.

At ten o'clock the band stopped playing and they queued up in the corner for tea and coffee and a selection of cakes and biscuits. By this time some of the girls had found boys they wanted to spend the rest of the evening with, but Josie and one or two others sat together trying to look uninterested in boys who leered at them across the room.

Promptly at half-past ten the musicians resumed their places on the platform and couples started to dance while several of the girls danced together.

The music disguised the screeching of brakes from outside the hall as an open-top tourer drew up abruptly outside the front door. There were five people in it, three boys and two girls, and the boy driving the car said, 'There's music in there, dance music, come on, let's see what's going on.'

The girls said they preferred to drive on, but none of them were exactly in a position to protest since it was Nigel Peterson's car and he was driving. In sulky silence the girls followed him out of the car and one of them said, 'We're hardly dressed for a dance, we've been to a point-to-point meeting.'

'Don't be such a spoilsport,' Nigel said, 'it's only a village hop, hardly a hunt ball.'

They stood within the doors, five young people wearing country tweeds, and those in the hall looked at them in surprise. Nigel Peterson was well known in the area. His father was a baronet and owner of Rawcliffe Hall on the outskirts of the town. A local magistrate, and with a finger in practically every enterprise within the town, Nigel was his youngest son. He invariably drove his car at breakneck speed around the country lanes and had been cautioned a great many times by the police, but very little had been done about it.

Nigel had not been in a good mood. Anthea McKinley should have been at the point-to-point meeting with him, but she had let him down at the last minute. She did it constantly because she was well aware how much he fancied her. Now he stood leaning against the wall eyeing the dancing couples with a look of cynical boredom.

'Come on, let's go home,' the other girl said, 'This is not for us. Besides I'm tired.'

That was the moment Nigel looked across the room and saw Josie Marston sitting alone. She was wishing the dance was over, the set smile on her face uncomfortably false, but in the next moment she looked up in amazement at a handsome smiling face and a young man with a polished accent asking her to dance.

His friends read the signs well. There was little chance now of Nigel's driving them home, so instead they decided to make the best of it and join the dancers.

They were the focus of all eyes, some envious, some disdainful, some speculative, but neither Josie nor her partner cared. For the first time in weeks Josie was enjoying herself as she danced every dance, and Nigel's prowess on the dance floor was superior to any partner she had ever had.

When the evening came to an end at twelve o'clock and couples started to leave Nigel smiled down at her disarmingly and asked if he could drive her home. 'It's going to be a bit of a squeeze, but we'll manage,' he said.

'Thank you, there's no need, I only live just along the road, and I have people going my way.'

'Oh well, if you're sure. Do you come here every week?'

'Mostly.'

'I'd like to bet you're a school teacher,' he said laughing.

'Whatever gave you that idea?'

'You mean I'm wrong?'

'Yes, totally.'

'Then what do you do?'

'I work at Silverstone's in the fashion department.'

'Of course, it couldn't be anywhere else.'

'I must go, my friends are waiting for me.'

'Do you live with your parents?'

'No. With my brother and his wife.'

Politely she held out her hand which he took and gallantly raised it to her lips. 'You haven't told me your name,' he said softly.

'There's no need for you to know it, I've never seen you here before and it's highly unlikely you'll come here again.'

He threw back his head and laughed. 'I might surprise you,' he said, and from the doorway a girl called out, 'Come on Josie, we're waiting for you.'

He bowed. 'Goodnight Josie,' he said with a smile. 'Nice name.'

They teased her about him on the way home, the son of the lord of the manor, a man from a different world of fast cars and horses, hunt balls and foreign travel. Philosophically Josie thought, it was good for one evening, there's nothing more.

Three days later when she was leaving Silver-

121

stone's on their half-day closing he fell into step beside her and, taking her arm, said, 'I know you don't have to work the rest of the day; have lunch with me and we'll drive off somewhere.'

She looked at him in amazement. 'I'm expected home for lunch,' she said. 'I've made plans for this afternoon.'

'Can't you cancel them? I've cancelled whatever plans I had.'

'Then you shouldn't have without knowing if I was free.'

He laughed. 'When you know me better you'll find out how impulsive I can be. Say you'll come, my car is just round the corner.'

'I'll have to let them know at home.'

'You do that. I'll take you home.'

'No. I'll come back to you. I won't be long.'

Edith would be furious, and she'd put two and two together and make five. Josie would have to grovel, so with that in mind she bought a huge bunch of tulips from a barrow near the house and rehearsed her excuses.

As she had predicted, Edith was annoyed, and curious, very curious, but in reply to her questions she simply said, 'It's just a friend who's turned up unexpectedly, I'll see you later,' then thrusting the tulips into her arms she made her escape.

The car was large and racy as she'd known it would be, and there were many passers-by who gazed at them with open-mouthed curiosity. Josie felt pretty sure Edith would know all about her adventure by the time she arrived back home.

They drove out into the country and he drove

very fast, so fast that she said, 'Do you need to drive so fast?'

'Don't you find it exhilarating?'

'I find it dangerous in these narrow lanes.'

'You sound like my mother.'

'I just think it's unnecessary that's all.'

'Right, I'll slow right down,' and he did to around twenty miles an hour and he laughed at her expression.

'It's just as dangerous to drive at this speed as it is at the other,' he said.

'Can't you drive normally?'

'I can, but it isn't nearly as much fun. Have you ever been to the Coppins?'

'No, what is it?'

'Only the best restaurant for miles.'

The restaurant was all he had said it would be. Expensive with restrained elegance. Josie was glad of her tweed coat with its marmot collar, and Nigel was attentive, distinctly attentive while the girl sitting opposite with two older people looked across at them constantly.

Nigel had greeted them when they entered the restaurant, stopping to chat for several minutes. He did not introduce Josie and she had the distinct impression that he was being obviously gallant to attract the interest of the girl. She was attractive in a rather bold way. A big girl wearing country tweeds with long dark hair and an air of well-bred assurance.

When she and her companions left the restaurant she smiled across at them and mouthed goodbye. Josie asked artlessly, 'Is she a friend of yours, Nigel?'

123

'She's one of the crowd.'

'She's attractive.'

'I suppose so. She's an excellent horsewoman.'

His voice was curt, he didn't wish to talk about the girl, and changing the subject he asked, 'Fancy coming with me to a point-to-point meeting tomorrow?'

'I'm afraid not. I shall be at the shop tomorrow.'

'How about Saturday then?'

'Saturday is our busiest day.'

'Then we'll have to think of something for your day off. Do you like racing?'

'I've never been to a race meeting.'

'Gracious girl, what have you done with your life, I can see we'll have to do something about it.'

'Why didn't you ask the girl sitting over there to go with you?'

'She'll no doubt be riding her horse in the ladies' race. Her name's Anthea by the way.'

'Oh well, it was just a thought.'

Their friendship was light-hearted. Josie constantly reminded herself that Nigel came from a different world and Edith was quick to remind her that she'd done very well to capture Alec Dawson who came from a very respectable family who were not without money, but this friendship with a baronet's son was doomed to failure from the outset.

She spent money recklessly on clothes that earned her sister-in-law's anger, and the girls she had gone to school with, gone to dances with, now left her alone. Some of them were envious, they thought she was getting above herself, and even her best friends found it difficult to cope with the new Josie with her upper-crust accents and expensive clothes.

Throughout the summer she saw Nigel constantly. She'd never had anything to do with horses, but now they went to race meetings and point-to-point gatherings, and she mixed with his friends. The men were affable, the girls rather less so. It really didn't matter, Nigel was attentive. The only thing that bothered Josie was Anthea's amused smile and her air of assurance with Nigel.

Anthea had a string of male escorts wherever she went. Her background was established money, she treated most of her men friends with casual equanimity and Josie constantly felt that her presence in their midst was Nigel's attempt to make her jealous.

When she accused him he merely laughed saying, 'Of course I'm not trying to make her jealous, Anthea's old hat, we've not been around together for ages.'

Life at home was difficult for Josie. Her brother constantly advised caution, her sister-in-law was scathing, indeed only her niece Kathy listened to her stories of the good time she was having.

When Nigel invited her to go with him to the hunt ball Josie honestly believed that his feelings for her were genuine. She chose a dress in heavy peach parchment satin sparkling with bugle beads and she had to dip deeply into an already depleted bank balance to pay for it. She was gratified with Nigel's admiring compliments, but she was thrilled and totally captivated with the venue for the ball.

Maplethorpe had been the seat of the Fortesque family for generations and Earl Fortesque followed in his father and grandfather's tradition of allowing the local hunt to hold their annual ball there. Josie wouldn't have been human if she'd failed to be completely captivated by the stately pile in the midst of its extensive parkland. Like Cinderella in the fairy tale she'd floated entranced through the gracious rooms with their priceless porcelain and pictures.

The ballroom was already filling up with men wearing hunting pink and their ladies sparkling with jewels, but even so there were a great many admiring glances cast in her direction and Nigel looked particularly handsome as his laughing eyes gazed down at her as they waltzed around the room.

It was much later when Anthea made an appearance with her parents, and Josie had to admit that she looked particularly striking in a plain jade chiffon gown, her only ornament – a heavy jade necklace and long ear-rings to match.

The plainness of her dress put more sparkling creations very much in the shade, but Anthea's figure was voluptuous with broad creamy shoulders and blue-black hair that swung carelessly when she moved.

'I suppose I should ask her to dance,' Nigel mused. 'She's come unescorted so it's only polite.'

Josie had smiled, and had watched him walking across the floor to invite her to dance.

When the dance was over he did not come back

and another dance started. Josie felt that people were staring at her. Most of the men had brought guests, either friends or wives, but Josie sat there alone hoping that her expression was relaxed and untroubled.

Across the room Earl Fortesque stood chatting to a group of his friends and one of them said, 'I see young Peterson's with the McKinley girl, he seems to have forgotten the girl he came with.'

John Fortesque looked across the room and saw the most beautiful girl he'd ever seen sitting alone and staring in front of her with embarrassed distress.

'Stupid young fool,' he muttered angrily. 'Why bring a girl at all if he intends to leave her alone for most of the evening. I'll have a word with her.'

He sauntered round the room and after several minutes Josie found herself looking up into a calm remote face and eyes that were kind and lips that smiled gently.

'Would you like to dance?' the mouth asked, and all around them the conversation ceased as she melted into his arms. Afterwards Josie remembered very little of that dance, except that he asked if she was enjoying herself, and that he hadn't met her before.

She told him her name and she learned that he was in fact her host, Earl Fortesque, and he escorted her to supper.

Josie was unaffected. She told him where she lived and where she worked. She told him she'd been friends with Nigel Peterson for around nine months and he'd said quietly, 'He's behaving very badly my dear, I intend to have a word with him.'

'No please, I'd much rather you didn't. I can get a taxi and go home.'

'Do you want to go home?'

'I've loved being here, I'm so glad I came, but I don't want to see Nigel again this evening.'

'Very well then, I'll get my chauffeur to take you home. Come with me and wait in the drawing room until my car comes for you.'

The drawing room was beautiful as she'd known it would be, and while she waited she wandered round the room looking at family portraits and beautiful furniture and carpets. She was standing in front of a large portrait staring up at it when he returned, and joining her he said, 'My wife, Lady Fortesque.'

She was not beautiful, but she had a cool patrician air, and she was wearing a white satin gown and tiara in her dark hair.

'Thank you so much for taking care of me,' Josie said. 'Your wife will be looking for you.'

He smiled. 'I doubt that very much, she'll have a thousand and one things to do and a great many people to talk to. We rarely see each other at this affair.'

She drove home in Lord Fortesque's grey Rolls-Royce and as it drew up in front of her brother's house lace curtains from several windows were pulled aside, and eyes peered and ears strained until Josie ran from the car into the house. She ran straight up to her room and that was the night Kathy heard her sobbing, sobs that continued until the first morning light crept into the room.

Sitting in the living room staring into the fire Kathy was remembering the days that came after

128

that traumatic night. Nigel's telephone calls that were never answered, his appearance at the front door that were rebuffed by both her mother and Josie.

Josie went back to the Friday night hops, but they were not the same. The girls she had gone with before no longer sat with her, the boys who had been reluctant to ask her to dance before had no intention of asking her now, and even Alec Dawson had found another girl to escort and treated her to superior smiles as they danced around the room.

Josie stopped going.

Edith was quick to tell her that people were talking about her. Saying it served her right, that she should have known Nigel Peterson was not for her, that he had always been over-fond of Anthea McKinley whose father was very rich.

Instead of going to church on Sunday Josie now wandered the country lanes alone, since Edith saw to it that Kathy did not spend too much time with her discredited aunt.

It was on one of those country walks that she came face to face with Lord Fortesque riding his horse along the lane. They stared at each other and then he dismounted and joined her at the stile. It seemed strange in after years to think how that small meeting led to other things. The family quarrels and long silences, culminating in Josie's departure to live in a stone cottage on the Fortesque estate with its accompanying scandal. Then later, as their affair progressed, to the house he bought for her in a village several miles from home.

Kathy had wept long and bitterly at her aunt's departure, because with Josie's going it seemed to the lonely child that all life had left the house. On that last morning Josie had hugged her closely saying, 'Don't worry darling, I'm not going to forget you. Every Friday I'll come to see you, I'll pick you up at school and we'll have tea at that nice café in the High Street and then I'll drive you home.'

Edith had been quick to say that she wouldn't allow it, but her father had said more sternly than usual, 'Josie is my sister Edith, half of this house belongs to her, we can't stop Kathy seeing her.'

'She's my daughter, I don't want Josie anywhere near her,' Edith had said. 'Everybody talking about her, and him a married man with a family. I don't want Kathy growing up like her.'

Her father got his way, something he didn't often get, but true to her word whenever Josie was at home she collected Kathy at the school promptly at four o'clock and together they drove in Josie's new two-seater to the little café in the High Street, except in summer when they drove to some favourite place in the country. At six o'clock she would take Kathy home, chat to her brother, never to Edith who remained in the kitchen rattling cups and saucers.

She brought Kathy books and clothes, paintbrushes and paint-boxes, and took her to concerts and mannequin parades her mother never knew about, as Edith would have considered them sinful.

Kathy was the daughter Josie would never have, but although Kathy loved her because of Josie's lifestyle she had a lonely childhood when mothers cautioned their daughters not to get too friendly with the niece of Josie Marston.

The more Kathy thought about it, the more she remembered that Friday evening which was to change the course of her life irrevocably.

She had thought it would be something that would make her mother proud, a scholarship to St Winifred's, the best girls' school in the area, but her mother had been adamant that they couldn't afford it. That Kathy should keep her feet on the ground, find a job in some shop or factory, learn to sew and cook so that one day she'd make a decent wife for a good respectable man.

That had been Friday morning before the advent of Aunt Josie later in the day.

Chapter Ten

All evening memories of that Friday troubled Kathy's mind. Her mother's acid anger, her father's attempts to pacify her and then Josie's angry accusations that Edith was denying Kathy her chance in life.

None of them had asked for Kathy's opinion. She had escaped up to her room with the tears of frustration coursing down her cheeks, throwing herself across her bed while she listened to their voices going on and on, and she was remembering how hard she'd worked to achieve her results. She wanted to go to St Winifred's. She wanted to make something of her life, not simply accept the dull existence her mother had mapped out for her.

She had reckoned without Aunt Josie. Within days Josie had returned with other ideas and they had all sat in the little parlour to listen to her. Her mother's face had been grim and unyielding, her father's troubled, but Josie had been quick to assure them that if they would allow Kathy to take up her scholarship her clothes, her books, everything else she might need would be paid for.

'And who's going to pay for it?' Edith had demanded. 'Not you, why you've given up your job, what money do you have?'

'I've said it will be paid for, isn't that what matters?' Josie had retorted.

'No. I don't want people saying my daughter's being clothed by you. There are girls at St Winifred's who live close by, their fathers go into Albert's shop, they know we couldn't afford it.'

Josie departed in some degree of impatience and did not return for several days. When she did it was when Kathy and her father were alone in the house, her mother was at one of her meetings.

By the time she came home Albert was on his sister's side and Josie was prepared to be patient with her. Kathy would go to another school, a boarding school, and her fees would be paid for as well as anything else that she would need.

'But who is paying for it?' Edith demanded. 'I won't have Lord Fortesque paying for my daughter's education, he's not your husband, he's your fancy man whether he's a lord or not.'

'I don't care what you say about me,' Josie had retorted. 'Kathy is what matters, her future, her entire life. Surely you can't deny your daughter all the things you never had?'

'I had decency,' Edith retorted. 'I didn't live off somebody else's husband or take money from some man who should have been giving it to his wife and family.'

'You don't know anything about it, Edith, and I'm not going to explain, you wouldn't listen anyway. You see everything in black and white, never in shades of grey. Doesn't my brother have a voice in this?'

'She's my daughter,' Edith snapped.

'She's my daughter too,' her husband said firmly. 'Kathy is the only person who matters, surely we can't deny her the best possible start in life.'

'Boarding school,' Edith had snapped. 'Whoever heard of anybody going to boarding school in our walk of life. Everybody will know who's paying for it, we'll be the talk of the town.'

'It has nothing to do with the town,' Albert had said.

'We're well respected. I don't want people talking about us, all those people at the chapel, all those people who come into the shop.'

'Why don't we ask Kathy what she wants,' Albert said quietly.

Three pairs of eyes were turned on her, and in a whisper Kathy said, 'I just want to go to school. I don't want to leave and that be the end of my education.'

Rising to her feet and gathering up her furs Josie had said, 'Well, that I think, is that. I'll call for you at the school next Friday, Kathy, and we'll have a ride out somewhere now that the weather is improving.'

Nobody saw her out. Edith sat for the rest of the evening with a frozen face while her father looked uncomfortable. Kathy was sorry. She tried to interest her mother in some aspect of her homework but was uninterested and in the end she went up to bed slamming the living room door behind her.

The following Friday Aunt Josie drove her to her new house several miles away. It was the first time Kathy had been there.

It wasn't a particularly large house but it was set against a backdrop of woodland, a russet red-brick house with Virginia creeper climbing up to the first-floor windows and surrounded by green lawns and a wide curving drive. Kathy thought it was a mansion, larger than any house she had ever seen, but when she said as much Josie laughed, 'Don't tell your mother it's a mansion darling, she'll put her worst possible construction on it. Actually it's really quite small, but I fell in love with it the first time I saw it.'

It was a pretty house, and Aunt Josie had always had good taste. They ate afternoon tea in a room with large windows overlooking a small pond and Kathy clapped her hands with glee at the sight of a procession of ducks waddling down to the water.

She loved every room in that house, and every

aspect from the windows, and Josie said, 'You're going to do great things with your life darling, I just know it. One day you'll have a house as beautiful as this, I'm sure.'

'Nothing could be as beautiful as this,' Kathy breathed.

Josie laughed. 'You'll see,' she said.

From outside on the drive they heard the sound of a car and Josie, smiling down at her, said, 'We have visitors Kathy, come and meet your benefactor.'

A tall man was letting himself into the hall when they descended the stairs and Josie went immediately into his embrace while Kathy stood back in some embarrassment. Josie turned and held out her hand, 'Lord Fortesque, this is Kathy,' and she found herself gazing up into the kind, handsome face of a man with dark hair, silvered at the temples, with nice grey eyes and a charming smile.

He held out his hand and took hers, saying softly, 'You're as pretty as Josie said you were. I've been hearing what a clever girl you are Kathy, I hope we can be friends.'

She liked him. He treated her like a grown-up, but she kept their meeting within her heart, she never told her mother that she met the man Josie loved.

She understood why Josie loved him. She remembered all those boys leaving the village hall after the Friday night hops. Young boys swanking about their conquests, too young, too brash, none of them very sure where life was taking them, and here was this handsome man with a sophistication none of those boys would ever aspire to, even when they grew up.

At their meeting Kathy saw no further than that. She had no conception of the things that troubled her mother with her rigid upbringing in a small town, and where women like Josie were judged harshly as being no better than they should be.

Miraculously all the things Kathy would need for her new school began to appear when Josie brought the uniform she would be expected to wear. Gym clothes and tennis rackets, and at the beginning of September it was Josie who drove her into Gloucestershire where her school was situated.

It had looked so beautiful that afternoon in its peaceful setting. Cool green lawns and the river meandering gently between its banks, a building of warm stone with large open windows, and girls strolling across the lawns in companionable friendship. It was a setting that had not prepared Kathy for the coldness that came later.

She was not one of them. Those girls had known each other for years, their families had been friends, they had moved in the same circles, they were poles apart from the girl who descended upon them that warm September afternoon with her country accent and her wide-eyed curiosity. She had so desperately wanted to make friends, but somehow or other they knew who she was and how she had managed to arrive in their midst.

They did not include her in anything. Instead they gave her a wide berth outside the classroom, but in the classroom Kathy excelled, she was better than any of them. This too made her a pariah, and by Christmas she was hating every moment of her new life, the school and the girls who were her daily companions.

In the quiet of her room she wept long and bitterly. Her appetite suffered and her mother was quick to say that the school was doing nothing for her, she was unhappy.

When Aunt Josie asked her about the school she burst into tears and out came the dismal story of girls who ignored her, her sad lonely life that only got better in the classroom. Josie was troubled. Somehow or other the girls had learned how Kathy came to be at the school and for the first time she began to doubt the wisdom of the part she had played.

Kathy was dreading going back to school. She was afraid of her mother finding out that she was unhappy because it would have proved her right all along, but as she drove with Josie along a road banked high with snow and in the face of a wind that tore through the branches of the trees in undisguised fury her expression was as bleak as the weather.

Josie embraced her outside the car, her face anxious as she said, 'Things will get better, darling, I promise, it's all so new to you, they have to get to know you.'

'They don't want to get to know me, Aunt Josie.'

There was nothing else to say and Josie sat in her car watching Kathy trudging across the icy ground. There was an air of dejection in every stride she took, and she studiously avoided looking at the girls who were walking in pairs or small groups towards the door.

Kathy had already decided that if they didn't want to know her she didn't want to know them. She would work hard and prove to her teachers and everybody else that she was worth educating. The morning it all changed was a surprise to herself and the other girls.

She was sitting in the school library where she invariably went instead of the common room where they were having coffee. She was immersed in a history tome when the door opened and Jane Fortesque entered the room, and after a few moments she walked across to where Kathy was sitting and pulled up a chair.

In a soft breathless voice Jane asked, 'What are you reading?'

Kathy looked up in surprise, then turning the book over so that Jane could see the title she went on with her reading.

'Aren't you having coffee?' Jane asked.

'No. I prefer to do some reading.'

'You never come into the common room.'

'I did when I first arrived, when nobody spoke to me I decided to come in here instead.'

'Kathy, I'm so sorry. I feel awful about it. It was all my fault, I knew who you were and I resented you. The other girls have been my friends for years, when I told them they resented you too. It was wrong of us.'

Kathy closed her book and stared at her.

'Why are you being friendly now then? I'm still the same girl, I can't change anything.'

'I know. It doesn't matter. I want you to come into the common room to be with us. I've talked to my friends to make them understand.'

'What is there to understand? Your father is still paying for my education, nothing has changed.'

'My father talked to me over the holidays. I love him very much, he has made me see so many things in a different way. I knew that things at home were far from perfect, it seems I always knew, but he made me see that what he is doing for you in no way hurts me. He loves me very much, he will always love me.'

'But surely you knew that. What do you know about my Aunt Josie?'

'I've known for years that my parents went their own ways. I also knew that they would never openly split up, it's inconceivable. I do know about Josie, I've known for ages. She's beautiful, and my father loves her. He told me that he loves her.'

'But he won't ever marry her.'

'No. He says it isn't important.'

'Josie loves him, I think she would like to be his wife, but she'll always be regarded as the bad woman, won't she? It really isn't fair.'

'No, perhaps not. It's how things are though, I can't think they will change.'

'Was it because of your mother that you resented me?'

'No, it was because of me. My mother's never seemed to worry about anything outside her horses and her dogs. She and my father are polite to each other, they keep up appearances. They go to functions together when it's expected of them,

139

but at home they're rarely in the same room.'

'Have you brothers and sisters?'

'I have one brother, Andrew. He's nice, but I hardly ever see him, he rarely comes to visit. He has his own estate in Hampshire.'

'He isn't married?'

'Yes. He's often overseas but when he's home I go with my father to stay with them. Mother won't leave her dogs.'

'Are you quite sure you want to be friends with me, Jane? It doesn't matter any more, I've become accustomed to being on my own.'

'Please, Kathy, I do want to be friends.'

At that moment the school bell sounded to say that coffee time was over and the girls should go back to their classrooms. Jane said hurriedly, 'There won't be time now, but please join us at lunch.'

'I'm already on another table.'

'Then I'll ask for you to be placed with us.'

'Who will that be?'

'Ginevra Midhurst and Alanna Van Royston.'

'Won't they mind?'

'No. They'll be pleased that I've asked you.'

That had been the start of several years when the four girls were inseparable. Long weeks at Ginevra's home, school holidays in Scotland or the English Lake District, and always with a friendship destined to last at least until their time together in Gloucestershire finished. After that the other three went to a finishing school in Switzerland and Kathy went up to Cambridge to read law.

If her mother was proud of her she never said

so, unlike her father who was happy to tell everybody how well his daughter had done. Aunt Josie said, 'You could have gone to Switzerland darling.'

Kathy laughed. 'Never in a million years, Aunt Josie. I want to study law at Cambridge, I don't want to put that sort of gloss on what I already have. What have I got to do with Switzerland? They'll learn to ski and speak better French, then they'll all come back at the end of it and marry into the nobility. We both know that that isn't all it's cracked up to be.'

The years passed. Christmas cards came from them, letters at infrequent times to tell her how they were enjoying themselves, and when Kathy obtained her degree long letters of congratulations and presents. They never met, but Alanna at least supplied the newspapers with copious reviews of her activities.

Kathy and Josie had read of her exploits as Josie remembered the American girl with her beautiful face and expressive eyes.

Kathy could remember them sitting on their beds in the dormitory they shared, listening to Alanna's stories of her various homes in America and elsewhere. Her larger-than-life handsome father with his string of women friends, his penchant for making lots of money and losing it just as quickly, and her mother who preferred travelling around Europe and whom she rarely saw.

Sitting in front of the living room fire with the sound of the rain pattering on the window, waiting for her father to come home from his meeting, Kathy had spent all evening remembering, and for the first time in months she felt troubled. Two things had brought her immediate future into perspective, Ginevra's invitation to her wedding and Mrs Greavson's invitation to tea the following day.

Glancing up at the clock on the mantelpiece she thought that her father would be home soon so she got up and went into the kitchen to make coffee. It was almost ready when she heard her father's key in the lock and she heard him opening the hall wardrobe to hang up his coat. He came immediately into the kitchen carrying a wet umbrella.

'Have you been in all evening, love?' he asked.

'Yes. Did you get very wet?'

'No, George Thompson drove me home, he dropped me at the corner. It'll not be too nice in Cheltenham if this continues,' he said with a smile.

'Actually Dad we're not going into Cheltenham, Anthony's mother invited me to tea instead.'

'That's nice.'

She grimaced, and he said, 'Don't you want to go?'

'I don't think so. Mr Greavson says his sister-in-law's a terrible snob.'

'Well, that shouldn't worry you, Kathy.'

'Anthony's father's a doctor in the town, he'll know all about Aunt Josie and her belted earl, as the townspeople call him. I don't want an inquisition from Anthony's mother.'

'Surely she wouldn't. I know Doctor Greavson, he's been buying clothes from the outfitters for years. He's a very nice man, well respected.'

'I'm sure he is. Mr Greavson said as much, it's his wife he isn't too keen about.'

'Anthony's nice enough, with him and his father you can handle the mother. I sometimes wonder, Kathy, if you wouldn't have been wise to take a job in another town a long way away from here, it all bothers you so much, even after all this time.'

'I wanted to come home to be with you after Mother died.'

'I know, but I'd have handled it. Have you decided what to do about the wedding invitation?'

'Not really. I doubt if I'll go.'

'Ginevra wouldn't have invited you if she hadn't wanted you to go.'

'She might, out of courtesy.'

'No. You are an old friend, she'll want you there. I was looking at the invitation, she's said you could take an escort. Why not ask Anthony?'

'No. It would make us seem like a pair.'

'Well, you've seen a lot of him lately. He'd probably enjoy the experience of rubbing shoulders with the nobility.'

'I'm sure he would. I have to think about it.'

'Even his mother wouldn't object to his escorting a young lady to the wedding of an earl's daughter, to a marquis no less.'

Kathy laughed. 'You're getting to be quite a snob yourself Dad. Like I said, I have to think about it.'

143

That was as much as he could get out of her. He settled down to listen to the news and Kathy washed up the coffee cups, after which she said she'd go to bed and wished him goodnight.

She lay for a long time staring up at the ceiling. What had Anthony told his parents about her? That she worked in the same firm, had an honours degree in law and was considered one of the firm's most up and coming solicitors? His father knew her father, knew the shop where he had spent all his working life, and he had no doubt heard a great deal of the gossip concerning her aunt and how Kathy had received her education.

Anthony had never asked any questions about her past. They laughed together and talked about their work. He talked about his friends at the tennis club; he was taking up golf and encouraging her to do the same. She often wondered if the senior partner of their firm had discussed her with his brother or Anthony. Somehow she didn't think so.

They didn't live in the old part of the town, and the people who lived near them were newcomers and hardly likely to concern themselves with old scandals. Times were moving on, things that were scandalous twenty years ago hardly raised an eyebrow today, and yet she was troubled.

Even the advent of a bright sunny morning failed to assuage her fears.

Saturday was the busiest day of the week at the shop and she watched her father walking jauntily down the street, neat and dapper as always, and because it was Saturday, wearing his usual car-

144

nation button-hole.

As she looked down on the busy street people were already rushing along with their shopping baskets. Two boys came into view pushing a large handcart piled high with early spring flowers. The winds of early February seemed far too early for daffodils and tulips, but their cheerfulness did little to encourage Kathy to feel in the least cheerful about the afternoon ahead.

Chapter Eleven

The early promise of a nice day gave way to heavy rain and strong winds before lunch, and by the time Anthony picked her up, on time as always, the day had disintegrated into chaos.

'Good job we didn't go into Cheltenham,' Anthony said cheerfully, 'we'd have got drenched.'

Kathy merely smiled in agreement, and he went on, 'I played a round of golf with Dad this morning and we managed to finish before the heavens opened. What did you do?'

'Very little. I was on my own, it's my father's busiest day.'

'I'm wanting a new sports jacket, I might pay him a visit next week.'

'If you're lucky he might give you a discount.'

He grinned. 'Can he do that when he doesn't own the shop?'

'He doesn't own it, but he does run it. The owner leaves him free to do what he likes.'

'Do you know this area at all?' he asked.

By this time they were driving along wide smooth roads lined by large new houses, each with its conservatory and smooth green lawns. Even in the wet misery of a February afternoon they looked prosperous with their drives occupied by ostentatious cars.

Without answering him Kathy was looking around her with interest and when the car turned in at the last house with a garden twice as large as any of the others, Anthony said cheerfully, 'Well here we are. Mother doesn't like cars to park outside the dining room window so we'll have to run for it. This is as near as I can get without arousing her displeasure.'

The rain was pelting down as they ran through the puddles towards the front door and they arrived laughing in the porch, shaking the rain from their hair and their raincoats.

Anthony took her coat in the hall saying, 'I'll put them in the morning room, they're too damp to put in the cloakroom with the others. Come into the drawing room and meet the parents.'

She waited until he'd deposited their wet coats, then he held the drawing room door open for her and held out his hand. Only one person sat in the room, Anthony's father, in a large armchair in front of the fire; he rose to greet them with a warm smile.

He held out his hand and Anthony said, 'This is Kathy, Dad, where's Mother?'

His father smiled, 'In the greenhouse arguing with the gardener.'

'Not again!'

146

'I'm afraid so, we'll no doubt hear all about it when she makes an appearance. So you're Kathy? I've heard quite a lot about you from my brother.'

'You didn't tell me, Dad,' Anthony said.

'Well, it was all extremely good. I've been looking forward to meeting you. Now do sit down and make yourself comfortable. I'd ask you to join me in a drink but I rather think tea is on its way.'

Kathy took a seat on the settee with Anthony and his father chatted easily with them until they heard the sharp closing of a door, and he looked at Anthony with raised eyebrows.

The door opened and a fashionably dressed woman of medium height entered. Her iron-grey hair was immaculately styled and she had a pretty, expertly made-up face. On this occasion her colour was heightened and without looking at either Anthony or Kathy she addressed her husband.

'John, I really do think you should do something about the gardener. Is it my greenhouse or is it his?'

'I rather think it is ours my dear. What's brought this on?'

'I wanted some blooms for the house but he says they're not ready even when they have heads on them the size of one of my hats!'

'I rather think he was nursing them along in time for the show.'

'Some of them are ready now, there'll be others in time for the show.'

'The house isn't short of flowers, Clare, why

147

do we need more?'

'He gets pleasure from them in the conservatory, I would get pleasure from them in the house, it's time he accepted it.'

'He's an expert gardener, my dear, do we really want to fall out with Henry?'

'He should be told that that is what he is, our gardener, nothing more. He doesn't own the flowers.'

'But he has grown them, if Henry leaves us tomorrow there's a stream of people waiting to take him on.'

'You're too soft with him, John.'

She transferred her gaze to Anthony, and without acknowledging Kathy's existence said, 'If your father won't speak to him then you should, Anthony, I can't manage him on my own.'

For the first time she appeared to notice Kathy, and Anthony rose to his feet pulling her up after him.

'This is Kathy Marston, Mother, surely your quarrel with the gardener didn't make you forget you'd invited a guest?'

'Of course not, but I was justifiably angry.'

She came forward holding out her hand which Kathy took with a smile.

'I'm very pleased to meet you my dear,' she said, 'I'll just go and tidy up then I'll be back to chat with you. I want to see how Mrs Hodson is coping with tea.'

With a brief smile she left them and Doctor Greavson said with a small sigh, 'I hadn't realised she'd dragged in Mrs Hodson on a Saturday afternoon, but I'm sure the good woman can cope without supervision.'

It hadn't taken Kathy long to realise that James Greavson was entirely correct in his summing up of his sister-in-law, or that she was not going to like her. It became doubly clear during the rest of the afternoon when she was subjected to a bombardment of questions about her role in Anthony's uncle's firm of solicitors, and where Kathy had acquired her degree – after her first amazement that she had actually got one.

Her opening remark had been, 'Anthony told me he had met a very nice girl at work. Just exactly what do you do in the office, dear?'

'Kathy's a solicitor, Mother, she has a law degree,' Anthony said sharply.

His mother raised her eyebrows. 'Really, I didn't know. Girls are emerging in all walks of life now aren't they? Anthony has a degree from Oxford.'

'I know,' Kathy replied. 'I took mine at Cambridge.'

That was the end of conversation about her role as a solicitor.

'So you live in Pelham, this side of Pelham?' she asked.

'No, we live in the town.'

'Actually in the town?'

'Actually. My father refuses to move. Maybe he will when he retires.'

'How is your father?' Doctor Greavson asked. 'I saw him a few months ago when I went into the shop. He looked very well then.'

'Yes, he is well thank you.'

'So you have a shop in the town?' Clare went on.

'My father works in one, the gents' outfitters, Marlowes.'

'Really. But didn't you say your name was Marston?'

'It is. My father doesn't own the shop, he's worked in it all his life.'

'Really. It has a very good reputation I believe.'

Kathy was beginning to feel tired of this ridiculous woman with her airs and pretensions. She found herself wondering if Anthony was oblivious of them even when she felt sure her husband was not. Once or twice she met the amusement twinkling in his eyes, and she felt better for it.

Tea was an excellent affair served by Mrs Hodson, a large woman wearing a floral-patterned overall, her brown hair tied back from her face by a piece of string. After she'd left them to it Mrs Greavson said testily, 'I do wish she'd dress herself up on a Saturday afternoon, and do something with her hair.'

'I rather think we've done very well to get her here on a Saturday afternoon at all. From the look of the trolley she's been very busy,' her husband said evenly.

'Are you enjoying working for my brother-in-law?' Mrs Greavson asked.

'Yes, very much.'

'I suppose he has other girls on his staff.'

'Not with law degrees, Mother,' Anthony said.

'I expect your parents were very pleased when you did so well at Cambridge,' Mrs Greavson said.

'My father was pleased, my mother died nearly

ten years ago.'

'Oh, I'm sorry. Did you want to come back to your home town to work?'

'There was an opening here. I've spent most of my life away from home, I thought it might be nice to come back.'

'Anthony spent some time in London, we agreed that it would enhance his career. Working in London is so much more interesting than working in a small town.'

'Why did you leave London, Anthony?' Kathy asked innocently.

'Well, with an uncle owning a firm of solicitors I'd have been mad not to come when there was an opening for me.'

Kathy smiled, and for a moment his mother seemed disconcerted. She decided to change the subject.

'I do hope Mrs Sherwood isn't going to make simnels for the show this year. I'll admit they are very good but nobody else gets a look in.'

'Why not take some of Mrs Hodson's along?' her husband said.

'How could I when she takes them herself?'

'What are you taking this year, Clare?'

'I'm hoping to show flowers if the gardener will allow me to take them, and I might take a jar or two of my chutney. I hope you'll be around to help us, Anthony. There's so much fetching and carrying to do and your father never gets involved.'

'When is the show, Mother?'

'After Easter, the third Saturday in April.'

'Kathy'll come along won't you darling? She

151

could sell ice cream to Eskimos. Find her a stall where the men will find something, she'll do wonders for it.'

'Perhaps she doesn't enjoy this sort of thing,' his mother said.

'The third Saturday in April is out anyway, I've been invited to a wedding on that day,' Kathy said quickly.

Anthony looked up with raised eyebrows.

'You didn't tell me about it,' he said smiling.

'There hasn't been much time. I only received the invitation yesterday.'

'It doesn't really matter Anthony, you'll be able to be there,' his mother said with something like relief.

Mrs Hodson came to clear away and Dr Greavson said, smiling, 'Thanks for all you've done Mrs Hodson, the tea was excellent. You'll be able to get off home now.'

'As soon as I've put the kitchen to rights and washed the dishes,' she replied.

Kathy stole a surreptitious look at the clock. The time was going so slowly and conversation was flagging. Surely they would be able to get away soon and as if in answer to her unspoken plea Mrs Greavson said, 'We're going over to the Fletchers this evening John, they've invited us for a game of bridge.'

He frowned. 'When did they invite us? I was rather hoping for a night in.'

'Really John, they asked us over last Saturday when we were leaving. We can't not go at this late stage.'

With a resigned sigh her husband got up from

his chair, and Anthony said, 'Kathy and I will get off then, we'll have a drink at that new place near the crossroads, Kathy.'

Doctor Greavson squeezed her hand warmly at the door, and his wife held out her cheek for Kathy to kiss. 'I'm so pleased to have met you' she said, 'I'm always pleased when Anthony brings one of his young ladies home.'

Kathy felt like laughing. The woman was too obvious, but Anthony appeared not to notice. At least he made no attempt to deny that there had been several young ladies.

Driving along the tree-lined road he seemed in high good humour as he said, 'That was very nice darling. You got along very well with Mother. Everybody gets along well with Dad.'

She smiled.

'What's all this about a wedding invitation? Is it here in Pelham?'

'No, it's in Berkshire.'

'Who do you know in Berkshire?'

'A girl I was at school with. I expect she's invited some of the others, it will be nice to see them again.'

'Do you want to go?'

'Of course, why do you ask?'

'It's not going to be much fun going on your own. Hasn't she asked you to take a friend?'

'Actually she has, but it can't be you, Anthony, you'll be kept busy with your mother's show.'

He was silent, and stealing a look at his face she could plainly see the uncertainty written on it. In the next breath he said, 'Is it going to be a big affair, morning dress and all the trimmings?'

153

'Oh, I'm sure it will be.'

'Family of some note are they?'

'I always found them very nice people. I was fond of Ginevra.'

'Ginevra! Rather upmarket, isn't it?'

'How do you mean?'

'Well, the name, I've never heard it before.'

'I believe it's been used once or twice within her family.'

'We'll talk about it some more, Kathy, that's if there's nobody else you have in mind.'

'And your mother's show?'

'Let me worry about that.'

Over breakfast several mornings later Anthony raised the subject of the wedding invitation.

'Kathy didn't like to say I'd been invited, Mother, when you went on about my helping you with your show. You always have so many helpers, I'm sure you can do without me for once.'

'No, Anthony, we can't. I've already told the committee members they can rely on you.'

'Any other year they can, but this year I really do think I have to say no.'

'Really, Anthony, everybody at this wedding is going to think of you two as an item. You haven't known the girl long, what do you know about her?'

'What do you mean, Mother?'

'I have been making a few enquiries. After all you are our only son, we don't want you making any mistakes about your future.'

'I'm not with you, Mother.'

'Do you know for instance that her father's sister is in a long-standing affair with an earl,

154

somebody she met when she was going around with Baronet Peterson's younger son. The earl does happen to be married and with children, but he educated your lady friend, sent her away to boarding school and paid for everything. You knew, didn't you, John?'

'In my profession I don't listen to gossip,' her husband replied testily.

'Well, it's true never the less. I'm quite sure your brother knows all about it.'

'Whether he did or not it didn't stop him engaging the girl.'

'It stands to reason, doesn't it. Her father doesn't own that shop, he merely works in it, how could he be expected to pay for his daughter to go to boarding school and on to university out of his earnings? I want you to be very careful, Anthony. I'm quite sure by inviting you to this wedding she intends something more permanent to come out of it.'

'You *have* been busy, Clare,' Anthony's father said coldly.

The two men left the house together and at Anthony's car his father said. 'Don't take too much notice of everything your mother says, Anthony, I liked the girl and your uncle thinks very highly of her. This is a small town and when scandal rears its ugly head everybody in the town knows about it. Whatever the girl's aunt has done nobody knows the full story, and none of it reflects on the girl herself.'

He watched his son drive away.

He had never been sure how carefully Anthony listened to his mother. They had always been

155

close and he'd been glad to send the boy away to school and proud of him when he'd done well at Oxford, but that particular bond between mother and son had remained too positive. Clare would have a say in what Anthony did with his life, and he had never had any doubts about the mischief she could cause.

His brother James had never liked her, they were like two cats when they met and Christmas get-togethers had long since become things of the past.

Clare had been a pretty, quietly spoken girl when he first met her, the only daughter of a town councillor who owed a lucrative engineering works in the next town. He'd joined a practice with two other doctors and quickly become popular, even more so when the senior doctor retired through ill health shortly afterwards.

They had lived in the town in those days, in a medium-sized stone house next to the practice, but it had been Clare on the look-out every weekend for something more ostentatious. Clare who had discovered the new property outside the town, and Clare who had selected the largest house of the lot. It was nowhere near as convenient for him doing his rounds but Clare loved it and Anthony was on her side. He said they should have moved years ago, it was nearer the tennis club and the golf club.

Mother and son were like-minded about a lot of things and John sensed the future would not be without its problems.

Anthony pursued the subject of the wedding invitation. They could make a weekend of it, drive down the day before and find some nice inn or hotel to stay at and drive back on the Sunday.

Kathy was less enthusiastic. She followed Anthony's predictable reasoning. Some hotel where she would be expected to respond to his advances, a situation which no doubt his mother was also well aware of. Then there was the wedding itself. But for his mother's show she'd had every intention of declining, it was only Clare's insistence that her son be on hand to help her that had prompted her to mention the wedding at all.

There were a great many questions James Greavson wanted to ask, but even a legal eagle had reservations about appearing too intrusive.

Taking his wife into his confidence he said, 'I can't think it was a success, you know what Clara's like, nobody'll be right for her one lone lamb.'

'Anthony's a nice boy,' his wife said in his defence.

'Well of course, but Clara'll make it her business to find out everything she can about Kathy and in her narrow-minded little soul some of it will be suspect.'

'Why, what do you mean?'

'We'll talk about it again, I'm due on the golf course. I'll have a word with John, we might accept that dinner invitation he's been issuing these last few months.'

'You said you didn't want to see Clara any more than necessary.'

'I know, but this is different.'

Valerie Greavson wasn't exactly over-fond of her sister-in-law either. She'd always been aware of Clara's acid tongue and her pretensions. Her husband put up with them but had the ability to switch himself off. Anthony teased his mother about them, but was more inclined to take them on board. She wouldn't enjoy a dinner engagement with them, but James had had something on his mind that could only be settled with a confrontation.

Later that evening he confirmed that they were to dine with his brother and his wife a week on Sunday. It was an evening Valerie was hardly looking forward to.

Chapter Twelve

Clare was a good cook with the assistance of Mrs Hodson, and as always the table was impeccable, from the array of cut-glass and silver to the arrangement of carnations in the centre.

James asked innocently, 'Nice flowers Clara, from your greenhouse?'

'No, from the florist. I never ask for flowers from the greenhouse.'

'Really, why is that?'

'We have a gardener who thinks he owns the lot.'

'Oh dear.'

Her husband smiled. 'The quarrel between

Clare and Henry is an ongoing thing. He'll come up trumps for her show I've no doubt.'

'I've a good mind not to ask him.' Clare said haughtily.

'Where is Anthony this afternoon?' her brother-in-law asked.

'I don't know, he only tells me what he wants me to know, he's probably with that girl who works for you.'

'Kathy Marston, you've met her then?'

'Yes, he brought her to tea.'

'Nice girl, very competent. She has a good law degree you know; she's the first qualified woman solicitor we've had on the staff.'

'I suppose you went into her credentials?'

'Well of course, haven't I just said so? Law degree taken at Cambridge, what more could we want.'

'I mean her personal details.'

'Well, she's a single girl living with her widower father in the town. To my knowledge she's never been in the hands of the police, not even for a parking ticket, I'm not with you, Clara.'

'Not even about her education?'

'Oh, it's an excellent one. Girls' upmarket boarding school, then university. She came with all the details it was in our interest to know.'

'All of them?'

'Can you think of anything else?'

'I can think of how she received her education.'

'From excellent teachers I should imagine.'

'Or who paid for it?'

'That wouldn't interest me in the slightest, why should it?'

159

'I've been learning quite a lot about that young woman. Her aunt is embroiled in a long-standing affair with Earl Fortesque, a married man with children. He paid for her education, I really do think it's quite disgusting. Did you know about it, James?'

'About the affair yes, about Kathy's education, no. It's nothing to do with anybody beside his Lordship and Josie Marston.'

'So you know the aunt, do you?'

'I was introduced to her once at a dance. She was there with Nigel Peterson. I thought she was the most beautiful girl I'd ever seen.'

'Really James, what has Valerie got to say about that?'

'It was long before I met Valerie. Josie Marston was a corker, she worked in the fashion department at that big store in the High Street and I knew her brother who worked in the gents' outfitters. They were a very respectable family.'

'Until the girl ditched Nigel Peterson for a more aristocratic lover.'

'Well, young Peterson's run the gamut of glamorous females. His reputation doesn't bear looking into so I'm pretty sure there was not much future for Josie with him. I should think Fortesque was a much better bet.'

'Even when he was married.'

'Nobody outside the three of them knows very much about the state of his marriage. This long-standing affair with Josie has lasted through a good many years and shows no signs of coming to an end. It's something the aristocracy seem to handle rather well.'

'Well, I think it's disgusting. I don't want Anthony to get involved.'

'With what? Kathy or her aunt?'

'If their friendship becomes serious he'll have it all his life, everybody remembering the aunt; it's a scandal that won't go away.'

'This is small-town gossip Clara, small minds with nothing better to talk about. Why are you so pessimistic about them anyway?'

'She's been invited to a wedding, some girl she was at school with, and she's invited Anthony to escort her. Everybody will think of them as a pair. I don't want Anthony pushed into something he can't get out of.'

'I don't think Kathy's the sort of girl who would push Anthony into anything he doesn't want. He might even enjoy the wedding.'

'What do you mean by that?'

'It's probably an invitation to a society do, after all they were the sort of girls she was at school with. If that's the case you can conceivably dine out on it for the best part of next year.'

'I'm not very likely to do that, James.'

'It depends, Clara. If Anthony comes home talking about dukes and duchesses, not to mention several peers of the realm, nobody around here will be able to beat you on the social scene.'

'I'll get some more coffee,' Clare snapped and departed out of the room.

Her husband said, 'You're baiting her James, and you know it doesn't take much. I liked the girl Anthony brought home, she was pretty and very nice, I also know something about Clare's prejudices.'

161

'Don't we all,' his brother breathed.

Clare returned with the coffee, asking, 'More coffee anyone?'

'Yes please, Clara,' James said holding out his cup, and Clare snapped, 'I wish you wouldn't call me Clara, James, nobody else does and you know I prefer Clare.'

'I know you do my dear, that's probably why I do it, I'll try to remember in future.'

'You won't, you never do.'

'Doesn't Anthony know the names of the people who are getting married?'

'I don't ask him anything about the wedding. If he wants to go he'll go whether I like it or not; if he wants to talk about it when he comes back that's up to him.'

'I think that's very sensible, Clara, sorry, Clare. You and John can sit here and listen to him talking about what is probably destined to be a very prestigious affair indeed.'

The rest of the evening passed reasonably un-eventfully. They played bridge and the two men discussed their golf, while the two women talked about fashion and what they wanted to do for holidays, it was later on their drive home that Valerie said, 'You really did antagonise her, James, perhaps she has a point about Anthony and his lady friend.'

'Not she. Only prejudice and a scandal that erupted years ago.'

'But it's still going on.'

'Yes, but not here in Pelham and not that it affects anybody in the town. They should all mind their own business.'

'Was she really as pretty as you say she was?'

He grinned. 'Yes she really was. We were at a rugger ball, a group of young chaps just out of the egg, most of us still had feathers sticking all over us, and there was this girl, elegant, beautiful, dancing round with young Peterson whom none of us could stand.'

'Why was that?'

'Probably because he was landed gentry, the son of a baronet, and aware of it. He thought all the girls wanted him and he had the best-looking girl at the dance.'

'What happened to him?'

'He married some girl his family picked out for him and drank himself into an early grave. His marriage didn't work out, apparently he always wanted Anthea McKinley, but she married a man old enough to be her father, somebody who was extremely rich. Peterson's father had almost bankrupted the family so she wouldn't have entertained Nigel.'

'Life in the town seems very circumspect now, James. It seems to me that that was an affair on the grand scale.'

'People needn't seem so smug, Val, behind some of those curtained windows in many of those urban streets everything isn't quite as pristine as they'd like it to be. With Josie Marston, scandal reared its ugly head because she was a beautiful girl and he was somebody out of the top drawer. Noble, rich...'

'And married.'

'That too. But what do any of us know about the state of his marriage? So many of those

163

people have wives and husbands found for them, nobody can tell a man, or a woman either, who they are to fall in love with.'

'She can't get any real satisfaction from being his mistress though, it isn't a perfect relation-ship,' Valerie persisted.

'Perhaps not, but it's certainly lasted, and I've seen them together. They look a very devoted pair. They're quite evidently in love.'

'I wonder what his children think about it?'

'They're grown up. The daughter was at school with Kathy Marston so whatever animosity there was the two girls must have overcome it.'

'In her shoes I wouldn't exactly want to mingle with them at a wedding. Clara will want the full story. I rather think Anthony has a few surprises in store for him.'

James grinned. 'We'll be hearing all about it, that might just be one evening I won't mind spending in her company.'

Anthony continued to press Kathy on the subject of the wedding invitation. 'I can't think why you don't reply to it,' he said petulantly. 'I've said I'll gladly go with you and we'll take a look round for a suitable wedding present. Didn't they send you a list? They usually do these days and it stops presents from being duplicated.'

Kathy shook her head. 'The present isn't a problem.'

'But something is, Kathy.'

'Perhaps I'm not ready to face them all again.' Anthony remained silent. He did not want to tell her that his mother had made it her business to find out all she could about her past, or rather the past of her Aunt Josie.

She had been happy in Anthony's company, they had laughed together and it had all been so uncomplicated; now she looked upon what they had had together as something irretrievably lost.

Behind all his questions she saw his mother. Her pretty vapid face and birdlike inquisitive eyes.

What sort of people were the Midhursts? Was it likely to be a society wedding, and what would the guests be like? Was she absolutely certain that he needed to wear morning dress? After all he didn't want to let her down; and what would they be expected to give the happy couple as a wedding present?

His questions only served to make Kathy reticent. She would tell him nothing about the Midhursts that he could pass on to his mother, nothing about her schooldays that had brought them together, and when he asked her to show him the wedding invitation she shrugged it off with a smile, saying she'd forgotten where she'd put it.

'But you've answered it surely?' he prevaricated.

'Of course.'

'Mother's quite cross that I shan't be there to help with her show, I do think it would placate her a little if I could tell her something about this wedding we're going to.'

'Anthony, you needn't have come with me. Why didn't you go along with your mother to the show? After all if you don't know anybody it's not

165

going to be much fun for you.'

She hated herself for being secretive, but the old Anthony she'd almost been falling in love with would never have questioned her in such a way. He'd have been light-hearted about it, prepared to enjoy the day without thinking too much about the social background of the people concerned.

Innocently his uncle asked, 'I believe you're off to Berkshire with Kathy to the wedding of one of her old school friends.'

'Yes, after Easter.'

'Your mother's feeling a bit miffed that she doesn't know much about it.'

'I don't know much about it,' Anthony snapped.

James smiled to himself. Good for Kathy he thought, she was well aware that anything she told Anthony would be repeated to his mother, and the woman would put two and two together and make five.

'I hope you haven't made any arrangements for over Easter,' Clare said over dinner the week before. 'I really do think we should drive into Cumbria to stay with Aunt Philippa and Uncle Edmund for a few days. She says it's ages since she's seen you, Anthony, and they are your godparents.'

'Easter can be dire in Cumbria,' her husband said.

'Well, we needn't travel around, they have a large comfortable house and if the weather is decent you can do some sailing. The last time we went you and Anthony were never out of the boat.'

'What about your girlfriend, Anthony?' his father asked.

'We haven't made any arrangements about Easter. I rather think she needs to shop and spend time with her father.'

'Have you had thoughts on a wedding present?' his mother asked.

'I've left it to Kathy. She knows I'll go halves whatever she decides on.'

'You don't seem very well informed about who is getting married or anything about the respective families. Surely she's told you something?' Clare said sharply.

'Actually she's told me very little. I've stopped asking her.'

'It doesn't sound to me as though it's going to be a grand affair or surely she'd have elaborated on it. I thought the girls she was at school with were from the top drawer; evidently she wasn't in their league.'

'You don't know that Mother. You're only surmising.'

'Why doesn't she talk about them then?'

'Probably because for years everybody else in Pelham's been talking about something they know nothing about. Kathy doesn't want to talk about it and Anthony will find out for himself,' his father said testily.

'You'll see I'm right, Anthony,' his mother snapped. 'She doesn't want to discuss it because there's nothing of note to discuss. She wants to show you off to her friends, after all not every girl has a man friend with a law degree from Oxford and a foothold in his uncle's firm.'

'Kathy isn't like that, Mother.'

'Stick up for her all you like, but I hardly think this is the wedding of the year you've been invited to.'

Easter Saturday in the Marston household started much as every other Saturday. Her father pinned in his carnation and prepared to set out for the shop, first asking with a wry smile, 'What are you intending to do with your day, love? Isn't Anthony away?'

'Yes, Dad, in Cumbria.'

'Visiting relatives?'

'His godparents. I thought I'd go to the shops, I need a hat and shoes. I still haven't got Ginevra's wedding present.'

'What can you give her, love? She's a girl with everything.'

'I know, but there's sure to be something.'

She went with him to the door, picking up the post that had fallen on to the hall floor. Her father said, 'Anything for me Kathy?'

She leafed through the mail quickly, passing one or two envelopes to him, then she opened the door and watched him walking quickly down the road. His tall slim figure was surprisingly youthful and as he passed several groups of people he raised his hat in greeting.

Returning to the kitchen she scanned the morning post. Most of it consisted of junk mail until she came across a picture postcard and she stared at it curiously to find that it was a scene depicting the harbour of Funchal in Madeira. She turned it over, who did she know who was

168

spending Easter in Madeira?'

She read the signature with some surprise. She had not expected to find that Ginevra was in Funchal so soon before her wedding.

The postcard told her very little.

Enjoying the sunshine on this beautiful island. We're enjoying the sailing and the flowers, time is passing all too quickly. Please Kathy no wedding presents unless it's that darling little horse you saw before I did. Only joking. Love Ginevra.

Kathy sat back puzzled. Evidently Ginevra was not alone in Madeira but she'd never been very forthcoming. At school she'd annoyed Alanna, who was open and outgoing and even Jane who was naturally shy had often been nonplussed by her.

She was remembering the horse. A tiny jade horse, exquisitely sculptured, and which she'd picked up for a quite ridiculous price at an antique fair they'd gone to at a stately home. It was true she'd seen it before Ginevra, who was bemoaning the fact. It had taken all Kathy's pocket money whereas it would hardly have infringed on Ginevra's.

She went up to her bedroom and immediately to where the ornament stood on top of her tallboy, picking it up, and stroking the cold smoothness of the jade. Of course Ginevra could have it, and Anthony would have no obligation to contribute anything towards it. She opened the wardrobe door and took out the pale blue heavy shantung dress and jacket she had bought for the wedding. It was pretty, beautifully cut, and the colour complemented her blonde hair and blue eyes.

It had cost a great deal of money, and her mind went back to the rows between her mother and Aunt Josie on the subject of the latter's extravagance. What would her mother have had to say about this creation she wondered?

She was glad Anthony was away for Easter. More and more they were finding it difficult to talk to each other normally about everyday things. His mind was on the wedding and he was annoyed with her because he thought she had told him too little about it. He had every right to be exasperated, but she couldn't forget his mother's condescending attitude towards her and she was annoyed that that old scandal resurfaced time and again to intrude into the present.

Anthony waited for her on the office steps when they returned after the Easter break. He was smiling, and suddenly her heart warmed to him. He really was a nice man, he couldn't help his mother's attitude, and as he walked beside her into the building he said. 'Enjoy your Easter, Kathy?'

'Yes, Dad and I walked on Good Friday and we went to church on Sunday. It was quite uneventful. Did you enjoy Cumbria?'

'Yes, the weather wasn't too bad so we got some sailing in.'

'Does your mother like sailing?'

'Heavens no. She spent time with Aunt

170

Philippa gossiping, giving each other all the news. Two weeks to the wedding Kathy, we'll have to talk about the journey or if we intend to stay overnight somewhere.'

'Yes, we'll do that.'

'Mother was wondering what you intended to wear?'

'You can tell her all about it after the event.'

He smiled stiffly and left her to go into his office.

What was the matter with her? She was becoming paranoid. After all he'd made a perfectly natural remark and she'd gone all secretive again.

The first day after Easter had seemed a good time to call one of his meetings; it would be a quiet day, and as he surveyed the members of his staff James Greavson noticed that Kathy and Anthony were not sitting together, but rather at opposite ends of the room. He felt a faint twinge of regret. He liked Kathy and he liked Anthony, it was obvious something had gone wrong in their relationship and he did not think he needed to look far to find the culprit.

It would all come out in the wash, and he decided he would ask no questions of either of them. As soon as the meeting was over Kathy left the room, but Anthony stayed to chat about the godparents, both of whom were known to James and his wife.

'Kathy didn't go with you?' James couldn't resist asking in spite of his earlier decision to say nothing.

'No, just Dad and Mother. Kathy had to do

some shopping for the wedding.'

'Of course. Next weekend, isn't it?'

'No, the weekend after.'

Standing at the window staring out into the busy street James reached a decision. His golfing pal had a brother living in Berkshire and he might just know something about a wedding there. Of course there were likely to be a good many weddings around this time, but there was no harm in making a few pertinent enquiries.

Chapter Thirteen

Anthony's mother had made up her mind to stay aloof from her son's lady friend. She was annoyed that Anthony knew so little about the wedding in Berkshire and had made up her mind that it would in all probability be a hole-and-corner affair which was the reason the girl didn't want to discuss it.

Clare was unaware of the twinkle in her brother-in-law's eye when she said as much. James had made enquiries from his friend and had triumphantly informed his wife that on that particular weekend the Earl of Midhurst's daughter Ginevra was to marry her marquis.

'But you can't be sure, James,' Valerie said doubtfully. 'Surely Kathy would have told Anthony about a wedding as important as that one.'

'No she wouldn't. She wouldn't want his

mother to know, you know what she'd make of information like that.'

James was well aware that his nephew's feelings for Kathy were going through a period of frustration that seemed not to be troubling her in the slightest.

Anthony posed the question of a wedding present and Kathy produced the small jade horse Ginevra had mentioned.

He looked at it in some dismay. 'What's so special about that?' he demanded.

'It's jade.'

'I know it's jade, but it's so small, surely she'll expect something better than this. The last wedding I went to they presented me with a list asking for dishwashers and canteens of cutlery.'

'Ginevra loved this horse, she always wished she'd seen it before I did.'

'Oh well, there's no accounting for taste I suppose. Have they bought a house, do you know?'

'I'm sure they have.'

'You don't seem to know very much about the wedding Kathy, either that or you don't want to tell me.'

'Actually I don't know very much about it. I've never met the bridegroom and I only know the Abbey from visiting Ginevra's home.'

'Funny place to choose for a wedding, an abbey.'

'Not really. It's a beautiful old church in the village. I would have expected Ginevra to be married there.'

Anthony shrugged his shoulders and Kathy said quietly, 'You don't have to go. Your mother

173

would be glad of your help at the fête.'

'She's found other helpers, besides when I make a promise I keep it. I said I'd escort you to this wedding so I intend to.'

'Thank you Anthony, you're very kind.'

His mother thought that their friendship was on its way out and she was hopeful. The girl was extremely pretty and of course she did have that law degree from Cambridge, but she'd driven past the gents' outfitters where her father worked and past their home, a neat stone house on the corner of the High Street, with a small garden at the front and a short walk up to the front door. The house had looked well cared for with pristine paintwork and a polished brass door-knocker, but Anthony could do better for himself.

She said as much to her friend Mrs Perkins. The Perkins had a pretty daughter called Zoey and the Perkins had money. Zoey was stylish, good company and outgoing. She'd played tennis with Anthony and was taking up golf. They moved in the same circle, went to the same church, and whenever Clare brought Zoey into the conversation Anthony agreed that she was a nice girl.

Mrs Perkins too thought that there might conceivably be the prospect of something permanent for the young couple when his friendship with Kathy Marston came to an end. After all, an up-and-coming solicitor with an eye on a partnership in his uncle's firm must steer clear of a wife with a history of scandal, even if it didn't concern her.

174

When Mrs Perkins and Clare had their heads together inevitably the old scandal concerning Josie Marston surfaced and Clare said to her friend, 'It won't last long after this wedding they're going to. I can read the signs. Anthony knows very little about it so it's probably a very low-key affair or she'd talk about it. He'll find out her friends are not really his sort.'

'But didn't you say she was educated in a very upmarket girls' school?'

'Yes, but she wouldn't have many friends there, not from the way she got there. No, this wedding has nothing at all to do with her education. I've asked my brother-in-law, but he says Kathy's said nothing about the wedding to him. She would have done if it had been a society affair.'

'Yes of course. Zoey's helping at the fête, it's a pity Anthony won't be there.'

'We'll sort something else out; all we need is patience.'

It was the weekend before the wedding and Kathy was busy hoovering the hall when she saw a car drawing up in front of the house. Thinking it might be Anthony she went to open the front door.

Instead of Anthony however a tall elegant woman was climbing out of the front seat. With a cry of delight Kathy recognised her Aunt Josie and she hurried down the path to meet her. As they warmly embraced she thought Josie never looks any different, she's still beautiful, still slender and stylish, her face wearing the same enchanting smile that had captivated so many people over the years.

175

'Let me look at you,' Josie said laughing down at her. 'You're the prettiest thing, you remind me of me when I was your age.'

'I'll never be as pretty as you, Aunt Josie.'

'But you are darling. I suppose your father's at the shop?'

'Of course. Need you ask, it's Saturday, his busiest day.'

'I'm glad we're going to have the house to ourselves. I'm dying for a cup of tea.'

'Why didn't you write to tell us you were coming?'

'I decided on the spur of the moment. Why haven't you been to see me?'

'I'm a working girl, Aunt Josie, I haven't forgotten you but I do wish you'd never sold that lovely house. Why did you?'

'It was too near Pelham darling, too near Maplethorpe.'

'Are you happy with things as they are?' Kathy asked.

'Yes of course. They can never be what we want them to be, so we've settled for second best. Has Ginevra Midhurst invited you to her wedding?'

So that was the reason for her visit.

Kathy smiled. 'Yes. I didn't know if I should accept. The decision wasn't easy.'

'Darling, my ignominious past has nothing to do with you, you and Ginevra were good friends. Jane asked me if you were going.'

'Jane asked you!'

'Jane and I buried the hatchet a long time ago. We're good friends. I know it sounds incredible after what has happened but I've really tried with

176

Jane. Jane adores her father and life at home hasn't been easy between her parents. Nothing to do with me, Kathy, it was all pretty hopeless long before I came on the scene. She knows her father loves me and she's accepted it. Do you never hear from her?'

'A Christmas card, that's all.'

'I think she's looking forward to seeing you again so of course you must go to the wedding. Are you taking an escort?'

'Yes. Anthony Greavson, a solicitor in the firm.'

'Serious?'

'Not any more.'

'Oh dear. Is this something else I'm responsible for?'

'Of course not. I met his mother, I didn't particularly like her and I wasn't what she wanted for Anthony. We're friends, nothing more, but you can tell Jane we'll be at the wedding. Hasn't Jane found somebody to marry?'

'We worry about Jane. Oh, I know that sounds awful because I'm not her mother, I'm merely her father's mistress, but I'm very fond of her and I know John worries about her. She's cynical about life and it goes back to her childhood when her mother showed little interest in anything beyond her dogs and horses, and she became solitary and withdrawn. Then when I got involved she began to believe that her father didn't love her either.'

'Is she still like that?'

'In some respects. There are men who like her, would like to know her better, but she treats them all with a cavalier insensitivity that makes

177

them feel they're wasting their time. She views all marriages with the same jaundiced prejudice with which she views her parents' marriage. She's not very sure that Ginevra's wedding is one made in heaven.'

'But that's a terrible thing to say.'

'I know, but she seems to know something about her fiancé's past that could upset the apple-cart. I have no idea what it is, she hasn't said.'

'Ginevra has been in Madeira, she could be home by this time.'

'With her fiancé?'

'She didn't say. I suppose Jane and her parents will all be at the wedding?'

'Yes, and you mustn't let it bother you, Kathy. Jane received a separate invitation in case she wanted to take somebody along. I doubt if she will, but you just go and enjoy it, darling. Will Alanna be there?'

'I'm sure Ginevra will have invited her.'

Josie laughed. 'Oh well, if Alanna can successfully ride the storm I don't think there's anything for you to worry about. I have to go now darling, it was only a short visit. Give my love to Albert and tell him I'll see him soon.'

After a brief embrace Kathy waited while Josie drove away. All along the street heads were turned to stare after the expensive white car and then knowing looks were exchanged.

Kathy felt strangely unsettled after her aunt's visit. She was concerned about Jane and her bitterness. As a schoolgirl she had looked upon

178

the other three as girls who had everything, all the good things the world had to offer, with never a cloud on their horizons.

They'd been the girls who had talked about holidays abroad, in the south of France and the Caribbean. They talked about yachts and polo, hunt meetings and garden parties and, in Alanna's case, she talked about her father whom she adored, his string of women friends and his disasters on the stock market.

She had listened to them all without having anything to contribute. None of them would have been remotely interested in the small exclusive shop where her father worked. It was only exclusive to Pelham, outside the town nobody had heard of it. She would have seen their eyes become glazed at any talk of her mother's various interests, the Mothers' Union and Chapel every Sunday, the market stalls where she shopped for vegetables and their yearly holiday somewhere in Devon or Cornwall.

They didn't seem to mind that she had little to contribute, they were all too involved with themselves. Only now and again Jane said, 'You never talk about your interests, Kathy, you should tell us to shut up about ourselves.'

Kathy had smiled. 'I love listening to you,' she'd said. 'To me it's a whole new life, nothing exciting ever happens to me.'

Jane had looked at her with something like disbelief and she knew that she was thinking about Josie, Josie who was all too prominent in her father's life.

What would Anthony make of her old school

179

friends and what would he tell his mother afterwards? She had no doubt that Anthony would be totally captivated with the entire procedure and she was being unfair to him. She ought to be able to tell him about what to expect from the wedding but memories of his mother's patronising manner still irked her. She knew for a certainty that Anthony had already been got at by his mother and she wished heartily that he would make some excuse not to attend.

Clare hurried across the garden when she heard the sound of Anthony's car in the drive. He was unloading his clubs and golf trolley and she greeted him with a warm smile.

'Enjoy your golf, dear?' she called out. 'You've always been a bit scathing about mixed foursomes. Who did you play with?'

'Zoey Perkins, Mother. She's very good.'

'Didn't you want to stay for the presentation tonight or are you going back later?'

'No, I promised to pick Kathy up. It's the wedding next weekend, we have to make arrangements.'

'But you see her at the office, couldn't you have made your arrangements there?'

'We do have work to do, Mother.'

He was irritable and didn't want to discuss the matter. His tetchiness both intrigued and elated her. It was obvious there were dark clouds on the horizon where Kathy Marston was concerned.

It was evident he didn't wish to take Kathy to the golf club, and once this wretched wedding was over he'd surely see that Zoey Perkins was more his sort.

'Is your father staying on at the club or is he coming home to change?' she asked.

'I really don't know. I don't even know if he was playing.'

'We're dining with the Perkins tomorrow evening, you were invited too.'

Anthony shrugged his shoulders. 'I really don't know what I shall be doing tomorrow evening, Mother.'

He knew what his mother was about. It would suit her if he called it a day with Kathy and transferred his affections to Zoey Perkins. She never lost an opportunity to bring up that old scandal, but what she didn't seem to realise was that a scandal of years ago in her generation hardly raised an eyebrow in his. He'd never met Kathy's aunt, and if he and Kathy had problems they weren't connected with the past.

Perhaps his mother was right. Perhaps they were ordinary countrified people and the wedding would be a mundane affair and he'd wish they hadn't gone, but then his mother had always had high-flown notions on the sort of people he had to mix with.

He was well aware that she had hopes of Zoey Perkins, and he liked the girl. To be honest he had more in common with Zoey than he had with Kathy apart from their chosen careers, and Kathy was being decidedly obstreperous. Whatever her friends were like he'd tell her he was enjoying himself, make a show of being very nice to everybody and give Kathy a weekend to remember.

When he told her he intended to book in at some nice hotel or country club for the entire weekend she offered no opposition and Anthony planned that they would drive into Berkshire on the Friday evening and drive back sometime on Sunday.

With this in mind he started to ring round every upmarket hotel he could think of, and a great many others his friends could think of. For that weekend in particular there was no room at the inn. When he told Kathy he'd had no joy in finding accommodation she'd merely smiled. Kathy had known that every hotel and inn in the vicinity would be filled with Midhurst guests.

Anthony was annoyed. 'It will mean leaving home at some ridiculous hour,' he grumbled. 'Driving miles dressed up in wedding finery isn't exactly my idea of a pleasant start to the event.'

'Anthony, why don't you say if you'd rather not go,' she argued.

'Would you go on your own?'

'Of course. Ginevra is my friend and I've accepted the invitation. I shall however quite understand if you decide not to go with me.'

'I wouldn't let you down like that, Kathy.'

'Your mother would be pleased.'

'Why do you say that?'

'You could help with the fête.'

'I'm not interested in the bloody fête,' he snapped. 'We'll go to the wedding as planned.'

They were driving through the village of Feversham and Kathy said, 'I always loved this village, my aunt had a house at the corner of Sheppleton Lane, do you know it?'

'No, I really don't know much about the village.'

'Neither did I until Aunt Josie came to live here.'

Hearing Josie's name on Kathy's lips immediately intrigued him. Aunt Josie! Wasn't she the woman his mother had talked about together with all the scandal?

'Show me where it is,' he asked.

Kathy directed him down the leafy lanes towards the crossroads and the mellow stone house with its perfect lawns and Virginia-creeper covered façade. Anthony stopped the car to look at the house.

'Doesn't she live there now then?' he asked.

'Not for some years.'

'Where does she live?'

'She has a lovely old house near Cheltenham. This house was too near Pelham and Maplethorpe.'

'Why did that matter?'

'Oh, I'm sure you've been put in the picture about my aunt Josie and Earl Fortesque. She's been his mistress for years, she was younger than me when she first met him and it's gone on from then.'

'Why doesn't he marry her?'

'Because he already has a wife and she will never divorce him. Josie knew this from the outset, now I doubt if it's a problem.'

She stole a glance at Anthony's face. They both listened to stories like this every day of their lives where marriage problems were thrashed out in the courts; that it was Kathy's aunt was a

183

different story, and in his expression she sensed a certain distaste. Her aunt should have known better than tangle with the aristocracy, and involve Kathy in doing so.

'Have you met Earl Fortesque?'

'Yes, several times.'

'Did you like him?'

'Very much. He was kind, handsome and generous. He paid for my education.'

'Why, for heaven's sake?'

'I won a scholarship for a good girls' school, but my parents didn't have enough money to allow me to take it up. My father would have found the money, my mother wouldn't hear of it. Aunt Josie thought I should be given a chance and Lord Fortesque paid for it.'

'Does my uncle know about this?'

'He knows where I was educated, he didn't ask me who paid for it. I'm sure he's aware of it now. After all a tale never loses anything.'

'Why are you telling me all this today, Kathy? You never told me before.'

'If your mother hasn't already told you I'm sure she will. In which case you can tell her you already know. If she has told you then I've merely confirmed her story.'

'My mother hasn't said anything bad about you.'

She smiled.

'Anthony, you're her one lone lamb and she wants you to find a girl with no skeletons in the cupboard, a girl nobody's going to talk about in derogatory terms. This is a small town where everybody knows everybody else. Years ago my father said I should find somewhere else to live, somewhere where I wasn't so well known, but this is my home and I wanted to come back to it. My father's weathered the storm. People didn't stop going into his shop, he's liked and respected because he's earned that right, I have to be worthy of him.'

He started up the car's engine and they drove slowly past the house and down the lane. She was glad she'd been honest with him about the past, but she had no means of knowing how it would affect the future.

His good-looking face was thoughtful and at that moment she was glad that she didn't love him. Once she had thought that she would come to love him, now she was very unsure.

Alanna

Chapter Fourteen

There were willing hands to assist Alanna to climb out of the tender that brought her to the little jetty below the long white villa where she had spent long hot summers before the time came to return to England and school.

Her eyes scanned the long veranda with its trail of hibiscus, the line of palms swaying along the private bench, and as she climbed up the shallow stone steps towards the lawns above a large smiling West Indian was hurrying down to meet her. He reached and took the suitcase out of her hands, and his face was alive with welcome, disclosing two rows of huge white teeth in a mouth alive with humour.

'Mees Alanna,' he cried, 'we not know you come today.'

'I know, Jacob, it was a quick decision. My father's here of course?'

He laughed. 'Here yes, but not at home.'

'Why, where is he?'

'Come to the house, I tell you where he is, you want meal?'

'Not immediately. Who else is down here?'

'Maria he bring, that is all.'

When she didn't immediately ask any more questions he said, 'Where you come from, how you know where to find him?'

'I've come from New York, I went to the house

in Boston and it was closed up, then I went to New York and that was deserted too. I found out from the Johnsons that my father was here. I suppose he's hiding from somebody, creditors or a woman?'

Jacob laughed loudly.

'Where's the yacht, is he out on that?'

'He let it out to some people, he skipper it for them.'

She stopped short in the gardens to stare up at him.

'You mean my father has let some people use his boat? I don't believe it.'

'It true. I tell you he skipper it for them, six of them.'

'When is he likely to return?'

He shrugged his shoulders, a gesture she was familiar with, and said 'Two more days then they return home.'

'But who are they?'

With another shrug of his shoulders he said 'I not sure, English perhaps, perhaps French. They want boat for two weeks, your father said they could have boat but only if he skipper it. That boat his joy.'

'I know, that's what I can't understand.'

'You will, Mees Alanna, your father tell you all about it when he return.'

Maria came from the back of the house to greet them, ordering Henry to take Mees Alanna's belongings up to her bedroom, then asking if she would like tea.

'Yes, please Maria. I went to Boston and New York, the houses were shut up, what happened

190

to the servants?'

Maria shrugged her shoulders. 'They gone,' she said. 'Mr Van Royston paid them off, he keep only me and Jacob and two gardeners here.'

'Oh, well, I expect I'll learn all about it in due course.'

After Maria had left her she walked out onto the terrace and stood looking down on the long sweep of the bay. A strong feeling of nostalgia swept over her as she took in the soft white sand and the swaying palms, the azure blue sea breaking gently against the rocks and the scent of oleanders strong on the air.

She had loved Santa Lucia as a child and had wept long and bitterly at the thought of returning to England with its icy winter winds and rain-lashed playing fields. Of course her sadness had not lasted. She had come to love the years she spent in England and the friends she made there, but always undermining her contentment was the battleground on which her parents played out their marriage. Their hostilities, their extravagances that in the end had to be paid for in one form or another.

What particular problem would her father present her with now?

She found that Maria had unpacked for her and put her clothes away. She had not brought many things because she didn't know how long she would be staying, or even if her father was on the island. Now she was glad to change into a cotton skirt and strapless suntop.

She took the narrow path on to the beach and sauntered idly along its length, pleased that it was a private beach and she was not likely to encounter anybody else. She supposed she would have to linger on until her father decided to return home, but her life at the moment was like a whirlpool, endlessly spinning round with neither a beginning nor an end.

Why couldn't she have had parents who could give good advice and support when she needed it, instead of two people more concerned with their own predicaments than any she might have? Her mother had always been ambitious for her. She wanted a beautiful daughter who would marry well, preferably somebody very rich, famous, well connected. She'd fulfilled these ambitions by being beautiful, the sort of girl guaranteed to glamorise any glossy they cared to put her in, and she had married well. Her mother had been delighted with both of her husbands, the first a count, the second a prince. It was a pity they'd been penniless and arrogant in the first instance, rich, selfish and adulterous in the second.

Jacob and Maria stood in the garden watching her sauntering back to the house and Maria shook her head sadly, 'I wonder why she come,' she said dully. 'She too beautiful that one, too aimless, what she doing here?'

Jacob didn't respond. Instead he tripped lightly down the steps to meet Alanna at the foot.

'What you do for these days on your own?' he demanded.

She laughed. 'Unwind, Jacob. Sit in the sun and absorb the peace.'

'Your father be glad to see you.'

'I'm not too sure. Whenever we meet either he

has problems or I do.'

He laughed again. 'He problems all right, you sort each other out.'

Maria served her solitary meal in the small room jutting out at the end of the villa, from where she could hear the surf lapping gently against the rocks, see the moonlight glistening on the water, hear the soft throbbing of West Indian drums from a nearby village.

She mooched about the villa, looking into drawers in the desk her father used, but discovering nothing that would tell her why he felt the need to charter his yacht out. It was almost as if he'd thought somebody would come into the house to pry then realise there was nothing to find. She stood for a long time on the terrace where a soft scented breeze fanned her cheeks and blew her silken skirts against her sun-kissed legs.

Why couldn't she have come back to Santa Lucia and absorb its peace, feel its gentleness wash over her, why were there so many nagging perplexities waiting to surface?

She went up to her bedroom and opened her small travelling-case from which she took out Ginevra Midhurst's wedding invitation. She was surprised that Ginevra had invited her. How would they view her, those aristocratic solid English people who made up Ginevra's world. They'd know her as the American girl who was never out of the newspapers. They'd trot out the two men she'd married, foreign titles would mean little to England's upper crust. Polish and Austrian counts and princes had no standing, their countries could boast no monarchy or courts where titles meant something.

The fact that she was a rich woman whose princely husband had been more than generous in an effort to salvage his family name, in the end meant nothing to Alanna and even less to the world in general.

Of course she wouldn't accept the invitation. Ginevra had probably only sent it out of politeness. Her thoughts turned to Kathy Marston. Ginevra had probably invited Kathy in the same burst of generosity, Kathy possibly wouldn't go, how could she with the Fortesques being prominent guests? She'd probably asked Jane Fortesque to be a bridesmaid.

She replaced the invitation in its envelope and closed the case.

The days passed slowly, lazing in the gardens or swimming in the warm sea. Maria watched her comings and goings in dismal silence.

She had worked for the Van Roystons for a great many years, seen Alanna grow up, watched her change from a leggy, insecure young girl into an often tormented woman. Maria had deplored the lifestyle of her parents and witnessed firsthand the effect it had had on their daughter.

England had been good for her. She had delighted in its history, its calmness; but even in England she had come home with stories of devious goings on in the lives of people who had always seemed to exist in a state of pristine perfection.

Her marriages had been disastrous. Two handsome titled men who had both been totally unsuitable. The first one had married her for her money, which had been bequeathed to her by a grandfather in the hope that her parents wouldn't get their hands on it. He had tied most of it up so successfully that even Alanna had difficulty in getting hold of it, and the second, the prince, had moved on to an older woman who was willing to buy him.

The prince had been rich, too handsome and incredibly arrogant. Their marriage had been a tinderbox ready for lighting. A string of other women had sent shock-waves through the family and Alanna had rebelled. Their acrimonious divorce had occupied the front pages of every newspaper in America and in Europe as well. Alanna had come out of it embittered, considerably richer, but there had been a price to pay. The scandal surrounding that divorce followed her wherever she went and her ex-husband saw to it that the price she had exacted from him was well publicised. Getting her out of his life was worth every penny.

He blamed Alanna for every adulterous liaison, for every sinful episode in their union, and looking down at the girl stretched out under the umbrella in the gardens Maria wondered what was going through her mind. Had it been worth it? What would be the end to it?

Two days later, in the early evening, when the sun was setting in a blaze of golden splendour, she heard Jacob running along the terrace and his cries of 'Massa's home, Massa's home.'

Alanna jumped to her feet and ran out on to

195

the terrace to see him racing down the steps towards the jetty, and coming round the headland was the white boat. A lump came into her throat as she looked at it. Her name was *Lady Katrina* and she was beautiful. How many times had she heard her father say that the two most beautiful women in his life were his daughter and his yacht?

She stood at the top of the steps with her silken skirt blowing against her, her raven hair caught in the breeze, and to the man standing at the prow of his yacht she seemed like some Grecian goddess, his beautiful Alanna, and his heart sank with a feeling of acute shame that he had betrayed her.

He could rely on BooBoo to bring the yacht to anchor. He'd kept BooBoo on because the old man didn't ask for much, only to handle the boat, sail her wherever he wanted to go, live in the garden shed on whatever Maria could spare from the table.

Jacob was there to help with the gangway, his face alive with warmth, two truly genuine people who loved him for what he was, scamp or benefactor, rich man or destitute. Then he was climbing the steps and Alanna was waiting to greet him. He put his arms around her and hugged her close, then keeping his arm round her they walked into the house.

'Have you eaten?' he asked her.

'I was about to, Dad, but I'll wait for you.'

'Well, I need a shower and to change, give me half an hour love.'

It was like Alanna not to ask questions immediately. He complimented Maria on the quality of the meal she put before them, then he poured the wine and asked, 'Why didn't you write to tell me you were coming? I expected you for Christmas.'

She smiled. 'Really Dad, where would I have found you?'

'I was here.'

'You never came here for Christmas. You always preferred Boston.'

'This year I thought I'd have a change, besides the weather is better here.'

'You liked Boston because of the snow Dad, you always said the Caribbean was hardly your idea of Christmas.'

'Did I really say that? Well, I hankered after the yacht. What did you do with yourself?'

'I stayed with the Carstairs and we skied in Vermont. I also went to the house in Boston and found it closed up and all the servants gone.'

'I gave them a holiday for Christmas, they have families to go to.'

'And New York?'

'My, you have been travelling. Now you'll tell me that was closed up too.'

She nodded. 'Dad, what is happening?'

'We'll talk about it later, in the meantime let me tell you where I've been these last two weeks. I took some friends round some of the islands, it was their first time in these waters.'

'Friends?'

'Yes. Six very nice people, English, from Hampshire. They'd done some sailing in the Solent and the Med.'

'I didn't know you'd ever set foot in Hampshire.'

'I haven't. I met them over here.'

'So they're very new friends?'

'Well, yes.'

The silence was uncomfortable. He was telling her half-truths and she knew more than she was telling him. He looked at her helplessly and she said 'Dad, why don't you tell me what is happening? Henry told me you'd let those people hire your boat and you.'

'Jacob talks too much.'

'He meant no harm, he's one of the best friends you've got.'

'I know. They were six people who wanted to sail a boat round the islands; my boat was doing nothing and neither was I.'

'Very philanthropic of you Dad, six virtual strangers and your proudest possession.'

He scowled, looking at her doubtfully, and with something of his old quick temper he snapped, 'All right then, if Jacob's told you so much I suppose he's told you the rest. I charged them for the hire of my yacht and for my services too.'

'You needed the money, Dad?'

'Yes, I needed the money.'

'The entire experience was a great leveller for me. Those six people strutted round the islands wearing their yachting caps and other gear and BooBoo and I drank in the bars and some chap asked us if they were decent employers and where they hailed from.'

Alanna laughed. 'I don't suppose you enlightened him.'

'No, let 'em think what they like. They paid me what I asked them. The *Lady Katrina*'s the last thing I'll part with.'

'Is it as bad as that then?'

'I'm broke, Alanna. I went against Gerry Faversham's advice and put all my eggs in one basket. He warned me that they were on the slide but I thought I knew better, now Hamiltons have gone broke and the money's gone. Whatever I sell can't hope to salvage myself.'

'Have you told Mother?'

'She'll not lift a finger to help me. She'll hang on to whatever funds she's got and I can't say I blame her.'

'But does she know?'

'She soon will when she finds the two houses have gone. It won't make any difference, she'll not hand over a cent.'

'I have money, Dad, I can let you have some.'

'I'll not take a penny from you, Alanna. Your grandfather's money is well invested, and I'll not take any of that you got from your husband. My God, Alanna, you suffered for that, it's yours and I've no right to it.'

'The money means no more to me than the man did. If it helps to get you out of a hole you're welcome to it, Dad.'

'And I say I won't touch it. I've sunk pretty low in my time, but this time I'll face the music, nobody's going to say I've taken my daughter's money to get me out of a hole.'

'Oh Dad, you can't afford to be proud.'

'Leave me something, love. Now tell me about you, what are you doing with yourself, where

199

are you going?'

'I don't know. I'm rich and notorious. Some man might marry me to say his wife is the Alanna Van Royston everybody knows about, how will I ever be sure that that's not the only reason?'

'Alanna, you've been unlucky. You married two wrong 'uns, the next one could be different. He could marry you because you're the most beautiful, intelligent, kindest thing in his life.'

'And you're my father, if you don't think that who will. Where is my mother?'

'She was in Venice before Christmas, now she's in St Tropez.'

'Alone?'

'Heaven knows.'

'I'll have her address Dad, I've nothing better to do.'

'You mean you're going to Europe?'

'Why not?'

'I would have thought you'd had enough of Europe, two disastrous marriages there, and where exactly would you go?'

'I've had an invitation to Ginevra's wedding in April. I could go to England.'

Her father looked at her curiously. 'Who is she marrying?'

'Some marquis.'

'Oh well, if you're mixing with the British aristocracy you could pick up an earl or a duke, I doubt if they'd be as flighty as the last two.'

'Dad, the way I feel at the moment, the last thing I want in my life is a man. I'm not even sure I want to go to Ginevra's wedding.'

'Why shouldn't you go, what does it matter if

you're talked about? None of us knows what life is going to do to us and nobody has a right to sit in judgement, at least nobody on this planet.'

She laughed. 'Jane will be there, I'm not sure about Kathy Marston. I'm surprised she ever forgave us for snubbing her so unmercifully before we really got to know her. We were ignorant and intolerant, too young and incredibly smug. I've had a taste of how she must have felt.'

'Then you should go, let them see you don't give a damn, and wear the most extravagant, expensive thing you can find. Whether they like you or not they'll be pea-green with envy at what they see.'

'Oh Dad, that's what you always did, isn't it. Whenever you lost a mint of money you set your stall out and in the end it all came right.'

'But not this time darling, not this time.'

Chapter Fifteen

Despair had never sat easily on Max Van Royston's shoulders. For hours he sat slumped in his chair and one bottle of whisky after another disappeared from the table in front of him until Jacob carried him off to bed to sleep it off.

The days passed all too slowly. Alanna was lonely, her father was no companion, and she had no means to combat his slow disintegration. In his more sober moments she talked to him, told him he was ruining his life and doing little for hers, and he listened to her sorrowfully before the next bottle of whisky took its toll.

Then one morning four people arrived at the villa and Jacob announced that they had come to charter the yacht. They were English, reasonably young, and they wanted the boat and were prepared to handle it without his assistance.

Max was reasonably sober and when Jacob informed him what they wanted he snorted angrily, 'If they want to hire the boat, they hire me with it. No weekend sailor is going to take out the *Lady Katrina.*'

'Why not talk to them?' Jacob suggested reasonably.

'I don't need to talk to them about skippering the boat, nobody handles my boat as if they owned it.'

'At least you could speak to them, Dad,' Alanna said. 'Find out if they can afford your price.'

So between them Jacob and Alanna made him look reasonably respectable before they ushered his guests in to meet him. They were two men and two women, probably in their forties, English, and Max quickly learned that they were friends of the people who had first chartered the boat and who had now returned home.

'We've seen pictures of her,' one of the women gushed, 'she's so beautiful, and my husband knows about sailing, he'd take very good care of her.'

'What sort of sailing have you done?' Max asked.

'I've had boats in the Bristol Channel and in the Lake District, I've sailed around the Greek islands and I've been interested in sailing as long as I can remember.'

'It's an ocean-going yacht we're talking about,' Max snorted contemptuously, 'not some small craft you can hire from any marina.'

'The *Lady Katrina*'s my father's joy,' Alanna put in quickly. 'I'm surprised he's chartering it out at all. Have you made enquiries at the marina?'

'Well no. Our friends told us about this one.'

'My father handled it for your friends, I've no doubt he'd handle it for you.'

'You mean he wouldn't trust us?' the other man said.

'Would you trust your boat to strangers? I'm afraid if you want the *Lady Katrina* you will have to take my father too.'

They stared at one another in silence and Alanna knew what they were thinking. Here was this man smelling strongly of whisky, belligerent and caustic, with a black servant eyeing them with arrogant disdain and a daughter they felt they should know from somewhere. Alanna knew what was passing through their minds.

'How much would you be asking for the yacht and your services?' the first man asked.

'Come back tomorrow and meet me down by the boat,' her father said abruptly, 'we'll talk about money then, but where she goes I go. If you're not prepared to accept that then forget it.'

'How long are you talking about?' Alanna asked.

'Two weeks, perhaps a little longer.'

'Have you sailed in these waters before?'

'We've cruised the Caribbean on a cruise liner

203

and we hired a yacht in Barbados for a week. We both know what we're doing, we've had expert tuition.'

Her father's eyes were sardonic, but he offered no comment, and he left it to Alanna to show them out. At the top of the steps they stood looking down to where the yacht lay at anchor, taking in every exquisite line of her, even with her sails furled, and then they saw BooBoo stretched out on her deck.

'Who's the man?' one of the men asked.

'BooBoo. My father never sails without him, he's indispensable.'

'Then we'd have to pay for him too?'

'You will have to talk to my father about money, BooBoo wouldn't be any problem.'

She smiled and wished them good morning, and one of the women said, 'I'm sure I've seen you somewhere, Miss Van Royston, perhaps in England?'

Alanna smiled and turned away. She had never met the woman in England, no doubt when she'd had time to think about it she would remember where she had seen her, either in some upmarket magazine or on the front page of a newspaper.

They came back the next morning and she watched her father and Jacob walking down the steps to meet them where they stood on the jetty until he escorted them on to the boat.

He was sober, attired in pristine white and wearing his yachting cap jauntily on his dark hair, presenting an altogether more salubrious picture than he had done the day before. When he returned to the house several hours later he seemed in high good humour.

They were prepared to meet his price and accept his demands, and the next morning she saw him skipping jauntily down to the jetty while Jacob loaded crates of food on board, and she waited in the gardens to watch the yacht sailing smoothly out to sea. There had been much laughter and high spirits and she knew her father would be on his best behaviour; the *Lady Katrina* brought out the best in him.

For the rest of the afternoon she tried telephoning her mother in the south of France. Her mother should be told something of her father's plight, but she was unsure if it would do any good. At the end of the day she made up her mind that she would not stay on in Santa Lucia, she would fly to Europe.

It was early morning when the plane touched down at the airport in Nice and as she waited to retrieve her luggage she was the centre of all eyes. She was accustomed to being stared at and when a man came forward to help her she thanked him with a brief smile and walked quickly away.

His eyes followed her. Beautiful elegant women abounded in his life, he wrote about them, they filled pages of exotic steamy novels that film studios in Europe and America queued up to buy and he racked his brains to think where he had seen this woman before.

He watched her walking across the airport lounge dressed casually in a pale blue trouser suit, her blue-black hair swinging freely on to her shoulders, walking with a cat-like grace so that heads were turned to stare after her. She seemed totally oblivious of the attention she was creating and a feeling of regret washed over him. He would like to have known who she was, where he might meet her again.

By this time she was at the taxi rank and he hurried forward to stand behind her. She was going to St Tropez and, without a moment's hesitation, he stepped forward saying, 'Excuse me, Madame, but may I be permitted to share your taxi? I too am going to St Tropez.'

Her eyes flicked over him and he knew that she did not connect him with the man who had helped her with her luggage. She smiled, and in that instant he saw that her eyes were green, as jade as the Chinese ornaments in his apartment in Paris. She smiled and murmured softly, 'Of course.'

They drove several miles in silence. Conversation normally came easily to his lips, but for once he was unsure. There was something about this young woman that made him feel that she would not welcome trivial chitchat and he was surprised that she made the first attempt to break the silence.

'Where in St Tropez do you want the taxi to drop you?'

'Please, allow me to take you to your destination first, I am in no hurry. Where is it to be?'

'The Villa Rose.'

'Really. Then my villa is close by, I live at the Villa Marguerita.'

Alanna knew the villa, but she could not recollect ever having seen anyone there. It had usually been standing empty with the shutters closed and an air of emptiness about the place. As if he read her thoughts he said, 'I have not been home for some considerable time, I have been living in London and America. We were on the same plane from America this morning.'

She smiled. 'I didn't know.'

'Are you expected in St Tropez?'

'My mother is here; it is some time since we met.'

'So you don't live here permanently?'

'No.'

'Where then is your home?'

'I am in the process of looking for a home, until now it has been here, there and everywhere.'

'A citizen of the world.'

'Not really. Simply a bird of passage.'

'A very beautiful bird.'

Her eyes met his and in hers he read a veiled cynicism that said little for his flattery.

'If we are to be neighbours, Madame, perhaps you will tell me your name. I am Jules Moreau.'

Not by the flicker of an eyelid did she betray that his name was known to her. He doubted that if he'd said he was the angel Gabriel that those incredible jade-green eyes would have shown more interest, and yet surely she had heard of him. The author of innumerable books, some of which had been filmed. His picture was prominent in magazines and newspapers. Then suddenly he knew why she was familiar.

One summer's day, sitting on the deck of his friend's yacht in the harbour of Rhodes, he had seen her face on the front of a magazine his

207

friend's wife was holding and he had reached over to take it from her. He thought she was the most beautiful thing he had ever seen, the face he had seen in his dreams, every woman he had ever written about had possessed her face, but in real life until that moment he had never known it. Now here she was sharing a taxi with him and she was leaning back in her corner completely uninterested either in his name or anything about him.

The taxi was moving up the drive from the wrought-iron gates to the front of the white villa and she leaned forward in her seat to look out of the window, a small frown on her face. The curtains were drawn, the house had an unlived-in air, but he said quietly, 'It is very early, Madame, people are still in their beds.'

She looked at her watch.

'Of course. I hadn't realised it was so early.'

She reached inside her handbag and took out her purse and he was quick to say, 'Please Madame, allow me to pay the taxi driver. It is a very small gesture and you are after all my neighbour.'

She smiled and for the first time a degree of warmth crept into her smile. 'Thank you, it is very kind.'

He got out of the taxi and held the door open for her, then he carried her luggage to the front door. He smiled down at her. 'I'm sure we shall see each other again, perhaps in the gardens or in the town. You didn't tell me your name.'

'No I'm sorry. It is Alanna Van Royston.'

He smiled again and walked back to the taxi,

then as they drove away he raised his hand and she smiled.

Alanna could hear the sound of the bell reverberating inside the villa and she looked up at the windows anxiously. Suppose her mother had moved on? She was always unpredictable with too many ports of call, too many acquaintances she called friends. She rang again, and then after a few minutes her heart lifted at the sound of bolts being drawn back and a woman's sleepy face peered at her from round the door.

Alanna smiled. 'I'm sorry to be so early Celeste, is my mother here?'

'Why yes, but she still asleep. She expect you?'

'Actually no. Can I come in with my luggage?'

'Ah yes, come in come in, I help you.'

'I've been trying to catch up with my mother for days, Switzerland, Nice, Cannes. They told me in Cannes that she was here.'

Celeste's face was confused and Alanna laughed. 'I'm gabbling on Celeste, I'm forgetting your English isn't all that good. Could I possibly have a cup of tea?'

'Tea! Ah yes, in here Mees Alanna, I bring you tea, breakfast too.'

'No breakfast, just tea. By that time perhaps my mother will be ready to receive me.'

'She out very late last night. She not been in bed long, big party.'

'Yes well, Mother's at her best with a big party.'

'You will stay here now?'

'Perhaps for a little while, Celeste, I'm not sure if it will be convenient. Is Madame Germaine here too?'

'Non. She in Geneva then Gstaad, skiing you know. Your mother not want that.'

'No. It was kind of Madame Germaine to let my mother stay here.'

'Oh, she likes her here, she good company most of the time.'

Alanna laughed. 'Most of the time just about sums it up.'

'I get your tea,' Celeste said hurrying from the room.

Dolly Germaine and her mother had been school friends and grew up together in Boston where they enjoyed all the social activities moneyed backgrounds could provide. Dolly had been married twice, first to Henry Jamison who had died young and left her more money than she knew what to do with, and then to Pierre Germaine whom she had met in Switzerland, a man who was just as rich as her first husband, and considerably more doting.

Her mother both liked and envied Dolly. Dolly always had too much money, and two men who had lavished more on her as well as total devotion. Neither of them liked Max Van Royston who was handsome, a spendthrift and totally useless where money was concerned.

The fact that her mother had adored him for too many years no longer counted. Now she was both angry and disenchanted and Alanna felt that the task she had set herself would go unrewarded. Her mother would not go to her father's assistance – he had done it once too often.

She stood looking out of the window towards

the slope and the pink villa above.

Jules Moreau! She had known who he was as soon as he said his name, but she had been very careful to remain unimpressed. She was no longer the wide-eyed girl who had dallied with counts and princes and thought them the pinnacle of all that was wonderful. They were simply men, men who could be unkind, tyrannical, selfish and greedy.

The Jules Moreaus of this world had had their fill of naïve young women who had drooled over their fame and popularity, she had no intention of adding to the list.

Celeste came in with her tea and went around the room plumping up cushions and straightening ornaments. Alanna asked idly, 'Where was the party last night, Celeste?'

Celeste shrugged her shoulders, 'Some big house owned by film star, many people there, all famous.'

'I have no doubt. Do you know the man who lives at the Villa Marguerita?'

'He come seldom, never stay long. Rich man, famous they say. I never see him these days.'

'He came this morning.'

'How you know?'

'We shared a taxi.'

Celeste grinned. 'Your mother be pleased about that, she tell everybody she has a beautiful daughter.'

Alanna unpacked her suitcase and put her clothes away, but there was no sign of life from her mother's room. It was still very early, but she felt she was marking time. The gardens outside offered a solution, though she soon grew tired of strolling across the lawns, and the need to talk to her mother was pressing.

When she returned to the villa Celeste gave her a doubtful smile saying, 'I take your mother tea but she has not touched it. She still sleeping.'

'I'll go up to her, Celeste.'

'She no like it. I never go up before noon.'

Ignoring her advice Alanna went upstairs, opening the door of her mother's room cautiously. The gown she had worn the night before was thrown carelessly over a chair, her high-heeled gold kid shoes lay on their sides in different corners, her underwear lay scattered at the foot of the chair.

Her mother was fast asleep, lying on her back with a pad of eye lotion covering each eye, and irritably Alanna went to pull back the curtains from the windows.

There was a cry of annoyance from the bed and a voice said, 'No, no Celeste, go away.'

Alanna went to the bed and looked down at her mother's face. The make-up she had worn the evening before was still colouring her face, and she could smell her favourite Arpege perfume. She reached down and gently removed the eye pads from her eyes and slowly they opened, blinking nervously, at first unable to recognise her visitor. Then Alanna said gently, 'Mother, it's me, Alanna.'

Her mother moaned dismally and seconds passed, then she struggled up against her pillows staring at her daughter without any display of welcome.

'I should have let you know I was coming, but I did try telephoning you, Mother,' Alanna said softly.

'What time did you get here?'

'Very early, too early to wake you.'

'It's still too early to wake me, what time is it anyway?'

'After eleven.'

'Really Alanna, you arrive out of nowhere and expect me to get up to talk to you when I've only been in bed a couple of hours. Why have you come? Oh I know why you've come, it's your father, isn't it?'

'Among other things.'

'I'm not going to talk to you about your father before I've had a shower and made myself look respectable, and even then I've nothing to say about him.'

'While you're getting dressed I'll put away your dress from last night and all the other things you've left lying around.'

'Don't lecture me, Alanna.'

'I'm not. I'm trying to be helpful.'

'Did Celeste not tell you I was at a party last night and it was very late when I got back?'

'Very early when you got back, Mother.'

'Yes, well. You should have been there Alanna, everybody who is anybody in these parts was there.'

'Then you would enjoy it.'

'Yes I did, and now that you're here what are you calling yourself, Princess Austerlech I hope, a divorced woman does not revert to her maiden name.'

By this time she was staggering into her bathroom and Alanna sat on the edge of her bed in an endeavour to hear her voice through the half-open door.

'Well,' she called out, 'what do you call yourself, Alanna?'

'Certainly not Princess Austerlech. I left that title behind me with my divorce.'

The door opened and her mother's face, smeared in cream, peered out.

'Rubbish, Alanna. Until you marry again that's who you are.'

'It's not who I want to be.'

'Well I'll tell you now the name Van Royston will conjure up no eligible man for you. Your father's bankrupt so there's no money in it from that quarter. The money comes from Claus and all the world knows it.'

'I've only been with you ten minutes and already you're marrying me off to some man who is looking for a princess with money. Well this time the only person I shall take notice of is me. I'll join you on the terrace for breakfast. What would you like?'

'Fruit juice and coffee, it's what I always have.'

Alanna made good her escape. She had not come to Provence to talk about herself, marriage, or anything else beyond her father.

Chapter Sixteen

Alanna sat watching her mother daintily sipping her orange juice while outside the palms lashed across the window and a pale watery sun struggled to dispel the greyness of the day. Her mother shivered delicately.

'I really don't know what I'm doing here,' she complained. 'The Med can be dire in late January and February. I should have gone south to the Canaries or to Egypt where the sun can be guaranteed.'

'Or to the Caribbean, Mother.'

'Definitely not the Caribbean. I know what you're trying to do, Alanna, you want me to contact your father, you want me to salvage him yet another time and it's not going to happen. What sort of people have chartered his yacht and how is he going to pay his crew?'

'There isn't any crew. He's had to let them go.'

'Then how is he going to handle the yacht?'

'There's BooBoo and Jacob and Dad's no slouch when it comes to looking after the *Lady Katrina*.'

'Those people are surely not going to be satisfied with that.'

'They've done some sailing, they'll cope.'

'I never heard of anything more ridiculous, or pretentious. Seven people on a yacht as big as the *Katrina*. What sort of money are they paying him?'

'I have no idea. He must have been satisfied with it. At any rate it's better than nothing.'

'I've got my lawyers keeping tabs on him. I know about the house in Boston and the one in New York. The servants have gone, the houses are up for sale, without even a word to me.'

'He's been chasing you around Europe trying to get you to do something, when he didn't manage to get hold of you he had no choice. The houses had to go. I think he's got somebody interested in the house in New York.'

'Half of it belongs to me. My lawyers will see that I get what he owes me.'

'Mother he's your husband, you shouldn't be haggling about money, you should be supporting each other.'

'And I don't want a lecture from my daughter on the rights and wrongs of things. I should be in the same position as Dolly Germaine. I was always prettier, I always got the handsomest boys and Dolly settled for the studious plain ones. It wasn't a good policy, she got two rich, decent men and I got your father.'

'You did want him, Mother, you always boasted that you got the best-looking man in New York and the most exciting.'

'That was when I was too young to know the difference. I got a man who liked to surround himself with women and ran through my money as though there was no tomorrow. Ask yourself why your grandfather tied most of your money up so that your father couldn't get his hands on it.'

'I've offered to help him.'

216

'He'll snatch your hand off.'

'Actually he's refused to take anything.'

Her mother stared at her with her mouth open. 'Don't tell me he's developing a conscience at last? I don't believe it.'

'It's true though. He said for what I'd gone through with Claus I deserved every penny and he wouldn't touch it.'

'But he'd be prepared to touch mine regardless of what I've gone through with him.'

'Mother, there is no comparison. My father likes women, he hasn't a clue about high finance or handling money, but he never hit you, he never made you fear for your life, he never boasted about his conquests, how easy they were, and how there would be a hundred others.'

'No, perhaps not, but I'm sick of seeing Dolly living it up on men who dote on her, who would never in a thousand years be unfaithful, and are happy to shower her with all the things I would like and never got from your father.'

'So you're prepared to see him bankrupt, without a home; the house on Santa Lucia will have to go, probably the yacht too. I don't see how he can keep it.'

'That'll be the last thing he'll part with. He'll probably sail the seven seas like a pirate with half the world's police force looking for him. I don't want to listen to another word, I'm sick of it. Can't we talk about something else?'

'You can tell me about your parties and who you're hobnobbing with.'

'The parties have been wonderful, and darling the people I met there, all celebrities, men as rich as Crœsus, the women with their jewels and furs. Thank goodness I could hold my own up, but nothing to do with your father Alanna,' she added drily.

Alanna got up and walked across to the window. Her mother's indulgences sickened her; she had always been like this, it was her mother at her worst and at this moment she felt irritated where some other time it might have amused her. Her mother joined her at the window in time to see a white Mercedes driving past their garden and through the gates of the villa next door.

'It looks as though the villa is occupied,' she commented. 'I've never seen anybody there in all the times I've been here. I wonder who it is.'

Alanna didn't enlighten her.

'Dolly said she had somebody famous living next door, but when nobody ever came I was sure she was romancing. It had to be somebody famous.'

'Isn't Dolly coming to stay with you?'

'I expect so. She said I could live here as long as I liked, but they probably would be joining me before Easter.'

'So you're going to stick it out until then?'

'I'm not sure. It will depend on what's going on and if I'm invited. Somebody's going into the villa next door, it looked like a chauffeur, and there are two men in the garden. I'll ask Celeste, she'll know who lives there.'

Alanna had no doubt that her mother would poke and pry until she knew all about the man next door, including his wife if he had one.

Celeste had been able to tell her mother very

little about the man, either that or she was keeping her own counsel, so early in the afternoon her mother said she was going to take tea with some woman she had met at the party the evening before.

'She knows everybody, Alanna, she'll know for sure who our neighbour is. Why don't you come with me? I've told them all about you, darling.'

'All about me, Mother!'

'Well, I've told them that my daughter is the Princess Austerlech and that you're divorced from your husband. No doubt they've all read about it, after all Claus is quite famous on the racing circuit and he's very handsome. You needn't worry darling, none of those people are likely to think anything derogatory about your marriage to Claus, most of them have been involved in scandals of some sort or another. It's the world they live in darling.'

'I don't want it to be my world any more, Mother.'

'Perhaps not darling, but you can make the most of it while it lasts. Don't settle for mediocracy, you're beautiful, rich, and a past that might seem interesting never did a rich woman any harm.'

She watched her mother leave the villa driving her expensive new small car and wearing her mink coat, her head covered with a bright chiffon scarf. Minutes later she watched their neighbour driving away in the white Mercedes and she knew she wouldn't have long to wait before her mother returned with news of his credentials.

She came back in the early evening bubbling

with excitement.

'Our neighbour is famous, Alanna, he's Jules Moreau, the author. He writes big exciting novels about famous people, moneyed people with their affairs, their travels abroad, their dangerous lives. They have nearly all been filmed, you must have seen them, I know I have. He's not been seen around here for years, he's been in Hollywood and everywhere in the world where his books were being filmed. My friend didn't know whether he was married or not. He's probably been married several times and divorced. I asked her how old he was, she said probably in his forties.'

Alanna did not tell her mother that she had already met Jules Moreau, but she had no doubt that her mother would make it her business to make his acquaintance very soon. Her mother walked in the garden, something she had rarely done, particularly in grey days at the beginning of February, and with the pretence that she was engrossed in the shrubs that lined the paths.

Alanna squirmed with embarrassment and Celeste's cynical smile said it all. She was therefore not in the least surprised when several days later her mother hurried back inside with a smiling flushed face and eyes as bright as a bird's.

'We've met, Alanna, and he's charming and very good-looking. He saw me in the garden and raised his hand, I pretended I didn't know who he was and simply welcomed him home.'

'Did he tell you who he was?'

'I introduced myself, so naturally he had to tell me his name. I had to tell him that I had heard of him, actually, darling, it would have been very coy of me to pretend that I'd never heard of him. I've invited him to take tea with us one afternoon if he's not too busy.'

'I don't think the French are particularly interested in afternoon tea, Mother.'

'Of course they are darling. Besides he knows I'm American, they adapt don't they.'

'So you're going to ask him about his latest novel and the sort of people who are in it, and of course he'll be delighted to tell you how successful he is, how much money he makes and how his success has shaped his life.'

'Really, Alanna, I don't much like your cynicism. He's a perfectly charming man, you'll find out for yourself.'

'No, Mother I won't. I'm not going to be here to be trotted out for his inspection. You saw me marry a count, then a prince, both of whom you heartily approved of. I'm not about to add a famous author to the collection.'

'Alanna, that's terrible, and nothing was further from my mind. You're becoming very waspish. I know you've had a bad time and notoriety doesn't sit easily on your shoulders, but you have to put all that behind you. What you need is stability. A decent man in your life, somebody who will care for you and look after you. When that happens the past will be forgotten by you and everybody else.'

'Mother, I thought I had found that twice and twice I was fooling myself. I've reached the conclusion that nice decent men are not to be found, at least in my brittle existence. You enjoy your tea party with Monsieur Moreau and I'll go out and get my hair styled. May I borrow your car?'

Her mother sulked and studiously avoided any further mention of her tea party with a famous author.

Conversation was spasmodic. Alanna leafed through several magazines and her mother played patience at a small table under the lamplight and at ten o'clock said fretfully that she was going to bed. At the door she paused to stare back at Alanna, who smiled and wished her goodnight.

In her bedroom she sat in front of her dressing table smoking a cigarette out of the long ebony holder she favoured. Really Alanna was very difficult. She had found Jules Moreau utterly charming. He had a low musical voice and his English was perfect with only an attractive hint of a foreign accent. He was very handsome, tall and slender, his dark hair immaculate with only a hint of silver at his temples which gave him a very distinguished air. Conversation had flowed. He was interesting. Alanna would have been fascinated by him, and he had asked her about her family, if she was married, if she had children, and she had found herself telling him about her husband's unfortunate failings and Alanna's disastrous attempts at marriage.

He had been sympathetic. She had showed him pictures of Alanna and family photographs of happier days. He had remarked on the beauty of her daughter and had left her saying he hoped they would meet again very soon.

In the days that followed there was an uneasy

peace between Alanna and her mother and Alanna was bored. Bored by the shops and her mother's constant chatter about the people she had met and who were likely to invite them to their homes for some party or other.

At no time did her mother mention her father and his problems, it was as though she deliberately wanted to erase him from her memory.

She only saw their next-door neighbour entering and leaving, driving his white Mercedes up to the front door of the villa. Then one morning her mother gasped with delight as she opened her morning mail.

'Alanna, this is so kind. Jules has invited us to a small informal gathering on Friday evening, just a few friends, and the invitation is for both of us. You'll have to think what to wear, you brought very little luggage with you.'

'I didn't expect to be invited anywhere, Mother, I thought we'd be moving on, I really don't have anything to wear for Monsieur Moreau's little soirée.'

'I'm going to look at what you've brought, you're being difficult, I'm sure you have something.'

So she followed her mother as she marched upstairs to her bedroom where she proceeded to throw things out of her wardrobe and on to the bed.

'Well, there isn't much there and that's a fact,' she snapped.

'I told you, Mother.'

'Then we'll go out and get something. Sylvano's will have something, he's expensive, but you're not going next door looking like a ragbag.'

'I don't want to go next door at all, and the last thing I need is a new dress. I have plenty at the apartment in Paris.'

'Well, we're not in Paris now are we. What's that at the back of the wardrobe?'

She reached inside and brought out a simple black dress that shrieked class and which had cost the earth.

'Why did you hide this at the back of the wardrobe? It's just what you need. I never liked you in black, Alanna, black is for blondes, I liked you in jewel colours, jade and emerald, scarlet and vermilion. This will have to do, it's classy and anybody can see it's expensive.'

'Mother, I really don't want to go. I've hardly partied at all since my divorce from Claus. The first time I did I was the subject of everybody's curiosity, people standing around speculating on how much I was worth, what he was up to and who I was seeing. I can't think that this party will be any different and Monsieur Moreau's appetite has already been sharpened.'

'You're bitter, Alanna. Jules is a man of the world, he's not interested in tittle-tattle about you. I expect he's heard enough scandal to fill a library with his books.'

'I'll make a deal with you, Mother. I'll go to this party if you'll write to Dad. Just to tell him he's being thought about.'

'Oh, no, Alanna, that's blackmail. Leave your father out of this, I'll handle anything to do with him. We'll go to Jules's party, you will be nice to him, nice to everybody, and let people see that you may have been the subject of gossip, but you are a beautiful, charming woman and that scandal has affected you as little as water off a duck's back.'

So her mother replied in the affirmative to Jules's invitation and then spent hours deciding what to wear.

'I really do think most of my gowns are too formal, that little black dress of yours is just right, I should choose something quieter. We'll go to Sylvano's. Come with me Alanna, I might need your advice.'

'Mother, when have you ever taken my advice? Sylvano will help you.'

'Alanna, he's overpowering. He reeks of perfume and I can't do with him fussing around me.'

'You were prepared to have him fuss around me.'

'Well yes. But he's harmless. Gay you know. He'll be sure to have what I want so while we're in the salon you can take a look round. I'll treat you, darling, to something nice.'

'Mother, I don't need you to treat me. I'll come to the salon with you. I don't need a bribe.'

Alanna strolled around the salon, tired of watching her mother try on one dress after another, and Sylvano fussed and postured in an endeavour to charm his customers.

He was a tall lanky man with long blond hair and long slim fingers that gesticulated with every sentence he uttered. He was utterly feminine, but there was a decided charm about him that was

225

totally amusing and he set about charming Alanna so that when they left the shop her good humour was largely restored.

Her mother had chosen a heavy wild silk gown in French navy, and Sylvano had drooled on its glamour and how she would be the sensation of the evening, with Mademoiselle also who was so very beautiful. He then proceeded to show Alanna gown after gown and seemed totally desolate when she declined to try even one of them on.

'I told you what he was like,' her mother said, 'but you have to admit, darling, he has the most fabulous creations.'

'Is he always like that, Mother?'

'Either like that or in tears about some disappointment or another. Usually something quite trivial, when one of his models disappoints him or some love affair nobody knows much about.'

'Love affair?'

'Well, yes. Some man or other.'

Alanna was thinking about the two men she'd married, both of them macho and conceited, both of them glorying in a number of affairs, handsome, bold, as different from Sylvano as chalk from cheese.

As they got out of the car in front of the villa Jules was leaving his garden and he raised a polite hand in greeting. Her mother said, 'That's the sort of man I like, Alanna, charming, restrained, and old enough to have developed some sense.'

'He's younger than my father and you're always telling me he's never had any sense.'

'Nor has he, and he's too old to change now. Besides we're not talking about him. I won't have you spoiling my day.'

Her mother paused on the doorstep and looked down on to the harbour and the armada of yachts moored there.

'Jules said he owned a yacht. I wonder which one it is?' she mused.

'None of them look as majestic as the *Lady Katrina,*' Alanna retorted.

'Perhaps not. But Jules has the money to keep it and maintain it, I wonder just how long your father is going to be able to keep *Katrina.*'

Looking at the bitter expression on her mother's face Alanna wanted to ask if there was anything left of the love she had once felt for her father, or even if there'd been any love in the first place.

Her mind went back to her schooldays at that so English school where she was surrounded by aristocratic English girls who fantasised about what went on in salubrious backgrounds, but where one of them cried herself to sleep every night because her father was having an affair with another woman.

When she'd asked Jane Fortesque about it the English girl had been reticent; when she'd spent a week in Jane's family's home she had liked Lord Fortesque enormously, but had hardly got to know his wife who was so obsessed with hunting, her dogs and her charities that she was hardly ever in the house.

Every night before she went to bed she looked at Ginevra's wedding invitation with the realisation that only half of her wanted to go. She wanted to see her friends again, she wanted to see the countryside she had grown up in with its winding lanes and church spires across the hedgerows, but she knew in her heart that nothing would be the same.

Her own life had been a kaleidoscope of changing fortunes and her reputation deserved or undeserved had become common property. How would those old friends with their stiff-necked propriety regard her? Of course there was Kathy, Kathy might understand.

She should reply to the invitation, time was moving on and she would have to return to Paris to sort out something to wear for the occasion.

It was worry about her father that was making her indecisive. What would he do when those people who had chartered his boat returned to their homes? Would he have a home to return to? Her mother's intransigence both worried and angered her.

Chapter Seventeen

Alanna had had many thoughts on the people she thought Jules would invite to his home and it did not take her long to realise she had been wrong. She had expected film and stage celebrities, dollybirds and producers, starlets and newspaper moguls; she had not expected the sort of guests she was being introduced to.

228

He had invited only twelve people including herself and her mother, and they were men and women of Jules's age group; she was the youngest guest in the room. There was a famous artist and his wife, two other authors and their wives, a mountain climber and his son, and two other people who apparently had been friends of his for many years.

They talked about a great many interesting things that were happening in the world, not about themselves, until one man mentioned that he had recently bought a boat and was in the process of hiring a crew. At mention of this her mother talked about the *Lady Katrina* and Alanna went to stand at one of the French windows from where she could look down on the harbour.

There was a full moon and the scene was enchanting. Lights were strung out like jewels along the stretch of coast and in the harbour itself the lights on the boats anchored there vied with the silvered crescents beyond the harbour wall. She felt a prick of tears behind her eyes. It was so beautiful and her thoughts were on her father as she listened to her mother going on about his yacht when Alanna knew she wouldn't lift a finger to help her father to keep it.

She was aware that Jules had come to stand beside her and that he was aware of the hint of tears in her eyes.

'It's a beautiful sight, Alanna, even on a February night,' he said softly. 'Have you done any sailing?'

'When I was little I used to sail with my father.

We had a place at Cape Cod and he owned a sailing boat, nothing pretentious, but he could handle it himself. It was exciting, I loved that boat.'

'He parted with it?'

'Oh yes, always for something better, something bigger. Now he owns the *Lady Katrina*. She's beautiful and she's very big, an ocean-going yacht.'

'I know, I've seen her.'

'You have?'

'Yes. I saw her anchored at Santa Lucia about two years ago. She was the sort of yacht people talked about, and if they were rich enough, wanted to own.'

'Would you like to have owned her?'

'Of course, but she wasn't up for sale.'

'She may be, very soon.'

He looked down at her without speaking, and in a dull voice she said, 'My father bought her in a year when he was unusually affluent. Now he's no longer rich and he's having to find money to pay his debts. I think the yacht will be the last thing he parts with, but it may have to come to that.'

'I'm sorry. In that case perhaps I will be interested.'

'My mother is talking to your friend about the yacht. I wish she wouldn't.'

'Why is that?'

'Because she didn't want him to buy it, as she never wanted to sail with him. When he parts with her it will break his heart.'

He sensed the bitterness that had built up in

230

this girl. With two disastrous marriages behind her she did not need this conflict between her parents. He had met women like her mother before, rich spoilt women who knew how to handle the accumulation of money but never its loss.

Alanna attracted him strangely when he seriously believed he was immune to women. He had only been in love once, with Naomi, when he had been a young and struggling writer. She had wanted something else, somebody who could give her the things she craved, and she had left him for an English aristocrat with a stately home and a title.

Years later her marriage had crumbled and she had wanted to come back when he became rich and successful. He no longer loved her, he was unconcerned about what had happened to her. He was remembering his bitterness now and he felt enormous sympathy for the girl beside him.

'Where is your father now?' he enquired.

'Sailing in the Caribbean.'

'Will he join you here?'

'No. This isn't my mother's villa, it belongs to friends of hers.'

'I know, the Germaines.'

'Yes. She is a very old friend of my mother's, they were at school together in Boston. She's been kind enough to let my mother stay here, but where she will go from here I can't think.'

'And you?'

She shrugged her shoulders. 'I have an apartment in Paris, but I am looking for somewhere to live permanently.'

'And where do you think it might be?'

'I'd like it to be on an undiscovered island somewhere in the sun. I doubt if there is such a place.'

He laughed. 'No, I believe all such islands have been discovered a long time ago, and in the end perhaps you would hate it. People are very important, my dear, in the end we all need one another.'

'Do you really think so?'

'I do.'

She smiled up at him, and again he was touched by the sadness in her smile. Alanna Van Royston had been painted as a woman who had embraced life with little thought of what it would do to her. Titled husbands, one a money-seeker, the other a playboy. She had been gifted with great beauty and riches and whatever she did and wherever she went she had made headlines. Now this sad bewildered girl had come down to earth and she cared little for anything beyond running away.

'Come,' he said, 'let me get you another drink.'

She handed him her glass and watched him walk away to replenish it.

She liked him. She liked his tall graceful figure and his handsome remote face, she liked the low charm of his voice and the sympathy in his smile, but she didn't want to like him. Liking people led to loving people, and loving people led to misery and betrayal. She'd have one more go at getting her mother to contact her father, then she'd leave. There was nothing for her here.

Jules returned with her glass and realised immediately that she was regretting their few moments of closeness. Her beautiful face wore an expression of aloofness and with a smile and a murmured excuse he moved away to chat to his other guests.

The rest of the evening passed pleasantly enough. Conversation and polite farewells, and the climber and his son were escorting them to their front door while Jules stood in his garden bidding other guests farewell.

'Well,' her mother remarked as soon as they were alone, 'that was very pleasant, you were getting on well with Jules.'

'He was very polite, Mother, we talked about the *Lady Katrina*.'

'Why for heaven's sake?'

'He heard you talking about her.'

'Only because that man said he'd just bought a yacht, and he was interested. He'd actually seen the *Lady Katrina*.'

'I'm sure he had, who hasn't?'

'Why was Jules interested?'

'He has a boat, he's fond of sailing.'

'Would he be interested in your father's yacht? I'm sure it'll be up for sale pretty soon.'

'Oh, Mother, how can you say that?'

'I can and I do. Jules's friend is taking delivery of his yacht at Easter and he's giving a party on board to celebrate. We're invited.'

'Why would he invite us?'

'Everybody there tonight is invited. I said we'd be delighted to accept.'

'I'm going to bed, Mother, see you at breakfast.'

Her mother was pouring a gin and tonic in

233

spite of the fact that she'd been drinking most of the evening, and Alanna said with a smile, 'Aren't you afraid of turning into an alcoholic?'

'No. I drank wine most of the evening even though I prefer gin and tonic. Wine doesn't seem to have much effect on me.'

'Oh well, goodnight, Mother.'

Her mother settled into a large armchair with her glass in her hand, favouring Alanna with a sleepy smile. 'Goodnight dear, Jules likes you, I can tell. For heaven's sake don't let this one slip through your fingers.'

'Jules is a man of the world, Mother, I'm sure he has a great many women he's fond of, and neither of us is in the market for anything else. If you start your match-making I swear I'll leave.'

'Where will you go? Not to your father I'm sure, long before you get there there'll be no house and no boat; you'll be forking out your money for somewhere to live.' Alanna merely looked at her long and hard and climbed the stairs to her bedroom.

Alanna slept fitfully and next morning was downstairs while her mother slept on. Alanna didn't expect her to surface much before midday and she was surprised when half-way through the morning Jules appeared at the front door asking with a smile, 'I'm going down to the harbour, Alanna. I was wondering if you'd like to take a look at my boat?'

She hesitated, then, not wanting to appear churlish, she said, 'Thank you, I'll get my coat.'

They drove down to the harbour with few

words passing between them. It was a friendly silence however, not an oppressive one. He parked the car above the harbour steps then they walked along the path and Alanna looked with interest at the conglomeration of boats moored there, both large and small, but not one as prepossessing as the *Lady Katrina*. As if guessing her thoughts Jules said, 'These are little buckets compared to your father's yacht, Alanna.'

'Perhaps, but they're all beautiful in their way.'

He pointed to where a larger yacht lay at anchor in the centre of the harbour and Alanna caught her breath. The boat was beautiful, a two-masted yacht that even with her sails furled looked incredibly graceful. They boarded the dinghy to take them out to her.

He showed her round with pride saying, 'Is she anything like the yacht you had at Cape Cod?'

'Oh, she's much larger, that was only a small sailing boat, single-masted, skittish in a rough sea. Surely you wouldn't part with this, even for the *Lady Katrina?*'

He smiled. 'No, I probably wouldn't. I don't want a large crew to help me to handle her. I don't want a floating villa, I want to sail my boat because I want to feel I'm in control. I suppose your father employs several crew?'

'He did, but he's paid them off; he's handling her himself now with the aid of an old beach-comber and Jacob, our West Indian servant.'

He asked no more questions.

'I didn't ask you what she was called?' Alanna said.

'The *Cassowary*. It means the flightless bird.'

235

'That's beautiful.'

'I thought so. She sails like a bird, a seabird flying on the wind. You're cold. Come below and we'll have coffee, or something stronger if you prefer it.'

'Coffee please. I suppose the boat your friend bought is larger than this one?'

'It must be. He's throwing a launching party on her over Easter.'

'Yes, my mother told me.'

'Didn't he invite you?'

'I believe so.'

'You'll accept of course.'

'I'm not sure if I'll still be here.'

Most men would have been curious, asked questions, but Jules Moreau merely asked if she would like brandy with her coffee and Alanna felt strangely annoyed at the omission.

All the men who had appeared in her life had been too eager, too forthcoming, and when they had failed her the disappointment had been too catastrophic. Now she found herself wondering what sort of woman would make her companion betray an interest.

He was entertaining, worldly, casual, and all this was new to Alanna, and woman-like she found herself wanting homage from the one man who was showing none. By the time they returned to the car and driven up to the villa she had decided she would decline Ginevra's wedding invitation, telling herself somewhat dishonestly that it was concern for her father that kept her in St Tropez where she could work on her mother, rather than the more exciting aspect of the man living next door.

She had refrained from mentioning the wedding invitation to her mother because she was unsure what she would say. Half of her would want her to remain in St Tropez as her companion, the other half would think of all the British aristocrats who were likely to attend the wedding and how advantageous it would be for Alanna to hobnob with them.

From their garden they watched the arrival of the new yacht, quite the most luxurious to find a mooring there, and Jules too watched from his garden. Then he sauntered over to chat with them.

'Well,' he enquired, 'how do you like her?'

'She's beautiful,' Alanna replied while her mother said more conservatively, 'She's very nice, I thought she'd be as large as the *Lady Katrina*, but she isn't.'

'No,' Jules said with a little smile, 'I rather think the *Lady Katrina* would have the edge on most yachts anchored here.'

When they returned to the villa Alanna couldn't help saying, 'If you're so concerned about the *Lady Katrina* why won't you lift a finger to enable Dad to keep her?'

'She's the one thing he never asked me for money for. He bought her from one of the really good deals he ever made. Most of them collapsed almost before they were born, but that was a good year. He never repaid any of the money I'd bolstered up his disasters with and the only time he made money he spent it on that yacht. I resent her, he deserves to lose her.'

'Can you really be so vindictive towards somebody you once loved?'

'Did nobody ever tell you that hatred and love are very close bedfellows? They're both strong emotions, they mean something. I don't mean ordinary hatred between people who've done the dirty on you, I mean between people who have once cared deeply for each other. I know you think I'm an uncaring wife and mother, but you know very little about the life I had with your father.

'He never paid for your education, I did. He never settled money on you when you got married because he didn't have any. I did all that, now you'd like me to throw good money after bad and salvage him once again.'

'Perhaps if you'd refused to give me money when I married my life might have been very different. I might have attracted different sorts of men.'

'You blame me for that too, Alanna?'

'Forget about it, Mother, it's water under the bridge. I just wish we could be a family, we never seem to have been that.'

'We never will be. We're both volatile, selfish people who like our own way, it's time to move on. This time I think we should divorce, both make new lives for ourselves, let the law sort out our money problems.'

She looked at her mother's face, more resolute than she had ever seen it, and her heart sank. She wished there was somebody else she could talk to. She thought of Jules, but Jules wouldn't be concerned with her problems, he'd shown very little interest where she intended to move on to, or when it would happen.

As if she understood where her thoughts were leading her to her mother said, 'Jules has said he will escort us to the harbour at Easter; the party is to last several days, we have to think what we'll need for the occasion.'

For the next few weeks her mother would shelve the problems surrounding her father and would soak up every exciting moment of the Easter party on the new boat. That night after her mother had gone to yet another party, in somewhat of a huff because Alanna had refused to go with her, she decided to telephone her father in Santa Lucia.

Maria's voice answered her, somewhat hesitant, then recognising Alanna's voice she said, 'Your father here Mees Alanna, wait, I tell him.'

His voice was remarkably cheerful, she'd known it could never be anything else. 'Alanna love, how are you, where are you?' he carolled.

'I'm in St Tropez at the Germaines' villa with Mother.'

'Are the Germaines with you?'

'No, but I believe they're coming.'

'And how's your mother?'

'Very well, she's visiting friends.'

'As ever.'

'Dad, how are you, how did the sailing trip go?'

'Very well, we all enjoyed ourselves. They'd like to do it again soon.'

'And what are you doing now?'

'Unwinding. Catching my breath. I'm spreading it about that the yacht can be chartered, as long as I skipper her. I'm not willing to think of anything else.'

'The money you get from that won't solve your long-term problems dad.'

'Perhaps not, but it will enable me to hang on to the *Katrina*. I'm not bothered about the house. The one in New York's been sold.'

'So you have the money for that?'

'My creditors have it. Have you talked to your mother?'

'Yes. Dad, she won't help you, this is one time you can't rely on her.'

'Oh well, I wasn't expecting any help from that quarter anyway, it was always a forlorn hope.'

'I told you I'd help you, Dad.'

'And I told you I'd go to prison first, either that or blow my brains out.'

'Dad, please don't say such things, there has to be a solution. What about the house in Boston?'

'Your mother's put the kybosh on that. She's been in touch with her lawyers, the house hasn't to be sold. She can do that, she owns half of it.'

'She didn't tell me.'

'Of course not.'

'Then she should give you your half.'

'My dear girl, I've had that and more in all the time I've been married to her. She doesn't owe me anything, I owe her and she's got the upper hand.'

'Dad, I do worry about you.'

'Have you decided to go to your friends' wedding in England? You hadn't made up your mind.'

'I don't think I'll go. It's two weeks after Easter

and I'll need to go to Paris to collect some clothes. I expect they'll be relieved if I refuse.'

'Why will they be relieved? You've done nothing wrong except marry two hopeless, impossible men. If they didn't want you to go, why would they ask you?'

'Out of politeness I'm sure.'

'Rubbish, not even the stiff-necked British would be willing to cut off their noses to spite their faces.'

'If you don't like them, Dad, why did you send me to school there?'

'I didn't, your mother did. She thought you'd capture a belted Earl.'

Alanna laughed. 'You haven't lost your sense of humour, Dad.'

'No, I'll hang on to that as long as possible. No nice man in the offing, pet?'

'No, Dad.'

'There will be, love. This time I'll do the approving and disapproving before I walk you up the aisle.'

'Dad, you're impossible.'

'Well your mother approved of the last two. Next time don't let her have a hand in it.'

'Look after yourself, I'll be in touch soon.'

'Yes, well be sure to tell me when you're coming over in case I'm on the boat. She may be all I have left.'

How could her father be so light-hearted about his future? She thought about what her mother had said, that he could live like a pirate, sail the seven seas with half the world's police force searching for him?

241

Chapter Eighteen

Alanna's mother had little to say about her evening at the Contessa Sabrini's, and while she sat slumped in her chair with a gin and tonic in front of her Alanna surveyed her petulant face. She wanted to tell her about her conversation with her father, but she felt it was best left alone. Instead she said, 'You're not saying much about your evening out.'

Her mother looked up, and, picking up her glass, said, 'It was the usual thing, same people, same conversation, except that at the end of the evening four people arrived whom I didn't know, I hadn't seen them before.'

'Who were they?'

'One young man came over to me saying he knew me, or he knew of me. Said his name was Brian Garvey. I'd never heard of a Brian Garvey. Do you know him?'

'I don't think so.'

'He said he knew about me and your father and he also knew you.'

'Really, where had we met?'

'He said he'd met you in Havana and in Brazil. Do you suppose he's one of Claus's crowd?'

'I've no idea, Mother. He probably knows of me without our having met. After all, most people have. What was he like?'

'Youngish, brash, confident. Good-looking if

you like that type.'

'What type?'

'You know. He could be anything, one never really knows these days, film stars, musicians, aristocrats, they could all be from the same barrel.'

'You'll probably meet him again with the same crowd. Did the contessa know him?'

'I didn't ask her, but I assumed she did, either that or they were gate-crashing. Two men and two women. They were having a good time, plenty of drink going around.'

Alanna was not interested, she doubted if they would be included among Jules's friends.

She was finding their lack of conversation oppressive and for want of something else to say she said, 'Have you any idea when Aunt Dolly and her husband will be joining you, Mother?'

'Why do you ask?'

'I just wondered if you'd stay on here with them.'

'Where else would I go? America is out of the question, your father's intent on selling our houses there and he's dispensed with the servants. I couldn't stay with friends all of them knowing his financial problems. I really don't know what I shall do. What will you do?'

That was the moment when she could have told her about the wedding invitation, but something prevented her. Her mother might encourage her to go to England to hobnob with the upper crust; on the other hand she would moan about being left alone, but she really had to do something about Ginevra's wedding. Half of her wanted to go, the other half dreaded it.

Her mother was saying, 'Dolly hates the Med before the beginning of May, I doubt if they'll be here much before that. She's prepared to shiver in Switzerland so why think the Med's too cold in February?'

Just then the telephone on the small table rang and Alanna got up to answer it. It was Jules.

'I've been invited to view the new yacht to-morrow, Alanna. I was wondering if you and your mother would like to accompany me?' he asked.

'I'm sure we will. Mother is here, I'll ask her.'

Her mother pulled a face. 'What a nuisance. I'd love to view the yacht, but I have a salon appointment in the morning. My hair needs styling and I promised to pick the contessa up. Do make an excuse for me, dear, but tell him you'd love to go.'

Neither of them could see Jules' smile as he replaced the telephone receiver.

His telephone call decided Alanna that she would not attend Ginevra's wedding after all.

Alanna was enjoying her morning. The yacht was beautiful even when most of the morning she found herself comparing it with the *Lady Katrina*. They were escorted round by the proud owner, food and drinks were on hand and Jules said with a wry smile, 'I thought the launching party was due over Easter. I hadn't realised we were having a rehearsal.'

Alanna was thinking that she had been right in deciding not to go to Ginevra's wedding, so much so that the night before she had sat down and written a letter explaining that her mother was not very well and she was spending time with her in Provence. It was not strictly true, but she couldn't think of any other excuse. She wished Ginevra and her fiancé all the luck in the world and hoped they would be able to meet in the near future.

The letter was resting in her handbag and she hoped to post it on the way home. She refused to admit that her reasons for declining the invitation concerned Jules in any way. She did not want another man in her life, it was too soon, besides apart from the courteous behaviour of a man towards a young woman there was nothing to suggest that he might be interested in her. He had asked no questions about how long she was staying in St Tropez. Indeed, apart from the everyday courtesies, he had shown little interest in either her past or her future.

She stood at the rail looking out to where a group of young people were sunbathing on a smaller yacht moored near the harbour wall. There was much laughter and chatter and she found herself remembering that once she had been part of a group like that when Claus was in his element in the centre of a gaggle of admiring girls. Claus had paraded his conquests in front of her like trophies and if she'd seen the looks of contempt levelled at him from some of the men he'd never cared.

When they climbed the steps at the end of the harbour wall Jules said, 'Here are the car keys, Alanna, it's chilly standing about and I need to have a word with someone. Wait for me in the car.'

With the intention of posting her letter before going to the car she walked quickly, and it was only when she reached the postbox set in the wall that a man came towards her. She recognised him as one she had seen climbing aboard the smaller boat earlier in the morning. He was smiling, stopping in front of her, so that there was nothing for her but to stop beside him.

'You don't remember me do you?' he surprised her by saying.

She looked into his face and shook her head.

'Havana, Brazil?' he enquired.

'I'm afraid not. You say we met there?'

'Yes. My name's Brian Garvey, I worked for one or two seasons on your husband's cars, or should I say your ex-husband's cars.'

'I'm sorry I don't remember you. There were so many people around at the time.'

'Well yes. But you would remember my wife Marcia.'

Marcia Garvey, of course. The girl her husband became involved with in Havana, the girl who had finally pushed her over the edge so that she'd packed her bags and left him. Now here was her husband smiling down at her with evident amusement.

'You may not know it,' he said with a cynical grin, 'but she walked out and left me with absolutely nothing, then your husband left her. Did you know that?'

'No, but I'm sure he found somebody else.'

'Oh, he did. By that time I didn't want Marcia back. He took my wife, she took my money, but none of it worried you did it, Alanna. You

246

divorced him and did mighty well out of it. Money's a good thing to have if you're a woman. I see you're well on your way to capturing another rich man. Good luck to you, after Austerlech any man would be an improvement.'

With another smile and a flick of his hand he had left her to go striding across the square. She forgot about her letter; instead she flew to where the Mercedes was waiting and sank miserably into the front seat.

The journey back to the villa was taken in silence and looking at her pale, withdrawn face Jules could only feel surprise at what had caused it. She had been happy and smiling all morning, quite evidently enjoying herself, now she looked miles away.

She was remembering Marcia Garvey, blonde, pretty, one of a pattern. Slender, sunkissed, long-legged young women who had surrounded Claus in the nightclubs, on the racing circuit, on the boats. She couldn't remember ever meeting Marcia, but she must have done. The husbands had always seemed to melt into the background somehow, they were simply there as escorts, to buy the drinks and the clothes; the girls were there for Claus.

For the first time in months Alanna found herself remembering the trauma that had come after. The lawyers and their fat fees, the court scenes and the wrangling over money. Claus and her father loathing each other, and all along the line she'd beaten him so that he'd had to give her everything her lawyers asked for, and it had been Claus who had torn her reputation into shreds in his bitterness.

Jules stopped the car in front of the villa and as she fumbled for the door handle he said softly, 'Is something wrong, Alanna? You're very quiet. Didn't you enjoy it?'

She stared at him, suddenly aware that they hadn't exchanged a word throughout their drive from the harbour.

'I'm sorry Jules, I've been thinking of something else.'

'Was it the man I saw you talking to near the wall?'

'Yes. I didn't know him, but apparently he knew me.'

'Well, whatever it was it obviously upset you.'

She smiled. 'I'm sorry to have been such a poor companion. I expect by this time Mother's back from her salon, would you care to come in to have tea with us?'

'Thank you no, I have somebody coming to see me. I'll see you anon.'

He waited to see her entering the villa before driving away.

Her mother was still out so she went up to her bedroom and sat for some time staring at the envelope in her hands. She had forgotten all about it until now, then slowly she tore it into small pieces and let them fall into the waste-paper basket.

When her mother came into her bedroom half an hour later she found Alanna pulling all her clothes out of her wardrobe and throwing them on to the bed. Her empty suitcase lay open on the floor and in amazement her mother cried,

'What are you doing, Alanna? What is the meaning of all this?'

'I'm leaving, Mother. I'm going to England.'

'England!'

'Yes, to Ginevra Midhurst's wedding.'

'But you've said nothing to me about it. When is she getting married?'

'Two weeks after Easter.'

'But that's soon. You can't go, there's the party at Easter and you've said you'll go with me. You don't need to go now in any case, put those things away and come downstairs, we need to talk.'

'Mother, there's nothing to talk about, my mind's made up.'

'Is it anything to do with Jules?'

'Jules!'

'Well, yes. I thought you were liking him rather a lot, is there somebody else?'

'Oh, Mother, of course it isn't Jules. He's charming, he's been kind, it has nothing to do with him. I'm going to the wedding of an old school friend, I feel I should go, it would be terrible not to go.'

'But why so suddenly? Why start packing now?'

'I can't go to the wedding with any of these things, I need to go to Paris to pick up some clothes. I need to shop around.'

'And who will escort you to this wedding?'

'I don't need an escort Mother, I haven't had an escort for three years, why should I need one now?'

'Because everybody else will have one. Where's the invitation, let me see it.'

'It's there on the dressing table.'

Her mother picked it up and sat down weakly on a chair to read it. After a few minutes she said, 'It says here that you can invite an escort to go with you,' she said.

'I know but I don't have one and I don't want one.'

'Alanna, something's brought this on and I want to know what it is. What happened this morning? There's something you're not telling me.'

Alanna sat down facing her and her mother was instantly aware of the bitterness in her eyes.

'I met a man this morning who knew me when I was married to Claus. His wife left him for Claus, and I left him because of her. I didn't remember him at all, his name is Brian Garvey, but he knew all about me. All about the divorce, all about the money he'd had to give me, all about everything, and now he's here and in no time it'll be everywhere. You should leave too, Mother, get right away.'

'Don't be silly. It's history. Is this man back with his wife?'

'No.'

'Well, what's he blaming you for? You should be sympathising with each other.'

'He's angry because I came out of it stinking rich and he was penniless. Mother, I don't want to argue with you, I'm going to England to attend this wedding and where I'll go from there I really don't know.'

'I wonder what your father'll have to say about this.'

'Why don't you ask him? It'll give you two a chance to talk.'

'Oh no Alanna, you don't push me into anything as silly as that. When do you propose to leave?'

'Tomorrow, if I can get a flight to Paris.'

'Did you tell Jules what you proposed to do?'

'Of course not. He wouldn't be interested. He'll escort you to the party on the yacht at Easter. You'll enjoy it, Mother.'

That evening Alanna answered Ginevra's wedding invitation and booked her flight from Nice to Paris for the following morning. As for the evening, her mother played endless games of patience, drank several glasses of gin and tonic and retired to bed at ten o'clock without saying goodnight.

It was barely light when she crept into her mother's bedroom the next morning, but for once her mother was sitting up in bed wide awake, and as she bent down to kiss her her mother looked at her balefully.

'I haven't slept a wink, Alanna, I'm worried about you. How long do you intend to spend your life running away, and where are you running to? All those people who knew you as a girl, all of them knowing what's gone wrong in your life, I would have thought a wedding would be the last thing you would want to witness.'

'It will be nice to meet my friends again.'

'How many times have you seen any of them since you left that finishing school in Switzerland?'

'It hasn't been because they forgot to invite me. It was always I who couldn't go, I who lived at the other side of the world, I who was married.'

'You mean none of them are married?'

'Well, this is Ginevra's wedding and Jane isn't married. I don't know about Kathy Marston.'

'If you'd been going anywhere except to a wedding I could understand it, but you're annoyed because there's somebody here who remembers you. Don't you think it will be twice as bad where you're going?'

'It will be a chance for me to develop a second skin. Show them that I'm as unconcerned as they think I am. Mother, I have to go, the taxi will be here.'

'When will you be back?'

'Like I said, I don't know. Anyway Dolly and her husband will soon be here so you'll have company. I'll link up with Dad, sail the world with him, we'll be two pirates together.'

Later that morning Jules received a tearful telephone call from Alanna's mother. Unable to make anything of her on the telephone he went round to the villa to see her. It was evident she'd been crying and he sat listening to her version of all that had gone wrong in her daughter's life.

'One disastrous marriage was bad enough,' she cried, 'but the second one was worse than the first. He never left her alone until she said she'd marry him. He followed her all over the place from Europe to South America, from the States to Rome; wherever Alanna went he was there and he was so handsome and so romantic, any girl would have been flattered.

'He was no good of course. He was a playboy with too much money. Race horses and cars, polo and yachts, Claus had them all, and then he had Alanna. Once he'd got her he wasn't bothered about caring for her. There were other women, too many of them, and their lifestyle filled one magazine after another; then the court case and the money-wrangling. My husband's never been any good with money, but he did use the best lawyers to handle Alanna's affairs. All his setbacks have been disasters, hers were so lucrative the press made a picnic out of it.'

'Why are you so worried?' he asked her. 'I'm sure Alanna will enjoy her stay in England.'

'Of course I'm worried, Jules. Have you ever met any of those titled people who can look down their aristocratic noses at other people while they keep their own traumas under wraps? We Americans tend to bring everything out in the open, you French do too, but the British, they're hidebound by convention, they sit in judgement, things that are not quite nice are still frowned upon.'

'Just a little hypocritical, don't you think?' Jules murmured.

'Well of course it is, but if her old friends show their disapproval Alanna will be devastated. All that unconcern she shows is a façade, it hides too much hurt.'

'Will she come back here after the wedding?' Jules asked.

'She said not. She said she'd go out to her father and sail with him. I'm not sure if she'll find a house to go to, the one in New York's been sold and there's no way he's getting rid of the house in Boston, half of that belongs to me, so does the one on St Lucia. Of course he's pretty good at getting around difficulties. I should know, I've been married to him long enough.'

She was telling him these things because she was distraught, things that normally she would have kept to herself, and he was left wondering how much of her parents' antipathy towards each other reflected on Alanna.

'Why did you decide to have Alanna educated in England?' he asked.

For several minutes she stared at him non-plussed, then she said flatly, 'I wanted it for her. I wanted her to marry well, some member of the British aristocracy, and I believed it would be an opportunity for her. Instead she marries a Polish count with no money, followed by an Austrian prince with too much money and no morals. The money on Alanna's education was wasted.'

'Surely not. She's still beautiful, none of it has been lost, it is simply unfortunate that she was a rich girl in a careless world.'

'I want her to find a nice, decent man and get married again.'

He smiled. 'I know, a man with a nine to five job and a lucrative pension at the end of it. Do you really think that would be for Alanna?'

Sadly her mother shook her head. 'No. She'll probably go on making mistakes.'

'Then what do you really want for her, Mrs Van Royston?'

She looked him straight in the eyes and said, 'Somebody like you Jules. Older, wiser and in

254

control. I don't know very much about you, do I? Do you have a wife somewhere?'

'Alas, no.'

'Why is that I wonder? Not from choice I'm sure.'

'There was someone once when I was much younger, there is nobody now. But why do we talk about me, I thought it was Alanna we were talking about.'

'You must think I'm a very silly woman, Jules. I've not been good for Alanna, neither has her father, it's no wonder we're suffering now for all the things we did wrong.'

'I wouldn't worry too much about Alanna, Mrs Van Royston, I have the strangest feeling that Alanna will survive.'

Jules went home and thought about Alanna. From the first moment he'd seen her alighting from that plane in Nice she'd intrigued him. He knew her, and her history. She was the sort of beautiful girl that filled his best-sellers. Film stars jostled with one another to play her, but since he'd got to know Alanna he recognised the traumas hidden inside her. A wise man would stay aloof from those traumas, but his conversation with her mother had brought on a relentless surge of sympathy for her.

He had met women like Jessie Van Royston all too many times. Rich women who lived their lives in the world's playgrounds, women with beautiful daughters they were too ambitious for. He had little doubt that Alanna's mother had had a hand in both her unfortunate marriages, and from what he'd heard of her father he'd apparently contributed nothing apart from his adoration for her. He thought of her alone in Paris with the prospect of a society wedding in England in her mind.

In Paris Alanna was surveying her wardrobe. She had clothes for every contingency, balls and regattas, race meetings and garden parties. There was no need for her to look for something new. Anything Ginevra's wedding guests came up with she was able to do better. There was nothing like Paris to radiate style and elegance. If they wanted to talk about her she'd give them something to talk about, and then when it was all over she'd move on. There would be something else waiting round the corner.

Jane

Chapter Nineteen

Jane Fortesque stood in front of her cheval mirror looking at her reflection and thinking 'the dress is pretty and the colour suits me. I could have chosen something worse.'

She was tall and slender. Her hair was an indeterminate shade of medium brown, her eyes were hazel, and, if not strictly pretty, her face was interesting with good bone structure, well defined brows and a porcelain complexion.

Jane was remembering words she had once spoken to Ginevra Midhurst when they were school friends. 'They couldn't have called me anything else but Jane, that's what I am, plain Jane.'

Ginevra had been quick to say, 'But you're not plain, you'll be very attractive one day and you'll have a beautiful figure to go with it.'

Well, she had a good figure. She looked well on a horse, better than she looked in the ballroom, she thought, but she had stopped worrying about being considered beautiful a long time ago.

The sound of music, laughter and conversation drifted up from the ballroom below and she could imagine the scene. Men in hunting pink evening dress, women in exquisite dresses, older women who had worn their gowns many times before, but no longer had the urge to compete with the younger women for the older men who would be

259

sitting in the library or elsewhere drinking their whisky, swapping their hunting stories.

There would be groups of young men singing their ribald hunting songs and then there were the others looking around for something more permanent.

Jane didn't lack escorts or dancing partners. The hunt ball was always held at Maplethorpe and her parents gave ungrudging use of their home for the occasion. That she was Lord Fortesque's only daughter guaranteed that she would be well looked after by a host of young men, but tonight's affair would be like all the others that had gone before, and Jane had been attending these functions since she left school.

She heard a soft tap on her door and turning round she smiled at her father entering her bedroom. Jane had always considered her father to be the most handsome man she had ever met and tonight he looked wonderful in his hunting pink dress jacket and white ruffled shirt. He was tall and his hair, peppered with silver, only seemed to add to the distinction of his classical good looks. He smiled across the room at her and she went forward into his embrace.

'You look lovely,' he said, 'green suits you Janie, new dress?'

She laughed. 'Oh Daddy, you're hopeless. This is the dress I've worn for at least two hunt balls.'

'Why didn't you buy another then?'

'I bought something else instead, something I'll get more wear from. I'm very practical.'

'I'd like you to be a little less practical, darling. You could be having more fun.'

260

'Perhaps I'm a lot like Mother. I'll bet she's wearing that old brown thing she's had for ages.'

He smiled but didn't comment. Jane had always known that her parents were poles apart in how they thought, how they behaved and how they lived their lives. Between them was respect, a vague sort of friendship that stemmed from long years of knowing each other and growing up together in families who had been close, who had planned their future together before they left the nursery.

Those rigid autocratic families would never have believed that a woman would come along to disturb a marriage that had always seemed inviolate, and it had taken Josie Marston with her charm and her incomparable beauty at a ball similar to the one this night to shatter their complacency. Heads had been shaken, words had been chosen carefully, but nobody had ever believed that the affair would last, that years later she would still be a part of his life.

Jane stood looking in her mirror while her father fastened a gold chain around her neck, and his eyes smiled into hers.

'There's a very impatient young man waiting for you downstairs, Jane,' he said.

She raised her eyebrows. 'I suppose you mean Algy Barrington?'

'You're aware of it then?'

'I suppose so.'

'And it doesn't impress you?'

'I've known him too long and we know each other too well. I can't ever think of Algy as anything more than a friend.'

261

'Friendship is a very good foundation for marriage, Jane.'

'But we both know it isn't enough, don't we? You and Mother are friends, you don't love each other.'

He smiled ruefully. 'It's amazing how many people make it work for them, love.'

'Not you and not me. I'll join Algy downstairs now and I'll listen to him talking about horses and race meetings, dogs and all the crowd of young men like him who make up his world.'

'Your views might disappoint your mother, Jane.'

'Because Algy's mother is her oldest friend, because his father's rich and a great landowner, because we're out of the same barrel? Daddy, it isn't enough.'

'I thought you liked his friends.'

'They're all right. I know Larry Harbrook. He's chased after Ginevra Midhurst for years but she isn't marrying him.'

'I'm not surprised. His father's been a wastrel and squandered most of the family fortune.'

'But that's hardly Larry's fault, is it? Ginevra will never marry him, just as I shall never marry Algy Barrington.'

'Poor Algy. At least for this evening you can dance with him and be nice to him.'

Algy was kicking his heels at the foot of the stairs and her father gave her arm a little squeeze before he turned round and saw them. His good-looking face lit up with a smile and he stepped forward to take her hand in his.

'I thought you'd got lost,' he said, 'I seem to

have been waiting ages.'

'Why didn't you join in the dancing?' Jane said smiling.

'I preferred to wait for you. The next dance is a quickstep. May I take Jane off your hands, sir?'

Lord Fortesque smiled. 'Of course, enjoy yourselves.'

Algy was not the best dancer in the world, he had no natural rhythm. His dancing was energetic and evident of his pleasure. He insisted on chatting brightly throughout the dance and Jane would have preferred to remain silent to enjoy the music.

'Have you had an invitation to the Midhurst wedding?' he asked.

'Yes, this morning. Have you?'

'Yes, I and the parents. Larry's bound to be upset about Ginevra's marriage.'

'Surely you didn't think Ginevra would ever marry him?'

'No not really, but they have been an item for some time.'

'They were never an item, Algy, simply old friends.'

'Larry thought they were rather more than that. Do you know the chap she's marrying?'

'No, I've never met him, but my parents know his parents.'

'Hadn't Ginevra told you anything about him?'

'It's some time since I saw Ginevra. We exchanged Christmas cards and she wrote to me when it was my birthday, but she didn't mention her wedding or Larry.'

'I'm invited to take a friend. I suppose you can

263

take an escort, anybody in mind?'

'No. I shall go with my parents.'

'You could go with me.'

'I shall see you there, Algy.'

'Your father's dancing with Lady Willesden, she never gives up does she?'

'What do you mean by that?'

'The entire country knows she's chased after him for years waiting for some encouragement. I don't suppose it's ever been forthcoming and certainly is not likely to be now.'

'Why now?'

He blushed bright scarlet and for several seconds she enjoyed his discomfort before repeating her question.

'It's just that she's never got anywhere with him, Jane. Everybody knows she's tried, but at this late stage it's a lost cause.'

'Why is it a lost cause?'

'You know we all know he's friendly with somebody else, don't we? I don't suppose she's here.'

'No, Algy. Josie's only ever been to one hunt ball here. I don't suppose she'll ever come to another.'

Her face was bland, expressionless, and he stared down at her slightly nonplussed.

'It used to worry you, doesn't it any more?'

'No.'

'I'm glad about that. Your worrying wouldn't change anything, would it.'

For a few moments they danced in silence, then Jane said, 'Those people talking about my father don't know anything, they should watch what they say.'

'Nobody talks about him Jane, it's history now, people have accepted it. Your father's much liked and very well respected. He has his own reasons for doing what he does.'

At that moment she liked him better than ever before, and smiling down at her he said, 'I'll bet she's an improvement on Lady Willesden, I've never thought much of her.'

She laughed.

'Have you met her, Jane? Can you confirm that?'

'Yes, I've met Josie Marston several times. She's beautiful and she's nice. At first I thought I hated her, now I like her, it's easier that way.'

'Easier? For you or your father?'

'For both of us.'

'The floor's too crowded, shall we go and have a drink? We'll dance again when it's something a bit slower.'

'Oh, Algy, your dancing is never slower.'

He grinned. 'I'm aware I'm not the classiest person on the dance floor, but I am the most entertaining.'

'But not the most modest?'

'Here, sit here in the alcove and I'll push my way to the bar, what'll you have?'

'Dry Martini.'

She watched him making his way towards the bar, occasionally being impeded by friends who wanted to chat, or girls anxious to dance, and Jane's thoughts went back to her first meeting with Josie Marston.

She had gone with a group of girls and Madame Perrigon into Interlaken. They had

265

sailed on the twin lakes and looked at the shops, and they were sitting at a small café drinking mineral water and eating their croissants. Suddenly she'd been aware of Ginevra pointing across the road to where a man and woman were walking down the road. Ginevra said, 'Jane, over there, isn't that your father?'

Jane's eyes had followed her pointing finger and became suddenly aware of the hot blush in her cheeks and she turned sharply away. It was Alanna who said, 'Surely you're going to speak to him?'

'No, I don't want to.'

She had got up to leave the table and it was then that her father saw her and with a smile he walked across the road followed by his companion.

He held out his hand saying, 'Jane, this is wonderful, I didn't expect to see you in Interlaken.'

He had smiled at the other girls and greeted their teacher with charming politeness, then taking hold of Jane's hand he had brought her forward to meet his companion.

'This is Josie Marston, Jane. I've talked to her endlessly about you, darling, so much so that I expect she really feels she already knows you.'

She had looked up into a pair of sapphire-blue eyes and at a lovely face under a halo of pale gold hair, at a slim woman who was beautifully dressed. The woman's smile had been charming, holding her hand in a warm clasp.

At that moment Jane's antagonism for the other woman in her father's life resurfaced. She was hating her for being beautiful, resenting her smile, her elegance which no doubt her father had paid for, and she was hating Kathy Marston and wishing they had gone on ostracising her, but then her father was sitting at the table with her friends, treating them to rich cream cakes, and Josie was chatting to Madame who was obviously enraptured by the beautiful woman who was chatting to her as if they had known each other for a very long time.

Instead of travelling back to school in the bus they were treated to three taxis, and as he held her in a warm embrace her father whispered, 'I'm so glad we've seen you darling, I'm also glad you've met Josie at last. I must have bored her a great many times about my young daughter.'

'Are you staying in Switzerland long, Daddy?'

'For a few more days, dear, then I have to get back.'

'Is she going back with you?'

'Josie is staying here a little longer.'

She was ashamed of the relief she felt on hearing that, but in the next moment her father was saying, 'I'm looking forward to having you home for good, Jane. Only another six months to go.'

'Is Mother hoping I'll be home soon?'

'Of course, we both are.'

'Is Mother well?'

'Yes, and happy with her dogs and horses.'

Jane had known he'd spoken nothing but the truth.

Algy came back with the drinks and took his seat next to her at the table.

'To get back to the Midhurst wedding,' he began. 'Do you suppose the Van Royston girl will

267

be there? But more to the point, who will she be with?'

'I haven't heard from Alanna for ages. I'm sure Ginevra's invited her.'

'I hope she turns up.'

'Why do you say that?'

'Because there'll be more people there interested in Alanna than the bridal pair.'

'Alanna will cope.'

'Did you read what she got as a divorce settlement? She near bankrupted her husband.'

'Paper talk.'

'Not it. Wasn't he the playboy of the year? And he made a bomb on motor racing, he must have done to own the yachts he sailed, the strings of polo ponies, the homes he bought all over Europe and South America.'

'Alanna's family had money, she didn't marry him for his.'

'Perhaps not, but wasn't the money on her mother's side of the family? Her father's been a bit of a gambler.'

'How is it you're such an authority on the Van Royston family?'

'Well, you have to admit she's kept the newspapers happy this last couple of years.'

'I hope she comes to Ginevra's wedding, I would dearly like to see her again. There's Mother, I'll have a few words with her.'

Lady Fortesque had entered the room set apart to serve as a bar and stood in the midst of a ring of hunting men, men who admired her for her skill on the hunting field rather than her glamour.

Elspeth Fortesque was a tall, well-built woman

with a windswept look about her even here in the ballroom. Her face was bronzed, with good bone structure and fine eyes. Her hair so much like Jane's, was caught back from her face in a kind of chignon, emphasizing her prominent nose and high cheekbones.

Jane despaired. The brown silk gown her mother was wearing had seen service at more hunt balls than she could remember, but with it she was glad to see her mother was wearing the pearls which had been a wedding present from her father. They were beautiful and lustrous, but in spite of their beauty they did little to help her to compete with more elegant guests.

Lady Fortesque looked her best in riding clothes sitting astride one of her mounts, or riding side-saddle as she often did even when she was alone in such a venture. She felt no need to glamorize herself for an affair that gave her little pleasure.

She greeted her daughter with a smile.

'Is that Algy Barrington you were with?' she enquired.

'Yes, Mother.'

'That's nice. He's a very nice young man, Jane, I hope you realise that.'

Jane smiled. Of course her mother thought Algy was a nice young man. His mother was her oldest friend, his father, a Major-General, was her keenest rival at every dog show, every point-to-point, and the vast acres of land they owned in Bedfordshire and elsewhere were not to be disdained.

Jane decided that tonight was not the night to

get into an argument about Algy's credentials; there would be other occasions, a great many of them.

His father breezed up to them smiling broadly, 'Keeping my lad in order are you, Jane?' he quipped.

Jane smiled, and he continued, 'You're looking very pretty tonight my dear, I'm sure Algy's aware of it.'

'The room's full of pretty girls Algy will have noticed I'm sure.'

'He's only got eyes for you, Jane. Now we were talking about the Midhurst affair, why not come and stay with us overnight and we'll all go on together? It makes more sense than travelling separately. What do you say Elspeth?'

'Well yes, it seems like a good idea to me. I'll speak to John about it.'

'I think it's a very good idea to me. You and John can travel with Beatrice and me in our car, or we can travel in yours. There'll be room in it for my daughter Kate, and Algy and Jane here can travel in Algy's car. What do you say, Jane?'

'I'm not sure. Perhaps we should ask Daddy.'

'Well, it makes sense. The village will be over-run with cars, the fewer of them the better in my opinion.'

'The wedding invitation stated quite categorically that both Algy and Kate could take a friend, I feel sure it was Algy's intention to ask you my dear.'

It seemed to Jane at that moment that events were conspiring to place her with Algy Barrington. At Ginevra's wedding they would be surrounded with people who knew both families, people who would look upon them as a pair and possibly make remarks about how much they were looking forward to the next wedding. Jane's and Algy's.

By this time Algy had joined them and immediately he warmed to the subject of their arriving at the wedding as one party. Jane's mother was looking at her with some exasperation and she was glad when in a few minutes her father joined them and the invitation from Algy's father was issued again. Something of her panic must have shown in her eyes, because her father said evenly. 'It really is too bad, but a few moments ago I issued an invitation to the Forresters to travel with us on the day of the wedding. I do agree that the fewer cars there are cluttering up the village the better the Midhursts will appreciate it.'

'Oh well,' grumbled Algy's father, 'it can't be helped now, but we'll all meet up there. The young people can still be together.'

Chapter Twenty

It was the usual post-mortem over the breakfast table after the hunt ball and Jane listened in silence to three different points of view.

Her mother was ecstatically delighted that it had gone so well, her father more diffident and Andrew decidedly unenthusiastic.

'You've started something, Father,' he said

271

frowning. 'I hope you're aware that long after you've shuffled off this mortal coil I'll be expected to continue the festivities here at Maplethorpe.'

His father smiled. 'You forget that I didn't initiate the ball, Andrew, I believe it was my grandfather who first had the idea.'

'Surely you're in favour of it?' his mother snapped.

'Well, I know you are, Mother.'

'Of course. It's our way of life, you all know I'm not a great one for dressing up and one party after another, but this event is one that should continue.'

'There's even a doubt that the hunt will continue, Mother, there's a lot of controversy about it.'

'Fiddlesticks. Of course it will continue. People living in cities should have no say in how country people run their lives.'

Nobody disagreed with her; they had learned from experience that it was useless to argue about something that made up the largest part of her life.

It was Andrew who changed the subject by saying, 'What about the Midhurst wedding? I suppose we're all attending?'

'Of course. How about Elvira? The baby will be three months old by then and can conveniently be left with a nanny.'

'Yes, I'm sure Elvira will want to attend.'

Across the table Jane met her father's quizzical glance before he said, 'You got a separate invitation, dear, have you decided to invite somebody along?'

Before she could answer her mother said, 'The Barringtons said we should go together if you remember, but you'd already asked the Forresters.'

'That shouldn't interfere with any plans Jane wants to make,' her father said evenly.

'Of course it does, John. Algy Barrington invited her to attend with him, she can hardly invite anybody else.'

'Why not?'

Elspeth looked at her husband with the utmost exasperation. 'Because Algy's parents are our closest friends, because he's highly eligible, and because as far as I'm aware Jane isn't interested in anybody else.'

'But is she interested in Algy?' her father continued.

'If she's any sense she is,' Elspeth snapped.

Andrew chortled, 'Well well, so my little sister's being manipulated. How much do you like Algy Barrington, Jane?'

'No more and no less than I like half a dozen other men,' Jane said firmly, and for her pains received her mother's angry frown.

Changing the subject Elspeth said, 'I hope this marriage to Ginevra is going to work.'

'What do you mean, work?' Andrew asked.

'Well, wasn't there all that talk years ago when Dominic was terribly in love with that Irish girl who drowned? After that he never seemed interested in a woman, now I suppose he's got to think about an heir to the dukedom. After all his brother's a bit of a loose cannon, isn't he?'

They were unprepared for Jane jumping to her

273

feet, her face red and angry. 'I think it's dreadful that we should be talking like this about Ginevra's wedding, why can't everybody just be happy for them instead of raking up something that happened years ago? It's horrible.'

She left her mother glaring after her with a comical look of astonishment on her face, while her father and brother stared at each other before her father rose to his feet and followed her up the stairs.

He found Jane sitting on the window seat sobbing quietly into her handkerchief and he went to sit beside her. He waited for the tears to subside before he said quietly, 'Don't get so upset darling, old scandals invariably arise surrounding a marriage as prominent as this one is going to be.'

'Why should they? Why can't people simply accept that Ginevra and Dominic are very much in love. Why rake up some girl he knew ages ago?'

'I don't know Jane, it gives them something to talk about and speculate on.'

'They'll do the same about me if ever I get married, won't they?'

'What do you mean?'

'Daddy you know what I mean. They'll talk about Josie, they'll all know that the show you and Mummy will put on is a façade, that we're not the united family we're pretending to be.'

Through her tears she looked at her father's face; his expression was bleak, and she felt a sudden rush of contrition that it was her tears that had put it there. Then in the next moment she felt that he deserved it, he was the one who had put Josie Marston first.

He remained silent, staring through the window at the reaches of parkland but at that moment he was remembering the long years when he had tried desperately to come to terms with a marriage that shouldn't have been. A marriage that had been engineered by two sets of parents who knew nothing else. People like him and Elspeth married for expediency, for money, for land. He respected his wife, he had never loved her, but it was an age when children instinctively obeyed their parents and when they had known from the cradle onwards what was expected of them. When for the first time he fell in love the outcome had been more painful.

Love had been the last thing on John Fortesque's mind the evening when he first looked into Josie Marston's eyes, eyes filled with tears, because some silly young fool was treating her shamefully. He had not thought ever to meet her again, but fate had deemed otherwise, and if Josie's love had brought him a happiness he had never envisaged, it had also brought him much pain and many misgivings.

He stood for a moment staring down at his daughter's bent head, then he walked slowly across to the door.

Across the room their eyes met and with a little cry Jane jumped to her feet and ran into his arms. 'Daddy, I didn't mean it, I'm sorry,' she cried. 'I know you love me, I know nothing you do is anybody's business, only yours, but it was hearing Mother talking about Ginevra that started it. I understand why you love Josie,

275

honestly I do.'

He gave her a warm squeeze. 'Are you coming back to the breakfast table?' he asked.

'No. Tell them I've gone down to the stables, I'll take Gypsy out.'

'Your brother will be leaving soon, aren't you coming to say goodbye?'

'Tell him I'll ride over one day this week. I want to see the baby.'

'Don't ride too long, the weather isn't good and we're in for a storm.'

He opened the door and she said quickly, 'Daddy, you do understand about Algy, don't you? He's a friend, I don't like him in any other way. Mother keeps on and on about the land they own, their affluence. Does it have to be like that?'

'No, Jane, it doesn't. I would like to think that times have moved on a bit, that we all learn from our mistakes.'

'So, if I marry a dustman you won't mind?'

He laughed. 'I might think you were making a great mistake, just as devastating as marrying Algy Barrington might be.'

'Then you don't agree with Mother that I'm wasting a golden opportunity?'

'I'll always be on your side Jane, you'll always be my girl, I told you that years ago and nothing's changed.'

It seemed to Jane that she'd always been asking for his reassurance about her role in his life. Alanna had once asked her if she felt bitter because of her mother, but it had never been that, it had always been her own insecurity. Andrew had always been the favourite with her mother and Jane had been a sickly baby. Her mother wasn't naturally maternal and Andrew had been a robust adventurous child, the sort of boy who did everything well, good on the cricket field and at rugger, brilliant at polo and on the tennis courts, whereas Jane was only ever at her best with horses. Her times with them were the only times she earned her mother's approval.

Her father was the one who read bedtime stories and tucked her up in bed, the one who told her she'd been marvellous on the show ground when she'd jumped her horse effortlessly over the most difficult fences. Her mother had merely accepted her success as her own. To Elspeth, Jane's acumen was an extension of her own, it was expected, and anything expected couldn't be remotely classed as wonderful.

Elspeth had found fault where there was none. It wouldn't do for Jane to become complacent, she had to do well all the time, or better.

When John Fortesque returned to the breakfast table Elspeth said sharply, 'Well, what is the matter with her? What on earth was said to bring on that fit of temperament?'

'Nothing should have been said at all about Ginevra's wedding. They were great friends, your remarks were unfortunate.'

'Really, John, life isn't all sugar and spice, she'll have to realise that sooner or later. I hope the marriage is a great success, but one has to face the doubts about it.'

'Doubts that are nobody's business.'

'Perhaps not, but they exist all the same.'

'Isn't it time you were getting off, Andrew?

277

You've a fair drive up to Elvira's parents,' his father asked.

'Yes, I'm all packed up, I'll get off as soon as I've put my stuff in the car. We'll see you both at the Midhurst wedding then?'

'Of course.'

'I'd have thought she'd have asked Jane to be one of her bridesmaids, wouldn't you?'

His mother pursed her lips. 'If she decided to invite old school friends to be her bridesmaids there were plainly difficulties.'

'Difficulties?'

'Well, obviously. The Van Royston girl and the other one.'

Her husband met her disapproving glance over the length of the table. Elspeth never mentioned his mistress or her niece, whenever she referred to either of them it was in an oblique manner which he chose to ignore.

Andrew shrugged his shoulders. 'I'd have thought the Van Royston girl would conceivably add some spice to the affair.'

'And the other one?' his mother prompted.

'I have never met the other one,' Andrew replied diplomatically.

He rose to his feet and, kissing her briefly on her cheek, said, 'Like I said, we'll meet at the wedding; it'll soon be here.'

'How long do you suppose Elvira intends to stay in Scotland with her parents?' his mother asked.

'She'll be ready to come home any time I'm sure. Naturally she wanted to stay on for a while after the baby was born. He's a fine little chap,

I'm sure you'll both think so.'

He met his sister in the hall. Jane had changed into her riding clothes and his first thoughts were that she looked wonderfully well in them. Her mother was a large lady who looked equally well in riding togs. Jane was tall and slender, and her features were softer, more feminine than her mother's.

'I'm longing to see the baby, Andrew,' she said smiling. 'Do let me know when Elvira gets home.'

'Come over and stay for a few days,' he said, 'it'll get you out of Mother's hair.'

'You've noticed?'

'Particularly where Algy Barrington's concerned. Have you anybody else in mind?'

'No. I've known Algy too long, and he's like all the others who live for their horses and equine pursuits. There has to be something else.'

She waited until her brother drove away from the house then she went to the stable where a groom saddled her horse. It was a cold blustery day, a day when she should have been glad to stay indoors, but it was always the same these days; suppressed anger and discord between her parents, and between her mother and herself that feeling of disappointment and exasperation she never failed to arouse in her mother.

She kept to the country lanes, glad of her riding mac and the warm sweater she was wearing. She had not gone far when she became aware that somebody was calling to her. She halted her horse and turned to see two riders bearing down on her, waving their crops and evidently in high good humour. It was Algy and Larry Harbrook.

'We're stopping off at the pub,' Algy informed her, 'join us, it's too damn cold to be riding far.'

'I was already on my way back,' Jane lied.

Larry added his persuasion. 'Do join us Jane, it's ages since we met, I'd like to hear what you've been doing with yourself.'

So for want of a very good excuse Jane allowed herself to be coaxed into joining them at the inn. They tied up their horses at the rails near by and the warmth which met them when they entered the pub cheered them up considerably.

They found a table in the window where they could keep an eye on their horses and immediately Algy went to the bar to order their drinks. Larry grinned at her and her thoughts were that the two men were really very similar, cut from a pattern, young, good-looking and brash.

'Well what do you think about Ginevra's wedding plans? I suppose you've been invited?'

'Yes, of course.'

'Were you surprised?'

'That she was getting married? I don't think so.'

'At her choice of bridegroom?'

'Why should that surprise me?'

'Didn't you think it should have been me?'

'I really didn't know how serious you and Ginevra were about each other.'

'I was very serious about her. Of course her old man didn't consider me good enough, not enough money, not sufficient blue blood.'

'What about Ginevra?'

'She evidently agreed with him, hence the son

of a duke and prospects that I could never have provided.'

'I don't think Ginevra would marry a man she wasn't in love with.'

He threw back his head and laughed, cynical hurt laughter.

'I've never met her fiancé, what is he like?'

'Some years older than Ginevra, good-looking if you like that grave remote sort. I'm not sure she's going to have any fun.'

'Marriage is a serious business.'

'Well, she'll get that all right. He's been off the social whirl for years; they met at a race meeting a few months back and suddenly they're engaged and wedding bells are ringing.'

'I'll meet him at her wedding.'

'You know she's invited Alanna Van Royston, I suppose?'

'No I didn't know.'

'That'll cheer the event up, and I'm taking my latest girlfriend, she's a dancer in a London show. Give 'em all something to talk about.'

By this time Algy had returned and was sorting out the drinks.

'Dry Martini, Jane,' he said, 'lager for you Larry, is that right?'

'Yes. We've been talking about Ginevra's wedding.'

'I rather thought you would.'

'Are you staying with Algy's family for a few days?' Jane asked.

'I wanted to get right away from anywhere where I might have bumped into Ginevra. She's going up to Northumberland to stay with

281

Dominic's grandmother for a few days, but I didn't want to stay at home thinking about them up there together.'

Jane did not want to put too much credence on Larry's talk about Ginevra and her fiancé. His words were tinged with bitterness and a remembered pain, he wanted her to take sides, but she was unable to do that. From the years when she had been very close to Ginevra she had always thought she was a kind thoughtful girl; if she had hurt Larry it had been inevitable. She hadn't loved him, and marriage to him would have been impossible.

Larry didn't see it that way, he thought she was marrying for money and position and because her parents wanted it.

While Larry talked and Algy encouraged him Jane thought about her mother. Her mother was doing her level best to push her into a marriage with Algy because it would be lucrative and if she went along with it she would never ever get away from her mother. She would live close by, indulge in the same pursuits, live for ever under her mother's shadow; and if Ginevra could cut the ties that bound her to home and family, she could do the same.

Her father would be on her side, she felt sure of it, and perhaps to a lesser degree her brother and his wife. Elvira and her mother had never been close, her mother thought Elvira spoilt and selfish, Elvira thought her mother overbearing and interfering. Either way Elvira had been adamant from the outset of her marriage that she would spend time in Scotland with her parents and considerably less in the company of the Countess Fortesque.

She suddenly became aware that Algy was looking at her with a broad grin on his face, saying, 'You're miles away, Jane, you're wasting your time talking to her, Larry, she's sure to be on Ginevra's side.'

'I'm sorry, Larry,' she apologised quickly. 'There are other things on my mind, but they have nothing to do with Ginevra. I'm sorry that you're unhappy about things, but it's probably for the best in the long run.'

'I'd expect you to take her side.'

'Larry, there isn't any side. I don't know the man she is marrying, but knowing Ginevra I'm sure she's thought everything out very carefully.'

'You are too complacent, old boy,' Algy said with a wry smile. 'When I decide to take the plunge I'll be certain that the girl I've got my sights on feels the same way.'

'Any ideas who that might be?' Larry asked.

'I'm full of ideas, just waiting for the right moment.'

His eyes were on Jane and there was no disguising the underlying meaning of his words, and Larry laughed. 'It's like that is it, well I hope you have more luck than I did.'

'I shall have. This time I've got the family on my side which is something you never had.'

Jane decided she would not tell her mother that she had spent the morning in Algy's company.

It had started to rain when she rode into the stable yard and a groom came forward immediately to take charge of her horse, and she set off towards the house, surprised to see her father hurrying down the steps to his car.

He waited until she reached him. 'I told you it wasn't a good day to take your horse out, love,' he said, smiling down at her.

'Is Mother in?'

'She's going to a meeting this afternoon, something to do with the show in May.'

'I suppose she'll be asking me to go with her.'

'And you don't want to go?'

'I can think of nothing worse.'

He stood beside her, hesitation evident in his expression, then he turned towards his car. She looked after him for several minutes before she turned to walk up the steps. At the car door he turned and called after her, 'I'd invite you to come with me, Jane, but I'm not sure that you would want to,' he said.

'You're going to see Josie?'

'Yes. It's a gloomy unsettled day, I'm feeling the need for company.'

'It won't take me long to get out of these things, Daddy, can you wait about ten minutes?'

His face lit up with a smile. 'Of course, I'll wait in the car. No need to get all dressed up Jane, life at Josie's is very informal.'

As she rushed upstairs to change he went to his car to wait for her.

Chapter Twenty-One

Elspeth Fortesque stood in the window of the drawing room watching her husband and daughter driving away. She knew where they were going and it didn't worry her. What did irritate her however was the thought that Jane was not accompanying her to the meeting at the Barrington house.

Elspeth saw her life in black or white. She liked people to conform, to say what they meant and disregard having to take note of whether people's feelings were being ignored. She was proud of her upright stance on things that she considered important. She was a commanding figure on the Bench and on every committee that she served on, and they were many and varied. People respected her even when they didn't always agree with her, she prided herself on the fact that when she thought a thing and said a thing she never changed her mind. She hoped that in time Jane would be like her, but she was beginning to realise that her daughter would not be as malleable as she had hoped.

She doted on her son. She had been a good wife and mother, honoured her marriage vows and produced two children, an heir to the title and a daughter she was hoping would marry a most suitable man.

She deplored the fact that she did not get along

with her son's wife. Elvira came from the right stock. She was a Scottish peer's daughter, she had brought breeding, money and stability into the family, but Elvira would not take advice on how to bring up her children and run her home.

She spent long months in Scotland with her family, leaving Andrew to get on with whatever he was doing and hoping he would drive long distances to see her most weekends. Elspeth thought she was spoilt and selfish. When she said as much to her husband and her daughter they simply said they liked Elvira and Andrew was happy enough.

She'd hoped Jane would drive over to the Barringtons with her and spend the afternoon in Algy's company. Now she'd driven off with her father, and what sort of influence would her husband's mistress have on her?

She had seen Josie Marston only once and she'd looked very much as she'd expected her to look. Fashionable, beautiful, and there probably wasn't a brain in her head. Men were such fools about women. How and where John had met her was unimportant, that he got from Josie what he had no wish to get from his wife suited her.

Elspeth had never been much interested in the intimate side of married life. Women talked about being in love, whatever that meant, but she'd sat in court and listened to romantic traumas from a multitude of women, feeling glad that such emotions had never troubled her.

She couldn't understand how Josie Marston was content to be her husband's mistress, to stay in the shadows, to know that she would never be his wife; the entire thing was degrading to her. She was also grateful to her now that her husband never sought her bed and remained perfectly content to allow her to live her life free from any sexual demands he might have subjected her to.

Her fine eyes swept over the parkland, at the deer sheltering under the beech trees, and the ornamental lake churning in a grey solid mass and at the branches of the trees swaying ominously in the sharp wind. There would be a good many apologies for non-attendance at the meeting she felt sure, but hers would not add to them. She seldom missed a meeting, her dedication to whatever endeavour she supported was absolute and with this in mind she thrust her feet into her rubber boots and donned her heavy fawn trenchcoat and pulled an ancient waterproof trilby over her hair.

Her butler waited at the front door carrying an umbrella, but she waved him impatiently aside. 'Tell his Lordship that I may not be in for dinner. I'll probably stay at the Barringtons,' she instructed.

He watched her driving away with a wry smile on his face. The Fortesques were good employers and he repaid them with loyalty and a certain affection. They lived their own lives, but if he ever heard an unkind remark about them being expressed he would defend them loyally.

Elspeth could look forward to a meeting where she sat at the head of the table and made her views known to all present. Most of the people on the committee were ineffectual anyway. They had ideas that were largely impractical, and had only been elected to show the community at large that the landed gentry did not wish to take charge and that everybody's ideas would be considered.

The fact that ideas were singularly unforthcoming suited Elspeth, Algy's father and Viscount Elmsworth: they had the only ideas necessary.

The rain was coming down heavily now as she drove the last few miles to the Barringtons' house. As she drove at last through the gates she could see that there were very few cars parked in the courtyard. That proved how ridiculous it was to have such people on the committee when a few spots of rain could keep them indoors.

She parked the car and marched across the courtyard and through the door which the Barringtons' butler was holding open for her.

'Afternoon Jameson,' she said with a brief smile.

'Good afternoon milady, they're gathered in the study. Not too many of them I'm afraid.'

'They won't be missed,' she snapped as she handed him her trenchcoat and hat.

There were only six men in the study and they greeted her with smiles and words of welcome. They admired her. She was as knowledgeable about country pursuits as any man on the committee and she was a good woman at fighting her corner. None of them fancied her as a woman, none of them envied her husband, and as she took her place at the head of the table and brought the meeting to order Elspeth Fortesque was in her element.

Meanwhile her daughter and her husband were

driving through the village where Josie Marston lived, and Jane was thinking how pretty it was with its stone cottages and leafy country lanes. Stone bridges spanned the gurgling stream that ran along beside the village street and as they reached the centre of the village the lights from the inn streamed out across the square, cheering the wet misery of the day, and Jane thought the scene was beautiful with the square tower of the church and rambling churchyard behind the lych gate. It was a scene explicitly English and she said, 'This is lovely, Daddy, I hadn't realised the villages around here could be so pretty, I love stone cottages, I'd like to live in one.'

He smiled down at her. 'You'll like Josie's house, that's it on the corner there.'

She looked at the house, built of mellow stone and standing on a hill at the junction between two lanes. Ivy and Virginia creeper clothed the stone walls surrounding the house, and the house itself. The windows were diamond-paned. Even as they drove through the gates the front door opened and Josie stood there while a small white dog raced along the drive to stand barking excitedly at the car.

As soon as her father opened the car door the dog leapt into his arms and laughing he said, 'Meet Hamish, Jane. He's a West Highlander.'

Jane took the dog from him and he immediately smothered her face with ecstatic kisses. 'He's beautiful,' she said, 'I've always loved Westies.'

She stood back while Josie went naturally into her father's embrace, then he held out his hands saying, 'I've brought Jane with me, Josie, she's fallen in love with the village.'

Josie smiled and, holding the door open wider, she said, 'I'm so glad to see you Jane, it's such a dreadful afternoon you'll be glad to come in out of the rain.' The house was welcoming with its glowing fire and the tea trolley underneath the window already set out with all the trappings for afternoon tea. It was set for two and Josie said quickly, 'I'll get another setting, do make yourself at home Jane, I can see Hamish has already made you very welcome.'

Josie was gracious. She chatted easily about life in the village, and Jane asked, 'Have you always lived here?'

'No. I had a house very similar to this one and I loved it, but it was too close to Maplethorpe...' Her voice faltered and immediately her father said, 'You must ask Josie to show you round the house Jane, it's a beautiful old house and you love it don't you darling.'

His use of the word darling brought the warm colour into Josie's cheeks and Jane felt a momentary tinge of acrimony. What was she doing here in the home of her father's mistress? She was being disloyal to her mother, condoning what they were doing, and to cover her disquiet she made a fuss of Hamish who responded with short yelps of pleasure.

'Have you done anything about the church's drama group?' her father was asking.

'No, I've left it to them to approach me. They're having a meeting of the group this afternoon to decide on their next play. I expect I'll hear something soon.'

'You would enjoy it dear, give you an interest and you would get to know people.'

Politely Jane asked, 'Are you interested in acting, Josie?'

'I've never done any. They have a very good society, but I'm not sure if I have anything to contribute. The vicar and one or two of the members have approached me, that's as far as it's gone.'

'Is there a theatre in the village?'

'Nothing so grand. They perform in the village hall, but it's quite a nice building and there is a good stage and the seating accommodation is excellent. They have spent quite a lot of money on furnishings.'

'It sounds great.'

'Well, I'm not sure I'd be any good.'

What would they have talked about if she hadn't been there? Jane wondered, and yet, in the peaceful room with the light from the leaping flames of the fire falling on delicate chintz and soft muted colours, on water-colour pictures and a trolley set with fine English bone china and all that was left of Josie's excellent afternoon tea, she felt content.

'Has Hamish been for his walk?' her father asked, and immediately Jane said, 'I'll take him, I'd like to look around the village.'

'No darling, you sit and talk to Josie, get to know each other. I'll take Hamish, he's used to me.'

'I can let him out into the garden,' Josie said quickly, 'you surely don't want to walk in the rain.'

'I rather think the rain's eased off now, dear,

neither of us will melt.'

'I'll show you round the house if you like, Jane,' Josie said and Jane was quick to say, 'Can't I help carry the tea things into the kitchen?'

'We'll leave them for the time being, they will give me something to do when you've gone. Come see the house.'

Jane loved it. This was the sort of house she would like to live in, the sort of village she would like to live in, both of them a far cry from the vast parkland surrounding Maplethorpe and the huge rooms, half of them unlived-in.

All the dreams of her childhood returned as she walked through the house with Josie. While her friends had talked of stately homes and noble sons that were likely to be on the market she had thought about some nice man with a nice car an interest in gardening and a good profession. All right, it was bourgeois and quite painfully not the usual aspirations of a blue-blooded girl whose father could lay claim to an earldom that stretched back into the annals of English history.

Ginevra's engagement had made their mother more determined than ever that Jane should do as well or better, and stretching behind her lay the lonely years when her mother had concentrated too long on Andrew and not long enough on Jane, and when her father had fallen in love with a woman to the exclusion of everything else.

Josie looked down at Jane's pensive expression and as their eyes met she said softly, 'You can probably put the entire house into the size of your dining room.'

'Yes, but this is the sort of house I've always

wanted. Maplethorpe is wasted on me.'

'I can't think that's strictly true Jane, I think we all tend to think that the grass is greener on the other side.'

'Is that what you thought?'

She wished she hadn't said it. She didn't want Josie to think she was accusing her of being a gold-digger. Josie merely smiled gently and in an even, controlled voice said, 'I never had aspirations of grandeur Jane, I was an ordinary smalltown girl who went to parties and village hops, I had girlfriends and several boyfriends, I believed that one day I would marry a decent boy I'd known for ages, somebody my parents knew and liked. I never looked beyond my class; that they looked at me was unbelievable.'

'Understandable I think, you're very beautiful, Josie.'

'My father said it was that that made life difficult for me. The boys I'd always known were unsure if they'd be acceptable, while the boys who admired me but didn't wish to marry me were seemingly unafraid.'

'Are you putting my father in that category?'

'No. Your father wasn't a boy. He was a married man with children. He came to my rescue on an evening when I was hurt and miserable and the amazing thing is that it didn't stop there.'

'Do you love him?'

'Yes. He's the only man I have ever loved. I shall never love anybody else.'

'But surely it isn't enough Josie. You can't be together as you'd like to be.'

'I know. It hurts. I've accepted it and nothing is

going to change.'

'I know my father loves you. Neither of you have got what you want.'

'No, that's true. What do you want from life, Jane? Do you have a job, more and more girls from your walk of life are doing things in the city, in industry, in law?'

'You think my education was wasted on me?'

'Not at all. I merely wonder if perhaps you're not a little bored with the same round of hunt balls, horsy pursuits and the same sort of people who enjoy that kind of thing.'

'It's what I know, what my mother wants me to know. I'm not equipped for a profession, I didn't go to university, I went to finishing school where I was taught to ski, speak better French, learn which wines to serve with which dish and how to make the best of myself physically.

'I could get work, the family name would help me, but then what could I do beyond let the others do the work while I smiled graciously. I doubt if I'm equipped to survive in the harsh world of reality.'

'I can't think that's true. If you've never tried to be anything else how can you know?'

Jane smiled. 'Tell me about Kathy; of all those girls I was at school with she's the one who's really done something with her life, outside marrying the right sort of man that is.'

'You're thinking of Ginevra?'

'Yes. Shall I see Kathy at the wedding?'

'Yes, the last time I saw her she was hunting round for something to wear.'

'Is she taking someone?'

'Yes. A young man in the same law firm. Anthony, it is his uncle's firm, he too is a solicitor.'

'Is it serious?'

'I'm not sure. Kathy was rather noncommittal about it.'

'Did Kathy say if she'd heard from Alanna? I'm sure she has been invited?'

'I'm sure she has.' They looked at each other and laughed.

'Poor Alanna,' Jane said feelingly. 'I'm sure she never wanted her life to be so scandalous. I'm glad I was never a raving beauty, being plain has its compensations.'

'Only you're not plain Jane, never even think it.'

The tour of the house over, they walked down the stairs and had almost reached the hall when they heard the doorbell.

'I wonder who this is,' Josie said, 'unless your father's forgotten his key.'

She opened the door to find the vicar standing on the doorstep, greeting her with a smile and saying, 'It's stopped raining, but I'll leave my umbrella out here in the porch; am I intruding?'

'No of course not vicar, do join us in a cup of tea.'

He stared at Jane uncertainly, and Josie said, 'This is Lady Jane Fortesque, Vicar, Jane this is the Reverend George Kerr.'

They shook hands and the vicar said nervously, 'I can quite easily come round one evening, Miss Marston.'

'No of course not, we're going to have tea anyway. Jane's father has taken Hamish for a walk, he'll be back soon I'm sure.'

As she busied herself with china and waited for the kettle to boil she could hear Jane and the vicar discussing church affairs, the Mothers' Union meetings, the concerts in the village hall, the fêtes to raise money for the church's leaking roof, and she was glad that at least Jane's education had made it easier for her to entertain a singularly nervous man.

It was obvious to Josie that the vicar was unhappy with what he had come to tell her and she was wishing she were by herself. She had faced all the traumas of her life much better when she was alone, but as she handed round tea and cake his eyes refused to meet hers. At last she said gently, 'How did the meeting go, Vicar? I'm sure that is what you've come to talk about?'

'Well yes.' His hands trembled and he spilled tea into his saucer as he hurried to put it down on the small table beside his chair.

'I brought up the matter of you joining us Miss Marston, but it would seem at the moment that we have no vacancies. The position will be reviewed of course before the next show.'

'I wasn't aware that I had applied for a vacancy, Vicar. If you remember you approached me.'

'Of course I did, and I should really have discussed it with the committee before I took it upon myself to do that. We're really a very small group of amateurs. We'll be taking in others I'm sure when our popularity grows.'

'I quite understand, Vicar. Are you ready for more tea?'

'Well no, I really must be going, I have to call

on old Mrs Jackson, I promised her faithfully I'd be in to see her today.'

He rose to his feet and stood uncertainly in the middle of the room while Jane looked at him curiously. She was aware of his nervousness, of Josie's calmness which hid emotions that were painful and unwelcome.

He smiled at her toothily. 'Good afternoon, Lady Jane, I'm so glad to have met you. Perhaps we'll see you at one of our shows one day.'

Jane smiled.

Josie saw him off at the front door and returned to her guest. Her eyes were thoughtful and Jane knew that she was smarting still from the hurt he had dealt her.

'Were you looking forward to joining them, Josie?'

'I suppose so in a way. It would have given me a new interest. However since it hasn't to be I might as well forget about it. I hope your father hasn't got wet; it isn't raining now but it was when he went out. He spoils that dog.'

'I've only ever known labradors, spaniels and deerhounds. My mother breeds them and shows them.' Then she faltered; should she really be discussing her mother's foibles with Josie Marston? But Josie's thoughts were on other things as she piled china on to the tea trolley.

In the next moment the door opened and Hamish rushed into the room wagging his tail and greeting them with short sharp yaps.

'Hamish,' Josie admonished. 'You're wet, come into the kitchen so that I can wipe you down before you go leaping on Jane.'

She was glad to escape with the terrier. She did not want John to see her looking upset, she would tell him about it one day but not today.

It was quite dark as they drove back to Maplethorpe and the rain had started again. Her father's face was thoughtful and she knew he was thinking of the last few moments they had spent with Josie. The talk had been constrained, long silences and nerves.

Josie had wanted them to leave because she was finding it difficult to chat normally when she was churning up inside, and now her father was thinking it had been a mistake to take his daughter with him.

The silence between them was oppressive and she was glad when at last he said, 'You two got along all right, dear?'

'Yes, very well Dad, why do you ask?'

'Because she seemed a little upset about something. You didn't say anything to upset her Jane?'

'No, Daddy you know I wouldn't. The vicar came, he upset her.'

'How could he do that?'

'He isn't inviting her to join the drama group.'

He didn't speak, his expression said it all.

Dinner that night was served in the small dining room because Jane's mother was dining out, and as soon as it was over her father said, 'You haven't anything planned for this evening have you dear?'

'No, I have some letters to write, why?'

'I'll drive over to Josie's, I'm rather worried about her.'

She watched the lights from his car disappearing along the drive. Her mother returned to the house shortly before ten o'clock, her father did not return to the house that night.

Chapter Twenty-Two

The affair was almost over. Lady Fortesque had presented the prizes with her usual air of camaraderie, sympathised with the losers, congratulated the winners and expressed surprise that her springer spaniel had once again collected first prize and Major-General Barrington's black labrador first prize in the gun dog section.

Now people stood around admiring the cups and Jane reflected cynically that it would soon be back taking pride of place in the hall where it had been for as long as she could remember. Different dogs of course, but the cup had been a fixture.

It was one of the main events of the year, and always held in the grounds of the Barringtons' estate on Easter Saturday. It had been a cold but sunny day and children ran in groups across the short grass or clustered round the lake to feed the swans. There had been stalls selling home-made cakes and biscuits, others set out with dog food, dog collars and leads, as well as a collection of walking sticks and camping equipment.

There was a vast marquee where tea and sandwiches had been sold and one corner given over to serve as a bar. Algy and Larry were in charge of this and now that the show was over it was here the younger element were gathered.

Jane had driven her mother and her dog over from Maplethorpe and she was aware that her mother would be in no hurry to depart. She was in her element, giving advice to people who had shown their dogs, receiving congratulations from a great many others.

Dark clouds were gathering over the parkland and Jane decided to wait for her mother in the marquee where she was immediately hailed by Algy.

'Your mother's done it again Jane, and the old man, was there ever any doubt that they'd pull it off?'

Jane smiled, accepting the glass of dry Martini he handed to her. She took her place with the group of men and girls round the bar and one girl made it her business to join her there. Her name was Freda Hawtrey.

The Hawtreys were fairly new to the area, but they had been quick to enter into the life of the villages. They were evidently well supplied with money and both Freda and her father rode with the local hunt and her mother was a live wire on local church charities.

That Freda liked and admired Algy Barrington was very apparent.

'I was hoping to see you today, Jane,' she began. 'Algy tells me you're going to the Midhurst wedding in Berkshire. You're friends of the bride's family, aren't you?'

'I was at school with Ginevra.'

'And you're going to the wedding?'

'Well, yes.'

'I'm going to watch it with my mother, we're not guests, but Mother's simply dying to see Alanna Van Royston. Will she be there, do you know?'

'I'm sure Ginevra has invited her.'

'Gracious yes, she must have.'

'Does your mother know her?'

'Only by reputation darling. We spent a holiday in Santa Lucia several years ago and her parents were there. They have a lovely villa there and a yacht you would die for. Her father's a bit of a lad you know, we met them once or twice and we were invited to sail round the islands on the yacht, but unfortunately we were leaving before anything could be arranged.'

'Did you meet Alanna?'

'She was staying at the villa with her second husband for a long weekend. He was terribly handsome, and he knew it. I wasn't surprised when the marriage ended.'

'Why was that?'

'Oh there were too many women around him, she did awfully well out of it. I can't say I blame her, no doubt he deserved everything he got.'

'Why do you particularly want to see her again?'

'Well, she's news isn't she. I want to see what she's wearing, who she's with and how well she's bounced back. You were at school with her, weren't you?'

'Yes.'

'Was she the gold-digger everybody says she was?'

'There was no need for Alanna to be a gold-digger, she came from a wealthy family.'

'Well, on her mother's side. Her father's a bit of a loose cannon I believe.'

'Alanna didn't talk about her family. I liked her, she was great fun and very beautiful. I'm looking forward to seeing her again.'

'Yes, I'm sure you are. Good luck to her, that's what I say. There's Angela Marston with Johnny Carstairs, he'd better not let his wife see them together.'

Jane turned away with some distaste and Freda said quickly, 'I'm not really being bitchy Jane, nobody really cares any more, at least not our generation. All the bad feeling comes from the older generation, and people who are really too middle-class.'

When Jane stared at her she grinned. 'I'm middle-class Jane so I know what I'm talking about. People in your class have been having affairs for yonks and nobody really cares; it's only silly nosy people who have nothing better to do that chatter.'

Freda's bright blue eyes were filled with speculation and Jane was wishing she could make an excuse and walk away, but some strange instinct compelled her to stay. She fully expected that at any time Freda would bring her father into the conversation, but at that moment Algy joined them saying, 'Well, have you asked Jane if Alanna'll be at the wedding? She's been badgering me for days.'

'Yes, she'll be there,' Freda said.

'There'll be more interest in Alanna than

there'll be in the bride and groom.'

'Well, bad girls are more interesting than good ones,' Freda laughed.

'Why do you call Alanna a bad girl?' Jane asked. 'Simply because she's divorced a rotten husband?'

'Two blue-blooded ones darling, and taken one of them to the cleaner's.'

Algy looked at Jane uncertainly. He was aware that she was finding the conversation distasteful. Handing him her empty glass she said, 'I'll see if my mother's ready to go home. It's looking more and more like a storm out there.'

'Two weeks to the wedding,' Algy said, 'shall we see you before?'

'I'm not sure Algy, if not I'll see you there.'

'Me too darling,' Freda said brightly. 'Oh, not as a guest, but I wouldn't miss it for worlds. I suppose the village will be crowded for the event.'

Jane smiled, and was glad to move away.

Spots of rain were already falling as she left the marquee and she was glad to see her mother walking with Major-General Barrington across the grass together with their respective dogs adorned with their rosettes.

'Not off already, Jane?' Algy's father said, a bright smile illuminating his florid face.

'Well, I thought Mother might be ready to go home. There's going to be a storm.'

'I thought we'd have a hot toddy, you're not driving Elspeth.'

'No, but I think I should get Rory back, it's been a long wearisome day for him,' Elspeth said handing his lead to Jane. 'You take the dog Jane, this cup is very heavy.'

'He did well, Mother.'

'Well, yes, nothing unexpected in that, I knew he'd do well.'

'Your dog too, General,' Jane said.

'Of course. Your mother and I know what we're about where dogs and horses are concerned. Why aren't you more interested in such things, Jane?'

'I like dogs and horses, but I'm not interested in showing them.'

'Pity, with your mother behind you you'd do well.'

'I'll put Rory in the brake, Mother, and wait for you. There's a storm brewing.'

Her mother screwed up her eyes and looked at the sky. 'Heavens yes, what a good thing we've had the best of the day.'

By the time Jane reached the car park the rain was coming down and Rory stretched out at the back of the brake with evident contentment. He'd been walked, trotted and raced around the show ring, now after a bowl of fresh water he was well disposed to wait for his owner, and Jane was glad to get into the front seat to wait for her mother.

She would be in no hurry. She'd be surrounded by like-minded people only too anxious to talk about their dogs, and if she could hear the rain beating on the roof of the tent she'd delay joining her as long as possible. Fortunately there was a book in the dashboard compartment that she could read until her mother decided to join her.

People were hurrying to their cars now through the puddles that had formed across the parking lot, and it was hardly light enough for her to read.

She was suddenly startled by a rap on the window of the brake and looking up she found Larry Harbrook grinning at her and she lowered the window.

'Are you off then Jane?' he asked.

'As soon as my mother joins me.'

'They're all in the tent drinking hot toddies, she'll be ages. Mind if I join you for a while?'

She shook her head and he hurried round to the passenger's door.

'Are you staying with Algy?' she asked.

'No, I'm off home now. I'm going up to London for the weekend.'

'That's nice.'

'Yes it is. Heard from Ginevra?'

'Not since I received her wedding invitation.'

He grinned. 'It'll beat me if this wedding comes off. Did you know they were in Madeira?'

'Who?'

'Ginevra and her marquis.'

'Well, what of it?'

'I've always understood the honeymoon comes after the wedding, not before it.'

'You're surmising a lot, Larry.'

'You have to admit there's something odd about it. The wedding's in just over two weeks and both of them out of the country. I personally think we'll be receiving cancellation notices within the immediate future.'

'Isn't that wishful thinking on your part?'

'No, it's what a lot of people are saying and thinking.'

'How do you know they're in Madeira – not from her parents I'm sure?'

'From the old biddy in the post office, she doesn't miss a trick.'

'It must be lovely to be in Madeira right now when you look at that sky and the rain coming down.'

'Jane, Jane, forget the rain, think of the implications.'

'No, Larry. You want something to go wrong with this wedding because you're hurt and angry. I don't think we should speculate unkindly about it, we should wait and see.'

'I'm not hurt and angry, I'm over her, I've replaced her.'

She looked at his young indignant face and smiled. 'All right, Larry, if you say so,' she said gently.

'I hope you don't keep Algy Barrington dangling like Ginevra's had me dangling. If you do you'll lose him. It's make your mind up time, Jane.'

Jane had never been so glad to see her mother hurrying across the lot with her head down against the wind. Larry said quickly, 'I'd better get out of here, I'll see you soon Jane, but I doubt if it'll be at the wedding.'

He leapt out of the car, holding the door open gallantly for Lady Fortesque to take her seat, favouring her with a bright smile and saying, 'Just been keeping Jane company for a few minutes, your dog looks worn out.'

'Yes, well, we're all a little tired. I shall be glad to get home and out of this storm,' her Ladyship answered him, then smiled at him as he stood in the rain while they drove away.

'How long has he been sitting here?' her mother demanded.

'Only a few minutes. He's driving home to Berkshire.'

'He's not staying for the weekend then?'

'No, he's spending it in London.'

'Did he say anything about Ginevra's wedding?'

'Not really. He's been invited of course.'

She was aware that her mother was looking at her and that she knew something of what she and Larry had talked about. Her mother said nothing, however, probably mindful of the last time she had voiced her opinion about Ginevra's wedding and Jane's response to it.

Jane had little doubt that everybody would be speculating even when they probably knew very little. If Ginevra was out of the country with her fiancé there was probably a good reason for it, but she couldn't avoid her unspoken anxieties. Dominic's lost love, Ginevra's one-time romance with Larry, surely neither of these things was surfacing now.

Over the dinner table that evening her mother enthused about her success at the dog show and her father listened politely, his congratulations entirely sincere, and after talk of Rory's prowess in the show ring was exhausted her father said, 'Andrew telephoned, his wife and baby are home now, they'd like you to spend a few days with them, Jane.'

Jane's eyes lit up. She could talk to Andrew and his wife about things she could never discuss with her mother. They would laugh about Algy, be entirely relaxed about Ginevra's engagement, and there would be the baby to spend time with.

She left her parents sitting on each side of the fireplace, her mother with her needlepoint, her father reading, a nice solid picture of peaceful compatibility showing nothing of the tensions between them, and in her bedroom she thought about Josie, alone except for her little dog Hamish. Was the love of a man really worth all that?

She felt restless. She wished Larry Harbrook hadn't told her about Ginevra in Madeira, she wished the woman in the post office had had the good sense to mind her own business. Then she decided quite out of the blue to telephone Kathy Marston.

It was some considerable time since she'd spoken to Kathy; they'd exchanged Christmas and birthday cards, but that had been all, now she felt it was important to be one of the old crowd again, one of the four girls who'd weathered growing up together. She couldn't talk to Ginevra, she didn't know where to find Alanna, but she did have Kathy's telephone number and on a night when rain beat heavily against the window and trees tossed in the parkland, Kathy could be at home.

A man's voice answered her, but when she asked if Kathy was there he said, 'I'll get her for you, who is calling?'

'Jane Fortesque, who is that?'

'Kathy's father,' the man said and there was silence.

Kathy's voice was as she remembered, sweet

and lilting, obviously pleased that she'd called, and almost breathlessly Jane said, 'I'm so glad to hear you Kathy, I should have rung before, there wasn't really anything to tell you. Shall I see you at the wedding?'

'Yes, of course, that will be lovely.'

'Are you going alone?'

'No, I'm taking Anthony Greavson, we're both solicitors in the same firm, his uncle's firm actually.'

'Is he nice?'

'Very nice.'

'Is it serious?'

'No. I thought it could have been, now I know it isn't.'

'Sounds intriguing.'

'Not really. Perhaps we know each other too well, working together, seeing each other every day.'

'But you like him well enough to invite him to escort you to the wedding.'

'Yes, I didn't want to go alone. Have you heard from Alanna?'

'No, have you?'

'No.'

'I wonder if she'll be there, so many things have happened to Alanna. It would be nice to see her.'

'Yes, are you taking someone, Jane?'

'No. I'm going with my parents.'

'Is there anyone?'

'My mother would like there to be, we don't agree on the subject.'

Kathy laughed. 'Have you met Ginevra's fiancé?'

'No. My parents know his parents, that's all.'

Jane wanted to ask Kathy if she'd heard any rumours about Ginevra's engagement, but she realised that Kathy would be the last to hear. She didn't move in those circles. Incredibly, Kathy lived her life in the sort of environment Jane fancied herself in, respectable, ordinary; why wasn't she happy with her young solicitor?

She suddenly found herself saying, 'I visited your Aunt Josie a few weeks ago Kathy, did she tell you?'

'Yes, she did.'

'And you were surprised.'

'I suppose so. I'm very fond of Josie, she was the one most beautiful person in my life when I was growing up. She brought a certain glamour into it. I don't expect you to understand, Jane.'

'Oh but I do. She's beautiful and gracious. I like her, my father adores her.'

'You minded very much at one time.'

'I know. I don't mind any more. I've grown up.'

'I'm not sure that growing up has anything to do with it, Jane.'

'No, perhaps not, but I understand things so much better now. You're still living with your father?'

'Yes.'

'You've never thought of getting your own place?'

'Several times. One day I'll find something or someone, in the meantime I'm very attached to this old house and the main street near the shops and the market stalls. Most people would hate it, I've grown up with it.'

'Just like I'm stuck with this old house surrounded by miles of parkland. It will never be mine Kathy, one day it will go to Andrew.'

'And you'll be in something similar with a new husband.'

'That's the norm, maybe I'll change the pattern.'

'I do hope we'll be able to have a long chat at the wedding. I'll introduce you to Anthony, you'll like him.'

Long after she had put the receiver down Jane thought about their conversation. There had been something so confident about Kathy's voice, she had a good profession, she had done so much with her life, and now there was a man in it she could afford to disregard as being not what she wanted. She wondered why.

She would spend Easter with her brother and his family. That should take her mind off the forthcoming wedding and whether it was on or off. She was wishing heartily she had never spoken to Larry Harbrook, quite obviously he was bitter, revelling in any titbit of gossip he could find to unsettle her about the wedding and lift his own spirits.

If she went to stay with Andrew she would get away from Algy who was becoming more and more persistent, encouraged by her mother and his own parents.

A knock on her bedroom door heralded her father coming to say goodnight, and with a wry smile he said, 'What have you done with yourself all evening?'

'I telephoned Kathy Marston, it's ages since I

spoke to her.'

'That was nice, dear.'

'She's going to the wedding, taking some man she works with.'

'Yes. His uncle's firm of solicitors I believe.'

'You know him, Daddy?'

'No. I know his uncle, a highly respected firm, your friend has done well to find employment with them.'

'Kathy was always the clever one.'

'Yes well, she had to be, didn't she. When are you off to stay with Andrew?'

'Over Easter I thought.'

'That's a good idea, you'll enjoy it.'

'I don't suppose Mother will mind?'

'Why should she?'

'Perhaps I should ask her, she may have plans.'

'Not that concern you I'm sure. Her only plans concern you and Algy, I think you can afford to cool them a little, don't you dear?'

The Day of Days

Chapter Twenty-Three

Clara Greavson eyed her son with the utmost exasperation. She didn't understand Anthony these days because he simply refused to answer her questions. She wanted to know if it was really over between him and Kathy Marston. Oh, there was the wedding he'd promised to attend, but that surely didn't commit him to anything. In actual fact he seemed to know very little about it; and then there was Zoey Perkins. He'd been seeing more of her, they'd played golf together and dined out once or twice, but her oblique references to Zoey had met with blank stares.

Over the breakfast table Clare decided to have one more try.

'Have you bought a wedding present yet, Anthony?' she asked evenly.

'Kathy has it in hand, Mother.'

'From the wedding present list?'

'I don't know if there is a list, the bride has asked for a jade horse she's admired for ages.'

His mother raised her eyebrows. 'Jade! Isn't that terribly expensive, where are you going to find that?'

'Kathy's had it for years. Apparently her friend always wished it was hers, Kathy's decided to give it to her.'

'How unusual. I believed brides thought in

315

terms of dinner services and good china. Have you seen it?'

'Yes, Kathy showed it to me. It's simply a small jade horse on an ebony stand. Chinese, I think.'

'Well, it probably would be. How did she come by it?'

'Mother, I have no idea.'

His mother had her own thoughts about the jade horse. Probably a present from her aunt's lover, or how could the Marstons possibly afford anything in jade?

Anthony was wishing his mother would drop the subject of the wedding. Kathy had told him very little apart from the fact that she had known the bride at school and they hadn't met for a good number of years. He wasn't in a position to discuss it with his mother because he knew very little about it.

He had been unable to find accommodation anywhere near the Abbey; it seemed every establishment in the vicinity was fully booked and when he asked Kathy if she knew if some other popular functions were going on at the same time she simply shook her head.

They had decided to set off early in the morning and drive to their destination. Driving a hundred miles in morning dress and Kathy's wedding finery was hardly going to be comfortable, but there was no alternative. His mother had been predictably scathing.

'Berkshire is always crowded,' she'd said, 'after all people do want to visit Windsor and they probably live in a small house and are unable to accommodate wedding guests. After all you're not family are you, Anthony?'

He'd been so sure that Kathy was right for him. A beautiful clever girl sharing his profession, good at what she did, a favourite with his uncle, so what had gone wrong?

His father had liked her, his mother would have come to terms with it, but from that afternoon when he had introduced her to his parents something had gone out of their relationship. His mother was like a dog with a bone about Kathy's aunt and her aristocratic lover, but scandal like that didn't matter any more, it was archaic to think it did.

Kathy should have understood his mother's concerns and learned to live with it. If they had given themselves a chance to really get to know each other she would have seen that his mother was charming, and his mother would have discovered that Kathy was just what she wanted in a daughter-in-law.

He would escort her to the wedding in Berkshire, make the best of it, be nice to her friends and then he had little doubt that all they would have in common was their work. They'd be good colleagues, nothing more.

Kathy too knew that they had reached the end of the line. She could have tried harder, resolved herself into understanding his mother and forgiving her for her scruples, but she knew in her heart it wouldn't have worked out. Anthony was very much his mother's boy, his entire life had been conditioned that way and she realised that she didn't love him enough to change it.

Her father thought it was a shame that their

friendship had gone sour, his uncle too. Kathy was a great asset to the firm; in a liaison with Anthony they would have gone far, now every day he realised they became more and more distant. Perhaps this wedding would bring them together, make Anthony see what he was missing. When he said as much to his wife she retorted, 'Clara's the last person I'd want for my mother-in-law and Kathy's had the good sense to see it.'

'But she's not really important, is she?'

'Oh she's important all right. Forget about it darling, it's not going to happen. Anthony will marry some girl his mother totally approves of and Kathy will find somebody else.'

There was dissension in the Midhurst household where his Lordship was undeniably tetchy and his Countess worried.

It was Easter weekend and the wedding was less than two weeks away. Ginevra and her fiancé were still enjoying the delights of Madeira and her mother sat at the breakfast table with Ginevra's letter in her hand.

'Well,' her husband demanded, 'does she say when she's coming home?'

'No.'

'What does she say?'

'The weather is wonderful, they are seeing something of the island which is very beautiful, and we mustn't worry.'

Her husband snorted, and looking down at the envelope Lady Midhurst said, 'The letter's been on the way a week, there's probably another one coming.'

'She should say if the wedding's on or off.'

'I'm sure she will, dear.'

'But when, that's what I want to know.'

Lady Midhurst couldn't think that her daughter would be cruel enough to keep them in suspense much longer. Surely she and Dominic had resolved their differences by this time. Ginevra was expecting too much, the love she wanted would come later, grow with the years.

Her husband was rustling his paper irritably.

'You can bet all the village is talking about this wedding,' he said. 'They'll be asking themselves, where she is, why nobody's seen her around. Then those letters from Madeira, don't think the fact that they're there hasn't got around.'

'It's nobody's business but ours, dear.'

'They'll make it their business.'

Unknown to his Lordship and his wife their butler was having similar heart-searchings. Gossip among the staff was rife and he'd had to admonish them to refrain from chattering among themselves, their loyalty, all their loyalty rested with the family.

The village post-mistress was the worst offender and every time he went into the post office she was asking questions. His own re-strained behaviour only made her worse, and there was that malicious gleam in her eye that annoyed him intensely.

Lady Ginevra should be at home helping her mother with the arrangements, attending wedding rehearsals, opening wedding presents. With only weeks to go it was ridiculous that she and her fiancé were abroad.

As he walked through the parkland on a cold blustery day his thoughts were interrupted by the sight of a low-slung tourer driving through the gates and his eyes followed it as it made its way along the drive, finally coming to rest in the courtyard outside the front door. His eyes strained into the distance to where two people stood together, a man and a woman, then after a brief embrace the man got into the car and drove away.

The wind took his breath away as he hurried in the direction of the house, and then Ginevra was waiting on the drive and he hurried forward to take the single suitcase out of her hands.

He smiled. 'Welcome home Milady,' he said, 'I'll have your suitcase taken upstairs, I expect you'd like tea.'

She smiled. 'Yes, thank you Charlton, tea will be lovely. Are my parents at home?'

'Yes Milady, and very anxious to see you I'm sure.'

By this time her mother was already in the hall. She had seen their arrival, seen Dominic looking down at her with his grave sweet smile, followed by their swift embrace before he drove away and her heart had sunk. Why wasn't he coming into the house, was this it then, was it over?

Ginevra embraced her mother warmly, and her face was smiling serenely. It was not the face of a girl who had seen her fiancé driving away from her for ever, but then perhaps she hadn't cared.

She was too nervous to ask questions, but not so her father, who said, 'So you've decided to come home at last to put us out of our misery.

320

Why isn't Dominic with you, or has he left it to you to put us in the picture?'

'I didn't want him to come in now Father, and he does have a very long drive home. I'm sure his parents are as anxious as you and Mother.'

'I'm sure they are. Well, are we to have a wedding or are we to send the presents back and cancel the affair?'

'What an old fusspot you are. Don't you think I'd have been home sooner than this if things hadn't been working out? There is to be a wedding. Exactly as planned, and before you say another word, I am very happy about it and so is Dominic.'

Her mother burst into tears, tears of relief, and impatiently her father said, 'There's no cause to cry now, what would you have done if she'd said the wedding was off?'

Charlton was coming in with a maid to serve afternoon tea, and his Lordship said quickly, 'No tea for me Charlton, I'll have a whisky and soda, the ladies will have tea.'

Charlton took in the Countess's tear-stained face even when her expression was serene and happy. Oh, surely all was well, and even as he handed his Lordship his whisky and soda Lady Ginevra said, 'You'll be glad when these next few weeks are over, Charlton, and the house gets back to normal.'

Charlton smiled, 'The staff will cope Milady, we're all looking forward to it.'

'I'm sure you are.'

Later that evening her mother was able to hand her the letters of acceptance to their wedding invitations, and wryly she said, 'You will see that Alanna intends to be here as well as Kathy Marston.'

'I'm glad, Mother, I wanted them to come. Are they bringing escorts?'

'Kathy is bringing someone, not Alanna. I'm glad about that, it's difficult enough that she's coming on her own, speculation would have been rife if she'd brought a man with her.'

'I don't see why, she's a free woman.'

'Recently, and with her track record she should keep it that way for some considerable time.'

Ginevra laughed. 'Oh Mother, how old-fashioned you are. Alanna had a rotten playboy husband, two of them actually, there wouldn't have been all the fuss if her second husband had been a nonentity. The fact that he was a world class playboy made it difficult for her.'

'And how about you Ginevra, you should put my mind at rest after all this worry. Are you quite sure Dominic is who you want and has he put your mind at rest about how he feels about you?'

'It wasn't immediate Mother. We were really two strangers whom society put together. He had been desperately in love with somebody else; she was dead, but he'd never really been able to forget her. I haven't asked him to forget her, but simply to come to terms with the fact that she is never coming back and I should be given a chance.'

'And has he given you that chance?'

'Yes. He may never love me like he loved her, after all they were very young, it was first love for both of them, free and wild and emotional, with me he'll find something he never found with her, serenity and honesty.'

'Honesty?'

'Why yes. Melinda was mercurial. She teased and flirted and there were times when he felt unsure of her. How strange it is that that sort of behaviour makes a man keener and more anxious. It isn't in me to behave like that, Dominic will always be sure of me, I couldn't pretend anything I didn't feel.'

'I hope he'll appreciate it.'

'He has. I've seen it in his eyes, in his attitude, more and more every day, a sort of inner contentment, like coming home.'

'When will you see him again?'

'Soon Mother, he'll telephone me tomorrow, after all there's an awful lot to see to. He'll be here within a few days.'

Those were the words that reassured her mother. She would see them together, form her own judgement.

In the meantime Dominic was reassuring his own parents that all was well. The wedding would take place, there was no cause for concern.

His father thought it was a storm in a teacup, his mother thought common sense had triumphed over stupidity. The stupidity had nothing to do with Ginevra, Ginevra was just what Dominic needed, it had all to do with that silly Irish girl who had haunted him for too many years. Now at last he would relegate her to a misspent past and come to a proper understanding of where his future lay.

Their talk turned to more pressing matters. Dominic's choice of a best man and groomsmen, relieved that he had decided it would be his younger brother and that the groomsmen would be Ginevra's brothers and one of their friends.

'What about the bridesmaids?' she demanded.

'Oh Ginevra's nieces and two young boys. Ginevra will have it all in hand.'

The boulevards surrounding Georges Briacces' imposing fashion house were crowded with smart cars while a steady procession of expensively dressed women moved in the direction of the ornamental façade and artistically designed glass doors.

It was the highlight of Easter Week, Briacces' Spring Parade when he showed his offerings to the world at large. The women came in all age groups, nubile young girls and fat matrons tottering on their high heels, fashionable film stars and actresses, belles of high society and foreign aristocracy. Inside the building gilt chairs had been set out surrounding carpeted catwalks, while Georges Briacces himself wandered around greeting his guests with enthusiastic charm, kissing their cheeks and their hands, a small dapper man, faintly effeminate, waving slender hands and oozing affected charm.

There was music and the sound of women's voices and laughter. Georges was well pleased with his new creations, everything had gone really well and as always he expected huge sales. It was in the midst of euphoria that silence suddenly descended and all eyes turned towards the entrance where an elegant young woman surveyed the scene before her out of jade green eyes.

Alanna Van Royston was the focus of all eyes as she stood draped in sable, her blue-black hair framing a face of cool sophisticated beauty.

Georges rushed to her side, raising her hand to his lips, and beaming with gratification. 'Your Highness, how wonderful to see you. Why did you not let me know you intended to be here? I would have found you a special place.'

'I don't want a special place Georges, and I am no longer a Princess, I have reverted to my maiden name of Van Royston.'

'Is that so, then tell me what you hope to find, something for the grand occasion I feel sure.'

'A wedding in England.'

'Ah. Elegant, circumspect, nothing too outrageous. You will find something.'

For days Alanna had scanned the clothes in her wardrobes and there had been so many of them. Clothes for all occasions and each one of them carrying a memory of times she preferred to forget. Too much of a crowd, too many insincerities, too much money and not enough values.

As the models paraded before her Georges scanned her expression for any sign that one gown above all others gave her pleasure. It seemed nothing was what she was looking for until a subtle awareness crept into her eyes as the vision in white wild silk swept down the catwalk complemented by the large black straw hat adorned with its black organdie flowers edged with white.

Perhaps white was inappropriate, she thought. She did not wish to compete with the bride, but this dress was hardly bridal, it was simply something different, the sort of gown they would expect to see her in. Wearing this ensemble nobody would be disappointed.

She wasn't sure about the hat. Her mother had always maintained that black did not go with her blue-black hair, but Georges enthused that the flowers edged with white enhanced the beauty of her face.

Her mind went back to other weddings she had attended in England where pretty blues and pinks had been prevalent, and she smiled cynically at the thought of raised eyebrows and unspoken criticism.

She had not been surprised to find that accommodation was difficult to find in the villages surrounding Saunderscourt, but there was her mother's friend Avis Mannheim living only a few miles away. When she telephoned them to ask if she could stay with them for just two nights prior to the wedding Avis was delighted.

Alanna knew that Avis would be avid with her questioning about her parents, the state of their marriage, and the scandal surrounding her own marriages. It didn't really matter, she could put up with it for two nights.

It was decided that she would take the afternoon train out of London and Avis and her husband Ralph would meet her at Reading station, a scheme which suited Alanna since there would only then be two evenings when she would be subjected to their scrutiny and their questions.

Since her arrival in Paris she had had several telephone calls from her mother which all followed the same pattern.

'Alanna, I really don't think you should go to this wedding in England, at least not on your own.'

'Why ever not, Mother. I am on my own.'

'That's just it darling. All those girls you knew will have escorts, perhaps even husbands.'

'I don't think so. They hadn't when we exchanged Christmas cards and the usual letter.'

'But they'll be surrounded by families, people they know, they'll be taking escorts.'

'Mother, it doesn't matter.'

'Well it matters to me. I don't want you to be the subject of gossip.'

'Mother, this is Ginevra's wedding, they'll have more to think about than me and the sort of mess I've made of my life.'

'Stop saying that Alanna, it wasn't your fault. It was the media's fault, they got it all wrong.'

'Some of it, Mother, not all of it.'

'Well anyway. Why don't I come up to Paris and stay with you for a few days, then we can go off somewhere, on a cruise ship, Egypt, the Far East.'

'You could go to Santa Lucia if you're so interested in travelling, Mother.'

'I don't want any of that, Alanna. I'm not ready to see your father. Have you heard from him?'

'I've spoken to him on the telephone.'

'What's he doing about that boat?'

'Why don't you ask him? We didn't speak of it.'

'I can tell you're determined to go to this

327

wedding; what are you going to wear?'

'I haven't decided.'

'I suggest something unobtrusive, a nice pastel dress and hat that goes so well with your colouring. Nothing sensational Alanna, that's what they'll all be expecting to see.'

Now whenever the telephone rang she cringed. It could only be her mother issuing the same old strictures.

Her father would not telephone, he was off on his boat with yet another group of people who had been anxious to charter her. She sensed in him a desperation. He'd never worried about money, somehow or other he'd always believed that it would surface just when he needed it, now for the first time in his life he was being made to realise that it wasn't going to happen.

He had really believed her mother would relent, and by this time he must surely have got the message that he was on his own. Alanna was simply hoping that he would not do anything foolish, but allow her to help him.

Chapter Twenty-Four

Although it was the end of April there had been a keen frost in the night and Ginevra stood at her bedroom window looking out across a parkland shimmering with silver. The weather forecast had been for a fine sunny day, but cold.

She surveyed her wedding dress draped from

the top of a wardrobe with its long train extending the length of the room. It was beautiful, its lines elegant and uncluttered by frills and flounces, but the heavy parchment satin was adorned by countless pearls and exquisite embroidery.

It was early, barely seven o'clock, and the wedding wasn't until two in the afternoon. By the time they left the Abbey the onlookers would be ready to go to their homes and get out of the chill April breeze.

She expected there would be a great many onlookers. The villagers had been filled with anticipation for months and she had no doubt that they would line the main street and the country road leading up to the Abbey. The village with its surrounding farmland had been built around Saunderscourt. The Lords of the Manor had built the schools, and the village church had had a hand in every detail of village life. From the library to the park on the outskirts of the village Ginevra's ancestors had played a prominent part. The name of Midhurst was everywhere from the statue erected to her great-grandfather in the square to the long list of benefactors who had sat in the courthouse, acted as governors at most of the schools, provided playing fields and tennis courts, and served on every committee connected with village life.

They had seen Ginevra and her brothers grow up, and their gratification that she was to marry the son of a Duke reflected on all of them. If this wedding had been doomed not to take place the trauma would have been too terrible to contemplate, and yet she would not have hesitated. If she really believed that Dominic could never love her, then she would not have gone through with it.

Those first few days in Madeira had not been easy, they were both trying too hard. Dominic had deliberately chosen a small unpretentious hotel on the hillside above Funchal, a place where they were unlikely to meet people they knew, and unlike Reid's where they would have been sure to meet acquaintances or friends known to both of them.

It was one morning when they walked into the town so that Ginevra could look at the shops selling Madeira's exquisite embroidered tray-cloths and bedlinen that she heard her name being called by a woman standing looking at a large tablecloth two assistants were holding out for her, and, dismayed, she recognised Aunt Esmeralda, her mother's youngest sister.

She smiled uncertainly, and her aunt said, 'What on earth are you doing here Ginevra and your wedding only weeks away?'

Just then Dominic joined her and her aunt's face registered comical amazement.

'Gracious, you're both here,' her aunt said, and Dominic with easy charm said, 'to get a little sunshine to bolster us up. I suspect you're here for the same reason.'

'Is your mother here too, Ginevra?' her aunt asked.

'No, just the two of us.'

Her aunt's face betrayed some doubt, even disapproval, and Dominic said easily, 'We believed

330

we should get to know each other earlier rather than later. This was an inspiration.'

'I see.'

She didn't see, and Ginevra was quick to ask, 'Are you staying at Reid's?'

'No, we're on a cruise ship, that one out there, we're on our way back from the Canaries. We were rushing to get this holiday in before your wedding and here you both are with similar ideas.'

Her aunt was nervous, not wanting to say the wrong thing, and Ginevra thought, she knows about Dominic and Melinda, everybody knows about them.

She had little doubt as soon as her aunt returned home she would be on the telephone to her mother, who would be tearful, expressing every doubt she had about her future with Dominic.

'Where are you staying?' her aunt demanded.

'A lovely small hotel overlooking the harbour.'

'Not Reid's?'

'No, we wanted something quieter.'

Every word she uttered enlarged the hole she was digging for herself and in the end it was Dominic saying evenly, 'Well, we'll have to leave you to select your tablecloth Lady Acton, you'll find they have a very wide choice.'

His hand was firm under her elbow as they exchanged smiles and farewells and then they were outside the shop and walking back towards their hotel.

Ginevra was wishing they'd met anybody else but Aunt Esmeralda. Of her mother's three sisters she was the most difficult. She thrived on scandal, had created some of it herself in her early years. Now she was married to a man twenty years older than herself, a taciturn, withdrawn man who hated all the things that had so captivated his wife in her youth. Now they seldom visited London and seemed to spend all their time in the country where he owned a vast estate and a large crumbling house which he prized and she deplored.

The sight of her niece and her fiancé in Madeira would be something Esmeralda could get her teeth into and conceivably find her something to think about outside her rather dull existence.

Ginevra couldn't really imagine how her aunt had been able to get him on a cruise, indeed her mother had said 'Don't be surprised if they don't come to your wedding dear, it'll be Henry, not Esmeralda.'

There had been magic in those few weeks in Madeira. The blue sea and the warm sunshine, the lush hills reverberating with the sound of goat bells, and pealing church bells. There they had swum together, walked together and discovered themselves. For the first time in years Dominic found that Melinda was receding in his memory and he was finding Ginevra. Young, pretty, a girl with an enquiring mind and a searching honesty.

He asked himself why he'd been content all those years with the cherishing of a dream. Melinda had kept him chained to her, by her quick-silver mind and the fact that he had never felt truly sure of her. She had been the first girl he had ever loved and he had been so young and ready for love.

Suppose she hadn't died? He had never been able to visualise marriage to Melinda even when he had wanted it. Her wants had been many and varied. Her desires, once realised, had been short-lived. Would he too have been discarded once she had possessed him? He had asked himself these questions hundreds of times, but then she had died and the questions remained unanswered.

In those long years after her death all he could remember was her beauty, her laughter and her passion, and in his foolish heart he had told himself that of course their love would have lasted. Now he was discovering that Ginevra was not the tease Melinda had been. Ginevra wanted things that were within reach, there were no demands for fanciful things, only genuine attempts to please him, to know him, to give of herself.

He began to see that with Melinda his life could have been exciting and unpredictable, with Ginevra it would be caring and serene.

She had seemed so incredibly young, too young he'd thought, but there was a maturity about her and as the days passed he felt himself becoming more relaxed, more youthful, more like the man he had once been before Melinda had bewitched him.

During the last few days since they had arrived home Ginevra had been constantly aware of the speculation in her mother's expression, the unspoken question, 'Ginevra, are you sure?'

She was sure. She loved Dominic and he would love her. It was almost there, she could feel it, all that old fascination was fading into the past, now he was seeing her and their future together.

There was a small tap on her bedroom door and her maid entered carrying a tray with her morning tea. The girl smiled and wished her good morning. 'It's cold Milady,' she said, 'but it's a lovely mornin', it's goin' to be a lovely day.'

Ginevra smiled. 'Thank you Polly. It's going to be a busy day.'

'Gracious me yes, Milady. The kitchen staff 'ave been up since six-thirty, all the comin' and goin' there's goin' to be today. The dress is beautiful, you'll look lovely, Lady Ginevra.'

'Thank you Polly. It is a pretty dress isn't it.'

She thought about the day in front of her. The banquet and the guests; her gaggle of young bridesmaids and the two page boys, both of whom had been reluctant. One the son of her eldest brother and his wife, the other the son of Dominic's sister. Both of them deploring the fact that they'd be tricked out in velvet, even when the bridesmaids were loving the idea.

At eleven would come the hairdresser. The house would be bursting with caterers, waiters and bartenders. Her father would be locked in his study no doubt fuming, and her mother would be endeavouring to do a hundred and one things at once.

What would Dominic be doing at this moment? They were all staying with their close friends the Forresters who owned an Elizabethan castle about twenty miles away. Ginevra had spent two weekends there where she'd first met Dominic's parents. Weekends in rooms where Good Queen Bess would have felt at home, with their dark low ceilings and winding staircases, tapestry-hung walls and wandering passages where at any moment she'd thought to encounter the ghost of some long-dead Elizabethan.

She had been warmly welcomed by her host and hostess, and had found Dominic's parents charming and unpretentious. They had been surrounded by a motley collection of dogs, and she had listened to her host telling her the history of the place, how long it had been in the family, and the rather more alarming story of the ghost of a nun who appeared regularly in the west wing and announced her arrival with melancholy sighs.

Across the table she had found Dominic smiling at her, and lightly he said, 'I've been coming here for years, Ginevra, and I've never seen the lady.'

There were several people present who unfortunately had seen the nun, and they took great delight in telling her about the vision, while the younger members of the party embroidered on it with gruesome delight.

She was wondering idly why Jane wasn't bringing someone. She knew that Algy Barrington held hopes about Jane, but the Jane she knew was not for Algy. The Barringtons were Jane's mother's friends and Jane had never conformed to the sort of girl her mother wanted her to be. Besides Algy was too much like Larry. Good company, brash, too full of themselves. If Jane married Algy they'd end up like her parents with one or both of them in love with somebody else.

Kathy Marston was bringing an escort and she believed she knew the type of young man he would be. Young, good-looking and ambitious. Clever too as Kathy was clever. Some young man who would provide her with a very nice house and contented lifestyle. They would never be short of money, they'd both have careers and if they had children they'd go to good schools and make careers for themselves. She really did feel that Kathy's life would be the most predictable of the lot, steady, well-organised, nothing to worry about. And then there was Alanna.

Alanna would come to the wedding alone, beautiful, elegant, perhaps a little dazzling. Even as a girl Alanna had always had the power to out-shine everybody else, with her beauty, her clothes, her attitude.

Notoriety would have only served to make Alanna more uninhibited. If people expected to see a woman famous for her beauty, her men and her money she wouldn't disappoint them. Well why not, underneath was the real Alanna, warm and loyal, a woman who had never deserved some of the things fate had done to her.

The door opened and her mother came into the room wearing her silk robe, eyeing at once the wedding dress hanging over the wardrobe.

'You'll look so beautiful, Ginevra,' she said, the tears springing readily into her eyes.

'Shall I ring for another cup of tea, Mother?'

'No dear, I've already had mine. I simply

thought we'd have a quiet chat. It's going to be impossible later on with all the children here and everybody else milling around.'

'I don't expect you've seen much of Daddy this morning.'

'No, he's in his study, it wouldn't surprise me if he has locked the door.'

Ginevra laughed. 'I'm sure he'll play his part with great aplomb when the time comes. You've both been so good, putting up with me and my problems, from now on Mother I hope it's going to be plain sailing.'

Her mother smiled. 'Don't rely on it, dear, life's never quite like that.'

'No, I suppose you're right. I don't expect Alanna had any qualms about her future and look how it ended up.'

'Why didn't you ask Jane Fortesque to be your bridesmaid? You've been friends such a long time and I'm never very sure that a gaggle of children does much for the wedding ceremony.'

'I couldn't ask Jane without asking the others. I know I've known her longer, but we were all together for many years and I thought just as much of Kathy and Alanna as I thought of Jane. By choosing children I'm not offending any-body.'

'You couldn't have asked Kathy with Jane's parents in the congregation, and Alanna would have eclipsed you. I'm not at all sure that I've chosen the right colour for my outfit.'

'Of course you have. You always looked elegant in cream.'

'I thought I should have selected something a

little more colourful.'

'No, of course not. The tan hat and shoes are lovely. I wonder what Dominic's grandmother will be wearing?'

'Something very well worn my dear, from days that were more given to frills and flounces. She'll bring out her feathers and her furs, her jewels and her eccentricities, but everybody will tell her she's looking marvellous and she'll survive the day a lot better than many other people.'

Along the drive came a procession of cars and vans. The caterers and their staff, the florists and the family. Then a large car brought the children and the hairdresser. It seemed to Ginevra that it would all never come together in time.

She could hear the high-pitched laughter of the children, hear them running up and down the stairs until somebody admonished them to be quiet, then minutes later Ginevra's door opened and her young nephew stood in the doorway surveying the room. He was seven years old, a fair-haired, handsome young boy, the spitting image of what his father had once been. Ginevra held out her arms and he ran into them.

'Is that your dress?' he asked, eyeing the creation on the wardrobe door.

'Yes, do you like it?'

'I suppose so. I don't like that velvet thing I have to wear.'

'But Alistair, you'll look wonderful in it, and velvet is so right for the cold wind.'

'When I was a page-boy for Aunt Isabel and her husband I wore a sailor suit. It was nicer.'

'You wore a sailor suit because Uncle Alex was

in the Navy, and it was a naval wedding.'

'Well, what sort of wedding is this when we're all wearing crimson velvet? Mummy says it's Tudor.'

'The clothes have been copied from Tudor times, I thought they were beautiful. The little girls were delighted with them.'

'Oh, they would be. I don't think the other page-boy likes his; he agrees with me that it's silly.'

'Why don't you go and put your suit on and then come back in here and let me see you.'

'It's too soon to put it on.'

'Well, then, there's nothing I can say, is there?'

At that moment his mother came into the room eyeing her son with a certain amount of annoyance.

'I told you not to go worrying Aunt Ginevra this morning Alistair, he's been on and on about his page-boy suit, I've told him it's beautiful but he won't have it,' she said, and Ginevra looked into her eyes and laughed.

'I can understand how he feels, do you remember those awful frilly lace frocks we had to wear for Alice Atherton's wedding? We hated them.'

Her sister-in-law dissolved into laughter. 'I know, they were dreadful weren't they. I spilled orange juice on mine so that I had to take it off. I never knew what happened to it.'

'I shall spill something on mine then,' Alistair said adamantly.

'Oh no you won't, young man. You will be a very good boy and not let the side down. What do you suppose the other page-boy will think if you misbehave?'

'He doesn't like the suit either.'

'But I'm sure he'll behave himself. The children were very well behaved at the rehearsal.'

'Yes, all of them.'

'We didn't wear the clothes then,' Alistair said sourly.

'Well, today's Aunt Ginevra's big day and you have to do your part to make it perfect. Do you understand, Alistair?'

He looked up at his mother with cocky assurance, but meeting her stern gaze his expression changed, and in little more than a whisper he said, 'Yes Mother,' and opening the door a little wider she indicated he should leave.

'I can't understand this fashion for children as attendants,' his mother said. 'When I married I had four very old friends and everything ran like clockwork.'

Ginevra laughed. 'You had me, Celia. I was twelve, I tripped over your train. One of the others took hold of my arm and dragged me upright, I had bruises for weeks.'

'Doesn't that bear out what I mean, darling? You were twelve, these children are much younger. I'll be keeping my fingers crossed that nothing goes wrong.'

'Have you seen Father?'

'John's gone along to his study. I expect he'll stay in there until everything has quietened down.'

'How is my brother?'

'Very well. David Reagan stayed with us over

340

the weekend and travelled here with us. John was so delighted that you'd asked him to be one of your groomsmen, we've all been friends such a long time.'

'David came here for years in the summer holidays. I had an awful crush on him at one time, he was so good-looking and terribly nice. He never looked at me twice.'

'He probably thought you were too young in those days. He's never married you know, I don't even know if there is anybody.'

'I'm sure there must be. Didn't John think to ask? Perhaps we should have invited her if she exists.'

'David's always been a rather private person, and you know John, he's got to be pushed and prodded into asking personal questions.'

Celia walked up to the wardrobe and looked up at the wedding dress. 'It's beautiful Ginevra, Marcia Beaumont is quite the best isn't she.'

'I've always liked the clothes she's made for so many people I know, she's done a good job on that one.'

'Yes indeed. Is Alanna Van Royston coming to the wedding?'

'Yes.'

'I only met her once, that was when she was at school with you and she was around fifteen. Very beautiful, very assured. Is she coming alone?'

'Yes, I believe so.'

'Oh well, she'll no doubt create a diversion when there's a lull in the festivities.'

'You sound like my mother, she's been going on and on about Alanna for weeks. Nobody should sit in judgement on her because nobody outside Alanna really knows the full story. I hope she'll enjoy herself, look absolutely sensational and confound every mean and spiteful thing anybody says about her.'

Chapter Twenty-Five

Clare Greavson hadn't slept well on the night before the Midhurst wedding. Her mind had been spinning around between her son's appearance at the wedding with his erstwhile girlfriend and the church fête. Would her chutney be as good as last year? Had she made enough of it? Would Mrs Hodson's cakes take the first prize as usual or would that new woman at the church surpass her?

Clare liked to bask in Mrs Hodson's reflected glory when she went up to claim her prize, but the new woman had supposedly been a house-keeper or cook to some quite well-established family so she could be a professional, Mrs Hodson was only a daily woman even if she had brought up six children.

Clare heard the sound of Anthony's bedroom door closing quietly, then his footsteps on the stairs. Her husband was sleeping soundly in the next bed; nothing ever seemed to disturb John's slumber, not even the prospect of inferior chutney or his son's choice of girlfriends.

She went to the window and opened the

curtains slightly to reveal a grey sky and faint rosy streaks, it was a fine morning. She saw that it was just after seven and, donning her dressing gown, she crept out of the room and down to the kitchen.

Anthony looked up from the kitchen table with a smile.

'What are you doing up at this hour Mother, worried about the fête?'

'And you.'

'Why me?'

'Because I'm worried about where you're going from here. You're going to a wedding you know very little about, with a girl you see little of these days, and what is Zoey going to think?'

Anthony frowned.

'Mother, I'm not concerned about anything Zoey thinks. She's a nice girl, I like her but that's all there is. I know you'd like there to be something more, but you have to let me work things out. Beside, you're assuming too much when you say it's all over between Kathy and me.'

'But I thought you only saw her at the office.'

'That's true, but surely you've heard that romance can be rekindled.'

'Not a good idea, Anthony. When something has gone sour it can never be the same.'

'I know that you'd like to think that, but let's wait and see shall we.'

'What have you had for breakfast? You've a fairly long drive ahead of you.'

'Coffee, orange juice. I'm not very hungry and Kathy said she'd pack a flask and make sandwiches.'

'Gracious me, aren't you having a meal at the friends' house?'

'The wedding's at two Mother, the reception will follow. Kathy thought we might have trouble getting a meal in some hotel near by, hence the picnic.'

'It sounds as spartan as the wedding. Kitted out in wedding finery, and eating sandwiches and drinking coffee in some layby, followed by a wedding and quite probably a nondescript reception, then home again. Really Anthony you should have made it quite plain from the outset that this wasn't your scene.'

'You'll hear all about it when I get home, Mother.'

'You needn't bother, I'm no longer interested.'

She meant it, but she did think he looked remarkably handsome in his pale grey suit and cravat several minutes later. He was doing Kathy Marston proud; she hoped the girl appreciated it.

The town was hardly coming to life as Anthony pulled up outside Kathy's front gate. A newspaper boy came down the street whistling cheerfully, almost falling over the kerb as he glimpsed Anthony's elegant figure emerging from his car, and standing to stare at Kathy walking down the path to meet him.

Anthony had known she would look beautiful. He had told her many times that he liked her in blue, and the blue she had chosen was a soft gentle azure, the colour of a summer sky, and under her large straw hat the colour of her dress her beautiful face smiled a welcome.

He took the basket she was carrying from her

344

and placed it in the back of the car.

Anthony smiled down at her. 'You look very beautiful Kathy, there'll be nobody there as pretty as you.'

'Tell me that later. I rather think you'll be agreeably surprised.'

Kathy was thinking how nice he looked. He was handsome, she felt proud to be seen with him, but something vital had gone from their relationship and she knew that she was not entirely blameless. Perhaps she should have discounted his mother, perhaps she had attributed to her more importance than she actually had, but behind her were old slights and traumas she could never face again.

Anthony's mother did not approve of her and had made it very plain. She had heard from several people that Clare Greavson had other ambitions for her son and none of them included Kathy Marston. They could never go back to their old camaraderie, that had gone for ever. Where once there might have been gentle banter now normal conversation didn't come easily, but Kathy had made up her mind that before they reached their destination she would tell Anthony all he needed to know about the wedding. It would no longer matter that his mother knew all there was to know, but if she'd known about it before, the gossip would have been insupportable.

The journey was uneventful. There were several traffic jams to negotiate in the towns they passed through, but as they came to the area Kathy remembered, she sat forward in her seat to absorb the view. They paused at last at the top of a long hill and Kathy said, 'There's a lane to the left a little way on, Anthony, you can pull in there. It leads to a small glade where we can have our sandwiches and from where you can see the village and the Abbey.'

While Kathy attended to the refreshments Anthony looked down on the view of Saunders-court in all its magnificence and beyond it the village and the squat tower of the stone Abbey.

Kathy too looked at the view of far distant towers and meandering parkland, of tall chimneys and mullioned windows, of ancient ramparts and the exquisite symmetry.

Anthony's face was reflective and she said gently, 'It is beautiful, isn't it? The Abbey is very old, fifteenth century, and happily it escaped all the mayhem associated with Henry the Eighth. The village is so proud of it and the Midhurst family make sure it is kept in pristine perfection.'

'That's an enormous place, who lives there?' he asked pointing to the hall.

'The Earls of Midhurst. It is called Saunderscourt.'

'I suppose the National Trust have it.'

'Actually no. The family still live there. I believe the gardens are open to the public for a month in the summer.'

'You'll know about this place through your friends I suppose?'

'Yes. I spent time here during school holidays, I loved it. I learned to ride and I knew every corner of those grounds down there.'

He was staring at her now. 'You mean you actually went into the grounds of that hall?'

346

'Anthony, have you forgotten that you and I were invited to Ginevra Midhurst's wedding? I haven't told you very much about it, but I have mentioned her name several times. Didn't you remark that Ginevra was unusual, a little pretentious, perhaps?'

He was staring at her now in wide-eyed amazement and she found herself rushing to explain.

'I wanted to tell you all about it right from the moment I received the invitation, but that was the weekend you took me to meet your parents. Your mother made it very difficult. She knew about me, my family history, even my education, and she disapproved. She did not want me for you, Anthony. I was hurt and I was angry. I could have flaunted that wedding invitation in front of her, make her see that if she disapproved of me other people didn't, so I made up my mind I'd tell you nothing to pass on to your mother. If you decided not to come then it wouldn't matter, but you'd promised to come and you were keen not to let me down. I've made it very difficult for you and I'm sorry, but I couldn't have played it any other way.

'If you'd backed down and said you couldn't come I wouldn't have blamed you and it would have solved the problem.'

'You mean you'd have come on your own?'

'Of course.'

For a long moment he sat looking down on the scene before them, a small frown on his face, his thoughts perplexed, and she felt at that moment that she was a century older than Anthony. He turned to look at her, 'I thought you and Mother

347

were getting along quite well, Kathy, what did she say or do that was so terrible?'

'She tried very hard, but underneath was her disappointment. She'd heard gossip about my family, and since that day I'm sure she's heard considerably more. Anthony, it doesn't matter, we're friends, I'm glad about that.'

'Have you told any of this to my Uncle James?'

'No, why should I?'

'Because he's never really got along with Mother, they usually scrap like cat and dog, that's whenever they take the trouble to meet.'

She smiled. 'I do have the feeling that he's not really surprised we're going our separate ways.'

'Are we, Kathy? Has it really come to this?'

'I'm sure in time you'll think it's for the best. Shall we enjoy today, it's what I want.'

He nodded, and after a few minutes said, 'Any more coffee Kathy? The sandwiches were great.'

Half an hour later they drove through the main street of the village and found it lined with local people wearing their Sunday best, with the children carrying flowers and eagerly waving to every passing car carrying invited guests.

'I told you it would be like this, Anthony,' Kathy said. 'I'm not surprised all the hotels and inns in the vicinity were booked up solid.'

They were now in a procession of cars and Anthony said anxiously, 'Where are we expected to park the cars, there must be a car park somewhere.'

'There is at the side of the Abbey, they're all heading that way.'

'Good job it's fine.'

'Yes, for April it's a lovely day. So many people thought June would have been a better time but April in England can be special.'

'Robert Browning thought so.'

The procession had veered off now and in front of them was the large car park half-filled with a collection of pristine cars that made Anthony's pride and joy seem ordinary.

People were leaving their cars to walk back to the front doors of the Abbey, men in morning dress and women in their finery, hats and floating draperies, and over all was an atmosphere of smiling conviviality.

More cars were driving up to the entrance and people were alighting from them to join the advancing throng. At that moment a large black car was depositing a woman who stood for a moment looking up at the Abbey, a woman wearing a white, wild silk gown and a black hat decorated with black and white organdie poppies. She stood hesitantly staring around her and Anthony was saying, 'I say Kathy, isn't that the American woman who's just divorced that Austrian prince? You know, the racing driver, the chap who's had to give her millions?'

Alanna's face registered delight and she was waving and smiling as she waited for them to join her, and Anthony's eyes were literally popping. She embraced Kathy warmly, and then Kathy was introducing Anthony and he found himself looking into a cool beautiful face that for months had adorned the magazines his mother was so fond of.

They shook hands and Alanna said, 'I'm so

glad to see you Kathy, I hope we can sit together in the Abbey, this is the part I was dreading.'

She favoured Anthony with a warm smile and thought, 'He's good-looking, very English, nice too, and ordinary.'

They walked together up the Abbey steps and Anthony's thoughts were more than confused. His mother would dine out on this for months, Alanna Van Royston and the Earl's daughter, all these aristocratic guests. And there was so much more to come.

A young man was greeting them at the door, smiling down at the two women and saying, 'Alanna and Kathy, I remember you very well.'

Alanna smiled. 'David Reagan, don't you remember Kathy, they took us fishing and we disgraced ourselves by chattering; they never asked us again.'

Kathy smiled. She did remember it. One warm August afternoon sitting on the banks of the river with Ginevra's brother John and this tall smiling young man, then he was taking her hand in his and smiling down at her.

He led them down the aisle to their seats and even among that select gathering there was a stir of interest at the sight of Alanna. Her face registered no emotion and as they took their seats Anthony asked 'Is he the bride's brother?'

'No, the bride's brother's friend. I don't know him very well but he often spent time here in the summer.'

Anthony was reflecting that this was a world Kathy knew and he didn't. It was part of her life that was alien to the world they both lived in, but she was comfortable with Alanna and the handsome man who had ushered them to their seats.

Within minutes he was ushering another party into the pews in front of them and this time another girl turned with a warm smile, and he asked in a whisper. 'Who are they?'

'The Earl and Countess Fortesque. That is Jane, we were at school together.' Anthony was bemused. Jane Fortesque's smile had been warm and this was the daughter of the man who was having an affair with her aunt Josie.

Jane Fortesque was attractive rather than strictly beautiful. She was wearing pale pink and it suited her light brown hair and slender figure.

Lord Fortesque was handsome, tall and elegant with silver sculptured hair and a clear-cut aristocratic profile. His wife was a raw-boned woman wearing a large navy-blue hat and navy-blue heavy silk dress. The sort of woman who would look well on a horse, with weather-worn features and proud unsmiling demeanour.

Kathy was more interested in the man sitting in the front pew, the man who was to marry Ginevra. He was good-looking, but she could see little of his face until he turned to smile at people sitting around him. For the main part he sat quietly chatting to the younger man sitting next to him and Alanna whispered, 'He's rather handsome, Kathy. Oh I do wish them well.'

Kathy saw at that moment that her face was bleak with memories that were painful and in a sudden rush of compassion she took hold of Alanna's hand and gave it a warm squeeze. Alanna smiled, saying, 'He's nice, your young man, is it serious?'

Kathy shook her head, and Alanna couldn't help thinking, 'I'm glad, he is nice, but not for you, Kathy.'

A young man had come forward and was entering the Fortesque pew, greeting Jane with a warm smile and taking his place next to her. Jane had looked surprised, but her mother was smiling at him genially, her father rather less so.

Kathy and Alanna exchanged glances. 'Who is he?' Alanna mouthed. Kathy shrugged her shoulders. It rather looked as if there was someone in Jane's life after all. The man was disposed to chat, and Jane silenced him with a shake of her head and Alanna said, 'Nothing doing there Kathy, at least not on Jane's part.'

Kathy smiled. 'How can you be so sure?'

'I've become a student of human nature since we last met. He's keen, she isn't. Her mother would like her to be, her father thinks otherwise.'

Kathy looked down with a smile and Anthony whispered, 'Who is he?'

'I have no idea, some man Jane evidently knows.'

Reflecting, Anthony thought, Kathy was unlikely to get an invitation to Jane Fortesque's wedding, the man was chattering again and Jane was telling him to be quiet. He couldn't see that lasting.

Two women accompanied by a teenage boy were taking their places in the second pew and Kathy whispered to Anthony, 'Ginevra's sisters-in-law and Lady Celia's eldest son.'

'Which is which?'

'Lady Celia is the blonde one, the other is Lady

Victoria, she has two daughters, they're probably bridesmaids.'

'I suppose the boy is the Earl's heir?'

'After his father.'

'Of course.'

Another stir in the congregation heralded the arrival of the Countess of Midhurst wearing dark cream silk and a brown straw hat. She looked decidedly elegant and from the front pew Dominic and his brother turned their heads to greet her.

Across the aisle smiles were exchanged between Dominic's parents and the bride's family, and Alanna murmured, 'How terribly civilised it is.'

Kathy looked at her in surprise. 'Civilised?'

'Why yes. My first marriage was burdened by too many ex-mistresses, although I didn't know it at the time. In the case of my second marriage the mistresses came later!'

'You're very bitter Alanna, it's understandable.'

Alanna smiled. 'I should forget about it, today of all days, but it's occasions like this one that bring it all back to me. This is what my mother warned me about.'

'Your mother didn't want you to come?'

'Not really.'

'But you did, regardless.'

'Of course. Are you going to the reception?'

'That was the idea. Are you?'

'I have to think about it.'

There was a great expectancy in the air, the feeling of something tremendous and inevitable as the organ lulled that vast congregation into gentle nostalgia.

It was the fanfare of trumpets that roused them and brought them to their feet and then the choir walked slowly down the centre aisle and the Earl escorted his daughter in their wake.

Dominic stood with his brother at the foot of the steps leading up to the altar and as she drew nearer he took his place beside her and their eyes met. To all those watching the warm tenderness of his smile was apparent and only a handful of them heaved sighs of relief.

Dominic's mother looked down at her mother with a degree of exasperation. The old lady had been responsible for raising problems nobody had dreamed existed, now happily they'd been resolved, but the old lady was still capable of interfering. They'd had words about it, but the Duchess had told her daughter that she'd done it for the best and time would prove her right.

Ginevra's mother was grateful that her worries appeared to be over. The happy couple were exchanging their vows with a calm certainty she hadn't expected weeks ago.

Her husband took his place beside her with a sigh of relief. Then after a few minutes murmured, 'I hope the old windbag doesn't go on too long when the register is being signed; it's been a long day.'

She gave him a long hard look.

Everybody agreed that the bride looked enchanting and Dominic looked happier than the cynics in the congregation had expected. The children looked sweet and picturesque in their Tudor costumes, even the two boys seemed aware of their importance and the need to behave. They were not fidgeting, and their doting parents heaved sighs of relief that for the moment all was well.

Alanna's thoughts were miles away. She was thinking of her last wedding in that little chapel at the edge of a lake in the woods near Vienna. The bridegroom had been romantically handsome, the congregation gay and flattering. The sun had shone out of a clear blue sky and at night the orchestra had played waltz music and they had danced in an atmosphere of Old Vienna.

She had thought those looks of love were destined to last for ever, but they had evaporated as quickly as a summer storm, they had meant nothing. Now looking at Ginevra and Dominic gazing fondly into each other's eyes she prayed that their looks of love were genuine and meaningful.

Kathy was aware of the tears rolling slowly down Alanna's face. There were few in that congregation who would expect Alanna Van Royston to weep with the trauma of a remembered pain.

Chapter Twenty-Six

The bride and bridegroom followed the bishop into the recesses of the Abbey where they would sign the marriage register, and then followed the procession of immediate family members to support them.

There were no problems on the bride's side of

355

the church, but there appeared to be a certain degree of anxiety from the bridegroom's side.

'Really, Mother,' the bridegroom's mother protested, 'I really don't think you should go into the vestry, it's always so dark in there and there are several very worn steps to negotiate.'

'I intend to go,' the old lady protested. 'I have come to see my grandson marry and I intend to be a part of all the proceedings. After all it's thanks to me that matters have sorted themselves out.'

'It's also thanks to you that we spent several very sleepless nights,' the Duchess murmured.

'Nonsense. Better sleepless nights now than in a few years' time. Here, help me down this step, these old pew doors are far too small. I'll walk with Andrew.' Andrew came forward gallantly to take her arm, while her other hand gripped her walking stick grimly.

His parents looked at each other with resigned fortitude, and slowly they followed the other members of the family into the vestry. A seat was immediately found for the old lady and the newly-weds went forward to greet her.

'It's so dark in here,' she grumbled, 'I can hardly see your faces. Isn't there any more light in here?'

A young priest came forward immediately carrying a lamp which he placed on a table near her chair.

'That's better, thank you young man, now may I be allowed to have a quiet word with my grandson and his wife without a crowd standing around.'

Dominic's eyes twinkled as he looked down at her. This was his grandmother at her most autocratic, but her eyes were kind as she looked up at Ginevra.

'You make a very beautiful bride Ginevra, I hope Dominic has told you so,' she said softly.

Ginevra smiled. 'He has, many times, Grandmother.'

'Your mother hasn't forgiven me for interfering, but I felt I had to. Have you two forgiven me?'

'There's nothing to forgive,' Dominic said, 'You were right.'

'How was I right?'

'You showed me that I'd been cherishing a dream that should have been allowed to die a long time ago.'

'That's a start, where did it go from there?'

'I discovered Ginevra, I also found love and warmth and regretted my stupidity for those wasted years.'

'Yes, well, they've gone and now you have each other and the future. Will you come to see me one day? I doubt if I'll ever leave my castle again, I'm too old.'

'You know we will, but I've heard you say that before.'

'I mean it this time. Now where is that brother of yours? It's high time he found himself a wife instead of chasing daydreams.'

'Then you should tell him, Grandmother.'

'I have, many times. When do young people ever take any notice these days?'

'I took notice, Grandmother.'

357

'Yes, but then you've only just started to take notice, you didn't when you were Andrew's age.'

Dominic laughed, and his grandmother said, 'They're ready to move out now, and I don't want to hold everybody up, I'm very glad I came, and I'm well content with what I've seen.'

'We'll talk again at the reception,' Ginevra whispered.

'I'm not sure that I can sit through that.'

'We'll look after you, I'm sure you'll enjoy it.'

As they moved away Dominic whispered, 'She'll enjoy every minute of it and endeavour to be the centre of attraction.'

Throughout the absence of the bridal party the congregation had listened to the organ, indulged in whispered conversation and largely sat in silence, immersed in their own thoughts.

Anthony Greavson was finding it difficult to believe that he was sitting next to Alanna Van Royston. He could smell her perfume, engage her in occasional comments, observe the fleeting expression in her incredible green eyes. What a lot there would be to tell his mother – she'd dine out on it for months. She'd be furious that Kathy had kept him in the dark about what was in store for him, and of course there would be no going back for them, it would be too late for his mother to try again with Kathy.

Alanna was wishing the entire thing was over. Whenever she looked round her she was conscious of several pairs of eyes staring at her, weighing her up, and she was not looking forward to the reception. There would be too many people milling around, too many people who thought they knew all about her. Kathy was lucky to have this rather nice man as her escort, at least he wasn't somebody they could gossip about.

Jane sat between Algy and her mother and she was seething with annoyance. Her mother's face registered self-satisfaction. She was glad that Algy had joined them making more than plain that he and Jane were an item. Jane resented both of them. She didn't want Algy beside her, she wasn't his property and never would be. If he continued to monopolise her at the reception she would have to tell him, then there would be trouble with her mother. She turned in her seat and caught Kathy's eye, and then the eye of the man sitting next to Alanna. Undoubtedly he was Kathy's escort, Ginevra had said that Alanna was coming on her own.

Sitting further back Larry Harbrook too was wishing the wretched affair was over. He shouldn't have come. Ginevra had looked beautiful as he'd known she would, and her Marquis was undisputedly handsome and the looks they had exchanged were warm and loving.

The girl sitting next to him was entirely bemused. She sat wide-eyed and curious, totally engrossed in an alien world. He'd picked her up at the station apprehensively worried in case she was wearing entirely the wrong clothes, then feeling agreeably surprised that she was not.

She was wearing a pale blue dress and coat and a black hat and as she took her place beside him in his car she whispered, 'Do I look all right?'

'You look great, Anita.'

'I got permission to borrow the rig-out from the theatre. I must be careful not to harm it.'

'Didn't you have anything of your own?'

'Nothing that would do for this affair. I spend all my time at the theatre, I wear trousers and tracksuits, something like this would be a waste of money.'

'Well, you look very nice. Looking forward to the reception?'

'I can't go to the reception, I have to get back to the theatre.'

'You didn't tell me.'

'I thought you'd know. The show has to go on. I hope you'll be able to take me to the station.'

He'd been annoyed. He wouldn't be able to introduce Anita to Ginevra and she'd probably think he'd been stood up, then with a grim smile he thought Ginevra wouldn't care whether he'd been stood up or not.

Alanna whispered to Kathy, 'I don't think I'll go to the reception, Ginevra won't mind, I've attended the wedding, this is what's important.'

'But why, Alanna?'

'I'm lost on my own without an escort and too many people know me, or know of me.'

'What does it matter? You're with us, we'll look after you.'

'That's kind, Kathy, but there have been too many occasions when I've had to suffer the stares and uncomfortable silences whenever I've walked into a room. I could go in there and announce I'm Alanna Van Royston, I've divorced two husbands and I'm as rich as Crœsus, I'm a predator so lock up your sons.'

Kathy looked at her in shocked surprise. 'Alanna, nobody's going to be thinking that, you're imagining it.'

'Am I Kathy, am I?'

That was the moment when the organ swelled into the wedding march and the bridal procession emerged from the vestry to start their long walk down the centre aisle to the door. The congregation rose to its feet and slowly, wreathed in smiles, the procession of bride and groom, attendants and family commenced their progression, and from all sides of the church smiles of approval followed them.

Now the pews were emptying and Anthony stepped back to allow the two girls to leave before him and Kathy looked at Alanna's face anxiously. She was determined to stay with her, it was ridiculous to say she didn't intend to go to the reception, and in front of them Algy had taken hold of Jane's hand as they followed her parents to the door.

Outside the Abbey the crowds were already milling round the cars. The villagers were cheering, moving ever nearer to the bridal car, and Kathy said anxiously, 'Stay with us Alanna, Anthony's car is parked just over there.'

Alanna shook her head and Kathy could see that there were tears in her eyes, while Anthony looked on doubtfully. Now Kathy too was aware of them, discreet stares, whispered comments, and Alanna said, 'I'm leaving you now Kathy, I'll be in touch,' and Kathy watched helplessly as she hurried through the crowds away from the Abbey.

There was nothing she could do, and as they made their way to the car Anthony said, 'Where is she going? The cars are parked over here.'

'She says she isn't coming to the reception.'

'Why ever not?'

'She has her reasons, all of them good ones I'm sure.'

'She's really rather nice.'

'Does that surprise you?'

'Well, she's not at all as the media presented her.'

'Hard, avaricious, greedy. That was never the Alanna I knew, she was generous and warm, fun to be with; why were they so mean to her?'

'They only repeated the things her husbands said about her.'

'And Alanna didn't say anything, she didn't get all that money for nothing, she suffered for it.'

'Where do we go from here?' Anthony asked.

'We go with the rest of them to Saunderscourt.'

Alanna was hurrying down the road through groups of people who stared at her curiously, a wedding guest in her finery, hurrying away from the rest of the guests, and it was only when she had reached the edge of the crowd that she felt her arm taken in a firm grip and she stared up in amazement at the man smiling down at her before she burst into tears.

Jules Moreau had watched her leaving the Abbey, watched the woman she was with talking to her urgently, holding her arm in an attempt to detain her before Alanna broke free and walked quickly with head down through the throng of people. That was when he had to hurry to catch

362

up with her and now he watched helplessly as the tears rolled down her cheeks.

He was holding her close to him, waiting anxiously for her to explain her actions, then in a choked voice she said, 'Jules, what are you doing here?'

'I'm here to see you.'

She stared up at him helplessly.

'Your mother showed me the wedding invitation, you were invited to bring an escort, I didn't see why it couldn't be me.'

'Did my mother ask you to come?'

'No, she doesn't know I'm here.'

'Are you sure?'

'I'm quite sure. If I'd felt satisfied that you were being looked after by some man or other I wouldn't have approached you. As it is I saw you hurrying across the road as if all the hounds of hell pursued you.'

'I look a mess, I've ruined my make-up, what are we going to do?'

'I suggest we sit in my car while you repair your make-up, then we can either drive off somewhere or go to the reception. It's up to you, Alanna.'

For a long moment she was silent, then she said, 'Half of me wants to drive off somewhere where nobody knows us, but I can't go on running away. I want to see Ginevra and her husband, I want to see the other people I knew before I made such a mess of things. What do you want to do, Jules?'

'I think we should go to the reception, confound the critics and enjoy ourselves. I don't think there'll be a single person there who knows me personally, they only know me by reputation, some of it good, some of it bad, and most of it supposition. We can face them together, Alanna.'

She threw her arms around him in a rush of gratitude. At that moment, with this man she felt she could face the world.

By the time she had restored her face to its pristine perfection most of the cars had already left. It didn't matter, she could be expected to make an entrance, she wouldn't disappoint them.

At the reception Ginevra and Dominic stood in the long beautiful entrance hall waiting to receive their guests. With them were their parents and Dominic's grandmother sitting resplendent in a velvet chair. There was no sign of weariness in the old lady's smile; there had never been a time when she had failed to rise to the occasion.

Larry Harbrook took Ginevra's hand and raised it to his lips.

'Are you alone, Larry?' she asked him, surprised.

'Yes, Anita had to get back to London. Lovely wedding Ginevra, you look beautiful.' He passed on to shake the bridegroom's hand and Dominic favoured him with a sweet smile.

Anthony followed in Kathy's wake as she greeted their hosts, embraced Ginevra and was introduced to Dominic. He felt he was walking in a dream, that at any moment he would wake up. Then Kathy was introducing him to Lady Jane Fortesque and he was smiling into the eyes of the girl he had seen taking her place in the Abbey pew.

She had embraced Kathy warmly, and now

they were chatting amicably about old times and Jane suggested they should look for somewhere they could sit together.

'Where is the man you were with in the Abbey?' Kathy asked.

'I don't know, he's somewhere around.'

Her tone of voice indicated that she didn't really care where he was and once again Anthony found himself escorting Kathy and one of her friends.

What his mother had told him about Kathy's aunt and Jane Fortesque's father, whatever it was, certainly hadn't made any difference to the way the two girls were chatting and laughing about old times. At that moment they were joined by the man who had ushered them into the church, and Jane, taking his hand, said, 'How nice to see you again David. I do hear about your comings and goings from my brother Andrew. You remember David Reagan, don't you Kathy?'

Kathy smiled.

'I expect you were glad to forget the afternoon we took you fishing and accused you of frightening away the fish,' he said with a smile, and then Kathy did remember, the tall, handsome boy Ginevra had admired, and her brother, not a little angry with them that they had chattered on all afternoon when they were supposed to remain silent to encourage the fish to bite.

'What are you doing with your life, Kathy, are you married?' David asked.

'No. Anthony is a partner in the firm of

solicitors I work for. We're old friends.'

While Kathy chatted to David, Anthony chatted to Jane and she suggested that they should move towards the buffet table and help themselves to food. There was so much of it and in such variety.

Anthony was very much aware that he was liking this girl with her straight gaze and friendly air. For one uncomfortable moment he noticed her mother's haughty stare from across the room. Unconcerned by it, Jane was chatting on disarmingly about herself, her love of horses, dogs and country pursuits, and Anthony asked, 'Do you play golf, Jane?'

'No, but I'd rather like to. We have a nine-hole course my father had made at the back of the house. Daddy uses it and has offered to teach me, but I've been so tied up with Mother and the horses that I've never taken him up on it. You play of course?'

'Yes. Some days I'm good, the next I'm terrible, it's that sort of game.'

'But you enjoy it?'

'Yes, enormously.'

'Does Kathy play?'

'No. I rarely see Kathy these days outside the office. We work in my uncle's firm, I expect she's already told you.'

'Some, I wondered if there was more.'

He smiled. 'It started out that way, now we're good friends, nothing more.'

'Then if I asked you to help me with my golf she wouldn't mind?'

'No, I'm sure she wouldn't.'

Anthony found it hard to believe that he had escorted Kathy to a wedding where he suddenly found himself attracted to her friend, a girl who was smiling into his eyes with evident enjoyment. Across the room his eyes encountered the frowning gaze of the man who had sat next to her in church and he said hurriedly, 'Doesn't your friend play golf?'

'Which friend?'

'The man sitting next to you in church.'

'Algy Barrington. He's an old friend, we've known each other all our lives. We know each other too well, at least that's how I see it.'

'And he doesn't?'

'No.'

'I wouldn't like to tread on anybody's toes, Jane.'

'Algy doesn't play golf to my knowledge, but even if he did it really wouldn't matter. We're friends, nothing more. There could never ever be anything more.'

Anthony had once again encountered her mother's formidable frown and across the room Jane too was aware of it. She looked up into Anthony's face with a candid smile. 'My mother likes Algy, the two families have always been close. My father is rather less enthusiastic. Surely it doesn't preclude you from helping me with my golf?'

'No, not at all.'

'Then please get in touch and tell me when you are free. I'll give you my telephone number before we get separated.'

'Need we get separated?' Anthony said evenly.

367

'It rather looks as though Kathy's found herself another friend.'

They looked along the table to where Kathy was chatting animatedly to David Reagan and Jane said, 'David is a friend of Ginevra's brother, they were at school together and at university. He spent weeks here in the summer. He will remember Kathy from then.'

'Where does he live now?'

'In London. He's a barrister.'

'Then they'll have a lot in common. He isn't married?'

'No. I don't even know if there is anybody.'

'He's very good-looking.'

'Yes, he is; does that bother you?'

Anthony laughed. 'At one time it might have done, not any more.' That was the moment Algy Barrington arrived at Jane's elbow saying, 'The families are meeting in the Orangery, Jane, are you coming?'

'Perhaps I'll join you there later.'

'Your mother asked me to tell you.'

'I'm sure she did. As I said, I'll join you later, Algy.'

He glared at Anthony before moving away to join another man who was staring at them curiously.

'Who is the other man?' Anthony asked.

'Larry Harbrook. Ginevra's old boyfriend. That didn't come to anything either.'

Chapter Twenty-Seven

Kathy Marston was finding her companion both charming and easy to talk to. She remembered him clearly now as the handsome boy Ginevra had had a crush on years before, the boy who had been nice to the group of young girls who had descended upon Saunderscourt during their summer holidays, even when they must have seemed too young and too giddy.

'So you work for a firm of solicitors,' he said smiling down at her, 'did you qualify?'

'Yes, I took a law degree at Cambridge and went on from there.'

He seemed surprised and she knew why. Her other school friends had gone off to Switzerland as other upper-crust girls were doing; she on the other hand had gone to university and he was intrigued by the difference.

'You're working in your home town then?' he asked.

'Yes. My mother died many years ago. I live with my father in a terraced house on the main street. Does that sound terribly uninteresting to you?'

'No of course not, why should it?'

'Well you have to admit it isn't very adventurous.'

'Going to Cambridge and getting a law degree is adventurous enough Kathy. I took my law degree at Oxford.'

'Really. That's where Anthony took his.'

'I suspect he's a little younger than I, and we were probably at different colleges.'

'So you're a solicitor too?'

'No, I'm a barrister.'

'Better still.'

He laughed. 'I have a flat in the city but I do have other ambitions.'

'In law, do you mean?'

'No, my ultimate ambition is to find a house in the country, not too far out of London, with a garden and a dog.'

'You're not married David?'

'No. I'm still searching. Like you perhaps.'

'That is when you find your nice house and the dog, when you've stopped searching?'

'Yes, and you?'

'Oh yes, a nice house and a garden, a dog too, but a husband is a vague shadowy figure who hasn't as yet materialised.'

'And you would have to think about your father, I suppose?'

'Gracious no. I sometimes think he would like me to branch out and leave him in peace. To be honest I think he despairs of me.'

'And it didn't work out with Anthony?'

He was too astute, he knew there had been something, now he waited for her to deny it, and in a small voice Kathy said, 'Do you have a mother, David?'

'No. My mother died when I was twelve, my father never remarried and I don't see him nearly enough. He lives in Cornwall, a lovely old house on the banks of the Fal.'

'So you only see him when you get away for holidays?'

'And sometimes not even then. He goes off to the Bahamas and I have other interests.'

'What are they?'

'Golf and sailing.'

'Doesn't Cornwall lend itself to those?'

'Not all the time. Dad and I have never lived in each other's pockets.'

She looked across the room to where Jane and Anthony were talking earnestly together and David said, 'They appear to be getting on remarkably well Kathy, does it bother you?'

'Not at all.'

'Do you ever get up to London?'

'Occasionally. I have promised myself that I would go more often, to see the shows. The only theatre in our town is one given over to amateur dramatics and musical groups.'

'Why don't I give you my telephone number so that you can ring me if you feel like visiting the metropolis? Tell me which theatre you would like to go to and I'll get seats for us.'

'That would be lovely David, thank you.'

'You promise?'

'Yes, of course.'

'Then I must circulate, I'm not carrying out my duties too well but I'll get back to you.'

She watched him walking away from her, chatting to various groups on his way, but she was reluctant to return to Anthony who seemed totally engrossed in his discussion with Jane.

She looked towards the door where Ginevra

371

and Dominic were still chatting to groups of their guests, and then she saw Alanna, and with her a man whose face was strangely familiar. Where on earth had Alanna spirited him from?

At that moment Alanna saw her, and raising her hand she turned to her escort and indicated that they should walk over to join her.

From all round the room people were staring at them: Alanna, elegantly beautiful and smiling a radiant smile, while with her was a man most of them recognised, Jules Moreau, French, rich and famous.

Kathy found her hand taken in a firm grip and she looked up into a smiling face, at blue-black hair edged by silver wings set against a tanned complexion out of which grey eyes appraised her calmly. Alanna was saying, 'I sat with Kathy in church, I didn't know Jules was coming, Kathy.'

He smiled. 'I was detained, luckily I arrived here to prevent her running away.'

'Where is Anthony?' Alanna asked.

'Over there talking to Jane.'

Alanna eyed them, then with a smile said. 'They're apparently enjoying each other's company, but he's neglecting you Kathy.'

'No he isn't. I've been talking to David Reagan, he's only just moved on.'

Alanna laughed. This was the old Alanna, romantically inclined, always ready to see the beginnings of romance even in the most mundane encounters. The Alanna she had met earlier in the day had somehow gone, and in her place was the friend she remembered, warm and fanciful, not the cold disillusioned woman who had sat grim-faced beside her in church, with tears of resentment coursing down her cheeks.

What was there between Alanna and this Frenchman, she wondered? She was not the only one speculating on their sudden arrival.

Ginevra was listening to the comments around them.

'You know him of course,' her aunt was saying. 'He's famous, an author and of course some of his books have been filmed. I must tell Henry - he's quite a fan of Jules Moreau.'

Esmeralda moved away and resignedly Ginevra's mother said, 'I don't know where she'll find him, I haven't seen him since we left the church.'

'He was in the library reading the papers,' her husband said drily. 'You'd think there was enough going on here without recourse to the daily papers. I'm surprised he came.'

'Oh, well, he's better out of the way,' the Countess said.

Her husband had had enough. His shoes were pinching, he had indigestion and the guests didn't look as if they were ever going to move. His wife read the signs well.

'Really dear there's nothing at all to get upset about, the wedding's been absolutely wonderful, everything has gone like clockwork. There'll be time to put your bedroom slippers on when everybody's gone. Please put a smile on your face until the end of the festivities.'

Ginevra and Dominic were circulating among their guests watched closely by his grandmother. She was well pleased with what she saw.

Jane's mother was rather less enthusiastic.

'Who is that man Jane is spending all her time with?' she asked her husband testily.

'I haven't any idea,' he replied. 'They seem to be enjoying each other's company.'

'I know, but who is he?'

'Suppose we join them and Jane will introduce him.'

'I think it's quite dreadful how she is ignoring Algy. He was kind enough to join us in church and since then you'd think he didn't exist. She's treating him as badly as Ginevra is treating Larry Harbook.'

'You would hardly expect Ginevra to fuss over Larry Harbrook on her wedding day to somebody else,' her husband objected.

'Well, no, but for Jane to do it to Algy... I shall have something to say to that young lady in the morning.'

'I'm sure you will my dear.'

'Who is the man Alanna Van Royston is with?'

'His name is Jules Moreau.'

'French?'

'I believe so.'

'Another foreigner to add to the other two she's discarded no doubt.'

Lord Fortesque moved away to join his daughter and her companion, and Jane said, 'Daddy, I want you to meet Anthony Greavson. He works for the solicitors in the next town, you know them, don't you?'

'Very well. Are you related to James Greavson?'

'He's my uncle. My father is Doctor Greavson.'

'I know them both.'

'Anthony escorted Kathy Marston, Daddy, they work for the same firm.'

'Ah yes, and where is Kathy now?'

'Over there with Alanna and her escort, and David Reagan.'

The four of them were evidently enjoying one another's company, they were chatting and laughing together, and he said softly, 'Why don't you join them? They're old friends, you'll have a lot to talk about.'

Ginevra's mother looked around the guests and came to the realisation that she had been worrying herself needlessly.

Alanna Van Royston had commanded a great deal of interest, but it had been largely well disposed. She looked enchanting and her escort was obviously well connected since a great many people were anxious to smile and greet him. Kathy Marston too had occasioned no hostility. Indeed they comprised a very happy group, and Lord Fortesque had now joined them and it was all entirely civilised.

Her husband had conquered his early irascibility and was now chatting to Elspeth Fortesque, and no doubt talking about horses and their attributes. Occasionally Elspeth looked across to where her husband was chatting and smiling in the company of his daughter and other young people.

Waiters were still attending to the needs of the guests, it would seem their appetites for food and wine were unending, so thought Lord Midhurst as his eyes swept along the table still surrounded by guests choosing what they would like.

Ginevra and Dominic had gone upstairs to change out of their wedding clothes and Esmeralda, joining her sister, said, 'Do you know where they're spending their honeymoon?'

'I haven't asked. They're driving up to London from here, where they go on from London I have no idea.'

'I should think they've already had their honeymoon in Madeira,' her sister stated waspishly.

'That is an assumption you shouldn't be making, Esmeralda.'

'I'm sure it's an assumption most people will have arrived at.'

'Not me, and not her father. Where is Henry?'

'I don't know. Probably asleep in some quiet corner.'

'He really is the most unsociable man I have ever met. How did you manage to get him on a cruise liner?'

'With the utmost difficulty. I told him if he didn't come with me I would go to Florida to spend time with Joan Marple. He knew that would cost him more money than we could ever spend on a cruise.'

'How have you tolerated him all these years?'

'Didn't our parents make it very plain to us before we married that certain men were right for us? If we found out later that they weren't we had to grit our teeth and get on with it.'

'I suppose you're right. The younger generation think differently, perhaps it's just as well.'

'The Dowager Duchess is bearing up well, she's surely in her nineties.'

'I'm not sure. Ginevra is very fond of her.'

The Dowager Duchess had spent an exhausting and rewarding day. She had spent most of it sitting down, but surrounded by well-wishers and attendant grandchildren. Now she was wishing the festivities would come to an end, she was tired, it was time to leave.

Ginevra and Dominic were back in their midst, Ginevra looking enchanting in pale grey and arctic fox, Dominic wearing his camel coat and evidently both of them dressed for travelling. With smiles and echoing good wishes from every corner the guests followed them out to the front door where they filled the courtyard and stood on the steps until the happy couple had driven away, the cheers and laughter followed them along the drive.

Now was the moment for the guests to take their leave and one by one or in groups they were drifting away to find their cars. It was already dusk and Anthony looked down at Kathy asking, 'I suppose we should leave now, Kathy?'

'Yes, have you enjoyed it?'

'Yes, it's been wonderful.'

Lord Fortesque had joined his wife and, taking Anthony's outstretched hand, Jane said with a smile, 'I've enjoyed meeting you Anthony, we shall meet again I hope.'

'Yes of course, you are expecting me to telephone you?'

'Yes, I shall look forward to it.'

David had taken Kathy's hand in his and was saying softly. 'Think about the show Kathy, something you would really like to see.'

The three girls embraced one another warmly,

then Jane joined her parents and the others went to their cars.

Lady Fortesque eyed her daughter in some degree of asperity.

'I'm very annoyed with you Jane,' she hissed. 'You've hardly exchanged a word with Algy Barrington all afternoon, I don't blame him for being furious. Who was that young man you spent so much time talking to?'

'His name is Anthony Greavson.'

'Yes, but who is he, who brought him?'

'Kathy Marston.'

'You mean he was her escort and he was neglecting her to chat you up?'

'He wasn't neglecting her, Mother. Kathy introduced us, I thought he was nice, they are not engaged or even romantically involved.'

'But who is he, who are his family?'

'He's a solicitor, in his uncle's firm. My father knows the firm, and Anthony's father, who is a doctor in the town.'

'He's hardly in the same league as Algy Barrington.'

'He's promised to help me with my golf.'

If she'd said he was helping her to become a deep-sea diver her mother couldn't have been more astounded.

'Help you with your golf! Why, your father can do that, he's asked to help you often enough and you've never shown much interest.'

'Well Anthony's going to telephone me. You'll like him Mother, he's really very nice.'

'I'll speak to your father about this, he won't be very pleased.'

'I've already told my father about it; he didn't offer any objections.'

'Like I said, I'll speak to him about it. Your friendship with this young man doesn't have my approval.'

From the next group Jane's father read the picture well. His wife was displeased, his daughter adamant, and from across the room Algy Barrington was with the Harbrook boy and they were drinking too much.

Alanna introduced Jules to her mother's friends while she explained to them that she hadn't known he was coming, and now she would have to collect her belongings as they were driving up to London.

Avis and Ralph Mannheim were intrigued by this smiling Frenchman whom they only knew by reputation, but very much desired to know better. Was he going to be Alanna's new venture into matrimony, they wondered?

Alanna read the signs well. They wanted them to stay on, they wanted to be able to say they knew all there was to know and she was equally adamant that they must leave.

She thanked them for their hospitality, promised to be in touch very soon, and to their regret in a very short space of time they were driving away and Alanna said, 'They're really very nice Jules, very old friends of Mother's but I'm sure you wanted to get away.'

'I know that you did.'

'Jules, I'm so very grateful to you for coming all this way simply to give me some support when I was feeling particularly isolated. It's been wonderful thanks to you, I don't want you to keep it up, I'm sure you're very anxious to return to Provence.'

'Actually Alanna I'm in no tearing hurry to return home. Why don't we spend some time together in London? I suspect you never really knew either of the men you married, wasn't marriage something you rushed into with your eyes closed?'

Slumped in her seat her expression was bleak and he looked down at her with a smile. 'Don't think about them Alanna, but I am right.'

Of course he was right. She'd been young and frivolous, blinded by dissolute young men with aristocratic titles. She had longed to be loved, and neither of the men she had married had cared enough to give her the commitment she yearned for. Now here was Jules Moreau, older, sophisticated, and with something of a reputation for love affairs that had not lasted. What did she really know of him? As if sensing her thoughts Jules said: 'We don't really know one another Alanna, only what we've heard of each other. Most of it is hearsay, none of it can stand up to examination. You've been portrayed as a man-eater and something of a money-grubber. I've been depicted as a womaniser, too rich, too immoral, an ageing Casanova if you like. Why don't we make our own minds up about each other?'

'Why do people say things that aren't true?' Alanna asked dolefully.

'The media have to write about somebody; if the true story isn't known then they have to invent one. We know the truth of it. Actually I've always been a very private person and that merely makes people try harder.'

Alanna relaxed. She was glad they were not returning to Provence and her mother. The less her mother knew about them the better, but mixed up in her anxieties was her parents' marriage, her father's money problems. Looking up at Jules sitting beside her, for the first time in her life she felt that here was a man she could share her problems with.

Kathy and Anthony drove home largely in silence, both of them obsessed by the strange fates that in the course of one day seemed to be altering their lives.

She liked David Reagan, she had sensed in him a warm uncomplicated human being who would be genuine, and he had been so anxious that they should meet again.

Beside her Anthony's thoughts were on similar lines. He thought about his mother. She would be waiting anxiously to question him on every aspect of the wedding, and he made up his mind that he would say nothing about Jane Fortesque. After all what was there to tell her?

He'd promised to help her with golf, that was hardly something for his mother to get excited about. No, he'd tell her about Alanna and Jules Moreau, about the ancestral pile, the wedding guests, the bride and bridegroom, the clothes the women were wearing; that would be enough to be going on with.

Kathy was remembering happily that David did not have a mother to complicate matters.

Back at Saunderscourt Steven Charlton was expressing to his staff his sincere thanks for the way they had handled the day. Most of them were glad that it was over and that they could now get back to normal.

He listened to the young maidservants enthusing about Lady Ginevra's appearance, the looks of her husband and the different outfits of the women guests, while the housekeeper merely sat in front of the fire with her shoes off and her eyes closed.

Tomorrow they would put the house to rights, in the meantime his wife would be waiting to hear about every aspect of his day. His Lordship's congratulations were still ringing in his ears, sentiments he had been happy to pass on to all concerned.

Chapter Twenty-Eight

Clara Greavson was in a bad mood and her husband was aware of it. As their son helped himself to another cup of coffee she regarded him with the utmost exasperation.

Anthony was aware of it, and as soon as he had finished his breakfast he got up from the table saying he must be off, he had urgent calls to make before he got to the office. His parents heard the closing of the front door and then the sound of his car on the drive, and John Greavson asked, 'What's going on between you and Anthony?'

His wife reached out for another piece of toast and snapped, 'I'm furious with him. I've had to wait for him to tell me about that wedding, and when he does talk about it he says very little. It was obviously a hole-and-corner affair.'

'What makes you say that?'

'If it had been a decent occasion he'd have been anxious to talk about it. He's obviously back with that Marston girl again.'

'Are you sure?'

'Well, he's not been at the golf club has he, and Zoey Perkins hasn't seen hide nor hair of him. Her mother is quite put out about it.'

'I don't see why. You and her mother pushed the friendship, perhaps it was never Anthony's idea.'

'We'll have James and his wife over to dinner on Saturday evening, he'll know what's going on.'

'Not a good idea, Clare.'

'Well, I think it is.'

'I don't know what you've got against the girl. Times have moved on, and this old scandal has obviously run its course. The younger element are not going to care and the older people have probably forgotten about it. Besides you can hardly hold Kathy responsible for her aunt's actions.'

'You annoy me so much John. Of course people talk about it, I hear them at the meetings I go to and at the church.'

'Mothers of daughters who are jealous of Kathy's acumen, no doubt.'

'Not at all, but decidedly out of sympathy with the way she acquired it.'

'If you're so anxious about Anthony and his comings and goings why don't you ask him? And if he is back with Kathy invite her over, try to be nice to the girl.'

'I was perfectly nice to her the last time she was here. I can't help it if I don't think she's right for Anthony.'

'Well, my brother thinks a lot of her, he won't like it if you spend all evening pulling her to pieces for something that was never her fault.'

His wife merely frowned, but the determination on her face spoke volumes.

'I'm off to the surgery,' he said. 'You must do as you please about my brother and his wife.'

Clare did exactly that. Later in the morning she telephoned her sister-in-law who was so surprised by the invitation she couldn't think of an immediate excuse and Clare was off the telephone before she could gather her scattered wits together.

When she informed her husband of the invitation he said tersely, 'Why didn't you tell her we were already going somewhere else?'

'She took me by surprise.'

'You could have told her you would have to consult me first.'

'James, she was on and off the telephone so quickly I couldn't think. If you want to cry off you must tell her.'

After a few minutes he said, 'Oh well, it might be amusing. She'll be on about the wedding. I don't know what Anthony's told her, but I know for a fact it was a magnificent affair, we can expect Clare to dine out on it. She'll bore us to death for most of the evening.'

In actual fact it didn't take James long to realise that Clare knew very little about the affair. She was asking the questions. 'Did Anthony tell you about the wedding James, he said he'd enjoyed it?'

'I believe they both enjoyed it.'

'I rather think they're back together. You'll be pleased about that James, you like her I know.'

'Yes, nice girl. So you think they're back together again?'

'Well, he's been off every weekend without saying a word and he's not been at the golf club has he, John?'

'Was he away all last weekend then?'

'Oh no, he was out Saturday and Sunday. He's being very cagey.'

'If it'll set your mind at rest he wasn't with Kathy Marston. She asked for Friday off, went up to London for the weekend.'

Clare's eyes opened wide. 'Are you sure, or was she simply throwing red herrings in your path?'

'Why should she? She was going to some show or other, came back Monday morning and said she'd had a marvellous weekend.'

'Then I wonder where Anthony was?'

'Why not ask him?'

'Oh I will, never fear.'

The opportunity came on Saturday morning when she found Anthony loading his golf trolley into the back of his car. Clare's face lit up with a smile and Anthony cursed under his breath. He'd hoped to avoid his mother.

'How nice dear,' she said. 'You're going to the

385

club. Is Zoey playing with you?'

'No Mother. I'm playing somewhere else.'

'Where?'

'I'm late, Mother, I've got to go. I'll see you later.'

She stood on the drive staring after his car. He was being secretive and that wasn't like Anthony. There was another girl, somebody he'd met at that wedding, somebody she wouldn't approve of or he'd have told her about it. All of this could be laid at Kathy Marston's door. She blamed her for everything.

Elspeth Fortesque had stood at the window watching her daughter greet Anthony Greavson before she climbed into the front seat of his sports car and drove off in the direction of the golf course at the rear of the hall.

She had to admit that he was good-looking, tall and slim and fair-haired, he had a charming smile and Jane's face lit up whenever he looked down at her. She didn't like it, but what was worse, her husband seemed unperturbed by the state of affairs.

The Barringtons were distant, Algy had gone off to Malta with Larry Harbrook in a brown sulk and when she had told Jane of his displeasure she hadn't cared.

Jane had introduced the boy to her father, but as yet she'd kept him well away from her mother. Elspeth determined that she would get to the bottom of what she deemed to be an entirely ridiculous situation. After all, who was he, what sort of family did he come from? His father a

386

country doctor, his uncle a solicitor. Of course it was a lucrative and honourable profession, but he was not in Algy Barrington's league.

Jane couldn't remember a time when she had been happier. She was enjoying her golf lessons and Anthony's company. They laughed together and found they had a great many ideas in common. Their friendship was warm and light-hearted, but there could be more, and it would have to come from her.

Anthony was overwhelmed by her title, her family's ancient name, and he didn't think she could ever think of him as a serious suitor. He thought of her as a socialite, a girl who might dally with him but who in the end would turn to somebody like Algy Barrington. Anthony didn't know that all her life she had yearned for stability and a life away from the world of hunt meetings which her mother found so fascinating. She hated the baying of hounds and their chase after some defenceless animal. She hated the superficiality of numerous affairs between people in her mother's world, even when she had to admit that her mother was never involved in scandal and that it was her father who had strayed.

How mixed-up it had always been, for the first time in her life she was experiencing normality, a normality that her mother would call obscure.

Her golf was improving and Anthony was a good teacher. As they drove back to the hall she saw her mother's car leaving the gates and in a rush of shyness she said, 'Would you like to join me for lunch, Anthony?'

'Are you sure you're parents won't mind?'

'Mother's just gone out, that was her car, I'm not sure if my father's at home.'

Anthony hesitated. He doubted if he would have been invited if her mother had been at home, and he was experiencing the same hurt pride that he hadn't understood in Kathy.

Jane held out her hand, 'Please Anthony, I'd like you to come. I'll show you round, you said you'd like to see the inside of this place.'

At that moment Lord Fortesque came out of the house and ran down the steps towards them. He smiled and held out his hand.

'Well, how did the golf lessons go?' he asked.

'Very well, I am coming on. Anthony says.'

'Good. And now what are you two young people doing?'

'I've invited Anthony for lunch. Will you and Mother be out?'

'Your mother's gone over to the Fieldings and I have an engagement in town. Enjoy your lunch, both of you.'

His affability decided Anthony that he should accept. They lunched in a small room overlooking the mere and then Jane took him round the house. Anthony's thoughts strayed to his mother; what would she make of all this?

He found himself looking at portraits of Fortesques going back to the fourteenth century, men in suits of armour or rich silks and velvets, men and women in powdered wigs, bishops' robes, or officers' uniform in the service of the Crown. It was as grand as Saunderscourt, and when at last Jane showed him portraits of her parents he looked at Countess Fortesque's haughty profile and thought about Josie Marston.

They were in the ballroom when they heard Lady Fortesque's voice calling, 'Jane, are you in there?'

She had seen Anthony's car standing outside the house and she'd hurried inside to confront them wherever they were.

Anthony was aware of her cool stare and the fact that although she smiled when they were introduced there was no warmth in her manner and only hostility in her eyes. At that moment his thoughts went back to the afternoon he introduced Kathy to his mother and for the first time he understood her reluctance to tell him about Ginevra's wedding.

'I've been showing Anthony around the house, Mother,' Jane said.

'It is rather impressive, isn't it? Of course some of the rooms are hardly ever used.'

He nodded.

'We throw the gardens open to the public in August, but for the rest of the year it is simply our family home.'

'Of course.'

'I thought you might ride with me this afternoon Jane, but it's getting rather late.'

'I was just leaving,' Anthony said quickly. 'Thank you so much for lunch, Jane, and showing me round.'

'I'll come to the car with you,' Jane said. She knew that her mother watched them running down the stairs and crossing the hall.

'Will you telephone me, Anthony?' she asked.
'You're sure?'

'Why do you feel the need to ask?'

'I don't think your mother approves.'

'No she doesn't. My mother's thoughts don't stretch beyond Algy Barrington, but she's flogging a dead horse. I don't want Algy now, I never have, and I am old enough to choose my own friends. Please telephone me Anthony, I'm enjoying our lessons and your company!'

He smiled. 'I'll telephone you in the morning.'

The town was busy with weekend shoppers as he drove through it and headed for home. He didn't want to go home, he wanted to be with people; he had a lot to think about, so instead of driving down his road he went on towards the golf club.

The car park was full, but he couldn't see his father's car. He did however spot Zoey's small saloon. He harboured no guilty feelings about Zoey, they'd been golfing pals, nothing more, in spite of whatever his mother might think. She was sitting in a corner of the room with other men and girls who raised their hands and smiled when they saw him. He joined them, and they made room for him to sit next to Zoey.

'Has Dad been playing?' he asked.

'Your mother said they were having visitors this evening, your aunt and uncle I think,' Zoey answered. 'Didn't you know?'

Anthony frowned. His mother hadn't mentioned it, but he knew what the visit would entail. She'd ask questions about anything James could tell her about Kathy, himself and whatever his uncle had been able to pick up about the wedding.

Conversation was easy, they'd known one another a long time and he was in no hurry to go home. He would linger on until he felt sure his parents' visitors had left.

That manoeuvre didn't save him from the inquisition that came over breakfast on Sunday morning.

'You were late last night, Anthony, your aunt and uncle were here and it was late when they left.'

'I was at the golf club, Mother.'

Her face brightened. 'Was Zoey there?'

'Yes, we had a drink together, quite a crowd of us actually.'

'Did you play at the club then?' his father asked.

'No, I called on the way home. You're playing this morning aren't you, Dad?'

'Yes, I'd better get off, we're out early.'

Anthony's heart sank, he knew that as soon as his father left his mother would start her questioning.

'Your uncle was saying you and Kathy had enjoyed the wedding you went to,' she began.

'Yes, I told you, Mother.'

'But not much about it.'

'Did my uncle fill you in with the details?'

'No, he didn't. I don't think he knew very much. He told me Kathy Marston was in London over the weekend, she'd been to a show, had a lovely time, did you know?'

'Yes, I knew. I'm glad she enjoyed herself.'

'You didn't want to go with her?'

'No Mother. I told you it was over between us, why should we go to London together?'

'I didn't know what to think, you tell me very little these days, Anthony.'

'Perhaps there's nothing to tell.'

'Has she friends in London?'

'Well, obviously.'

'A man?'

'I believe so.'

'Do you know him?'

'I've met him.'

'Well, who is he, is he acceptable?'

'How do you mean Mother, acceptable?'

'Well you know, Anthony, is he in the same league as yourself?'

'I should think he has considerably more going for him. He's a barrister, has a flat in London, and his father has a title, I'm not sure what it is.'

If he'd said his father came from Outer Mongolia and was a Robber Chieftain his mother couldn't have been more dumbfounded.

'How did Kathy Marson come to meet somebody like that?' she demanded.

'But it was you who told me she'd been educated in salubrious surroundings, Mother. Naturally she knows people like that. She met him at the wedding, but she knew him years before.'

'What about this wedding, Anthony, was it worth going to?'

'It was a wedding to end all weddings, Mother. Lady Ginevra, Kathy's old school friend married a Marquis. We sat in church with Alanna Van

Royston, *the* Alanna Van Royston you've been drooling about in those magazines you read. She was another of Kathy's school friends. Oh, and another one was Lady Jane Fortesque, the daughter of the man who is in love with Kathy's aunt.'

For once his mother was lost for words.

At last she said, 'Why didn't you tell me all this before?'

'Because everybody would have known. In actual fact, Mother, Kathy didn't enlighten me for the same reasons. She'd had a surfeit of gossip, she didn't want any more.'

'Really, Anthony, as though I would gossip about it.'

He smiled grimly.

'Are you telling me she left you on your own at that wedding to go off with this new friend?'

'No, Mother. We were together as a group. I met Jules Moreau, the French author, you've read about him too.'

'Who was he with?'

'With Alanna.'

'Is she really as beautiful as her photographs? What was she wearing, something quite outrageous I feel sure.'

'She was very nice. Not at all as the papers depicted her.'

'Did she talk about her husbands?'

'Of course not Mother. Do you want more coffee, I'll make some more, this has gone cold.'

While he made fresh coffee he knew his mother's mind would be busy with all he had told her, he hadn't heard the end of it, she would question him over the weeks and months again and again.

She sat at the breakfast table deep in thought as he helped her to more coffee and it was only when she sat opposite that she looked up to ask, 'Didn't you meet a nice girl, Anthony?'

'A great many nice girls, Mother.'

'Anybody special?'

'I'm hardly a catch for a rich titled society girl.'

She frowned. 'But of course you are. You're a solicitor with great expectations in your uncle's firm. Your father's a respected doctor and there's never been a hint of scandal about anybody in our family.'

'Scandal doesn't seem to bother the aristocracy, Mother.'

'Obviously not if they're prepared to accept Lord Fortesque's long-lasting love affair. But seriously Anthony, you never talk to me, you go off every weekend with your golf clubs and we don't know where you're going or who you're meeting. Have you met somebody?'

'Yes Mother, I met a girl, I'm helping her with her golf. That's all.'

'But who is she?'

'I'm not prepared to tell you. There's nothing in it, we're friends, that's all.'

'But where does she live, locally?'

'Not far away.'

'Is that all, will there be nothing more?'

'I doubt it.'

'Why?'

'Because like I said, Mother, we come from different worlds. You thought I was too good for

Kathy Marston, I think her parents might think she's too well connected for me.'

'No, Anthony, I won't have it.'

'Well naturally you're prejudiced in my favour.'

'Aren't you going to tell me her name?'

'Jane.'

'Nothing more?'

'Not at this moment, Mother.'

'But you're seeing her again?'

'Perhaps.'

He was maddening. She'd never known Anthony be like this before, he'd always told her everything, they'd been so close.

Why couldn't this girl be for him, what a thing it would be, all their friends, the people at the club, John's brother James and his wife. And she'd be such a good friend to her, make her so very welcome.

She was already thinking about the sort of house they would have. Not a modern one like this, some large stone-built house in the midst of huge gardens with a long drive and terraces.

There would be dogs and horses. Anthony had never had much to do with horses, but his wife would want them, and when they had children they'd go to famous schools and by this time James would surely have made him a partner in the law firm.

She was so busy with her thoughts she didn't see Anthony get up from the breakfast table, it was only when he opened the door to leave the room that she looked up to ask, 'Are you seeing her today, Anthony? You've been missing for the last few Sundays.'

'I'm not exactly sure what I'm doing today, Mother.'

He knew he had promised to telephone Jane, but he decided he wouldn't do it from home, his mother was clever, by fair means or foul she'd discover who he was telephoning.

His golf clubs were still in the car; she wouldn't know about that, all the same as he got in and drove away he knew his mother watched from the window. She wouldn't be able to contain herself. She'd be anxious for his father to get home, he wouldn't put it past her to telephone his aunt and uncle, friends perhaps, and when nothing came of his friendship with Jane she'd be mortified.

No sense of failure occupied Clare's mind. Anthony was her wonderful handsome son who any girl would be proud of. She'd stop talking to Zoey and her mother about him, she was feeling rather pleased that he'd not got too involved with Zoey Perkins.

Chapter Twenty-Nine

Anthony found it easy to confide in Kathy during the next few months and he found her sympathetic and encouraging. She dispelled his fears, and through Kathy he discovered a new Jane, a Jane far removed from the narrow confines of the life he believed her to have.

'You've fallen in love with her, haven't you Anthony?' Kathy asked searchingly.

'Yes, but it's hopeless. I can't compete with the likes of Algy Barrington.'

'But it isn't Algy Barrington Jane wants. She's had years of Algy, it never worked out.'

'I hardly get a smile from her mother. She doesn't like me spending time with Jane.'

'How about her father?'

'Oh he's all right, very friendly actually.'

'Well then. In the end, Anthony, it's what Jane wants. Have you told your mother about her?'

'Only that she's called Jane. Nothing else. I don't want my mother spreading it around that I'm seeing Lord Fortesque's daughter.'

He grinned. 'I've come to realise that in many ways you were right about my mother, Kathy, at the same time she is my mother.'

'Of course, and I think you're being very sensible to keep Jane under wraps for the time being.'

Anthony was so deep in his own problems he never asked Kathy about David. It was left to his uncle to inform him that she was leaving the firm and going to live in London. Indeed James Greavson had been delighted to be able to pass this piece of information on to Anthony's mother.

'What will she do in London?' Clare had asked. 'Is she going to work there?'

'I believe so,' he'd answered her maddeningly.

'You mean she's leaving her father here or is he going with her?'

'I believe Mr Marston has become rather involved with a widow lady some friends have introduced him to.'

'Who is she, is she local?'

'I doubt if you'd know her, Clare, she doesn't live in this area.'

'Is it serious?'

'I believe so.'

'I suppose you'll be sorry to lose her. Has she got somewhere to live in London?'

'Actually she won't be living in London, I believe they're looking for a house in Richmond.'

'They?'

'Oh didn't I say, Clara? She's getting married, she'll continue with her job I'm sure, at least for the time being.'

'Who is she marrying?'

'He's a barrister, so they're in the same profession, so to speak. She's very happy, we're all delighted for her.'

'I can't understand how two people can go together to a wedding and find people there they want to get involved with.'

'Is that how it happened? I didn't know.'

'Well, that's where Anthony met this girl Jane, and where she met this man she's been going up to London to see.'

'Kathy tells me she knew him years ago when she was a schoolgirl actually. Anyway it's worked out beautifully for her, how is it working out for Anthony?'

'Don't ask. I suppose he'll tell me when there's anything to tell.'

James and his brother smiled at each other across the table, and after a few moments Clare said, 'I see that Alanna Van Royston is back on the front pages again. This time it's Jules Moreau, the author she's involved with. Anthony met her at the wedding you know, he said she was beautiful, just like her pictures, and very nice.'

Any talk of Alanna could naturally be expected to occupy all conversation for the rest of the evening.

Indeed the glossies were making the most of Alanna and her Frenchman. She was pictured lazing on the deck of his yacht, dancing in his arms in some exotic nightclub or partying on a tropical beach under a moonlit sky.

Newspaper hounds followed her progress from one Mediterranean venue to the next, and always by her side was Jules, handsome, protective, adroit at shielding her from people who were too pushy, too intrusive.

Alanna's mother was delighted on one hand and irritated on the other. She wanted them to put her in the picture, tell her exactly where it was all going, but both Alanna and Jules kept their feelings to themselves.

Her mother had left St Tropez and was renting a villa in Antibes in the hope that Alanna would spend some time there when Jules was engaged with commitments that were urgent. She learned very little from those visits.

'You tell me nothing, Alanna,' she grumbled. 'Are you as cavalier with your father?'

'I haven't seen him for a long time, Mother.'

'But you speak to him on the telephone. That must be costing him a fortune.'

'I worry about him, Mother. He doesn't telephone very often and when he does all he says is that he's coping. Chartering his yacht, and that can't go on indefinitely.'

'Why not? Is he running out of clients?'

'Wrong time of year, Mother. The hurricane season will soon be on them.'

'Then I suppose he'll shut himself away in the house and live on the bottle.'

'Jules and I plan to go over there in January, I'm worried about him and I want Jules to meet him.'

'I don't see why, your father won't impress him with his respectability.'

'Oh, Mother, can't you find something good to say about him?'

'Do you have anything good to say about either of the men you married?'

'That's different. I remember that Dad was always kind, always fun to be with. Oh I know you had your differences, but the things you hate about him now were the very things that made you fall in love with him.'

'Jules won't be impressed, you'll not do yourself any favours by introducing him to your father.'

'If he's so easily put off me then it wasn't meant to come to anything anyway.'

The more her mother talked the more Alanna's concern about her father grew. It was Jules who said, 'Why not fly over to see him, Alanna? I can't come with you right now but in the early spring I'll join you. That gives you time to talk to him about me.'

Her mother was furious.

'You can't go Alanna, Jules shouldn't have suggested it, besides what about me?'

'What about you, Mother? You're happy here with people you like, partying, you're seldom alone. I'll keep you posted about what is happening over there.'

'You needn't bother. I can tell you what will be happening over there.'

From the gate Alanna looked up at the façade of the villa, noting its shabbiness. It needed a coat of paint, but then at this time of year many of the houses looked far from their best. Already the wind was sweeping wildly across the lawns and as she walked up the steps towards the house she drew her furs closer to keep out the chill.

Standing outside the closed door she felt a strange feeling of dread, it was so silent. Looking down towards the jetty she could see the *Lady Katrina* lying there with her sails furled, looking strangely dejected.

She lifted the bellrope and pulled on it, hearing the sound echoing plaintively beyond the door. For what seemed like an eternity there was no sound, then slowly the door opened and Jacob was staring at her incredulously before his face broke into a broad smile and he cried, 'Mees Alanna, God be praised, you come home.'

He took her small suitcase and ushered her in before him, and all the time her eyes swept the curving staircase and then from the back of the house Maria came, hurriedly wiping her hands on her apron, her smile warm, laughing a little at the flour remaining on her outstretched hands.

Alanna laughed. This was normality. Maria telling Jacob to take her suitcase to her bedroom, saying, 'I make tea Mees Alanna, your father in there, he be glad to see you.' Then in the next moment her father was in the hall, his face wreathed in smiles, holding out his arms and clasping her in a warm embrace.

Her father's embraces had always been the same, the smell of cigar smoke and whisky or rum. This embrace was different, clinical almost, and she stepped back regarding him with an incredulous smile.

'I'm on the wagon, love,' he said with a grin. 'Could be I've learned my lesson at last.'

'But since when?'

'Since the doctor warned me if I didn't pull my socks up I was on the way out. I'm not ready to go yet love, not till my little girl's settled.'

'And when will that be Dad?'

'I've been reading about you and that French fella. I want to meet him, I hope he's nothing like the other two.'

'No, Dad he's not. I've been so worried about you, how are you coping?'

'Just about. I earned money on the yacht, not enough to salvage me of course, but I'm still here. It takes more than that to kill Max Van Royston off. How's your mother?'

'She's very well. I stayed with her for a little while.'

'I suppose she had a lot to say about me.'

'Dad, why didn't you do all this years ago, lay off the booze, leave women alone? You wouldn't be in your present predicament if you'd behaved.'

'I know. Now tell me about you, love. Tell me about this Frenchman, he's been as prominent in the scandal columns as you have. I never thought

402

yours was justified, how about his?'

'He's nice, he's wonderful, I love him to death and he's also a wonderful friend.'

'That's a good start Alanna, that was what was missing with your mother and me, friendship. When am I going to meet him?'

'In the spring.'

'Are you going to marry him?'

'He hasn't asked me. One step at a time, Dad.'

He had to be content with that, but for the first time in months Max Van Royston began to think the tide was turning.

Ginevra sat in her rose garden in the May sunshine reflecting that the year had been good to her. Beside her on a rug slept her baby son Oliver and there was an air of wellbeing and contentment about her. Ginevra was in love with life, with her husband and the beautiful house they called home.

Her parents had been spending the weekend with them and she had watched Dominic escorting her father across the park, pointing out to him the things they loved most about the gardens before they disappeared in the direction of the stables.

Her parents were ecstatic about Oliver and Ginevra wouldn't have been human if she hadn't felt delighted with her role as wife and mother. She had achieved everything that had been expected of her, but with love rather than duty.

She read Jane Fortesque's letter for the second time, only putting it down when her mother took the chair beside her own.

Her mother could chat about everything under the sun regardless of the fact that her daughter seemed unduly preoccupied. Ginevra was only half listening and after a while her mother said, 'Who is your letter from Ginevra?'

'Jane Fortesque, Mummy.'

'Really. What has Jane to say for herself? I haven't seen her mother for ages, but then she's so involved in the summer with county shows and the like. What is Jane doing with herself? I hear she isn't seeing very much these days of Algy Barrington.'

'No, Mother, I rather think that is over.'

'Elspeth won't be pleased, she very much wanted it.'

'Jane didn't.'

'But Ginevra, he's so well connected, they're great landowners, and they're wealthy, I always thought Algy was nice enough.'

'Like Larry was nice enough, Mother.'

'Well yes, but he was never in the same league financially.'

'Nothing changes, does it?'

'What do you mean, Ginevra?'

'You know what I mean. Money marries money, keep it all in the family. I wasn't prepared to go along with it and neither will Jane.'

'What is happening then?'

'I shouldn't be talking about it.'

'Ginevra, I'm your mother, you can talk about it to me.'

Ginevra sat back with a thoughtful frown on her face before saying. 'You'll keep it to yourself. Mother?'

'I'm hardly likely to be talking to Elspeth about it am I?'

'I hope not. Jane's fallen in love with a young man she met at my wedding. He's a solicitor in his uncle's firm, he's been teaching her to play golf, her mother doesn't approve.'

'I'm not surprised. How about her father?'

'He's happy with the situation.'

'What is the problem then?'

'He's concerned with their different stations in life. Jane doesn't give a toss. It's her mother who is worrying him.'

'Well, of course. I can understand Elspeth's feelings.'

'I'm sure you can, Mother. I can't. This is a different age, a different generation. Jane was always impatient with so many things in her family life.'

'Not least of all her father's mistress, I shouldn't wonder,' her mother said drily.

Ginevra decided not to elaborate on that subject and in the next moment her mother said, 'How did that young man come to be at your wedding?'

'He escorted Kathy Marston.'

Her mother's eyes opened wide.

'You mean he was actually Kathy's young man and he fell for Jane?'

'No, Mother, he and Kathy were friends, they may have been more at one time, but that had finished. They were both free to move on.'

'And he moved on to Jane, who did Kathy move on to?'

'To David Reagan. They're getting married

next year. At the moment they're house-hunting.'

'Really. David Reagan, I am surprised.'

'Why?'

'Well David's never brought a girl to see us, or taken one to your brother's house, we always thought he intended to remain a bachelor. Of course Kathy's very pretty and I expect he knows all about her.'

'All about her aunt. He knows she's beautiful, has a Cambridge law degree and is exceptionally bright. He's also in love with her and that should be enough for anybody.'

'Ginevra, you're tetchy. I like Kathy, I always did, I'm not saying anything disparaging.'

Lady Midhurst sat back in her chair to contemplate matters. The world was changing and not entirely to her liking. Young people marrying out of their class, Jane moving downmarket, Kathy Marston moving up, and what about Alanna Van Royston? Impetuously she said, 'You'll be telling me next Alanna is getting married for the third time.'

Ginevra laughed. 'I wondered when the conversation would get round to Alanna.'

'Well she's back in the news with a vengeance. Do you think it's serious with this Frenchman?'

'I don't know. I thought he was very handsome, and they seemed to be hitting it off remarkably well.'

'I didn't see him with her in the Abbey, she was sitting with Kathy Marston and a young man.'

'Yes Mother, that is the young man Jane is in love with. Alanna brought Jules Moreau to the reception.'

'Why not the wedding, I wonder?'

'I don't know. We chatted to them, but there were so many people around. He was charming.'

'Well yes, the French can be charming.'

Ginevra laughed. 'Oh Mother, what a jaundiced view you have about everybody who isn't upper-crust, dyed-in-the-wool English.'

'I'm not like that at all.'

'I love you like that, Mother, don't ever change, but don't ever mind when I disagree with you.'

Kathy and David drove down to Cornwall on a warm hazy day at the end of August. He was taking her to meet his father.

David's father had come back from the Bahamas to meet his son's fiancée, and to spend some time in the house on the banks of the River Fal where he had lived with David's mother until her death several years before. After that somehow the house had seemed lonely and desolate. Kathy was unusually quiet.

'You're not worried about meeting Dad are you, Kathy?' David asked.

'Perhaps, a little.'

'I wonder why?'

'Well, I told you about meeting Anthony's mother.'

'You'll have none of that to put up with darling. Dad's down to earth, just be yourself, he'll love you.'

He was exactly as David had depicted him. He was very like David, tall and slender, but with silver hair. They possessed the same warm smile.

Kathy stood with him in the garden looking out

across the placid river and the myriad of river craft sailing on the broad water.

'It's very beautiful,' Kathy murmured, 'why did you leave all this to live abroad?'

'It's also very beautiful where I do live, but nothing was the same when Elizabeth died and David was away. Anyway I knew David would flee the nest one day. I was beginning to despair of him, I thought he'd never find a girl he wanted to marry.'

'We've found a house with a view very much like this one,' Kathy said. 'David fell in love with it first, and then when I saw it I realised why. Now I think he must have been thinking about this house.'

'I can't wait to see it.'

'Will you come to stay with us there?'

'Well, of course, I'll be glad to. I don't need two houses, I should sell one.'

'But which one?'

'I come here when I want to see England again, now I shall be able to come to stay with you. I don't think David would like me to part with this one though.'

Kathy agreed that it was a hard decision to make.

'David tells me your father is a widower, Kathy.'

'Yes, my mother died some years ago. He has a lady friend, I'm so glad for him.'

'You'll be having the ceremony in your home town, I suppose?'

'I'd much rather get married here in Cornwall.'

He raised his eyebrows in surprise.

'Won't your father mind that?'

'No, he'll understand.'

He didn't ask questions and Kathy resolved that she would ask David to tell his father why she preferred to marry well away from the town that had sat in judgement for so many years on something that had given her so much distress.

She wanted Aunt Josie at her wedding, Aunt Josie who had been her joy as well as her benefactor.

Weddings in June

Chapter Thirty

The Villa Hibiscus had undergone a transformation since Alanna's arrival there.

Smooth green lawns stretched to the top of the cliff and the villa sported new paintwork and gardens that were a riot of colour. Waiters in pristine white moved among the guests, their dark faces wreathed in smiles, and mingling with the sounds of laughter and conversation were the strains of an orchestra.

There were other guests on board the *Lady Katrina* since Max Van Royston never lost an opportunity to show off his yacht. He was in his element escorting Jules's friends around watched by a benevolent BooBoo and Jacob.

Most of the guests had arrived the day before, and they had enjoyed the hospitality of the villa and the yacht. Max entertained them with the customary bonhomie that was his trademark while from the terrace his wife looked on with a certain cynicism.

Every day since her arrival she had asked herself what she was doing here, but no power on earth could have kept her away from her daughter's wedding. Alanna had captured Jules, and Jules had restored Alanna's reputation. They were quite evidently very much in love and people moved on, didn't they, and old scandals would be forgotten surely in the face of permanence in Alanna's life.

It was Alanna's money that had paid for the restoration of the villa, Alanna's money that had enabled her father to keep the yacht, and Alanna's money and taste that had ensured that the villa was ready to receive her wedding guests.

To be sure, Max had said he wouldn't touch a penny of it, but there was no alternative and Alanna would not allow Jules to contribute. Lying out to sea another boat was moored, the *Cassowary*, the yacht on which Jules and Alanna intended to spend their honeymoon. Jessie smiled grimly to herself. Max boasted about the *Lady Katrina*, but the *Cassowary* was in her opinion more beautiful and considerably less ostentatious. But then that was Max, a part of him she had fallen in love with before she was old enough to know any better.

Her friend Dolly Germaine joined her on the terrace and Jessie said acidly, 'Look at Max, in his element down there, acting as though he's responsible for all this.'

Dolly laughed. 'I don't see why you're so put out, Jessie, hasn't he always been like this?'

Jessie didn't comment, and Dolly went on, 'When you told us Alanna was to marry Jules Moreau we did have our reservations; after all there's been as much talk about Jules as there has about Alanna. I wonder how much of it was true.'

'I should think hardly any of it. A man as well known and handsome as Jules lays himself open to gossip. I remember when Alanna went off to school in England, I thought I was sending her into an environment that would look beyond her

414

beauty. I suppose it did in a way, but her beauty caught up with her in the end. It brought her two disastrous marriages. This time I hope it's been kind to her.'

'What about you? Have you thought what you'll do when the marriage is over and there's just you and Max left?'

'Max won't change, Dolly. In all the years I've forgiven him for one indiscretion after another it never worked out. I vowed and declared that there would be no more forgiving and no more going back.'

'He's older now, Jessie, he's hardly the gay Lothario he was then. Don't you think the time has come for him to realise it and pay some heed to what he's thrown away?'

'That's just it. He's always crawled back asking for forgiveness, he'll never recognise the fact that he's older and time's caught up with him.'

'What has Alanna got to say?'

'She's always been her daddy's girl, she'd like us to be together, he can wind Alanna round his finger like he used to wind me.'

The two women looked down to where Max and a group of people were climbing up the steps on their way from the yacht.

Max was loving every minute of it, climbing with his arms round two girls young enough to be his daughters, and Jessie said grimly, 'Can you see him changing Dolly? Not while there's girls like that ready to flirt with him and flatter him.'

'He's surely reached the age when he knows such attention to be worthless.'

'I suppose so, but it gives him a boost, and I'm

no longer prepared to put up with it.'

When they reached the terrace Max looked up and saw his wife and her friend watching them, and there was an air of embarrassment in his attitude when he moved away from the group. Joining his wife and her friend on the terrace he greeted them with a bright smile even when his wife's caustic expression brought him down to earth.

'I'll leave you two together and search for my husband,' Dolly said diplomatically. 'Everything is wonderful Max, this is one wedding to remember.'

She moved away and Max said. 'Why don't we sit down Jessie. What can I get you to drink?'

'Nothing, thank you. I was about to go inside to see Alanna.'

'Oh, she'll be getting into her wedding finery, you look beautiful Jessie.'

'This isn't what I'm wearing for the wedding.'

'Well, what of it, you still look beautiful.'

'Flattery comes easily to your lips, Max.'

'Why do you always think I'm flattering you? I'm perfectly sincere.'

'That's because sincerity and you are not very good bedfellows.'

'I'm trying, Jessie, you could meet me half-way.'

'I've met you more than half-way for too many years. I'm here to keep the peace until my daughter's wedding is over, then I'm leaving.'

'Where will you go?'

'The world's a big place Max and I have enough money to buy what it takes. Thanks to you the house in New York has gone, the house in

416

Boston is an empty shell, I do own half of this one however.'

'Then why don't you stay here, or at any rate come back to it when you've exhausted every other notion you can think of?'

'I think you should go down there to greet the minister, he's looking a bit out of his depth in this conglomeration.'

Max followed her gaze and saw that indeed the minister had arrived and was standing uncertainly on the lawn below them.

'Are you coming with me, Jessie?' Max asked.

'No, I'll get changed, there isn't much time.'

She saw Jules standing with a group of his friends and when he saw her he raised his hands in greeting and favoured her with a smile. He looked remarkably handsome in his formal morning attire and a feeling of gratification swept over her. Alanna had been so lucky to have met Jules, fate in the end had been more than kind.

She found Alanna and her one bridesmaid in her bedroom. The two girls had known each other all their lives; distance and circumstances had separated them many times, but they had never lost touch and Edwina Blancharde had seemed the perfect choice to Alanna. She was blonde and pretty, a perfect foil for Alanna's darkness, and she was looking beautiful in the deep rose gown and the halo of white gardenias in her hair.

Alanna had chosen a classically simple gown in parchment satin. Around her hair was a diamond-studded band and she had chosen to carry a posy of cream roses. Jessie's eyes filled

417

with tears. She had seen her daughter looking beautiful in two other bridal gowns, gowns that had been extravagant in their richness; somehow today the gown she had chosen represented stability and the sort of good taste that had been lacking in those other more flamboyant creations.

'Mother, you're not dressed yet,' Alanna exclaimed.

'No, I'm about to get changed. The minister's arrived, I've left your father to greet him, he'll be in presently.'

Alanna's eyes met her mother's appealingly. 'I hope you're friends, Mother,' she said.

'For today at any rate.'

'And after?'

Her mother shrugged her shoulders. She didn't know.

The guests were taking their places in the chairs set out for them on the lawns, the minister stood before his altar and the choirboys waited on the terrace for the arrival of the bride.

Looking at Jules waiting patiently for his bride there were women in that congregation who had admired him, wished he loved them, women he had dallied with for a while in meaningless affairs, but today was different. They saw in Jules a dedicated sincerity none of them recognised, Alanna Van Royston was the woman he loved, Jules Moreau was lost to any other.

Max's face was alive with pride as he escorted his daughter from the house to where Jules waited for her. The music and the words they exchanged were lost on the breeze, but when the

418

ceremony was over and Jules held her in his embrace there were tears in Jessie Van Royston's eyes as she sat next to her husband, and he covered her hand with his in unspoken understanding.

It was early evening when the wedding guests crowded together on the clifftop looking down on the dinghy that was taking Alanna and Jules to where the *Cassowary* lay at anchor. From the deck of the *Lady Katrina* Jacob and BooBoo waved ecstatic greetings and as Jules and Alanna sailed away all they were aware of was the sound of music and laughter on the midnight wind.

Josie Marston walked across the lawns of the hotel towards the edge from where she could see across the river's estuary towards the open sea. It was early, and as yet the river traffic was light.

She stood looking down at the scene before her, her expression pensive, a little sad, and strangely alien to the sweetness of her face.

Over the years she had visualised Kathy's wedding day and it had followed faithfully in the pattern she had once dreamed her own wedding would be. Frothy white lace and flowers, bridesmaids in sweetpea colours, a host of men in formal morning dress, and so many guests. It had never happened for herself, and because of her it was not going to happen for Kathy either.

She was thinking of her conversation with Kathy in her bedroom the evening before when she had said, 'Why did you decide to get married in Cornwall, Kathy, why not at home in your own church?'

She had not missed the fleeting shadow that had crossed her niece's face before she said, 'Both David and I wanted it here, it's so beautiful and I really don't have close friends in Pelham any more, only the people I work with.'

'Yes, but surely they would have wanted to be there?'

'Well hardly. Jane is getting married tomorrow so naturally all Pelham and miles around is agog with that.'

Josie hadn't pressed the point. It was embarrassing for both of them, but they both knew in their hearts why Kathy had decided a wedding in her home town had been impossible. It would all have been too much.

Slowly she walked back to the hotel and as she entered the foyer she saw that her brother and his lady friend were waiting for her.

She liked Millicent Jason. She had been a widow for five years and she'd met Josie's brother at some function he'd attended in the town. They'd found themselves sitting next to each other at dinner and friends seeing them getting on so well together had seen to it that there were other occasions when they could meet. Millicent was totally unlike Kathy's mother, probably that was the reason Josie got on with her so well.

She was nice-looking, dressed well and had a sense of humour which was something Edith had never had. Best of all in Josie's opinion however was the fact that she made her brother happy, happier than she had ever known him.

'Are we ready to go into breakfast?' Albert said.

'Isn't Kathy joining us?' Josie asked.

'I'm sure she'll come down when she's ready.'

'I'll go to her room, Albert, you and Millicent go in, we'll join you later.'

She found Kathy finishing her packing, and, looking up with a bright smile she said, 'I'm almost finished Josie, have you been waiting for me?'

Her wedding dress was hanging outside the wardrobe, a white silk confection, plain yet exquisitely styled, and standing before it Josie said, 'It's lovely Kathy.'

Her face was strangely pensive and with a little smile Kathy said, 'We always talked about my wedding Josie, you wanted me in lashings of organdie and a long floating veil; are you very disappointed?'

'It isn't really disappointment Kathy, it's simply that I never thought you'd be marrying anybody so far away from home. I've done this to you Kathy. I've paid the price for everything I've done, but more than that I've exacted sacrifices from you.'

'Please Josie, I do wish you'd stop blaming yourself for everything that's gone wrong in our lives. I owe you so very much, my education, my career, even David.'

At her aunt's look of surprise she went on, 'Yes Josie, even David. But for you I'd never have known Ginevra Midhurst, never have gone to Saunderscourt, never met David.'

'I wonder if either of us would have been content to be small-town girls, marrying boys we met at the local hops, working in the same town, surrounded by the people we'd known all our lives? I thought it would be enough for me, and then overnight it all seemed to change. I can't help feeling bitter, Kathy. Tomorrow afternoon Jane Fortesque will have her fairytale wedding, her father will be a part of it, I wonder if he'll even spare me a thought.'

Kathy looked at her in shocked surprise.

'Of course he'll be thinking about you and wishing you could be there. Josie, you know he loves you very dearly, besides I don't envy Jane her fairytale wedding, or her mother-in-law.'

Josie laughed.

In a few minutes Kathy said, 'She'll be the most marvellous mother-in-law to Jane that any girl ever had. She'll revel in talking about her son's wife, Lady Jane, and she'll never stop counting her blessings that it's Jane he's married and not me.'

'You minded once, darling.'

'Yes, but not for long. I don't mind in the least that we're marrying in Cornwall in a little church where we're not likely to be surrounded by anybody. Just the four of us, David, his father and his best man.'

'Who has David asked to be his best man?'

'Another barrister, a man he was at Oxford with, an old friend.'

'Have you met him?'

'Several times. He's a bachelor, and very nice. He had thought to ask Ginevra's oldest brother, but then he didn't think he'd be able to make it the day before Jane's wedding. They're all invited to that one.'

As soon as they joined Albert and Millicent in

the dining room her father passed over the morning paper. 'Take a look at that Kathy, your friend's in the headlines again.'

From the front page Alanna and Jules smiled at her and Kathy clapped her hands with glee. 'How wonderful,' she exclaimed. 'How beautiful she looks and how happy. Oh, I do hope that this time it's going to be perfect.'

The headlines were rather less enthusiastic, their snide doubts however were not reflected in the joyful faces of the couple concerned.

Josie had felt sure they would arrive at an empty church and that nobody would be remotely interested in her niece's wedding. Instead she and Millicent found themselves walking through the tiny churchyard between an avenue of smiling faces, and inside the church music from the organ swelled over pews that were already occupied.

It would seem the entire community had turned out to attend David Reagan's wedding. Across the aisle David's father sat with his housekeeper, Mrs Giles, and as they took their places in the pew he smiled a welcome.

'What a lot of people,' Josie whispered.

'They've seen David grow up here, Josie, they're not unexpected,' he said.

David and his best man smiled at her amazement, and then behind them was a hush of expectancy, the organ music changed to the bridal march and Kathy and her father came walking slowly down the aisle. David's look of love said it all, and Josie making room for her brother next to her favoured him with a tearful smile.

What did it matter that the wedding dress was timeless and largely unadorned? That instead of the floating veil her head-dress was a halo of cream roses; the little church was beautifully decorated with flowers, the congregation was warmly sincere, each and every one of them concerned only with wishing them joy.

After the ceremony they were surrounded by smiling faces and well-wishers and Josie whispered to Albert, 'It isn't the pomp and ceremony that makes a wedding is it, Albert, it's that look of love David gave to Kathy when she joined him at the altar, it's what comes after that's important. The years of understanding and caring.'

This was what she had had from John Fortesque, understanding and caring, without these any words breathed over a prayer book were not enough.

It was late afternoon the next day when Josie let herself into her front door and from the kitchen Mrs Pearson her daily help called out a greeting.

'I've had Hamish out for his walk. I wasn't sure what time you'd be home so I've made sandwiches and there's a flask of coffee waiting for you. How did the wedding go?'

'It was lovely Mrs Pearson. Kathy looked enchanting.'

'Aye well, she's a lovely girl. You look tired, was the traffic bad?'

'Not really, but I'm glad I don't have to go out again today.'

'The vicar called. He didn't say what he wanted and he didn't stay long. If it's about that theatrical group I'd 'ave nothin' to do with them.'

Josie laughed. 'I don't think it will be anything to do with them Mrs Pearson, it's more likely to be concerned with a donation towards some church fund or other.'

'Aye well he's good at that. I'll get off now. I've put a match to the fire and I've put the mornin' post and your newspaper beside your chair. I'll see you Friday as usual.'

Josie went to the front door with her and watched her stepping briskly along the road. Mrs Pearson was a treasure, a woman designed to defend her against any gossip overheard, a woman who asked no questions even when she must have asked herself many questions about her employer's lifestyle. To Mrs Pearson Josie Marston was a lady, and the gentleman in her life was nothing to do with her or anybody else for that matter.

Her morning post consisted of several circulars and she sat back in her chair to think about Kathy's wedding and the one that would take place the next day.

John Fortesque and his daughter were very close and he would miss her. She had been the one bright light that had relieved the greyness of his days in that great beautiful house and with Jane gone from it his life with Elspeth would become more and more a duty.

She thought back on her life and saw it for what it was. Something that the young Josie Marston had never wanted. That other Josie had thought about a husband and children. Summer holidays by the sea and long cosy winter evenings and pleasures shared. She had paid dearly for loving another woman's husband and her future was shrouded in obscurity.

Would John spare her a thought in the hustle and bustle of his daughter's wedding? And when it was all over would he be able to come to terms with what was left?

Chapter Thirty-One

Clare Greavson surveyed herself in the long mirror and felt well pleased with what she saw. She had chosen azure blue for her son's wedding, a long crepe-de-chine dress and a large hat exactly the same colour. It had been very expensive.

She had kept the dress a secret from everybody including her husband. He liked her in blue and she had managed to have her fine kid shoes dyed to exactly the same colour. She'd not been so lucky with her small handbag, but pale grey snakeskin looked very nice.

John and Anthony were already dressed and waiting downstairs, but as she made her way down she paused a little anxiously; nothing, absolutely nothing had to go wrong today. She had to keep her end up with her new daughter-in-law's family. She had met them only briefly and she wasn't at all sure that Lady Fortesque

426

approved of the match. She'd made an effort to be charming, but underneath Clare had been aware of some hostility, a vague disturbing undercurrent suggesting that she had visualised somebody entirely different for her daughter.

When she'd said as much to her husband he'd said, 'Well, they seem perfectly well suited to me and Jane's father's been exceptionally amicable.'

Anthony had merely grinned cheerfully saying, 'The old man's very nice, I don't much care what Lady Fortesque thinks, Jane doesn't.'

'That's not a very nice way to think about her mother,' she'd remonstrated, and he'd merely said, 'She'll come around, Mother, I get along with her father and her brother and his family, that's enough to be getting on with.'

Making her entry into the breakfast room her husband and son looked on and watched while she gave a little pirouette for them. 'Well,' she demanded, 'what do you think?'

'Very nice dear, not too showy.'

'Well, of course it's not showy, I don't want to compete with the bride's mother.'

'There's no danger of that,' Anthony said with a broad smile. 'Lady Fortesque comes into her own when she's riding to hounds, she's not exactly a fashion plate at any other time.'

'But she'll make a special effort today I feel sure,' his mother said, and Anthony decided to let his mother make up her own mind about his future mother-in-law and her dress sense.

'Did Mrs Hodson say anything about the wedding?' Clare asked. 'I can't think why she's been invited, Anthony, after all she's only been our daily for the past few years.'

Her husband looked up with a frown. 'She pushed Anthony out in his pram,' he remarked acidly. 'She's worked for us over twenty-five years, cooked, cleaned and washed for us. She's entitled to see him married, I think.'

'But what will she be wearing?'

'Mother, I don't see what you're worrying about. Jane's invited her nanny, and a great many of their old servants, it's what they do apparently, and I don't think you need to worry about what she'll be wearing. She always looks very nice at the church do's.'

Clare felt restless. She picked up ornaments and looked for dust, she eyed her husband and son doubtfully but could find no fault with their apparel, and her husband said more irritably than he intended, 'Do sit down Clare and drink a glass of sherry, you're making me nervous.'

'I'm nervous,' she retorted. 'I want everything to be perfect.'

'And it will be. Anyway it's not your responsibility.'

'Isn't it time you were going, Anthony?'

'I'll know when it's time to go, Mother, in the meantime take a look at this, Alanna Van Royston's been married in Santa Lucia.'

She snatched the paper from him and looked down at the smiling girl on the front page with her bridegroom.'

'Jules Moreau, the author! She won't be at your wedding then?'

'No, Mother. Nor will Kathy Marston. She married her barrister yesterday.'

'How about her aunt, she surely won't be at the wedding?'

Both Anthony and his father decided to make no comment on that statement.

The time was crawling. She thought about the Abbey crowded with guests and the roads leading up to it, and later the reception at the Fortesques' stately home. Wasn't this what she'd always wanted for Anthony, some upper-crust girl like Jane? She and Jane would be wonderful friends, they'd lunch together, chat over the telephone, she'd be a wonderful mother-in-law and grandmother to their children. Indeed since Anthony's engagement to Lady Jane her own status in the community had risen, particularly on her various committees. Indeed on several of them she was merely waiting to take the next chair.

Her thoughts turned to her brother-in-law. James annoyed her, he provoked her and today would be no exception. It was time he made Anthony a partner in the firm, he deserved it, especially now with his connections. She'd hoped Jane and Anthony would find a house near by, but instead they'd opted for a sixteenth-century stone manor house several miles away, a house that would never in a thousand years have been her choice. It had huge open fireplaces and small leaded windows, it was picture-book charming, but it would probably need a fortune spent on it to make it more habitable.

Of course Jane had good taste, she had opted for chintz and oriental carpets, burr walnut and English oak for the kitchen, but there again the kitchen with its huge range and thick walls had depressed her. What was so wrong with a nice modern kitchen with modern facilities? But then Jane hadn't been brought up to do much for herself, she'd soon get fed up in that ancient kitchen when she had to cook in it.

Jane had listened to her criticism with a slight smile. She had shown them from room to room, the low ceilings and wide window ledges, the stone floors and wide oak beams, and if they had delighted Jane, they had appalled Clare.

She had been careful not to criticise anything in front of Jane but she'd made her adverse views known to Anthony.

'What does Jane's mother think of the house?' she'd asked pointedly.

'I don't think she's seen it, she's tied up with a great many other things. Her father thinks it's charming.'

'Well, of course, isn't it very similar to the house his mistress lives in?' she'd retorted caustically.

'Incidentally, Mother, Jane gets along with Josie Marston very well. She likes her.'

'But not enough to invite her to the wedding, I hope.'

Anthony decided to ignore that last remark, and his father merely favoured his wife with a pointed look that spoke volumes.

'Why don't we have coffee?' he said getting up from his chair.

'I really could have done with Mrs Hodson this morning. The wedding isn't until this afternoon, there would have been plenty of time for her to

430

get ready for it, it's not as though she's an important guest,' Clare commented in some annoyance.

Neither her son nor his father commented. They were accustomed to Clare's frets and worries whenever she was faced with something different; she had never faced anything quite as daunting as her son's wedding before so her grievances were to be expected.

At that moment the florist arrived. White carnations for Anthony and his father, a spray of orchids for Clare which she immediately thought were quite wrong for her dress. She'd chosen orchids because they were exclusive and expensive, now she thought their greeny colour quite wrong for the blue of her dress, carnations would have been preferable.

'I suppose the Fortesques' flowers will have come from their greenhouses,' she said sharply. 'If we had a proper gardener we could have done likewise.'

'Have you seen the greenhouses at Maplethorpe, Mother? Ours would fit into one small corner.' Anthony asked.

'I'm merely saying our gardener doesn't make the best of what we've got.'

Her husband produced coffee and they sat down to drink it. Never in her life had time crawled so slowly. Why hadn't the young couple decided to get married in the morning? That way it would all have been over and done with mid-afternoon and her nerves wouldn't have been in such a state.

She very much doubted if Jane's mother would

431

be so distressed. Indeed at that precise moment Jane's mother was handing her horse over to one of the grooms in the stable yard. As always she had ridden him round the estate, something she did every morning come rain or shine, and as she strolled unhurriedly towards the house Jane watched her from her bedroom window with a strange half-smile on her face.

The hour her mother had spent riding Willow round the parkland was far more important to her than anything that would come later, ever her daughter's wedding. It was a wedding her mother didn't want.

Her mother didn't dislike Anthony, she regarded him as a nice enough boy but totally unsuitable for the daughter of the Earl Fortesque. He was an inept horseman, hated point-to-point meetings and racing in general, found nothing to contribute to the people she surrounded herself with and the fact that he was a solicitor in a respectable law firm counted for nothing.

Algy Barrington had found another girl, Serena Lloyd-Bancroft, a baronet's daughter, hardly in the same league as Jane, but his father had informed her they were due to announce their engagement any day. She couldn't believe that Jane had thrown it all away to marry Anthony Greavson.

She had made her views very plain, that they hadn't been endorsed by Jane's father annoyed her. She considered him complacent, to the point of stupidity, but he'd merely said it was Jane's life, Anthony was the man she wanted and at least he had a decent career. He doubted if the likes of Algy Barrington could have made it in any profession beyond anything to do with horses.

Elspeth had been quick to point out that men in Algy's walk of life didn't need professions, there was money to be made in land.

Her dealings with her husband were at an all-time low. It didn't unduly worry her, they'd often been unharmonious. She knew she had always had his respect and he had never shown her anything but kindness. These days however she sensed an impatience in him, all to do with Jane's wedding, she felt sure. He had always spoilt Jane.

Jane turned away from the window and walked slowly into her dressing room. The dress was the first thing that caught her eye. It was a beautifully cut creation in cream parchment satin, the cream veil was plain but with it she would wear the tiara her grandmother had bequeathed her. With a wry smile she doubted there would ever be an occasion to wear such a bauble again.

Cream satin court shoes stood side-by side on the floor and it only needed the cream roses, when they arrived later in the morning to complete the ensemble.

Some lingering feeling of regret washed over her. She would be leaving Maplethorpe, but then it would never have been hers, and yet she loved it. She had loved her childhood in the great house, the sweeping parkland and the formal gardens. Maplethorpe would always be her dogs and horses, her loving father and brother, things not even her distant mother could take away, that she was leaving it for a small stone house on the edge of a town didn't matter. It was the sort of house she had always dreamed about, warm and comfortable, the sort of house that would be a home.

She was aware that Anthony's mother didn't like it. She would have preferred them to have gone in for something only a little smaller than Maplethorpe so that she could have talked to her friends about it. Or something ultra modern, but then she had felt no need to consult Anthony's mother whom she neither liked nor disliked.

That Clare was a snob Jane recognised, Anthony laughed about his mother's pretensions, and Jane had no doubt that Clare would lean over backwards to get along with her new daughter-in-law. None of that was important, she was more concerned at the moment with her parents' marriage.

Her father was unhappy, her mother oblivious. When she left Maplethorpe later in the day where would they go?

Several hours later she stood once more in her window watching the two cars that were taking her mother and her attendants to the Abbey. The children had piled into the last car squealing with excitement; her mother travelled alone.

Before leaving her mother had called into see her, Jane had stood in the middle of her room waiting for the examination and when it came she was not surprised at the banality of her mother's comments.

'You look very nice Jane, I'm glad you didn't go in for something floating or heavily embroidered, one sees so much of it these days.'

'I'm glad you changed your mind about wearing the same dress you wore for Ginevra's wedding,' Jane commented.

'Nobody was interested in what I wore then and they won't be today. You know I hate formal wear, I doubt I'll ever wear this outfit again.'

The outfit was predictable beige, her only sop to glamour being the three rows of exquisite pearls Jane's grandmother had bestowed on her.

'I'll get off now,' her mother said brusquely, 'the sooner we get those children away the better chance they have of settling down. Why did you decide on children, Jane?'

'They'll love it, Mother.'

'Probably, but shall we?'

She had stood at the window watching her mother step sharply down the terrace steps and into the car. She was remembering the number of times she'd been a bridesmaid for different members of the family, and how the mothers of the brides had been in tears, enfolding their daughters in warm embraces, enthusing on the way they looked. Not Lady Fortesque though. Her mother would have been more emotional beholding a pure-bred Arab.

She looked in the mirror once more. The dress was classically simple, its beauty relying on the material and its cut. For the first time in her life Jane thought she looked beautiful.

Her father waited for her at the bottom of the stairs and his eyes lit up with delight at the sight of her. Unhesitatingly he took her into his embrace saying, 'Jane, you look wonderful, I'm very proud of you, darling.'

She hugged him. 'You look wonderful too Daddy, you always do.'

'Did your mother call in to see you?'

'Yes, she thought I looked very nice.'

He smiled. 'Your mother doesn't enthuse about anything Jane, we can't expect today to be any exception.'

'I had hopes that it might be, Daddy.'

He smiled ruefully, and Jane said somewhat anxiously, 'She's not very pleased that I'm marrying Anthony, but I love him, he's nice, he's what I want. I think most brides are walking into a new way of life but me more than most perhaps. It's the sort of life I want.'

'Then it's nobody's business but yours, Jane. I'm happy for you, Andrew is happy for you, your mother'll come around.'

'I'll think about you in this great big house, you're going to miss me terribly.'

'Yes, I know.'

'You'll come to see us often Daddy?'

'Of course. You mustn't worry Jane, we are all responsible for what we do with our lives, what I do with mine is something that you mustn't worry about.'

She looked at him anxiously, and with a smile he said, 'I think it's time to go darling, I've given the servants leave to draw lots as to which of them get to visit the Abbey, the rest of them are waiting there on the terrace.'

So between a row of servants wreathed in smiles they walked to the waiting car.

Sitting behind her son in the Abbey Clare Greavson was more overwhelmed than she had been in her life. She had wanted constant re-assurance that she looked her best, every bit as flawless as numerous elegant women sitting in the pews around them.

She longed to lean forward to ask Anthony who exactly they were, but decided against it. In the pew behind them James Greavson and his wife looked around them with interest. Eventually James said, 'Clare'll never forget today or let anybody else forget it either.'

'She looks very nice,' Valerie whispered.

'Well, of course, what did you expect.'

Clare turned round to smile at them. 'I'm glad it's a lovely day,' she said, then turning back to her husband she whispered, 'Valerie's wearing mauve, she looks quite nice. I expect it's new for the occasion.'

At that moment there was a stir in the pews around them and the Countess Fortesque took the pew opposite. After a few moments she inclined her head the merest fraction of an inch in Clare's direction, and Clare whispered to her husband, 'She's wearing beige, terribly severe, I don't think it does much for her.'

Her husband didn't comment. The music swelled, the long march of the bishop followed by the choirboys and the gentlemen of the choir made their way down the centre aisle, and then Lord Fortesque was there, escorting his daughter and her retinue of children behind them.

Anthony stepped forward to wait for her and the opening hymn was ready to be sung.

In everybody's opinion it was a beautiful wedding of two young people evidently in love,

437

not a wedding that had been manufactured as so many weddings were in the Fortesques' sphere of life, but one both parties had entered into with expectations of shared interests and love.

John Greavson stood chatting to his son while he waited for Jane to join him for the start of their honeymoon. His expression was slyly amused as he said, 'Your mother's made a mental note of every noble guest she's met, it will sustain her for the rest of her life.'

Anthony laughed, looking across the room to where his mother stood chatting easily to Earl Fortesque. 'They appear to be getting along very well,' his father remarked.

'I've always found Jane's father very nice,' Anthony said.

His father nodded. He was thinking about Josie Marston who had loved this man for too long and he was asking himself if it had all been worth it. Here was Lord Fortesque surrounded by his wife, children and friends and where was Josie, probably alone and thinking about the role her lover was playing today.

Lady Fortesque was standing in the centre of a group of people she appeared to have much in common with. He recognised Major-General Barrington and his wife, the hunting, shooting and fishing crowd. Throughout the reception Lady Fortesque had barely taken time to speak to guests she had little in common with.

Jane arrived looking exquisite in a pale blue dress and floppy hat and immediately everybody surged out of the hall to where Anthony's car was waiting to whisk them away. Good wishes were being called, Jane threw her arms around her father, her mother was well back so she received a wave and a smile, then they were driving away and the rest of them were strolling back into the hall.

Soon now it would be over and John couldn't help his feeling of relief. It would be nice to get out of his monkey suit and into grey flannels and a sweater. There was work to be done in the garden before it went dark, the rose beds could do with a watering, and as he set about looking for his wife Mrs Hodson tugged at his arm.

'It was beautiful Doctor Greavson,' she said, 'I cried like a baby she looked so beautiful, and Anthony too. I couldn't help thinking about the times I pushed him round the village in his pram. We never thought then that he'd be marryin' anybody like Lady Jane.'

Clare joined them, and together the two women started to reminisce about the young Anthony, and when Mrs Hodson left to join her husband she said, 'She looks quite nice John, I'm glad I let her have that hat, I don't suppose she'd anything quite as nice of her own.'

It was dusk. The last of the guests were driving away, servants were putting the rooms to rights, waiters and caterers packed up and drove away and up in her bedroom Lady Fortesque couldn't wait to get out of her wedding finery quick enough. She put on an old tweed skirt and sweater thinking she'd collect a dog and walk down to the stables with him. She'd missed her afternoon ride and hoped one of the grooms had taken her horse out. She'd half promised to drive over to the Barringtons but later decided against it. She'd see them at the weekend at the agricultural show.

She met her husband on the stairs and he was still wearing his formal attire.

'I'm going to the stables,' she explained. 'I hope my horse has been out. Are you staying in for the rest of the evening?' she asked on her way down the stairs.

He paused. 'How long will you be gone, Elspeth?'

'I'm not sure, why?'

'I'll be in the library when you get back, I'll see you there.'

She stared at him. He didn't normally concern himself with how long she'd be out of the house or where she could find him when she returned to it. If he wanted to talk about the wedding she'd had enough of it for one day, she'd be in no hurry to get back.

Two hours later he was still sitting in the library staring into the fire. It had grown chilly and he'd put a match to the kindling, either that or his attack of nerves was making him feel cold. It was during the afternoon with the sound of music, laughter and conversation going on around him that he had come to a decision and now there was no going back. It was never going to be easy and it was like Elspeth to keep him waiting. She didn't want to talk about anything, after all they'd had very little to say to each other for some considerable time. At last he heard the sound of her footsteps in the passage outside the library, then she opened the door and stood looking at him. 'I don't want to talk about the wedding John, I've had enough of it for one day and you know I didn't approve. Anthony was not the man I wanted for Jane.'

'I don't want to talk about the wedding Elspeth, whether you approve or disapprove. Jane is happy and that is all that matters.'

'I don't agree. She will live to regret it. Give her a few years and she'll see how different her life could have been.'

'Come into the room Elspeth and close the door behind you. I don't want to talk about Jane, we need to talk about us.'

'Us!' Her eyes snapped angrily, but she closed the door sharply and went to stand opposite his chair.

'Sit down Elspeth, let us be civilised about this.'

Her expression was hostile, his burdened with regret, but his voice was firm when he spoke to her. 'Now that Jane's gone, Elspeth, I think we should come to terms with what is happening to us. We have a marriage that is no marriage, we barely speak, we only see each other to keep up appearances, we're two people who'll rattle round this great house living our separate lives, are you going to be content with that?'

'What is the alternative?'

'We separate. In actual fact we separated years ago, now we should do it properly, either separation or divorce. You will find me more than generous. I have the utmost respect for you Elspeth, you are the mother of my children, I can never forget that, but neither can I go on living this aimless, loveless life simply because we're man and wife.'

'I suppose you'll go to her.'

When he didn't answer she said, 'Does that mean that you'll bring her here to take my place? What are you expecting me to do?'

'Nothing Elspeth. You can remain here as long as you like. In any case one day it will belong to Andrew. You've always said you hated it here, so I doubt you'll want to remain here anyway. I don't intend to fight you about anything, take what you want as long as it doesn't take from Andrew.'

'I'll leave as soon as I can find somewhere else, I've never liked the house anyway, but I do like the area. I shall look for something smaller, somewhere where I can still have my horses. My friends will rally round I'm sure. After all people have known for years about her.'

'Over all these years, Elspeth, Josie has never asked for more than I was able to give her. It could have gone on like that, but our marriage is a sham, something I'm unable to tolerate any longer. Elspeth, be honest with yourself, you'll be happier without it, we were never in love, now we don't really like each other very much.'

For a long moment she stood staring down into the fire, her expression bleak, then with a little shrug of her shoulders she said, 'When do you intend to leave?'

At that moment he admired her courage and striding across to her, he took her hands in his, 'Elspeth,' he said gently, 'we can be friends. We have the children, we have many years to look back on, we can either accept what we cannot

442

change or we can bear nothing but hostility towards each other. I don't want that. I want us to give ourselves time, time to heal the wounds, then hopefully, time to be friends.'

She didn't answer immediately, then easing her hands away she said, 'It's too soon John, like you say we'll give ourselves time, perhaps.'

With a small bitter smile she turned away and walked out of the room.

For a long time he stood staring down into the fire, then making up his mind suddenly he lifted the telephone and dialled Josie Marston's number.

He heard her voice, at first unsure, then when she recognised her caller, warm and loving with welcome.

'I thought you'd be too busy to call me today John, how was the wedding?' she asked.

'Wonderful. Everything went fine; and Kathy's wedding?'

'The same. Only a handful of us, but the village turned out to wish them well. She looked lovely.'

'Of course. It's very late Josie, but I want to see you, I have something to tell you.'

For a moment there was silence, and when at last she spoke there was a hint of fear in her voice so that he was quick to reassure her. 'Josie darling, I love you, I'm coming over tonight, I have a lot to tell you, I'll be there in just over an hour.'

He was not to know that at that moment Josie sat down weakly on the nearest chair. Her hands were trembling, there had been something in his voice, but her fears had always been there that

443

she was in a relationship that was not meant to last, that what she had was all that there would ever be.

She went to stand by the door. A thin mist was drifting across the garden, but in the sky a full moon sailed omnipotently above the beech trees. There had been so many nights when she had waited for him like this; why was tonight any different, unless it was to talk about Jane's wedding and how much he was going to miss her.

It was so still, the small wind hardly rippled the leaves and yet there was a perfumed peace about it, the peace of an English country garden under the stars.

Again and again she went to the door and time seemed to be passing so slowly. She felt restless, unable to settle to anything, until at last she heard the sound of a car's engine and she could see headlights lighting up the rambling village street. In only minutes the car came to rest on the driveway where lights from the house streamed out into the darkness.

She watched him climbing out of the car and then he came towards her smiling. It seemed to Josie in that moment that suddenly the years dropped away and she was looking at a lover she had never really known, younger, less careworn, robbed of so many doubts and traumas, the expression of a man able to look forward with confidence rather than with a remembered pain.

With a little cry she ran forward into his arms.

When he turned to put the catch on the door she looked at him in surprise.

'I hadn't expected to see you today John, I thought you'd be far too busy to think about me,' she said softly.

He smiled and held out his hand.

Throughout the years Josie had been the one who had suffered the slights and prejudices, vulnerable and often lonely she had been cast as the scarlet woman, while he had remained largely inviolate, immune from hostilities directed at the woman he loved. Now she would no longer be alone, they would be free to face the future together.

The publishers hope that this book has given you enjoyable reading. Large Print Books are especially designed to be as easy to see and hold as possible. If you wish a complete list of our books please ask at your local library or write directly to:

Magna Large Print Books
Magna House, Long Preston,
Skipton, North Yorkshire.
BD23 4ND

This Large Print Book for the partially sighted, who cannot read normal print, is published under the auspices of

THE ULVERSCROFT FOUNDATION